Carey Corp and Lorie Langdon

BLINK

BLINK

Doon
Copyright © 2013 by Carey Corp and Lorie Moeggenberg

This title is also available as a Blink ebook.
Visit www.zondervan.com/ebooks.

Requests for information should be addressed to:

Blink, 5300 Patterson Ave SE, Grand Rapids, Michigan 49530

ISBN 978-0-310-74230-2

Any Internet addresses (websites, blogs, etc.) and telephone numbers in this book
are offered as a resource. They are not intended in any way to be or imply an
endorsement by the publisher, nor does the publisher vouch for the content of
these sites and numbers for the life of this book.

Thank you to the Alan Jay Lerner Estate and the Frederick Loewe Foundation for
use of the *Brigadoon* premise.

Cover design and photography: Mike Heath/Magnus Creative
Cover direction: Cindy Davis
Interior composition: Greg Johnson/Textbook Perfect

Printed in the United States of America

13 14 15 16 17 18 19 /DCI/ 20 19 18 17 16 15 14 13 12 11 10 9 8 7 6 5 4 3 2 1

Dedication

For the romantics, the visionaries, and the believers
who've crossed the bridge in pursuit of a dream;
especially Alan Jay Lerner and Frederick Loewe.
There but for you go I.

CHAPTER 1

Veronica

I skidded to a halt in the crowded corridor, totally unprepared for a showdown with the evil witch of Bainbridge High. Stephanie Heartford, the girl who stalked anything with an XY chromosome, stood in front of my locker flirting with one of the cutest boys in school. And not just any cute boy — *my* boy.

Eric and Steph gazed into each other's eyes, standing so close I doubted a piece of loose-leaf paper would fit between them. Eric's knuckles grazed the hem of her cheer skirt, brushing the bare skin of her thigh. A move he'd used on me, more times than I could count.

Stephanie glanced in my direction, her lips curling at the corners as she whispered into Eric's ear. He looked up with wide eyes, a guilty flush staining his cheeks. I knew we weren't the perfect couple, but I was *trying* to make things work. And he was — *what?* — flirting with my archrival?

Eric stepped back and Stephanie strolled away, her Barbie-doll-on-helium giggle ringing in my ears. Staring straight ahead, I skirted a group of gawking freshmen and stalked to my locker. My fingers trembled as I dialed the combination, threw my Bio text onto the shelf, and slammed the metal door.

Eric leaned against the wall a few feet away, his shoulders hunched and his hands jammed into his pockets. His expression was reminiscent of when we were kids and he'd steal the cookies from my lunchbox, then refuse to admit it despite the smell of Oreos on his breath. "Don't look at me like that," he said as I approached.

"Like what?" I arched a brow. No way was I going to make this easy for him.

"Like I ate your last cookie."

"Did you?"

"So what if I did?" He shook his head and stared down at the yellowed linoleum. When he looked up, his eyes pleaded with me to understand. "I'm never going to be that perfect guy who comes riding in to rescue you from your crappy life. I'm no hero, Vee."

He was so far from heroic right now that I laughed. The harsh, humorless sound felt like a rock in my chest, forcing me to take another breath before I could reply. "I never said you were."

"Not in so many words " He trailed off with a shrug, letting the accusation speak for itself.

My spine stiffened, and I clenched my teeth so hard a sharp pain shot from my jaw to my temple. "So this is *my* fault?"

Eric nodded. "Kind of—yeah. I'm your boyfriend but you insist on treating me like I'm still twelve years old. I deserve more."

Really? He was going to play the wounded puppy? A scream brewed in the back of my throat, but I refused to make more of a scene, so I removed all inflection from my voice. "And you get 'more' from Stephanie."

"Maybe … yeah." I took a step backward, but he followed.

"This is exactly what I'm talking about, Vee. I've just told you I want more and you freeze me out, like some kind of Ice Princess. Say something!"

I could think of lots of things to say. Unfortunately, most of them would get me expelled. So I settled on, "I hope *Steph* will make you happy."

His whole face hardened. "She already has."

I stared at him, waiting for some sign of remorse, but his eyes remained flat as he turned and strode away. Some of the girls from my cheer squad stood in a huddle nearby, watching. One of them shook her head, her frosted pink lips tilted in a smirk. Had everyone known about Eric and Steph but me? So much for watching your friend's back.

A red haze narrowed my vision as I put one foot in front of the other, forcing myself not to run, not to think about the gossip or the snide little comments now circulating at my expense. If Eric wanted to move on with someone else, he could've at least had the decency to talk to me instead of making me look like a loser in front of the entire school. I passed homeroom and went straight to the parking lot.

When I reached my faded-to-pink VW Bug, I dove inside, throwing my book bag onto the passenger seat. Hot tears spilled down my cheeks as I gripped the steering wheel, the leather stitching branding itself into my skin.

I'd known Eric forever. We'd grown up down the street from each other, played in the same graffiti-stained park, and wished on stars from his tree house. He'd been there those first terrible days after my family fell apart, holding my hand and reassuring me that my dad would come back. I'd thought we were perfect for each other.

How could I have been so blind?

Pushing my head back against the headrest, I squeezed my

eyes closed. My throat burned with the effort to keep sobs from escaping. That moron was *so* not worth it.

I sucked in a shaky breath, and an odd feeling skittered across my skin. Like the moment before you turn around to find the old man at the grocery store gawking at you. I blinked the tears from my lashes and wiped my cheeks as I searched the parking lot. A boy stood several feet away, watching me intently. He was gorgeous; like someone who'd just stepped off the pages of a magazine. Definitely not a student at Bainbridge High — I would've remembered *him*.

I looked away, stunned. Pretending to adjust my window, I fiddled with the handle, rolling it down and then halfway back up. When I raised my eyes from the lever he had moved closer, and I noticed his athletic legs were bare, topped by a blue and green plaid — Wait. Was he wearing a kilt?

Forgetting to be sly, my gaze traveled up his white, collarless shirt and back to his incredible face. His brows lowered and our eyes locked. I couldn't look away as he shoved his hand into the dark-blond waves of his hair, pushed it off his forehead, and stepped toward me.

"Don't cry, lass."

Somehow his low voice reached me from outside, reverberating all the way to the base of my spine. He lifted his hand, something white clutched in his fingers.

A girl lugging a ginormous backpack rushed by my door, blocking my view. I shifted in my seat and gripped the door handle, ready to fling it open and meet the stranger halfway the moment the girl passed by. But by the time she'd moved on, the boy had disappeared. Vanished without a trace, as if he'd never been there at all.

That was beyond weird. Had I imagined the whole encounter, or had he slipped away before I could see where he went?

In light of my best friend's campaign to convince me to spend the summer in Scotland, a wishful hallucination of a hot kilt-wearing boy was entirely possible.

Kenna had been after me for weeks to go on vacation with her. Since she'd inherited a cottage from her great-aunt, all I needed to swing was airfare. But even after teaching extra dance classes for months, I hadn't been able to save enough — which had nothing to do with my self-discipline and everything to do with my mom spending the rent money on tight clothes and boxed wine.

A muffled pixie-like jingle interrupted my thoughts. I dug the phone out of my purse. *The moors of Scotland r calling ... r u coming or not?!?*

Instead of replying, I hit speed dial. Since Kenna's dad had ripped her away from Indiana to live in Podunk, Arkansas, we talked or texted at least twenty times a day.

She answered on the first ring. "Hey, Vee. What's wrong?"

The girl could seriously read my mind. Rather than tell her I was going crazy, I opted for my other big news. "Eric and I broke up."

"That's gre – Ah ... I mean, I am sooo sorry." I could hear the smile in her voice. It was no secret she thought Eric was a jerk.

"Way to empathize." But for some reason I could breathe again. How did she do that? Maybe we did share a brain, like her dad always claimed.

"At least now you have no excuse for not coming to Scotland."

"Except being broke."

Or was I? I patted the dashboard in front of me and saw dollar signs. I didn't want to sell my Bug, but getting away from

Bainbridge for the summer — and my cheating ex — sounded better than ever now. "I have an idea. No promises though."

"Hey, I've got news too. I decided what I want from my dad for graduation."

"Okaayy ... that's good, I guess." Kenna was the queen of random segues, so I waited for her to connect the dots.

"In case you didn't realize, that was your cue."

My voice oozed mock contrition as I asked, "Oh, I'm sorry. Whatever could you be getting for graduation?"

"A plane ticket to Scotland for my bestie."

A baseball-sized lump stuck in my throat, making it impossible to speak.

"Vee? You still there?"

I swallowed, but my voice was still a strangled rasp. "I can't accept that."

Instantly serious, she demanded, "How long have you known me?"

"Since kindergarten."

"Have I ever taken no for an answer?"

"No ..." She was right. Memories of her goading me into jumping from a moving swing despite my fear of heights, her forcing me out of the bathroom when I'd been too nervous to perform in our fifth-grade talent show, and the time she'd coaxed me from a two-week pity party using brownies and the latest Harry Potter movie as incentive after my mom started dating Bob the Slob, all proved it was true.

"Happy graduation, Vee. Next week, we're off on an epic summer adventure."

We both squealed until the bell cut us off. As if someone would hear her, Kenna hastily whispered, "Call me after school, 'kay? Bye."

Despite the warning bell, I sat staring out my windshield.

I'd just broken up with my boyfriend. I should've been devastated, but I felt ... *good*. I was about to spend the entire summer in Scotland with my best friend, and maybe if I was lucky I'd find a hot kilt-wearing boy like the one from my deliciously detailed imagination.

I hauled myself out of the car and headed back toward the school, glancing over my shoulder to the spot where the golden-haired boy had stood. A flash of white caught my eye, a scrap of cloth fluttering in the breeze. As it began to swirl across the blacktop, I pushed dark strands of hair out of my face and turned to intercept it.

Capturing the piece of fabric, I spread the delicate square flat in my hand. A handkerchief, like the one my grandpa used to use to wipe tears from my cheeks when I was little.

A small picture embroidered in blue and green thread displayed two lions back to back, one with an arrow clamped in its teeth, the other holding a sword, a tilted crown on his head. Beneath the picture were four letters in italicized script:

JEKc%

The mystery boy's initials?

As I guessed at what the letters could stand for, the script began to blur. I blinked and looked again; not only were the initials gone, but the fabric seemed to grow thinner, until I could see my fingers through it. Frantically, I stretched the cloth between my hands and brought it closer to my face. But before I could get a good look, the material pulled apart and evaporated into thin air.

I stared at my empty hands, disappointment hitting me like a sharp, quick punch to the chest. The memento was gone as if it'd never been — as if *he* had never been.

❖ ❖ ❖

I lugged my gear out of the Bug and trudged up our crumbled walkway to the front steps. Moths buzzed around the yellow porch light, flying in my face as I juggled my bags and the gallon of milk I'd picked up on the way home. My leg muscles trembled with fatigue. After teaching preschool ballet, advanced modern dance, and two yoga classes, I felt like I could sleep for a hundred years.

Dropping my bags inside the door, I went straight for the jumbo box of Cheerios on the counter. I didn't have to open the kitchen cabinets to know they'd be bare.

Too exhausted to change out of my dance clothes, I sunk into the saggy floral couch and clicked on the TV. I refused to think about Eric and *Steph*, so I distracted myself by imagining how amazing it would be to go to Scotland. To immerse myself in the culture, experience new things — even if that meant trying stuff like oat porridge, kippers, and fried haggis. Okay, maybe *not* fried haggis. Sheep guts were totally disgusting. But it would be like a whole new world!

The front door slammed. Mom's giggle preceded her into the house, reminding me that my dreams of freedom were a long way off.

Enter Bob the Slob.

I set my cereal bowl on the table and readied myself to bolt as they came stumbling into the room, arm in arm. Bob had his baseball cap on backward and the sleeves of his flannel shirt cut off, revealing large arms that had long ago turned to fat. On the creep-scale of guys Janet had dated, this guy topped them all. Last weekend he'd not only spent the night, but a good portion of the day camped out on our couch in his tighty-whities, a Coors Light in one hand, the remote in the other.

"Hey dumplin'! What're you up to?" Janet turned her wide, unfocused eyes on me. She'd been drinking — again. She wasn't a drunk, but she appeared to be finding more and more reasons to go out and *socialize*, as she called it.

Her wooly gaze settled on me and sharpened. "Jeez, Veronica, go put some clothes on!" Bob's eyes flowed over my skin-tight leotard and sheer wrap skirt with obvious interest. There was no way I was going to stand up and walk out of the room now. Suddenly, a blanket smacked me in the side of the head. Janet's way of helping me out.

"Um, thanks, Mom "

"Sure, Punkin! Do we have any leftovers or anything?" she yelled as she wobbled into the kitchen on platform sandals. Bob watched me with narrowed eyes and a catlike smile as I positioned the blanket more strategically around me.

"Ah no, Mom. I haven't been home much lately."

"Oh, okay." Janet stumbled out of the kitchen holding two glasses and a bottle of Arbor Mist. She squeezed into the same chair with Bob, and as he poured she stared at me critically.

Oh no, here it comes.

"Dumplin', I thought you were going to color your hair?" She took her glass and motioned with it toward my head. "Or at least get highlights or somethin'. Dark brown is just so dreary."

I reached back and twisted the length of my hair behind my head. She'd been nagging me to dye it for years, even offering to take me to the salon. But I'd only recently figured out it was because my hair was the exact shade of deep chestnut as my dad's. We also shared the same full mouth, and blue-green eyes. To Janet, I was a constant reminder of what she'd lost.

But she never seemed to remember that I'd lost him too. I still couldn't think about the day he went to the grocery store and never came back without feeling like I was having a mini heart attack.

"I dunno." Bob's fingers started to roam across Janet's mid-section as he stared at me. "I think her hair's purty that way."

I bit my lip. Bob had no idea what he'd just done. Janet drained her glass in one gulp and slammed it on the table. I needed to get out of there. Fast. "I'm really tired." I half-yawned as I gathered my things and stood, the blanket slipping from one shoulder.

Bob stopped nuzzling Janet's neck as his full attention shifted to me. His low whistle sent goose bumps skittering over my skin. "Well, well. Little Veronica, you've grown up rather nicely."

Gross!

"Veronica! I told you to go put some clothes on!" She shoved against Bob and stood in front of him.

"No problem," I threw over my shoulder as I clutched the blanket and stomped down the hall. Shouldn't I be able to walk around my own home without some perv eyeballing me? Last time I checked, this was my house too.

But apparently this was my day for incorrect assumptions, because just as I reached my bedroom door I overheard Mom say, "That girl's a selfish little leech, just like her father. I can't wait until we have this place all to ourselves."

Blindly, I pushed into my room, slammed the door, and threw myself down on my narrow bed. The sobs I'd been holding back since that afternoon crashed over me in waves, leaving me breathless. I cried until my head felt stuffed full of cotton, and my tightly held control lay shattered in jagged pieces around me. How had everything gone so wrong?

Maybe Eric was right about me. Since Dad left, Mom and I had lived in the same house, existing day by day, barely speaking. And with Kenna gone, there wasn't a single person in Bainbridge I considered a friend. Freezing people out seemed to be my special power.

A sudden chill racked my body. Rolling onto my side, I pulled the covers up to my chin, shaking with a cold that radiated from deep inside me. I squeezed my eyes closed, and a vivid image of golden-boy flooded me with warmth. *"Don't cry, lass."*

Clinging to the gorgeous figment of my imagination like a security blanket, I fell asleep to the lullaby of imaginary bagpipes.

CHAPTER 2

Veronica

Kenna and I strolled down the cobbled streets and crested a hill, me gawking like a tourist, which, technically, I was. Despite my weeks of research, nothing could've prepared me for the experience of actually being in this foreign land. From our elevated vantage point, Alloway appeared to be a cluster of whitewashed cottages and medieval stone structures nestled into an emerald landscape so vibrant it dazzled the eyes. Rooftops of every earth-tone variation and angle rose against an impossibly bright blue sky. It was like falling into an oil painting.

The softly rumbling Doon River flowed along the left side of the village. And just off the riverbank, the marble pillars and curved dome of a Grecian monument — dedicated to the poet Robert Burns — created a proud pinnacle that reached toward the heavens.

As we entered the village proper, the sidewalks teemed with people. Store owners propped open doors to let in the fresh breeze. Residents hurried down the crooked lanes, focused on their destinations but smiling. The torrential rains that had been present since we'd first arrived in Glasgow had finally stopped, leaving behind an iridescent coating that reflected the sun like beveled glass. Every light pole, glossy leaf, and brick storefront sparkled, reminding me of something from Narnia.

We followed a curve in the road, and a hint of fresh-brewed coffee wafted through the air to settle on my taste buds.

"Poet's Corner should be just ahead." Kenna tucked a strand of crimson hair behind her ear and pointed down the street. She'd wanted to stop in town before heading to the cottage so we could visit her favorite coffee shop. She claimed they had the best cinnamon hot chocolate on the planet.

Walking down this beautiful street with my BFF by my side, an entire summer in Scotland stretching before us, I had to suppress the urge to dance. And, as if to make the moment even more perfect, a tall, well-built boy wearing a kilt strode toward me. I noted the dark-blond waves of his hair, broad cheekbones, and strong nose. He radiated restless power. *Wow.* He was beyond gorgeous.

He drew closer, his gaze never leaving my face, and his mouth slid into a slow smile.

As he passed, his dark eyes bored into mine, and I tripped over a bump in the sidewalk. Recognition clicked into place and my heart cartwheeled into my throat. It was him — the boy who stood outside my car the day Eric and I broke up! What was *he* doing here?

I regained my balance, spun around, and almost slammed into an old lady. Apologizing, I stepped around her and searched the people on the sidewalk — a tall man in a knit cap, a young mother with two small children, a short middle-aged man grinning at me, but no beautiful boy in a kilt ... anywhere.

"Veronica?"

Kenna walked up beside me and touched my arm, but I couldn't speak. What were the chances of him being in Bainbridge, Indiana, and now in Alloway, Scotland? And what was with the vanishing act?

"Ken, did you see where that hot guy in the kilt went?" I searched the other side of the street.

"Um ... what?" I met Kenna's wide gray eyes, her brows arched in surprise.

"Come on, you couldn't miss him. Tall, blond, gorgeous —"

She was shaking her head in denial before I even finished. "I haven't seen anyone in a kilt, let alone a hot boy. And believe me, I've been looking."

I blinked several times as if recalibrating my eyes. I was totally losing it. Pain throbbed through my head and I paused to massage my temples.

"Are you okay?" Kenna waited patiently for me to finish.

Had I imagined him? *Again?* Maybe it was jetlag — or a brain tumor. Or maybe he had followed me from Bainbridge. Then why did he keep evaporating into thin air? *Just like the handkerchief in the parking lot.* I kept my eyes closed for several seconds, struggling to gain control, before opening them and focusing on my friend's concerned face. "Just tired. I could really use some caffeine right now."

"Then you're in luck."

She looped her arm through mine and led me down the walk to an adorable whitewashed building, a tiny oval sign announcing *Poet's Corner Café*. We squeezed past two round tables with sun-bleached umbrellas and entered the shop, a tinkling bell announcing our presence. The sharp scents of spices, rich coffee, and fresh baked goods swirled around us.

After getting drinks and scones, we camped out at a table by the front windows. I watched the street, letting the hot, rich liquid soothe my frazzled nerves. Kenna was right — best cocoa ever. But it didn't stop me from staring at every person who passed, searching for *him*.

Something in my gut told me my kilt-boy sightings weren't tumor related. Maybe I just needed a fantasy — to believe a better world existed for me than the one waiting back in Bainbridge. To have someone special in my life who wouldn't cheat with my rival or leave me ... so I was conjuring up the perfect boy.

Wait. Escaping into fantasy was a symptom of schizophrenia, wasn't it?

Kenna tapped her foot impatiently. "Are you going to tell me what's eating you?"

"Nothing."

"Reeaally?"

I pulled my gaze away from the window long enough to see her prop her chin in her hand to stare at me. "*My* Veronica would've already wolfed down that strawberry scone and gone back for seconds."

I glanced down at the calorific pastry on my plate and then back out the window. "I — "

A tall blond figure rounded the corner across the street. I shot out of my chair, hot chocolate sloshing onto my fingers as I pressed my face to the window. The man turned toward us and ... he was old enough to be my dad.

I sunk back into my seat and pressed a napkin to my stinging fingers. This was ridiculous. Chancing a glance across the table, I found my normally verbose BFF wide-eyed and speechless. I knew I had to start talking, but I couldn't explain what I didn't understand myself. "Would you still love me if I were crazy?"

A tiny smile lifted one side of her mouth. "I already do." The waves of her vibrant hair caught glints of light as she tilted her head. The sun reflecting in her dove gray eyes reminded me of when we'd first met, and I'd asked her if she was an autumn fairy. She'd said yes and that I could be one too. We'd been best friends ever since. I knew I could tell her anything, but right now the words wouldn't come.

So I forced my thoughts away from Golden Boy, took a sip of cinnamony chocolate, and changed the subject. "Was your dad still acting weird before you left?"

"Oh yeah, he kept hugging me and telling me how he's proud of me and knows I'll make the *right* decision."

"He didn't try to have the sex talk with you before you jetted off to the land flowing with legal ale and hot boys in kilts, did he?"

She snorted, causing several customers to turn in their seats and stare. "No. It's a little late for that anyway."

"Wait. What?" I leaned forward and lowered my voice. "Did you and your leading man from *Seussical* ... you know?" I wiggled my eyebrows.

"Me and the Cat in the Hat? No way — he doesn't even play for my team. I was talking about Weston." My blank stare prompted her to clarify. "The hot associate director from my internship."

Her audition in Chicago had happened months ago. I knew she thought the associate director was cute, but she'd never said anything about hooking up with him. "Ummm. Did you guys — "

"No — I mean, not yet. But who knows? We totally shared a moment after my audition." She rummaged around in her bag, pulled out her phone, and shoved it under my nose. "Here's Weston's picture. Talk about tall, blond, and yummy. And he included a handwritten note in my acceptance page about how he couldn't wait to start working with me in August. His penmanship was so ..."

I didn't hear the rest; the image of my own golden-haired dream boy filled my head, eclipsing everything else.

"Earth to Vee ... Did you hear what I just said?"

"Sure. The pedophile director was hitting on you ... yada yada yada." I pinched off a piece of scone, the buttery layers and sugary-yet-tart strawberries melting on my tongue. "Mmmm! This is amazing."

"Even better than Mrs. Russo's, right?" She slapped a hand over her mouth, no doubt realizing she'd mentioned Eric's mom. Her voice filled with apology. "Sorry. It just slipped out."

I tightened my stomach, bracing for the wave of pain — that never came. Instead, a lazy, enigmatic grin filled me with an overwhelming yearning that I'd never felt for my ex. Maybe Golden Boy was my subconscious's way of helping me move on?

"It's no big deal. I mean, Eric's betrayal was ... a big deal, but ..." I sat up straighter as I struggled to put my thoughts into words. "What I mean is, Eric's ancient history. He has nothing to do with Scotland or my future."

"What you need, my amiga, is a rebound guy. Some totally random Scottish hottie to get you over Eric." Kenna clapped her hands and bounced enthusiastically in her seat, having no idea how close her comment was to my fantasy.

She pointed, not so discreetly, toward the dark-haired boy wiping down the counter. "What about that cute barista? When I gave him my order, he couldn't tear his eyes off *you* long enough to even acknowledge me."

I scrunched up my nose, resisting the urge to count his numerous visible tattoos. "I don't know ..."

Kenna noticed that her exuberance had drawn the attention of the other patrons, so she leaned forward and whispered,

"Commence Operation MacHottie. I am sooo gonna be your wingman."

I stuffed the rest of the scone into my mouth before answering. "Just because you're saving yourself for Weston doesn't mean you can't have a summer fling too."

"Right. I can just picture exotic boys falling at your petite feet, while I get pity dates with their ogre sidekicks. No thanks."

I marveled at how clueless Kenna was to her appeal. She'd been turning heads since fourth grade, yet she acted as if she was invisible to guys. Like that was remotely possible.

"Next to your curves and coloring, I look like a member of the Lollypop Guild." I pursed my lips to the side and squinched up one eye.

She hooted a laugh. "Keep making that face and they might make you an honorary munchkin." She grabbed her bag and fished a tip out of her wallet. "We should go. The caretaker, Mrs. Dell, will be meeting us at the cottage soon."

I licked my finger and dredged it through the crumbs on my plate before popping the sweet morsels into my mouth. "Sure. Just let me get a bag of those scones to go."

"That's my girl."

🏵 🏵 🏵

When I was six years old, my dad took me to see a rerelease of Disney's *Snow White*. Every day for weeks afterward, I searched the woods behind our house for the seven tiny men and their little cottage, all while evading the evil queen and her huntsman. With childlike conviction, I knew my prince would come and that good would ultimately triumph over evil.

Dunbrae Cottage, with its rounded gables, thatched roof, and wild English garden, was surrounded by the same sense of magic, and it made me long for the girl I'd once been, the one who believed fairy tales could be real. But that naive faith in happily-ever-after had been ripped from me long ago.

Removing a pile of pajamas from my suitcase, I crossed the bedroom to the antique cherry dresser and placed them inside. Kenna had slipped into the hall to talk to her dad; he'd called to make sure she'd made it safely to Alloway. For some reason, that simple, loving gesture hit me hard. Maybe it was because I hadn't heard a peep from my mom in the last twenty-four hours.

"Seriously, Vee. You do realize these come in movie form?"

I whirled to find Kenna sitting on the bed, sorting through the books covering the bottom of my suitcase. "Besides, when are you going to have time to read these anyway? We're on vacation."

I walked over and gathered a stack of paperbacks topped by a tattered copy of *Pride and Prejudice*. They were my most prized possessions, procured from yard sales and thrift stores over the years whenever I had a few dollars to spare. No way was I leaving my treasures home with Janet. They'd end up as kindling in the backyard fire pit.

With the care of a mother tucking in her babies, I lined the volumes up on the dresser in alphabetical order. "Reading helps me fall asleep." *And not feel so alone.* But I didn't say that as I turned back to the suitcase and found Kenna bouncing lightly on the bed, clearly over the book conversation.

"So, what do you think of the place?" She stilled, expectation widening her eyes.

"You were right. It's just like a fairy tale. A better setting than anything you and I ever dreamt up for our plays." I scooped up a few more books and placed them on the nightstand, making sure the spines were perfectly aligned.

"The Reid-Welling Production Company! I totally forgot." Kenna's storm-colored eyes glittered with remembrance.

As kids, we'd fashioned costumes from the old clothing and junk, creating our own world of make-believe. "You were quite the little drama queen, even then," I teased, remembering how she would jump up and down and clap her hands in excitement every time I'd tell her about a new play idea, no matter how simplistic or sappy it was. I'd been content to take the supporting role — male lead, ugly stepsister, wicked witch, or whatever was required — as long as she liked my stories.

"And you were quite the storyteller. Must be all that *reading* you do." She waved her hand and spat the word out like it disgusted her as she walked over to the dresser and picked up a small, antique-looking clock. She turned it over and began to fiddle with the back.

"What are you doing?"

She flashed me an expression of impatience. "Setting the clocks ahead, silly."

"Why?" I had to hear this.

"So we won't be late for anything. You know how I hate being late."

I loved my friend but sometimes her logic confounded even me. "You could just try getting ready earlier."

Cutting me off with a shake of her head, she set the clock down. "Doesn't work."

"And this does?"

"Absolutely. One tiny adjustment and *voilà*" — she rolled her hands with a flourish — "more time."

I knew her ambition stemmed toward Broadway and not quantum physics; but there were so many things wrong with that statement, I couldn't help but respond. "Uh, you know time's not really adjustable, right?"

"Sure it is," she replied as she scooped up an armload of socks and dumped them into my middle drawer with my shirts and sweaters. "Haven't you ever heard of leap year?"

I shook my head with a laugh, chalking it up to Kenna's special brand of logic. After removing the rest of my books, I zipped my suitcase and then shoved it under the bed, nearly hitting my head on the four-poster frame as a knock sounded on the bedroom door. I peeked over the edge of the mattress as the door swung open.

"Hi there!" A girl with blonde, curly hair and a huge smile walked into the bedroom. "Sorry, I didn't mean to startle you. My mum sent me over to welcome you to the cottage, *since we're of an age.*" Her lilting brogue and open expression caused me to like her instantly as she extended her hand to Kenna. "I'm the caretaker's daughter, Allyson Dell. Ally for short. You must be Gracie's niece."

"Hi. Call me Kenna." The girl shook hands with my BFF, and I noted the sun reflecting off the silver and rhinestone piercings in her nose, upper lip, and left eyebrow. The sparkling jewels coordinated with her outfit, making her look less Goth and more chic. "And this is Veronica Welling."

Ally turned her vivid green-eyed gaze on me and I waved from the other side of the bed. "Nice to meet you, Veronica. Would you girls be up for some local culture tomorrow night? I'd like to take you someplace special and buy you your first ale."

"That sounds perfect." Kenna clapped her hands together enthusiastically just as my cell vibrated from the nightstand.

Janet's picture popped up on the screen. I didn't want to answer — no sense ruining my first day in Scotland. But *maybe* she was worried and calling to make sure I arrived safely. Excusing myself, I snatched up the phone and walked over to the window.

"Hi, Mom."

"Punkin, you aren't going to believe what's happened!" She was practically jumping through the phone with excitement.

No interest in how I'd survived my first flight *ever* — across an ocean, no less — or what my plans were in a foreign country. Typical Janet. "What's that, Mom?"

"Bob asked me to marry him and I said yes!" All the blood drained from my head and I gripped the phone so hard I heard a cracking sound. "We're getting married as soon as we can get the license, and then he's takin' me to the casino for a whole week! Can you believe it?"

"Uh … uh," was the only response I could manage, since my vocal cords seemed to have dried up and turned to ash. No way would I live in the same house with my new *step-daddy*.

"Well, is that all you're going to say?" A hard note crept into her voice.

I swallowed, stiffening my spine defensively. "Congratulations?" It was more of a question than a statement.

"Thanks, darlin'! When you get back all your stuff will be waitin' for you in the shed. Bob's boxing it up now, so he can use your room for an office." Bob the redneck pervert was boxing up my stuff? Including my underwear? I clenched my teeth with a snap.

"Since you got the Purdue scholarship, darlin', we figured you would want all your stuff boxed up anyway."

It was only a partial scholarship and she knew I'd had to defer until I'd saved up enough money to cover the rest of the expenses. We'd agreed I'd live at home while I taught extra classes at the dance studio — a plan she'd conveniently forgotten in lieu of her own self-centered interests. "I gotta go, Mom. I'm losing the signal."

"Okay, bye." *Click.*

I stood absolutely still and stared out at the swaying trees, every muscle in my body tensed against the emotion ballooning in my chest. Was it possible that anyone on this earth would ever love me enough to care about what I wanted, instead of plowing ahead with their plans and leaving me behind to pick up the pieces?

"Vee, what is it?" Kenna asked.

I glanced over my shoulder, realizing that Ally was still in the room. She didn't need to see how pathetic my life was — if she hadn't figured it out already. Trying to sound nonchalant, I answered, "Mom's getting married and it looks like I'm homeless."

"Oh no! Not Bob the Slob?"

"Yeah — the one and only." I glanced at Kenna only to see my own hurt and betrayal reflected in her face. I attempted a smile but failed miserably. "I'll be all right, but I'm really tired. Think I'll lie down for a bit."

Allyson's honey brows scrunched over her perfect nose as she clucked sympathetically from the doorway. "You poor thing. A good rest is exactly what you need. Tomorrow you'll be right as rain. You'll see."

With a nod at Kenna, she added in a lower voice, "I'll just show m'self out."

We listened in silence as Ally's retreating footsteps echoed down the stairs and out the front door. The cottage suddenly felt oppressive, tainted by Janet's selfishness despite the ocean between us. Why had I thought coming to Scotland would change anything?

When Kenna finally spoke, her voice trembled. "Vee ... you know you can always come to Chicago with me."

I held up my hand to stop her words before we both ended up bawling like babies. "Can you give me a few minutes ... please?"

"Sure thing, sweetie."

Watching the sun's retreat across the unfamiliar landscape, I waited until Kenna left before letting my head rest against the cool pane of the window.

I felt like a beach ball tossed around by the whims of everyone around me. Eric decided when our relationship was over, Mom packed up my crap as if it'd been my choice to move out, Dad left without asking if I would've rather gone with him, and although Kenna asked me to go to Chicago, that was her dream, not mine. I was sick to death of other people dictating my future.

When would it be time to find *my* destiny?

The sun had nearly set, and I squinted to discern the view against the fading light. Past a clump of overgrown trees, the sapphire river flowed through the lush, green valley and disappeared under a sliver of arching gray stone.

As I stared, the awareness of a presence in the room raised goose bumps on my arms. Icy cold shot down my spine, followed by a rush of hot blood to my face. Someone stood inches behind me. The boy who'd been haunting my every waking hour was with me — I could *feel* him.

A shadowy reflection materialized above mine in the window — dark, intense eyes, golden brows, and strong, full lips. Fighting the urge to turn around, I stood petrified — afraid he would actually be there, and terrified he would not.

"*Verranica.*"

My eyes widened in shock as the deep timbre of his voice flowed through me. His mouth hadn't moved.

"*Ye dinna need to be afraid of me.*"

Afraid? I wasn't sure what I felt, but I didn't fear him. "Who are you?" The words escaped my lips in a strangled whisper.

"*James Thomas Kellan MacCrae.*" White teeth flashed in

a cocky grin as his image became clearer. *"Or ye can call me Jamie, if ye like."*

"Are you ... real?"

"Aye."

Slowly, I lifted my trembling fingers to the cool glass. In our reflection, his large hand moved to cover mine. And I felt it — a whisper of energy against my flesh.

"Verranica ..." His soft brogue stretched my name into a caress laced with longing.

Suddenly, his image began to recede toward the river, and he reached for me as we drifted farther apart. Swirls of mist enveloped the stone path beneath his feet, winding their way up his body. *"Come to me ..."*

I stumbled forward and pressed against the glass. I could no longer feel him. "Wait!"

The door swung open behind me, breaking the spell. The boy vanished. I whirled to find Kenna walking into the room.

"Are you searching for something?"

My pulse fluttered like hummingbird wings, and I gripped the window ledge behind me as I swayed on my feet. What the heck had just happened? If I *was* losing my mind, it was a pleasant way to go. But a deep instinct told me I hadn't invented Jamie MacCrae in my head. He might be a ghost, perhaps, but definitely not a psychotic delusion. Wait, I didn't believe in ghosts. *Did I?*

Remembering Kenna had asked me a question I grunted, "Huh?"

"I thought you might've been searching for the bridge."

"What bridge?"

"The Brig o' Doon." Kenna drew out the last word with a perfect Scottish brogue, sending tingles skittering over my shoulders. "It's Alloway's most famous landmark."

The gray arch I could see from my window was the Brig o' Doon? I spun around and strained my eyes through the looming darkness ... wondering if it resembled the stone pathway from my vision. "Can we walk down there?"

"Sure, but not tonight. There's a trail from the backyard, but the caretaker, Mrs. Dell, warned me before we arrived that it's badly overgrown. No sense breaking a leg our first night here. Get it? Break a leg?"

Kenna's drama club pals back home would've appreciated the joke, but I couldn't even muster a chuckle. I shoved my hands in my pockets to hide their shaking, and turned from the window to see Kenna analyzing me, her head cocked to one side. "Are you okay?"

I stared at her for a moment, considering if I should tell her about the visions ... or hauntings ... or whatever. Instead, my brain circled back to the arch of ancient-looking stones I'd seen and the possible connection to the actual bridge outside my window. "So, why is the Brig o' Doon famous?" I was pleased my voice only sounded a few octaves higher than normal.

"Uh, *Brigadoon!*" At my lack of recognition, she added, "The musical by the immortal Lerner and Loewe?"

She hummed a haunting melody as she ran her fingers along my stack of books, knocking them over like dominos, and then turned to me expectantly. "Surely you recognize 'Almost Like Being in Love.'"

"Nope." She'd made me watch so many musicals over the years ... I certainly couldn't remember them all. I pressed my lips together and shook my head as I walked over to the dresser and righted my precious tomes, glancing at my copy of *Oliver Twist*. That musical I remembered, due to its grievous omission of the character Monks.

Kenna rolled her eyes. "You researched Alloway, right?

Robert Burn's poem, *The Tam o' Shanter,* is set on the Brig o' Doon. That ring a bell?"

"Of course. I just didn't realized that the Brig o' Doon was so close to the cottage." It's not like any of the roads we'd traveled had been straight. However, the more I thought about it, I did remember her telling me something a long time ago about a bridge near her aunt's and a dark-haired boy with a brogue that used to call to her. "Didn't your imaginary friend live under that bridge?"

Kenna snorted. "Not under the bridge — he wasn't the troll from *The Three Billy Goats Gruff.* Finn lived on it. I can't believe you remembered that."

It was a random thing to remember … or was it? What were the odds that both she and I imagined Scottish boys standing on an ancient stone path and calling for us to come? One in a million?

"Vee …" Kenna stalked toward me with narrowed eyes. "You're doing that twisty thing with your hair. I can read you like a script, remember? What's really going on?"

Not realizing I'd been tying my hair into a knot, I lowered my hands and pushed out a loud breath. It had always been hard to keep secrets from the girl who knew me better than anyone on the planet. "Remember when I asked if you'd seen that hot blond guy in the kilt earlier?"

"Yesss …"

"Well, I … ah … keep seeing him … everywhere. The same gorgeous boy in a kilt. Even once in Bainbridge, right after I broke up with Eric." I slumped back against the dresser and stared at my cuticles. It sounded even more insane when I said it aloud. But if I was going to tell her, I might as well tell her everything. "He was here just now. Before you came in, and he … ah … talked to me."

"Really? You know what my dad would say, don't you?"

I shook my head. Kenna's dad taught undergraduate psychology. Growing up, he'd had a psychological reason for everything, even why my dad walked out on us. Kenna crossed to the bed and sat on the edge, staring up at me with grave eyes. "He'd say 'Kilt Boy' is your anti-Eric."

"What's that supposed to mean?"

"He's your knight in shining armor. The perfect boy. Someone heroic who'd never choose their own interests ahead of yours." Her fingers absently brushed the quilted fabric of the comforter as she continued. "Think about it. He conveniently shows up after Eric dumps you, then again after your mom chooses Bob the Slob. Doesn't that seem a little bit convenient?"

She had a point. He had a knack for appearing just as my life was turning upside down. "So I'm crazy? That's the explanation?"

She stood and bridged the gap between us in a couple strides. "Actually, you're one of the sanest people I know. You're probably just hungry, sweetie. And tired."

As if on cue, my tummy growled like a ferocious animal.

"See?" Kenna patted me on the arm. "I'm sure you'll feel better with a full belly and a good night's sleep."

Maybe ... but that place deep inside of me that insisted I wasn't delusional didn't buy into the imaginary hero theory either. But to convince Kenna that I wasn't cuckoo for Cocoa Puffs, I needed some kind of irrefutable proof.

As I followed Kenna down the back stairs to the kitchen, my inner Nancy Drew went on full alert. I'd noticed tons of books in the library downstairs on Scots folklore and history. It seemed like the perfect place to start researching the mystery of the Vanishing Golden Boy. Besides, with the image of *Jamie's* pleading eyes as he faded away burned in my brain, getting any sleep was highly doubtful.

CHAPTER 3

Mackenna

Every truly happy memory from my childhood involved an old woman who dressed like a rainbow and the house she adored. I'd come to stay at Dunbrae Cottage the first time when I was six, right after my mom died. I remember living in a world enshrouded with grief, all drawn curtains and mourning clothes. Then Dad put me on a plane — alone — which was terrifying, except I did get as much soda as I could drink. After landing, I emerged from the breezeway to find an old lady wearing an emerald green dress and a fuchsia turban. Clutched in her hands was a sign that said "Welcome Mackenna" in pink glitter.

She hugged me tight, smelling like lavender and arthritis cream, and whispered, "I'm so glad you're here, sweetie." Then she took me to the airport gift shop and bought me a pink plaid dress. Mostly, I remember laughing with her as we left my black clothes in the airport bathroom trash. That was the first of many joyous summers, filled with wonder and sparkles ... Special Scottish seasons of love.

As I walked through my aunt's beloved cottage with my morning coffee, I indulged in my cherished memories — mornings spent journaling at the kitchen table, our afternoon sing-alongs in the dining room, and high tea in the living room, which Aunt Gracie always called "the parlor."

The wildly overgrown English-style garden, complete with croquet lawn and a bronze wall fountain in the shape of a lion's head, held a particularly special place in my heart. After breakfast, my aunt would sketch while I picked armloads of fresh lavender for her special green vase. The one she kept in the library and claimed came from another world.

As Gracie arranged the fragrant, purple flowers, she would tell the most amazing stories. My favorite was about an enchanted kingdom hidden away from evil witches in the mists of Scotland. Now as I admired the chaotic garden from the library windows, I questioned the wisdom of sharing Gracie's stories with my best friend. My aunt always indulged my imagination, going as far as setting a place at the table for my imaginary guests. But what Vee needed was less fiction in her life, not more.

I'd seen the haunted look in her eyes as she talked about Kilt Boy. Which made my decision as easy as an Andrew Lloyd Webber melody. My duty was to keep her from traveling farther down the yellow brick path of delusion . . . one that I knew from experience would inevitably end in misery and heartbreak. So I would not share any family tales of noble knights or fantastical kingdoms. I'd stick to practical traditions. Filling Gracie's vase with lavender, minus the story of its origins, would still be a fitting tribute to the woman whose love had shaped the direction of my life and a perfect start to our epic summer.

"Jamie — "

Holy Hammerstein! I spun toward the noise, ready to scream as my vision focused on Vee fidgeting in her sleep in the oversized chair in the corner. She was surrounded by books — legends and histories of Scotland, and biographies on the local poet Robert Burns. Apparently Sleeping Beauty had a restless night. Whereas I'd slept like the dead.

"Brig — Jamie. Stay."

Okay . . . that was random, and a little weird.

Vee made a tiny mewling sound, like an anxious kitten. Concerned, I crept closer. Other than the noises, she looked fine. More than fine — she was flawless, even asleep. Dark, sleek hair framed her heart-shaped face. Black, fluttery lashes — the kind you only see in mascara ads — daintily rested against the curve of her cheeks. Vee was petite, too, with porcelain skin. Stuff all that into a size-too-small cheer skirt and she was a teen dream. She practically screamed popularity, while I was an ex-Goth, theater-geek Amazon voted most likely to have ketchup on my boobs. But I guess that's what made the friendship unbreakable — counterbalance, not ketchup.

As if she could sense me staring like some kind of deranged stalker, Vee's eyelids fluttered open to reveal her confused, yet still brilliantly dazzling, turquoise eyes.

She bolted to her feet, brushing silken strands of dark hair away from her face. How did she get it to look so shiny? Even in the midst of night terrors, she still looked like she'd stepped off the cover of *Teen Vogue*. I, on the other hand, was in jeopardy of being mistaken for an iconic hamburger clown.

Vee turned in a disoriented half circle, blinking at the pile of books around her chair. "I must've fallen asleep."

"Ya think?" She stilled and regarded me with a narrow gaze that dared me to continue cracking smart remarks. *Geez, somebody woke up on the wrong side of the Atlantic.* Taking a more serious approach, I said, "You must've been having some dream. You were talking in your sleep and everything."

"I was?"

"Yep. So who's Jamie?"

Her face paled as she sagged against the back of the chair for support. "Have you ever had a dream so real you weren't sure if you were asleep or awake?"

Vee's voice sounded hollow, and I wondered what kind of crazy messed-up nightmares plagued her. "You mean good real ... like when I'm playing Glinda in the Broadway revival of *Wicked*? 'Cause I dream about that at least once a week. Or bad real, like that time I got caught in the zombie apocalypse in my underwear?"

Vee's already pale face blanched ghostly proportions as she answered, "I don't mean a dream exactly ... More like a vision you see during the day — so rich and colorful, the person so real that you feel like they've been there all your life, only you just couldn't see them before."

"Wait. Are we talking about Kilt Boy again?" When she nodded, I shoved my coffee into her trembling hands. She obviously needed it more than I did. What I needed was to tread carefully. Vee had the same haunted look from the previous evening. It was eerily similar to the phase where she saw her MIA dad around every corner and driving every passing car. "I think some people have more vivid imaginations than others. Aunt Gracie was like that. She used to capture all her dreams in a journal. Then in the margins, she would scribble all kinds of crazy notes."

"Journal? What did it look like?" She drained the coffee in one long gulp, set the mug on a nearby table, and crouched down to dig through the mound of books.

"You expect me to describe it? I was eleven the last time I was here."

"Like this?" She stood, holding up a thick book of worn, dark brown leather. In the center, a Celtic knot-like heart bore the letters G. L. for Gracie Lockhart. Vee flipped it over, regarding the rawhide tie that fastened the flaps. "Wow, it looks really old."

"It might be."

Vee stood and walked over to the bay window, cradling the book like a wounded bird. "I could go through it ... if you want. See if it contains anything important ... give you the CliffsNotes ... like when we were in school. I know how much you hate to read ... unless it's for a role. Which this isn't."

I didn't have to *read* her face to see through her act. She'd been a terrible liar when she'd tried the dog-ate-my-homework excuse on Mrs. Trimble in the third grade, and age hadn't improved her performance skills. The babbling was a dead giveaway.

She thought the journal had something to do with Kilt Boy. If I didn't find some way to distract her from her new obsession, she'd spend the whole summer with her nose buried in my aunt's journal and we'd never meet any actual boys in kilts. Feigning indifference, I held out my hand until she surrendered her treasure and made a show of flipping through the pages. "I'll look through it. But I doubt it will make any sense — Gracie cornered the market on cryptic. I used to think she was wonderfully mysterious, like Norma Desmond."

"Who?"

"Norma Desmond. From *Sunset Boulevard*?" My bestie shook her head blankly as I readied a smart remark. But the reply died on my lips when I realized she wasn't paying attention to our conversation. Instead, she stared at the seven-by-five-inch volume of leather and paper like it contained the cure for cancer.

The front bell chimed, causing Vee to leap into the air like a very nimble, and very startled, cat. She pressed one hand to her heart and then raked the other through her hair. "That's probably the caretaker, right? Ally's mom?"

"Adelaide Dell." Using my best *Mary Poppins* accent to loosen her up, I added, "Ally said her mum would 'pop round' today to see how we were getting on."

Still clutching the journal and humming, I stepped in time to the door and wrestled briefly with the deadbolt before opening it. The woman on the other side was ... surprisingly modern. With a name like Adelaide, I'd pictured a matronly, middle-aged woman with wisps of graying hair escaping from her bun and spectacles hanging from a chain across her bosom. This woman was reminiscent of an aging runway model. Her pale blonde hair brushed her chin in an asymmetric style. And her designer ensemble — wedged pumps, pinstripe suit, and flared navy blue raincoat — reminded me of something I'd seen recently in a Saks Fifth Avenue window. Despite the overcast skies, she didn't carry an umbrella.

"Good mornin' girls." The woman stepped into the foyer and waited for me to close the door before extending her hand. "You must be Mackenna. I'm Addie Dell. Well now, you've grown into a lovely young woman."

"Thanks." I didn't remember meeting her during my previous visits, but it had been seven years since the last time I'd been to Alloway. When I shook her hand, I complimented her on the renovations. "Everything is even more amazing than in the pictures."

"I'm ever so pleased the upgrades are to your liking." Addie's regal smile faltered slightly as her sharp green eyes slid past me. "And you, of course, are the friend."

Following Addie's gaze, I noticed Vee was still in her candy-striped sleep shorts and pink tank that read EAT SLEEP DANCE REPEAT. Of course, I was no better in my sweat pants and oversized *Les Mis* T-shirt. Feeling fifty shades of awkward, I hastily introduced my bestie to the woman who'd taken such meticulous care of my late aunt's legacy.

Addie clasped Vee's hand in both of hers and gave it a shake. Rather than let go, she lingered, staring with narrow, speculative eyes. "Allyson didn't tell me you were so ... *passionate.*"

The way she said it — almost like another word had been on the tip of her tongue — made me wonder what she meant. She finally let go of Vee's hand and focused on her shirt. "You're a dancer, I see."

Vee nodded but crossed her arms over her chest self-consciously as I stepped between them. "Sorry, you caught us in our pajamas."

Addie nodded politely, as if wearing pajamas instead of real clothes was a valid life choice. She pulled a sleek black binder from her designer bag and extended it to me. "Then I'll just leave this paperwork with you and scoot to my next appointment."

The "paperwork" was to transfer Dunbrae Cottage into my name. As Addie handed me the documents, her eyes widened. "Is that your aunt's journal?" When I nodded, she covered my hand, and the book, with her own perfectly manicured fingers. Her touch, cold but gentle, zapped me with a shock of static electricity. "I could've sworn that it was boxed up in the attic with the rest of your aunt's personal effects. How *ever* did you come across it?"

Vee stepped forward. "I found it in the library. With the books on Scotland."

Addie arched a thin, perfectly sculpted brow. "Did you now? How very peculiar. I must say, that is a most fortuitous discovery."

Since we were on the subject of my aunt's belongs, there was another item I needed to locate. I cleared my throat and Addie turned to me, unleashing a bright smile the exact replica of her daughter's. "Yes, dear?"

"Uh, my aunt had a green vase that she kept in the library. Do you know what happened to it?"

"I expect you'll find it in the attic with the rest of Mrs. Lockhart's personal effects." She cast a quick glance in Vee's direction before continuing. "However, if you don't, I'd consult wee Veronica here. She seems to be particularly clever in the area of finding hidden things."

With a friendly wave, Addie strode away on her stylish shoes. The minute her candy apple red Mini Cooper roared down the lane, the skies opened up. Cold droplets of rain pelted the earth in an angry staccato, making me anxious to get back to the sanctuary of the library.

As I closed the door, Vee asked, "Do you still want to go down to the Brig o' Doon today?"

"In this monsoon?" I shook my head. "We've got two whole months to play tourist. What I really want is to find Gracie's vase before we meet Ally tonight."

"What a coincidence." Her eyes flicked away and back, but not before I noticed her tracking the journal. "Because I was just thinking you might want to go through your aunt's things sooner rather than later."

Although Vee's words made sense, and my aunt's belongings did need to get back in their proper place, I worried her suggestion was some kind of ploy to separate me from the journal. I wouldn't keep it from her forever, just long enough to read it myself and determine if the contents would help or hurt her obsession with Kilt Boy. But in the meantime, I needed her out of the way so I could hide the book. "While I'm doing that, maybe you should take a shower?"

She hesitated, her eyes flicking again to the book in my hand. "I think I might try to take a nap first … I feel like I'm still suffering from jetlag."

A nap would work as well, but I wasn't kidding about her needing to bathe. Tucking the journal into my waistband, I replied, "Get some rest then. I'll wake you up in plenty of time to get clean and pretty for our first evening out in Alloway. Unless you want to show up at the tavern smelling like Stinking Beauty. But if you do, I can guarantee no kilt-wearing hottie is going to come within fifty feet, let alone kiss you."

CHAPTER 4

Veronica

Ye all ought ta be verra careful as ye traverse these hallowed roads this eve … or risk goin' the way o' Old Meg and lose yer own tail!"

With a flourish of his blue-veined hand, the old man finished his recitation of the *Tam o'Shanter* to raucous cheers and applause from the crowd. His shriveled face, covered in brown spots, reminded me of the dried-up crabapples that littered our backyard in Indiana. Strike that—Janet and *Bob's* yard in Indiana. Grasping my mug of ale, I took a huge swallow, the bitter liquid coating my tongue and flowing in a warm path down to my stomach. With the back of my hand, I swiped the foam from my upper lip and glanced across the table at Kenna. Her auburn hair caught glints of light in the otherwise dim tavern as she bounced in her chair applauding the old actor's performance. I envied her ability to live in the moment, enjoying every experience without the encumbrance of her past or any worry for her future.

Earlier, when she'd woken me from a three-hour nap, I'd

felt like somebody'd roofied my tea. My brain spun with the local legends and folklore I'd read the night before, desperately trying to make some connection to my waking visions. Even now, as I sat shoulder to shoulder with Kenna and Ally at the old Tam O'Shanter Inn, Jamie clung to my thoughts like Spanish moss. I couldn't help but wonder when he would show up again.

I let my gaze wander to the low beamed ceiling and the walls darkened with three centuries of smoke and grime. This place was straight off the pages of *The Legend of Sleepy Hollow*. A perfect backdrop for an ethereal visitation. Then again, on closer inspection, the eighteenth-century pretense didn't quite hold under the harsh flicker of electric torches and our server's neon-pink gym shoes peeking out from under her peasant skirt.

Returning my attention to the occupants of our cozy corner table, I watched Ally lean back in her seat, eyes half closed, soaking in the atmosphere. Kenna, on the other hand, craned her neck, her back hunched at an odd angle as if she were searching for something she'd dropped. "Hey, Ken, did you lose something?"

"Nope, just looking for hobbits." She straightened with a lopsided grin. "Doesn't this place remind you of the Shire?"

I barked out a laugh, the mouthful of ale I'd just swallowed in danger of spewing out of my nose. "I was thinking Sleepy Hollow, but yeah, I can totally see Bilbo here."

Ally laughed along with us and then raised her pint in salute. The flame from the candle on our table reflected on her bejeweled piercings, making her appear more elven or fairy than girl. As if choreographed, the slow strains of live bagpipes began to underscore her toast. "To Mackenna and Veronica and the beginnings of a marvelous new adventure. May new worlds be opened to them, and no matter where they roam, may they be vessels of something greater than themselves."

"Here, here." Ken and I clinked our glasses to hers before taking long drinks. My head began to feel like a balloon floating on a string. I turned to ask Ally if we could order some mozzarella sticks, or the Scottish equivalent, but her next comment swept away all thoughts of food.

She leaned forward, the sparkle of her emerald eyes eclipsing her facial jewels. "Now friends, are you ready to hear the *real* legend of the Brig o' Doon?"

"Didn't we just hear it?" Kenna asked before turning her attention back to the small stage where a fiddler joined the song, kicking up the tempo.

With a quirk of her perfectly arched brow, Ally caught my eyes. "The *Tam* is but a child's tale. I'm talking about the *true* history of the Bridge of Doon ... and what waits on the other side."

The image of Jamie MacCrae swayed before my eyes, his boot-clad feet firmly planted on an arch of gray stone, his deep, rolling voice calling, *"Verranica ... Come to me."*

Ally's rosebud lips quirked into a surreptitious smile before her intense gaze shifted to something behind me and she waved. "Alasdair! Come meet some new friends of mine from the States."

The wizened old man approached our table and inclined his head in an old-fashioned gesture of respect. "Ladies."

"Won't you join us for a pint, Alasdair? My friends here were wantin' to know more about the Brig o' Doon."

"Certainly." He took the seat across the table from me, rubbed his white-stubble-covered chin as he contemplated each of us with keen, blue-gray eyes. "This tale is not for the faint of heart, lasses."

Kenna's lips tilted slightly as she met his challenge. "I think we can handle it."

The old actor shifted his attention to me and I gave him a nod of assent, my voice trapped in my chest.

"All right, then." A grin creased the man's craggy face, lighting his countenance like a sunrise. "What most people dinna know, my fair lassies" — he rested his crossed arms on the table and lowered his voice in a theatrical whisper — "is that Robert Burns dinna create the legend of Brig o' Doon. He borrowed it from an even older tale."

I leaned forward and the clamor of the crowded pub faded away.

"Once upon a time, there existed a prosperous kingdom called Doon. It was rich with fertile lands and abundant mountain streams, its beauty beyond compare. The wise and just leader, King Angus Andrew Kellan MacCrae, was adored by all."

A slow shiver crawled up my spine. What were the chances of my dream boy and this mythical king sharing not one, but two names? I glanced at Kenna, her foot tapping to the music as she drew a series of circles in the condensation on her mug. Could I tell her about the connection? The answer was an easy *no*. She'd make some crack about "obsessive delusions" then never surrender her aunt's journal. I had to find out what Gracie knew.

With effort, I reigned in my focus and turned back to the old man. He angled toward me so that the candle's glow distorted the plains and recesses of his face, giving the appearance that his jaw unhinged as he spoke.

"But what is seen as light will forever be coveted by the dark. And so it was that the kingdom o' Doon was targeted by a coven of witches who desired to possess the realm for themselves. For years, they tried to seize the kingdom. No matter what strategy they employed — be it covert tactics to undermine the royal family or open warfare — they were thwarted at every turn.

"One legend has it that the witches raised an army of the undead to fight against the king's forces. But even against this aberration of nature, Doon's royal army reigned supreme. And yet, our witches didna give up." Alasdair paused dramatically to lean even closer to our captivated ears.

"'Tis purported that they made a pact wi' Auld Clootie hisself. A foul bargain that would deliver Doon into their hands. In exchange, the witches would place the Great Deceiver on the throne as their king, and all the righteous subjects o' Doon would be bound to him for eternity.

"So the kingdom was beset by catastrophe at ever' turn. First, illness struck the palace. The king's true love — his lovely queen — died, crippling the ruler with grief. Then the undead army returned in numbers so great not even the brave knights of Doon could keep them at bay. Finally, King MacCrae's infant son succumbed to the very illness that killed the queen and so many others."

The old man slumped back in his seat, silent. Several long seconds ticked by while we waited for him to continue. When he seemed disinclined to do so, I couldn't hold my silence any longer.

"That's it? Evil wins?" This tragic tale could not be the end of the legend!

"I was no' finished, young lady. Give an old man a moment to rest," he said with an impish grin and a wink.

After finishing half his ale in one long draw, Alasdair settled back into his tale. "So, bein' the God-fearing man that he was, the good king locked himself in the chapel and spent seven days and nights on his knees in prayer. He wouldna accept food nor drink, nor the counsel of his advisors. When he finally emerged, his youngest son was healed, and what was left o' Doon's army returned to the palace claiming the undead monsters had vanished.

"Gatherin' all his people, the king explained that their kingdom had been placed under an enchantment that would protect them from destruction at the witches' hands ... that they would, in fact, be an island to themselves and no one would be able to get in or out of the boundaries save for one day ever' hundred years."

No one at the table spoke for several seconds, and in the lull the sounds around me began to filter back into my consciousness. A haunting melody played in the background accompanied by a clear, sweet voice, *"Will ye go, lassie, go ..."*

By all logic, an enchanted kingdom was too perfect to exist — *didn't exist.* But I couldn't silence the voice in my head asking, *What if?* What if the boy who shared a name with the original king of Doon, the same boy who'd wedged himself in my otherwise lifeless heart, was out there somewhere waiting for me to find him?

"So," Kenna said with a smirk, snapping me out of my reverie. "How does one find this Scottish Shangri-la?"

"Ah-hah. You see, that is the great mystery. Many learned people have made it their life's work to discover the kingdom of Doon." His faded blue eyes narrowed. "But I happen to know of a reliable source that saw Doon with her own eyes." He lifted his glass toward Kenna. "To Grace Lockhart! God rest her soul."

Kenna sat straight up in her chair. "How did you know my aunt?"

"'Tis a small world, Mackenna Reid." With a tip of his head, Alasdair wished us good night and shuffled back to the bar, Ally following on his heels.

"He's such a liar. My aunt may have loved to tell tales, but I don't believe for one minute she thought any of them were real." Kenna turned to me and hitched a thumb over her shoulder at the departing old man. "Do you believe that guy?"

"I don't know …"

"Oh, come on, Vee, fairy tales don't exist. You of all people should know that."

She was right. I was no longer that little girl who wished on falling stars. I'd learned from experience hoping for the impossible just ended in heartbreak … but did that mean I'd stopped believing altogether?

I clenched my teeth and stared into my empty mug, the buzzy feeling its contents had given me long gone. "You're right." I pushed down my melancholy, and gave her a bright smile. "Make-believe can be fun sometimes, though."

Her gaze caught mine. "Sure. But like with acting, one needs to be able to tell the difference between fantasy and reality."

That was the thing, I *did* know the difference. And the more information I discovered, the less I could shake the feeling that whatever was happening to me was very real.

🦋 🦋 🦋

I listened to the clock in the library chime once and glanced at Kenna. She sat slumped on the living room sofa, snoring softly while a DVD of the latest *Les Miserables* remake played on the flat screen. Although she'd been the one insistent on a movie musical marathon, she'd not even lasted through Fantine's fall into ruin.

Mindful of the creaking wood, I crept up the stairs and down the darkened hall to her room. Why I was *creeping,* I wasn't sure. Once Kenna was out, nothing but a gaggle of zombies could rouse her … and maybe not even that.

My skin prickled with anticipation as I switched on her bedside lamp and began searching for the journal. I wanted to find proof for Kenna, but I also *needed* to see what was inside the tiny book — needed to find validation for myself that the voice inside my heart whispered the truth.

Both cluttered nightstands were empty of books. Moving to the dresser, I opened drawers and sorted through familiar articles of Kenna's colorful wardrobe. Sneakiness was not really in my nature, and a vague sense of guilt gave me pause until I reminded myself I was doing this for Kenna's own good ... as well as mine. The question of Doon's existence was already driving a wedge between us. She was too pragmatic to believe without concrete proof. And without evidence, she would continue to dismiss my instincts as literary-influenced romanticism — or in Kenna speak, nuttier than a squirrel on crack.

Opening the right bottom drawer, I pushed aside haphazardly folded piles of pajamas until my fingers connected with cool, smooth leather. I scooped up the journal, my hands trembling slightly as I carried it into the light. I carefully undid the tie and opened the fragile book to a random entry. The words blurred for a moment, forcing me to close my eyes to regain my focus. The pages felt stiff like parchment and smelled faintly of old sandals and lavender. Breathing deeply, I opened my eyes and began to read:

> *Nearly a century had passed since Cameron had been born, though in Doon this had been but the blink of an eye. With his midnight hair, smooth skin, and gray-blue eyes, it was clear he was not yet twenty years of age. He explained that Doon did not exist as part of the mortal world.*

I sat down, hard. Luckily the desk chair was there to catch

me. Kenna's *Uncle* Cameron? Skimming the rest of the page, I noted that Gracie described a picnic date, but I wasn't clear if she and Cameron were in Doon or the "mortal world" at the time, so I skipped ahead a few pages to a crude map labeled *The Kingdom*. There were bodies of water, mountains, house shapes labeled as *crofter, market, blacksmith*, clustered buildings marked as *The Village*, and a huge structure set at the end of a vast lake labeled *The Castle MacCrae*. I traced my finger from the bridge depicted at the bottom of the drawing past a forest, through the village, up to the castle, and wondered how far it would be on foot.

Pulling my mind back to the challenge at hand, I realized this proved nothing, other than the fact that the journal's author had an even richer imagination than my own. I flipped through the pages to see if anything caught my eye. Near the end, a single loose piece of paper drifted from the book and landed facedown at my feet.

I picked up the paper, and as I turned it over a shock ran through my entire body.

"Jamie."

The name left my lips as I stared at the lifelike drawing of the unbelievably gorgeous boy who'd haunted me for weeks. His eyes, dark and intense, smoldered at me from the page. Broad cheekbones, stubble-covered square jaw, perfect lips, slashing brows, and yes, the delectable dimple in his stubborn-looking chin were captured on the page in a perfect likeness.

The caption read *James Thomas Kellan MacCrae IV.*

My vision blurred as I choked back a sob. The picture confirmed what I'd known in my soul — Jamie was real.

The sound of heavy footsteps on the stairs forced me out of my daze.

Shoot!

Was this the proof I needed to show Kenna? Or would she come up with some explanation for this too? I needed more.

With a sigh of regret, I stuffed the small book in among Kenna's sleepwear and socks, and carefully shut the drawer. Switching off the lamp, I sprinted from the room and across the hall just as Ken's shadow stretched from the stairwell at the opposite end. In my own room, I eased the door shut and sagged against it ... the portrait still grasped in my trembling hand.

CHAPTER 5

Veronica

Kenna wove her way through a maze of trunks, boxes, and clothing racks, tugging at chains to turn on a row of dust-coated light bulbs. I followed behind, peering into every nook and cranny of the cavernous attic. I'd almost walked down to the Brig o' Doon a handful of times the previous night, but the rain and my fear had kept me tucked safely inside the cottage. I still had nothing tangible to connect Jamie MacCrae to the bridge. There had to be hundreds of stone bridges in Scotland. What were the odds, when I stepped onto the Brig o' Doon, that he'd be waiting there like a dream come to life? And what if he wasn't? What then?

Without warning, Kenna stopped. I nearly crashed into her, managing to dodge at the last second. A crease wrinkled her pale forehead. With a huff she bent to pick up a green glass vase filled with crumbling sprigs of dried lavender. "Sweet Baby Sondheim! How did I miss this yesterday? I searched through half the attic, and it was right under my nose the whole time."

Was Jamie right under my nose? I glanced at Kenna,

tempted to tell her again that the golden-haired boy was real, but her eyes were distant. Her lower lip trembled as she blinked into the artificial light. "I miss her so much," she whispered.

Pushing away my own preoccupation, I determined that my present priority had to be my best friend. Kenna'd always been there for me, and now it was my turn. I took her hand and gave it a gentle squeeze. "I know. She loved you and you'll always have that, right?"

"Right." She swiped the moisture from under her eyes and snuffled loudly. "I'm really glad we're doing this today. The cottage doesn't feel complete without her stuff."

Eons later we'd sorted almost everything into piles of sell, keep, or trash — but still hadn't found the boxes of Gracie's personal items Addie claimed were tucked in the attic.

With a sigh, I turned to the next trunk. The lid creaked open to reveal an old-fashioned bonnet. Rimmed in lace, its wide turquoise ribbons arranged in a neat line, it looked like a prop from a Jane Austen movie. I scooped up the hat, and its delicate material crumpled in my fingers like butterfly wings as I placed it on the floor. Underneath were what appeared to be the contents of a desk. It was odd that antique clothing would be packed with papers and envelopes addressed to … *Mrs. Grace Lockhart.* "Kenna! I think I found something."

Kneeling side by side, Kenna and I began removing the contents of the trunk: official-looking letters, boxes of old checks, address labels, and photo albums. Rain beat against the attic roof, filling the space with an escalating rhythm that matched my racing heart. Each drop proclaimed, *close — close — close.*

Kenna pulled out a book with a maroon cover. "Look! Aunt Gracie's scrapbook. It's filled with clippings about local history."

Close — close — close.

The trunk was nearly empty. Only one large padded envelope

remained. I reached in and lifted the bulky package. "Uh ... this one's addressed to you."

"Me? Let me see it."

Rain turned to hail, pelting the windows as I handed Kenna the parcel with her full name scrawled across the front. Underneath her name, it said, *From Grace Lockhart — In the event of my death.*

For long seconds Kenna sat in silence, flipping the package over and over in her hands, and then threw it into my lap. "You open it." Her gray eyes had darkened like the storm clouds that currently hovered over our cottage.

As I emptied the contents of the packet between us, lightning flashed nearby, causing the lights to flicker. When the electricity decided to stay on, we both stared at the floor where I'd dumped the single sheet of heavy paper and a clear plastic bag containing two rings.

Despite being completely illogical, I'd seen *something* the instant the rings had tumbled from the envelope. I carefully picked up the baggie, turning it back and forth. Surely the twinkling sparkles that'd hung in the air were a reflection of the storm outside ...

I took the gold ring from the bag and admired the intricate symbols carved in swirls around the band. It was beautiful ... Slipping it on my finger, I stared at the multifaceted red gem set into its center. A sudden rush of warmth spread along my hand, sending tingles throughout my entire body. My vision blurred and images flashed before my eyes ... lush rolling hills, a meadow bursting with rainbow-hued flowers, pristine snow-tipped mountains, and ancient castle turrets stretching into a cloudless sky.

With a snap, the images were gone. I sucked in a sharp breath and stared down at the ring. The scent of the crisp, sweet air from my vision lingered around me. I squeezed my eyes shut and searched behind my closed lids trying to get it back. A sense of such intense longing filled me that my heart ached in my chest. The place was like nowhere I'd ever been, or seen, yet it felt like *home.*

"Vee, you okay?"

I blinked several times before focusing on the blurred figure of my friend. "Um ... yeah. Check out this ring."

Determined to act casual, I handed Kenna the baggie with the other ring still inside, reluctant to let mine go for even a moment. I watched her face as she pulled out the silver ring and slid it on her finger. Its carvings were identical to the one I wore, the stone in its center a brilliant green.

"I don't remember Aunt Gracie ever having these." Kenna examined what looked to be a Celtic design. "They look like antiques."

"But do you *feel* anything?"

She searched my face as if waiting for a punch line. "Hungry, maybe ... *do you feel something?*"

"Ah, well no, of course not. It just feels — you know — heavy." I turned my attention to the envelope, checking to make sure that was all it contained.

Slowly, I looked up to find my friend biting at her lower lip as she battled her emotions. She reached toward the folded sheet of paper lying on the floor and then snatched her hand back like she'd been burned. "The letter from my aunt. Will you read it, please?"

I took the worn stationery and searched Kenna's face. Unshed tears filled her eyes, giving them a silvery shine. "Sure." An odd combination of trepidation and expectancy sent my already jittery nerves tingling as I opened the letter and began to read aloud.

My Dearest Mackenna,

At the time I write this, another chapter of my life is drawing to a close. Once again, my beloved Cameron calls to me. And I long to be reunited with him. This time, forever.

I paused and glanced at my friend. She stared at the floor, making it impossible to read her emotions.

As I scanned the next line of the letter, the paper began to shake in my fingers. Propping my elbows on my knees, I pressed on, relieved there was only a slight tremor in my voice.

I am one hundred and fifty-one years old and have lived a long, happy life full of love and purpose. My only regret, dearest Mackenna, is that I must convey your legacy in writing — for I would rather share this with you in person.

Remember the stories I used to tell you as a child? I pray, my dear, that your heart is still open to extraordinary tales, because I am about to tell you the most miraculous one of them all.

In 1882, at the age of nineteen, I finished my studies, and had just accepted a position as a governess in Glasgow when the visions began. I was haunted by a boy with black hair and whimsical gray eyes. He called to me from the Brig o' Doon.

My stomach catapulted into my throat. She had visions too?

Although I had not intended to detour on my way north, I felt drawn to the small village of Alloway. Along the journey, I stumbled upon an antique ruby ring in a curiosity shoppe and spent most of my meager traveling allowance to purchase it. From the moment I slipped it on my finger, I felt a sense of urgency and purpose.

I glanced at the ruby ring on my finger and then up at my best friend. She sat motionless, staring into the shadows.

The minute I laid eyes on the Brig o' Doon, my feet moved as if they had wings. I burned with the need to cross to the other side. As I reached the center of the auld brig, my ring began to glow.

On the far bank, the boy I'd been dreaming of stepped from the mists, his silver and emerald ring glowing in answer to mine. Behind him stood a glorious castle that grew sharper with each step. The ring had led me to Doon — a beautiful kingdom outside of time and place — where Cameron, my true love, waited. We were married that same day.

Cam and I spent twenty bliss-filled years in his kingdom before destiny led us back across the Brig o' Doon. Strangely, the world I remembered was gone. Over eighty years had passed on this side of the portal. The year was 1960.

Eventually, I was able to track my sister's descendants to America and reconnect with my only living relatives. I shared my secret with your mother when she turned eighteen, but her future lay elsewhere. Now I leave the legacy of Doon to your keeping, dearest Mackenna. The kingdom is your destiny, if you are courageous enough to embrace it.

All my love,

Aunt Gracie

The rain had stopped, plunging us in a shroud of silence as Kenna stared into her hands. Her mouth opened and closed but formed no discernible words. Unsure of what to say, I set the letter down and asked, "What do you think?"

She shrugged and twisted the emerald ring on her finger, her lips pursed and trembling.

I searched her profile and tried to put myself in her place. As far as I knew, she hadn't experienced any visions of her own, but surely she couldn't dismiss the words of the woman she'd known better than her own mother. When I spoke, it came out as a whisper. "This is all pretty extraordinary — don't you think so?"

"My aunt was always making up stories for me ... Pretending they were real. I guess she wanted to leave me with one last fantastical tale."

"It doesn't sound like a made-up story. Don't you think it lines up perfectly with what Alasdair told us at the pub?"

"He probably heard it from her." Beads of sweat dotted Kenna's forehead and upper lip.

"Maybe your aunt's journal would help clarify things? We could read it together."

"Just stop." She held up her hand, her eyes clamped shut.

I didn't tell her that I'd skimmed the first several pages — mostly genealogies, and family trees — while she'd been in the shower, or that I was already plotting to examine it again after she fell asleep. It would be so much easier if I could study the journal without the secrecy. I didn't want to lie to her. Maybe if she knew how similar my visions were to what Gracie and

Cameron experienced, and if I showed her the sketch ... "What if I could prove — "

"No — enough. I thought she just made those stories up for me, but apparently she went around telling the whole village she came from another planet." Kenna shook her head like a child who thought if she plugged her ears and closed her eyes she'd become invisible. Suddenly she sprang to her feet. "I can't deal with this right now."

As I listened to her retreating footsteps, I decided not to go after her. Maybe once she decompressed, she'd be more receptive to what I had to say. Plus, that would give me time to go through her aunt's things and find more proof. I carefully gathered the rest of Gracie's papers and tucked them inside the envelope.

My heart broke for Kenna and the confusion she must be feeling, but as far as I was concerned there was no doubt left in my mind. When I'd slipped on the ring, it was like a window opening to another world. I could see it and feel it, almost touch it. Despite past disappointments, I wanted the fairy tale — handsome prince and all. And if I didn't do everything within my power to find this magical place, this kingdom of Doon, I'd regret it for the rest of my life.

CHAPTER 6

Mackenna

Without conscious thought as to where I was going, I stormed into my bedroom, the door slamming in my wake. The walls trembled as my entrance dislodged a set of costume butterfly wings from an overstuffed shelf. The delicate keepsake spiraled to the floor in a gossamer swirl of silver, orange, and bright blue.

My first visit to Alloway had been sheer magic. Like something from *Mame*. My wonderfully strange, larger-than-life aunt converted her dining room into a stage, and we spent the entire summer cocooned in a world of make-believe — creating gorgeous sets and costumes to accompany our scripted stories of Scottish lore. I emerged from that summer a new creature; a confident, creative butterfly with an incurable obsession for theater.

Now, I resisted the urge to stomp the memento of my metamorphosis into shreds as I questioned whether Gracie's passion had been tinged with madness all along. Maybe I'd just been too young to realize the most influential person in my life was really the village wacko who believed her jewelry opened the mystical portal to a hidden kingdom.

The part of me that loved my aunt could've forgiven her — except that she'd infected Vee with her insanity.

My best friend was so susceptible. She'd spent her entire life trying to escape into literary worlds, yearning for something or someone to make her feel special and give her a legacy greater than being the neglected daughter of crappy parents. Now that she had Doon, she wouldn't let it go. Never mind that her quest would ruin our epic vacation and defraud the woman I'd idolized.

And since Vee had guzzled Gracie's Kool-Aid, I knew she wouldn't stop until she got to the bottom of Doon. If reading the journal would get this fantasyland out of her system faster, she could have it. Then hopefully we could continue our exploration of actual foreign lands with real Scottish hotties.

Grabbing the book from my dresser drawer, I shoved open my door and headed down the hall to Vee's room. But it was empty. The overhead light illuminated a square of paper on her undisturbed bed, and I recognized Vee's tidy cursive even before I could make out the single line she'd written. "K. Gone to check out the bridge — back soon. V."

Fabulous.

Vee's neurotic interest in the Brig o' Doon had her traipsing around the riverbank in the dead of night. What did she think would happen? That she'd click her heels three times and Doon would miraculously appear?

As I jogged down the steps to the main floor and slipped out the back, I realized this might work to my advantage. Vee would never accept that Doon was merely the delusions of an aging mind unless she had evidence. If that meant standing on the

Brig o' Doon with the rings chanting "Bibbidi-Bobbidi-Boo" to prove Aunt Gracie's kingdom didn't exist, then it was worth it.

I carefully picked my way over branches and rocks until the overgrown trail reached the illuminated path of the riverbank. The thunderstorms that had plagued Alloway the last two days had rolled through, leaving a tiny sliver of moon to guide me in the clear night sky. As I rounded the bend, I spied Vee sitting on a bench a few steps from the old bridge.

Aunt Gracie's ruby ring sparkled from her finger as she lifted it to the light. The way she gazed at it, I half expected her to crouch over and start crooning, "My precious."

As I approached, Vee's head swiveled in my direction, relief shining from her luminous doe eyes. "I knew you'd come."

"Of course. Remember that time as kids, I spent the whole night helping you search for the second star to the right? Or the time you read that museum story and I cashed out my entire piggy bank so we could hop a bus to Los Angeles and live inside Disneyland? And we would've made it if my dad hadn't busted us."

Rather than smile, Vee stubbornly shook her head back and forth. "This isn't like that. I just need to find more proof."

That was my cue. I pulled the leather volume from my back pocket and pressed it into her trembling hands. "Here ... It's not like I was going to read it anyway."

Walking past my bestie, I stopped at the mouth of the bridge. Due to the streetlamps, it was as bright as high noon. There was no swirling mist, and thankfully no mythical kingdom in the distance. An unwelcome pang of disappointment registered as I accepted my aunt's insanity. "What now, Vee?"

In the quiet, she walked up beside me, arms crossed over her chest. "How do you think the rings work?"

They don't.

But if she needed proof to get to that conclusion, might as

well get started. "Why don't we test them? Right here — right now."

Vee's eyes grew wide as I reached into my pocket for Uncle Cameron's ring and made a big production of placing it on my finger. Then I stepped onto the ancient cobblestones of the Brig o' Doon.

Nothing happened. Nada — zip — zilch.

Vindication coursed through my veins as I charged to the center of the arch and pivoted to face Vee. "This myth is sooo busted! There are no magical forces at work here. No alternate dimensions or fantastical portals. I'm wearing Uncle Cam's ring and I'm still right here in modern day."

With a half turn, I crossed to the far end of the bridge. "At least I believe I'm still in the present. The ultimate test will be when I step off the other end."

"Kenna, wait — "

Flinging my hand up to cut her off, I stepped onto the embankment with exaggerated movements and turned to challenge my best friend, my hands on my hips. "If Doon is supposed to be my legacy, where is it?"

Under the circle of lamplight, Vee's crestfallen face had a jaundiced glow. She'd been throat punched by disappointment her whole life. First, her dad did a Houdini act, vanishing into thin air. Then her mom, reverting to her natural state of selfishness, blamed Vee for ruining her life. Finally, Eric cheated on her with a girl dumber than a box of Beanie Babies and lied about it. No wonder she fantasized about escaping into a perfect society that would treat her like royalty.

I hated to shatter her delusions, but better now than after wasting the summer on some fantasy. "Now you," I said, trying to temper the harshness in my tone. "Cross the bridge."

Vee stayed put. She shook her head vigorously back and

forth as a distant clock began to toll the hour. Although I didn't count the chimes, I guessed midnight — and the irony was not lost on me.

Several tense seconds passed before Vee spoke. "What if nothing happens?"

"That's kind of the point, sweetie. Doon's not real. And I'm not moving until you admit it. I'll stay here all night if I have to."

"So you'd rather believe that your aunt was crazy than open up your mind to the possibility that Doon exists?"

Was it *Freaky Friday* all of a sudden? Had Vee and I switched bodies in the attic? "Do you *hear* yourself? You're supposed to be the logical one. What you're suggesting — you know it's impossible."

I expected her to answer defensively. Instead, she lifted her chin, her posture strong and confident as she replied, "This isn't about what I know. It's about what I feel, deep inside. It's about my destiny."

"You make your own destiny in this world. You can be anything, *do* anything."

"Then I choose to believe in Doon." With a deliberate step onto the bridge, Vee disappeared from the lamplight. As if someone cued spooky special effects, tendrils of mist began to curl over the sides of the Brig o' Doon from the riverbank below.

In the darkness, I could hear her measured tread on the stones. While I waited, the mists swirled and thickened, devouring the bridge until Vee's footsteps became muffled and then vanished altogether. Had she paused halfway across?

"Vee? Quit messing around."

The silence was as dense as the curtain of fog that'd sprung up out of nowhere.

"Vee?"

"Kenna?" She sounded miles away, but I would've recognized her panic at any distance.

"Hold on. I'm coming!" Using the wall as a guide, I began walking carefully across the bridge. After a few steps, I lost all sense of relative space. Realizing I could easily pass her in the oblivion, I called her name.

Her reply, while still distorted, sounded closer. "Here —"

I shuffled blindly forward, hands thrust in front of me. "Where are you?"

"I'm here." Her voice reverberated stage left. Turning in that direction, I stepped toward the center of the bridge. At first there was nothing but impenetrable mist, and then a disembodied hand reached for me. Vee's hand. Only it glowed blood red — like something from a horror movie. And mine, the hand that reached for hers, burned alien green.

"Ken!" Vee gasped. She pulled me closer until we could see one another clearly in the strange light. "*Look!*" She lifted our intertwined hands, our rings blazing between our bodies. "This enough proof for you?"

Too much. My lungs burned as my body went momentarily catatonic. I sucked in a shaky breath, wondering at the wheezy sounds coming from my throat. "This is not happening."

She met my eyes above the glowing rings. "I know you don't want to believe in anything you can't see or touch. I'm scared too. But we're supposed to see this through. I know we are. Do you trust me?"

I wanted to say no, but Vee's certainty in the midst of the creepiness compelled me to admit the truth. "Yes."

"Try to believe." When I nodded, she let go of my hand. "Put your palm against mine."

As soon as our rings touched, they glowed impossibly bright, like stage spots. Soon the red and green fused into a brilliant white beam that refracted through the mist like a prism. Fear kicked my heart into overdrive as I closed my eyes against the onslaught of blinding light.

Vee's voice, perfectly calm and clear as a bell, spoke reassuringly in my ear. "It's going to be okay."

Then the light vanished. In its absence, spots floated across my vision. Breaking my connection with Vee, I stepped back to examine my ring. To my great relief, it wasn't glowing green. It looked deceptively normal — like an antique handed down by a relative. Nothing more.

After a moment of contemplation, Vee said quietly, "I suppose you're going to tell me you didn't see that."

"No." Something had definitely happened. But even if our rings lit up like Christmas, it hadn't changed anything.

"You see?" Her reverent tone held no accusation as she spoke. "The rings are special."

"But it doesn't mean Doon is real. We're still lost in the fog on an old bridge in the middle of the night. *In Alloway.*"

"Maybe we didn't do it right." Although I couldn't see her face clearly, I could picture her concentrated frown in perfect detail. "I'll bet the answers are somewhere in Gracie's journal."

She reached into her pocket to retrieve the book, but I held up my palm to stop her. "Tomorrow, okay? I've had enough drama for one evening." Had I really just said that? I turned to go back. Everything would make more sense — logical sense — after a good night's sleep and a triple latte. "Right now I just want to go home."

"Wait!"

It was the way she said it that stopped me. The expectancy in her tone — awed and hopeful, and totally out of place given the circumstances — made my heart drop. Then she said, "Look."

The mist began to form lazy swirls that evaporated before

my eyes. I blinked, grasping for context as my lack of comprehension changed to shock. *Sacred Stephen Schwartz!* The bridge no longer spanned the river but ended in ruins at the halfway point. If I had taken two more steps, I would've been smashed into kibble against the rocks below.

"What the — ?" As if my brain finally caught up with my feet, I jumped back. My heart thumped painfully in my chest as I knocked against Vee.

One of her hands reached out absently to steady me. "Mountains."

Puzzled, I spun toward her. She wasn't warning me about the drop-off as I'd assumed, but rather gawking in the opposite direction. In the distance where the sea should have been, huge purplish mountains stood silhouetted against a rose-colored horizon. Between us and the far-off peaks loomed gleaming white turrets.

Vee's soft whisper tickled against my ear. "Are we where I think we are?"

What moments ago seemed like a fairy tale now appeared to be impossibly and unsettlingly real. Yet it couldn't be true. My entire body began to tremble. Keeping my eyes fixed on the terrible castle in the distance, I whispered back, "I seriously hope not."

CHAPTER 7

Veronica

All the hope in the world hadn't prepared me for standing on the soil of a mythical land, the sun rising where moments before the moon had dominated an inky-black sky. The realization that it should've been closer to midnight than morning must've hit Kenna and I at the same time. Instinctively, we clung to one another as we moved onto the riverbank. Somewhere in the distance a trumpet sounded, followed by the cheering of men — lots of them — their voices like shards of ice scraping across my skin.

My friend yelped and grasped me even tighter.

Struggling to gain my bearings, my gaze locked on mountain peaks that sprouted out of the ground like some monstrous version of Jack's magic beanstalk. The tiny hairs rose on my arms. How was any of this possible?

"I'm going back," Kenna declared, letting go of my shoulders.

I teetered precariously for a moment before gaining my balance. When I whirled around, Kenna was marching back toward the bridge, where tendrils of mist still swirled and coalesced, leaving only the first few feet of stone visible. Before my eyes, the undulating mass solidified into a giant barrier over seven feet high.

"Kenna, wait!" I began to run, but my legs felt mired in knee-high mud. "The fog's too thick!" If she tried to cross, would the ring light up and complete the ruined bridge, or would she topple blindly over the edge?

Just as her feet hit the ancient stones, she stopped. The wall of fog loomed before her, pulsing like a living beast ready to suck her in and never let go. I reached out and grabbed her arm, hauling her backward so that she stumbled away from the bridge and collapsed onto the grassy bank.

"This can't be happening! The stupid bridge was supposed to — " Her voice broke as she buried her face in her hands. "What do we do now?"

Kneeling beside her, I wrapped my arms around her shaking form. "Shh. It's okay. We'll figure it out."

I glanced back at what was left of the bridge. "But I don't think we can go back the way we came." Even if the Brig o' Doon had been crossable, I couldn't have forced myself to turn back.

Kenna lifted her head, and her wide gray eyes searched my face. "I can't be stuck here. My internship ... I have to be in Chicago in August."

"I know. Give me a minute to think." And by *think*, I meant *process*.

I pulled my knees to my chest and watched the morning sky awaken in brilliant Technicolor. As red, gold, and orange stretched over the landscape, it was like I'd just stepped from the broken farmhouse and onto the yellow brick road, the world shifting from black and white to dazzling color.

Occasionally, a roaring cheer or collective groan carried

through the valley, reminding me we weren't in Kansas anymore. Lush green hills rolled into the distance, and just visible beyond the trees, sun-bleached castle turrets stretched toward a cloudless sky, confirming the impossible truth. I'd seen this magnificent place before, felt it in my soul — in the attic, when I'd slipped the ring on my finger. My vision blurred as tears gathered in my eyes. We'd found it — Aunt Gracie's legendary kingdom. We were in Doon!

And since Doon was real ... *Jamie!* My heart stuttered and then skipped forward several beats. Was he really here, living and breathing, flesh and blood? I *had* to find out.

"Vee?"

I turned to meet Kenna's unblinking stare, her eyes brimming with tears. "I'm sorry I didn't believe you and treated you like you were a lunatic. You'd be totally in the right if you wanted to do an I-told-you-so dance." The words rushed out of her so quickly, it took me a second to decipher what she'd said.

I shrugged. "It's okay, I get it." I couldn't blame her for doubting my sanity just a bit; I had. "Being here is I told you so enough."

A grateful grin spread across her face and she pulled me into a hug. "Thanks." She let go and pulled back. "Now what's the plan?"

I'd stuffed Gracie's journal into the pocket of my hoodie for safekeeping. Pulling it out, I thumbed through the worn pages until I found the hand-drawn map labeled *The Kingdom* and then repositioned the book so Kenna and I could study the drawing at the same time. "Check this out."

Although I had the layout of the kingdom memorized, I traced my finger from the bridge past a forest and through the village, trying to calculate how far we were from the castle.

There was no scale on the map, but if we could hear the voices it couldn't be far.

I stood and stuffed the journal back in my pocket. Brushing the grass off my jeans, I turned in a slow circle to get my bearings. Based on the map, we needed to head toward the mountains, keeping the castle turrets slightly to our right until we found the lake. Then we could follow the shoreline around to the left until we got to Castle MacCrae.

Kenna cupped her hand over her eyes and squinted up at me. "Where are you going?"

I extended my hand and helped her to her feet. "I say we head for the castle."

We stumbled through the never-ending forest for what felt like half a day. I completely lost my way — a few times. Apparently expert navigation wasn't my strongest suit. All I knew for sure was that we were in a valley, the castle no longer visible over the trees. Thankfully, we could still use the escalating roar of voices as our gauge.

"Any brilliant theories about what's going on?" Kenna asked as she held a branch up for me to pass under.

I'd cheered at enough football games to recognize the almost manic fandemonium of a full-scale sporting event. "I'm assuming it's some kind of tournament."

Kenna froze in mid-step. "The kind where the losers get fed to the lions?"

"That would be the Romans. Not to mention the fact we probably would have heard roaring by now if that was the case."

"Oh, okay." Her head bobbed like a dashboard dog, and if I knew Kenna her mind was most likely racing through her tenuous grasp of ancient civilizations. "These people would most likely be from the middle ages, right? They're not going to burn us at the stake, are they?"

"They're Scots, Ken, not Puritans."

"Still." She clasped her hands and dropped her head to mumble a few hasty words. When she finished, she regarded me with a shrug. "It can't hurt to pray Doon's the singing, dancing, MGM-type civilization, can it?"

I wanted to laugh, but a riotous cheer from the unseen crowd made it sound as if they were right on top of us. I pointed straight ahead. "It's coming from the other side of those trees."

Kenna's cheeks drained of color as her mouth pressed into a determined line. "The sooner we find out what's going on, the sooner we can figure out how to get home. Let's do this." She took off at a jog and I followed on her heels.

We made our way through the tree line and stopped, tilting our heads back in wonder. On top of an enormous hill sat a massive stadium-like structure. From our limited vantage point, the stone walls and multicolored flags stretched to the sky like some medieval Superdome — so much for my friend's happy little musical theory.

An impossibly loud cheer exploded from inside the arena and rolled over us like the aftershocks from a bomb, raising the hair on my arms. My heart threatened to pound out of my chest, the instinct for self-preservation warring with my excitement — and the need to keep going.

I felt a tremor run through Kenna's frame as we huddled together. She took a shallow breath and wheezed, "Well, I've seen enough."

She turned to go back the way we'd come, but I grabbed her arm. Where had all her bravado gone? Usually she was the one dragging me kicking and screaming as she led the charge.

"Not so fast, scaredy-cat. Let's get a little closer and check it out." I clasped her hand in mine and pulled. She pulled back. The reversal of our normal roles would be amusing if I wasn't so focused. Nothing would stop me from searching every inch of this storybook kingdom for my kilt-wearing hero.

After a brief tug of war, she gave up with a huff and blew a crimson lock of hair off her forehead. "Fine. Where was all this tenacity when I wanted you to audition for *Hairspray*?"

We scrabbled up the hill and threw ourselves down behind the stone wall of the stadium, struggling to catch our breath. Not sure where to go from here, I indicated to Kenna with my own crude version of sign language that I wanted to get on her shoulders and look over the wall. Her brow lifted incredulously but then she nodded in agreement.

Grateful for Kenna's additional height, I arranged her long limbs in the proper squat pose, placed my foot on her thigh, and hoisted myself into a precarious position on her shoulders. Carefully, she rose to a standing position, both of us reaching out to the wall to steady ourselves. Without warning, visions of cheerleading formations flashed in my mind. Steph's cruel voice screamed at me to stop slouching like a toad. I stiffened my spine and reminded myself that, thankfully, that chapter of my life was over.

"For the love of Lerner and Loewe! What is taking so long up there?" Kenna demanded in a strangled whisper. "I'm not a human totem pole, you know."

Despite my inability to think of a snappy comeback, I was relieved Kenna had recovered her usual sarcasm. Swallowing my laughter, I peeked over the top of the wall. The arena was an oval about the size of a football field, with a dirt floor. Steep wooden bleachers filled with colorfully dressed spectators lined two sides of the playing field. To my left, I spotted a hidden opening leading under the bleachers.

I tapped Kenna's shoulder, and she lowered me unsteadily to the ground. Pointing in the direction we needed to go,

I followed as she crept along the wall to the gap and quietly slipped through. Moving between strips of light and shadow, we found space among sets of feet and settled with a decent vantage point. Through the slats, we could see most of the arena.

Directly in front of us, a square area marked off with ropes like a large boxing ring drew the focus of the crowd seated on the other set of bleachers. The audience became strangely quiet, their anticipation palpable as a whisper rushed through the stands like a wave.

"Good ladies and gentlemen, lads and lassies, this be the contest ye've been awaiting!" A cheer rang out. The disembodied voice continued. "Knight against knight! Champion versus champion! Brother against brother!" A roar went out, and the bleachers shook over our heads as people stamped their feet in approval. Sawdust coated our hair and lashes, causing me to doubt the wisdom of our hiding place.

"Never in the esteemed history o' Doon has there been a more anticipated event!" At the mention of Doon, I elbowed my best friend.

Kenna swatted my arm away and hissed, "Save your I-told-you-so dance until we're sure they don't have lions."

"Without further ado, may I present the brothers MacCrae!"

At the name "MacCrae," my focus zeroed in on two men, riding the biggest horses I'd ever seen toward the center ring. They were dressed identically, from their kilts and knee-high boots to the blue and green strip of plaid fabric draped diagonally across their bare chests.

As they dismounted, I focused on the closest guy, surprised how young he appeared despite his mammoth size. He was tall and broad with short-cropped dark hair and a boyish excitement that was obvious in his animated movements. His opponent, who faced away from us, was the complete opposite.

I watched as he lifted his plaid sash over his blond head, his muscles shifting fluidly beneath sun-darkened skin. Donning what looked like a heavy armored vest, he turned to reveal an all-too-familiar profile.

Jamie MacCrae.

My spirit leapt, straining toward him even as my knees buckled beneath me. Grabbing the bleachers, I pressed my face into the gap between two sets of dusty boots. My gaze fused to his awe-inspiring form as he pulled an enormous broadsword from the scabbard at his waist as easily as if it were a toy. He was even more beautiful in person than he'd been in my visions. His honey-colored hair, longer than I'd realized, curled slightly against his broad neck.

As he inspected his weapon, a fierce concentration marked his brow, contrasting with his brother, who grinned and posed for the crowd. Side by side, the dark-haired brother looked like a linebacker, and Jamie — a couple of inches shorter, but with perfect muscle definition — more like a quarterback.

As they entered the ring, the officiator's voice rang strong and clear. "I'll be havin' a clean fight. Ye both know the rules."

The man, now visible, paused and bowed to each warrior in turn. "Prince Jamie, Prince Duncan."

Prince Jamie? A freaking prince! *Are you kidding me?*

Breathlessly, I watched a slow, confident grin spread across Jamie's face as he bowed to his brother. The familiarity of that smile sent my pulse into overdrive, even as tingles of fear ran over my skin. He was about to fight his massive brother . . . with seriously sharp swords!

Then the smile gave way to intense focus and he attacked, pushing his burly opponent across the ring with powerful sweeps of his blade. Each strike was deliberate and lightning fast — like an avenging demigod straight out of mythology.

Kenna grabbed my arm in a vise grip and whispered, "I told you we had to be careful — it looks like they're going to kill each other. Who do you think's gonna win? The giant ogre or the surfer dude?"

"Wait. *What?*"

"I'm putting my money on the ogre."

The big one swung his weapon down toward Jamie's head, and I pressed the palm of my hand to my mouth to keep from crying out as Jamie blocked using the flat of his sword. With a mighty heave, he pushed his brother off balance and then punched him in the kidney. As the crowd went wild, I blew out a long breath and extricated Kenna's fingers from the flesh of my arm.

The dark-haired boy straightened and retaliated by smashing his ham-sized fist into Jamie's gut.

"Yes!" Kenna bounced on the balls of her feet. "That's how you do it."

She turned to me and, noticing my hands curled into tight fists, patted my shoulder. "Don't worry, Vee. This is *so* choreographed, faked for maximum entertainment, like world wrestling."

For a brief second, the brothers seemed frozen, their swords locked together. Then Jamie lifted the hilt of his weapon perpendicular above his head. The motion elevated his brother's sword, and the resulting momentum flung him past Jamie in an ungainly stumble.

Jamie spun, his blade slicing towards his brother's ribcage in a powerful arch. I sucked in a sharp breath. He *would* kill him! At the last second, the brother dropped and avoided Jamie's sword by what looked like centimeters.

At the end of his somersault, the boy Kenna kept referring to as the ogre sprang to his feet. With a smile, he winked at Jamie, and then bellowing "Ho!" shoved him halfway across the ring. As Jamie stumbled backward, his brother paused to lift his arm above his head and incite the crowd to its feet. He even blew kisses to a group of fawning girls on the opposite side of the stands.

Kenna scoffed. "What a jerk. I changed my mind. I'm rooting for Surfer Dude."

Reluctantly, I pointed to *Surfer Dude*. "The blond one with the long hair ... uh ... that's Jamie. The guy who's been appearing to me in the real world."

"Kilt Boy?" For once in her life, Kenna was speechless. She stared at me, mouth open and twitching until it transformed into a smile. Then she laughed — not in hysterics, but with real honest-to-goodness joy. "So that's what all this was about?"

From our cramped position, Kenna drew me into a bear hug. I pulled away and closed my mouth with an audible click, stunned that my confession hadn't set off my best friend's hypersensitive psycho meter. "What do you mean?"

She continued to grin as if the weight of the world had been lifted from her shoulders. "After we ended up over the rainbow, or whatever, I worried ... being Gracie's niece ... that I was here to do something. That I'd have to battle flying monkeys or drop a house on the white witch. But this is all about you, sweetie. I just need to figure out how to get us home."

I didn't know whether to hug her again or punch her. All I knew was the boy of my dreams was real, and as long as he didn't get himself killed in the next few minutes, I —

A hand like iron clamped down on my arm, followed by something cold and wickedly sharp against the side of my throat. A breath, close and stale, assaulted my senses as its owner growled, "Don't ye dare move, lassie, or I'll run this knife through yer gullet."

CHAPTER 8

Veronica

Although unable to see the threat, I clearly felt it on my bicep and the tender skin of my neck. I froze. If I cried out, would Jamie hear?

A second masculine voice cautioned, "I wouldna try anything if I were ye." Kenna's soft yelp confirmed she was also at some thug's mercy. My courage sank as I realized any resistance on my part would put her in danger.

Forced out from under the risers, I stumbled back through the stone wall and down the hill. Shuffling sounds behind me indicated that Kenna and her captor followed close behind.

As the boisterous cheers of the coliseum faded, so did my hopes Jamie would come galloping to the rescue on his big war-horse. Then again, we'd only been walking a few minutes. Maybe he would sense I was in danger and leave the tournament. I squeezed my eyes closed and tried to project my thoughts into his head, like he'd done with me. *Jamie, it's me, Veronica. I'm here in Doon. I need you!*

I opened my eyes, and waited expectantly.

Nothing.

Perhaps he'd heard me and I couldn't hear him.

Right. Or maybe I'd wake up back in Alloway, snug in my four-poster bed at Dunbrae Cottage, and realize this was all just a dream.

"That hurt, you big troll!"

I twisted around to see if Kenna was okay, but only succeeded in tripping on a bump in the path. My captor jerked me back onto my feet, practically yanking my arm out of the socket. I sucked in a breath through clenched teeth.

"Keep goin'," he demanded.

A sharp pinching sensation stung my throat, followed by warmth I knew was a thin line of blood trickling onto the collar of my hoodie. This was no dream. If my prince wasn't going to save me, I'd have to save myself. Too bad I hadn't paid more attention during those self-defense phys-ed classes. The only moves I remembered were the eye jab and the knee to the privates. Since the instructor had never mentioned how to accomplish this while being held at knifepoint, I decided to try reasoning with my captor. "Sir, I can explain — "

"Silence!" He tightened his grip on my already aching arm, and I decided to listen.

We walked a good distance and around a concealing bend before our abductors stopped. The knife still hovering near my throat, I moved with care as the creep holding me addressed his cohort. "Quit yer laggin', Fergus."

As I got my first good look at the guy restraining Kenna, I stifled a gasp of surprise. He was the size of an evergreen tree. At least a foot and a half taller than me, he had the sort of fair-yet-ruddy complexion that turned his skin every shade of mottled pink imaginable. His hair, a long shock of yellow, was baby-fine with two slender braids extending from his temples.

And his face — his face looked so young and innocent I had a hard time believing he would hurt anyone. Ever.

The man-boy, Fergus, regarded me for a moment with pale blue eyes and then frowned in a way that made me want to give him a cookie to make things better. "I was just thinkin', Gideon. Shouldna we inform the MacCrae?"

My captor — presumably Gideon — relaxed his grip slightly, allowing me to twist away from his blade to look at him. He had a good thirty years on Fergus. A few inches taller than me, he was bald and slight, but comprised of sinewy muscle as if he'd spent every day of his life running a decathlon. Weathered by sun and age, his bearing said hunter and tracker. More importantly, it said, "Don't mess with me."

Gideon glanced back the way we came. "Later. Fer now, let's get them to the castle. We'll be takin' the low gate."

Whatever the "low gate" was, it caused Fergus a moment of concern that he did his best to hide. He acquiesced with a solemn nod.

Encouraged by his hesitation, I addressed him. "Excuse me, Fergus?"

"Silence, lassie! You wenches will remain quiet unless spoken to."

Fergus grimaced. "Let the lass speak."

"And let her beguile me? Notta chance!"

"Och, Gideon, we donna know they're in league with the witch."

Witch? Cold slithered down my throat and dropped into my stomach, like I'd swallowed an ice cube. Maybe Kenna was right and the people of Doon were burn-witches-at-the-stake-Puritans after all.

Gideon tightened his iron grip on my arm. "There's magic

afoot, I tell ye. How did they come to appear in our land? The Brig o' Doon does no' open fer another fortnight."

Kenna took a step forward, but the giant didn't let her move far. "We used my aunt and uncle's rings."

"Show me."

When Kenna lifted her hand, Gideon yanked the ring off her finger so carelessly that she cradled her hand to her chest and bit her lip. He examined the ring with a catlike hiss, then looked at me with a manic gleam that gave his blue eyes a purplish glow. The tip of his knife bit in farther. "Yers too."

I wriggled the ruby ring from my finger and held it up. Like a savage, Gideon snatched the band and waved it in the air. "Is this not all the proof ye need, Fergus Lockhart? I'll no' be bewitched!"

The giant continued his attempt to make his partner see reason. "The witch has never been able to breech the borders o' Doon. Not on the Centennial, or in between."

Gideon's eyes bulged from their sockets. His red face revealed the fervor of his argument. "But her minions kin. These're clearly the witch's minions! Need I remind ye of the last time we underestimated that devil woman? Now move. Tha's an order!"

"Yes, Captain." The giant saluted, yet his eyes remained troubled as he watched his superior pocket the rings.

Gideon half-pushed, half-dragged me down a narrow trail. The path looked neglected — surely not the correct way to our destination, the castle. But as we curved back toward the lake, I saw a wall of stone rising from the rocky hillside. Between the imposing stone columns was a small door of heavy wood and black iron. The door looked like it hadn't been used in ages.

From around his neck, Gideon produced a large key on a rope and proceeded to wrestle the lock open. The prehistoric door gave with a whoosh, swinging inward to reveal a dark, dank corridor. With the help of a shove, Kenna and I entered the "castle" — but it wasn't a part of the castle I'd ever wanted to see, not in a million years.

As Gideon locked the door from the inside and the darkness swallowed us, he chuckled. "Welcome to the dungeons o' Doon, witches."

CHAPTER 9

Veronica

A dank, smelly dungeon wasn't exactly what I'd had in mind for my storybook castle. As Gideon forced me down a dim corridor lined with rusty iron cells, I wondered if I would meet Jamie for the first time from behind bars. Or if maybe Gideon would hold a private trial, convict us of witchcraft, and drown us in the moat before Jamie even had a chance to know I'd come.

Gideon shoved me through an open cell door and I stumbled forward, grabbing a table to right myself. Kenna rushed in after and the door clanked shut behind us.

"You okay?" Kenna leaned in and examined the cut on my neck.

"I guess." As good as expected considering we'd traveled through a magic portal, found an enchanted kingdom, and been immediately convicted as trespassers. "You?"

She pulled back and fastened her turbulent stare to mine. "They took the rings. *And* they think we're witches! What're we going to do?"

I shook my head. "I don't know."

Her eyes swept our surroundings, and hope filled her voice as she asked, "I don't suppose you have any mad cheerleader skills that could get us out of here?"

I snorted. "Like what?"

"Like the ability to backflip up to that open grate above the door."

"I'm a cheerleader, Kenna, not a ninja."

"Right." Mumbling something about *Sweeny Todd* under her breath, Kenna paced away and began peering into shadows and pressing random stones protruding from the walls. But there was no secret escape passage. Wishful thinker, that one.

It didn't take a rocket scientist to know the dungeon was inescapable — and disgusting. The only furniture in the room was crude: a rough wooden table with two mismatched stools; a lumpy potato-sack mattress with straw sticking out at odd angles; and in the farthest, darkest corner sat a rusty metal bucket whose purpose I refused to contemplate. As far as dungeons went, this place warranted a one-star review.

I pulled Gracie's journal from my hoodie and place it on the rickety table. As I did, Kenna circled and gestured toward my pocket. "Would you happen to have anything useful in there? A screwdriver or stun gun, maybe?"

I pressed my lips together for a second before answering. "You do realize who you're talking to?"

"What about a knife or mace?"

With a much-deserved eye roll, I listed the meager contents of my pockets. "I've got tinted lip gloss and an empty baggie. Oh, and this." I pulled out my cell and examined the screen.

"No bars — but look." A pale square of light illuminated the open journal as I turned my phone into a flashlight.

Clearly impressed, she whistled. "I never would've thought of that. That's why you're the brains and I'm the talent."

I ignored her as I turned my attention to the one thing that might help us out of this situation. The journal. "There's got to be answers in here somewhere."

Kenna resumed pacing the perimeter of our cell. "We can figure a way out of this. We're modern women with history and technology on our side. So let's think creatively ... Do you think they know what political asylum is?" I kept searching, unwilling to encourage her by answering.

Undeterred by my silence, her stream of consciousness continued unabated. "We'll think of something. We certainly can't stay here. That bed looks like you could catch scurvy from it."

I didn't look up from the journal as I admonished, "You can't catch scurvy from a mattress. You contract it because of a Vitamin C deficiency, and it mostly afflicts sailors."

"How do you know that stuff? And why? Anyway, you get the point. It's *icky* here."

Now I looked up. "It's a dungeon, Kenna. By definition, dungeons are *icky*."

She ignored my patronizing look and grumbled, "I'll bet if Fergus had his way, we wouldn't be in here."

Now *that* was a good idea.

I moved to the iron door and craned my head to see out of the tiny, barred window. As I'd hoped, a man-shaped shadow lurked just outside. In a tone similar to the one I used with my dance students, I called into the darkness, "Hello there? Can you hear me?"

Several seconds passed before an unfamiliar voice stiffly answered, "Aye."

"Do you know Fergus?"

"Aye."

"Can you please get him for us?"

Coming to my aid, Kenna pressed her face next to mine. "This is probably totally beyond you, but we're Americans and are, therefore, entitled to a phone call. But since you people don't have phones, we'll settle for speaking to Fergus."

"Nay."

I nodded and took a step back, giving her permission to let him have it with both barrels.

"Pleeeeeease?" That particular whine had gotten us more than our fair share of candy before dinner back in the day. It chaffed like sandpaper on a sunburn. "I reeeeeally need to speak to Fergus. It's a matter of life or death. Pleeeeaseeeee?"

From farther down the corridor I heard heavy, measured footsteps moving in our direction and then stop. "I'm here, lasses."

Kenna tipped me a satisfied nod and stepped back mouthing, "The talent."

Pressing my face against the bars, I asked, "Is that you, Fergus?"

"Who else would I be?" For a second I thought I'd offended him. Then his quiet laugh eased my concern. "What kin I do for ye?"

"We didn't just appear out of nowhere — we were led here by Kenna's aunt, Grace Lockhart."

"The red-haired lass is Grace Lockhart's niece?"

"Yes." From some distance away, I heard commotion followed by the unmistakable voice of Gideon.

Fergus whispered urgently, "Have faith, lass. A higher purpose is at work here, and ye are not without allies." Then our only hope moved out of sight.

I locked eyes with Kenna, and she gestured to the journal.

"Put that back in your pocket." She was right. We'd already lost the rings; if they confiscated the journal, we'd be screwed.

The gate at the end of the cellblock creaked as multiple sets of footsteps drew closer. Our door swung open and Gideon barged in flanked by several stone-faced guards. Each man had a weapon belted above his kilt. "The MacCrae wishes ta see ye. Come wi' me, witches. And take care ta hold yer tongues."

I could only hope the MacCrae would listen to reason, or at least allow me to speak to Jamie.

🌀 🌀 🌀

We wound our way up narrow, torch-lit stairs that seemed to go on for a mile. I swallowed compulsively, trying to force moisture into my parched throat, but only succeeded in upsetting my already-churning stomach.

At the top of the stairs, Kenna and I followed Fergus's hulk-like form down a dim corridor, Gideon's overbearing presence our ever-present shadow. We entered a circular room smelling of stale wood-smoke and dust. Sun streamed through a bank of diamond-paned windows, causing me to blink like a rat coming up from the sewer and almost slam into Fergus as he stopped.

After returning Kenna's wobbly smile, I let my gaze wander. Two guards stood on either side of the circular space, hands locked behind their backs, the dark brown of their leather vests blending with the rectangles of wood paneling that covered the walls. An unlit candelabra hung on a long chain, almost brushing Fergus's pale hair. I tilted my head back, following the gilded chain of the chandelier to an oak-paneled ceiling carved into geometric sections that when viewed as a whole resembled a blooming flower. If I hadn't been shaking in my Nikes, I would've been impressed.

An unnatural hush fell over the room, and all the guards pivoted to face forward. Since I couldn't see around the giant wall of Fergus, I assumed the MacCrae had arrived.

"Where are the lasses?" asked a deep, melodic voice.

I knew that voice.

Fergus stepped aside to reveal the boy of my dreams sitting on a throne-like chair. A jewel-encrusted circlet rested atop his blond head, but something more than the crown held the room in thrall. Despite his casual posture, he radiated a natural authority, as if he'd been born to command men. His somber regard moved from Fergus, down to me, and stopped.

Slowly, he rose to his feet. All the sounds in the room faded away as our gazes caught and held. Something like hunger filled his dark eyes as they roamed over my face to my lips and back up again.

My heart beat so hard, I feared everyone in the room would hear it. Longing exploded across my body and I stepped toward him, lifting my hand. I'd been waiting for this moment—

His whole body stiffened and he scowled at my outstretched hand. I could almost feel the cold radiating from him as, without a word, he turned his back, the fur-trimmed hem of his cape fluttering against my outstretched fingers.

The blood drained from my head and pooled somewhere near my feet as sounds rushed through my ears like a roaring tide. I stumbled back several steps. Didn't he recognize me? He'd been the one stalking *me*, for heaven's sake!

"Gideon," Jamie barked as he sat back on his throne. "Approach."

"My laird." Gideon moved from behind me and bent in a stiff bow. "These *girls* utilized the witch's magic to infiltrate our borders. For the safety o' the kingdom, they must be imprisoned."

Kenna stepped forward, palms held in front of her. "Whoa,

there. I'm not going back to that hellhole. You can't hold us without evidence. We have rights!"

Gideon spun to face us, grasping the hilt of his sword. "Not in Doon ye don't, witch. Now hold yer tongue."

Kenna put her hands on her hips and stepped toward him, raising herself up to her full height. "Make me, you bald rent-a-cop!"

Her bravado was admirable, but in this case I was pretty sure it was going to get us skewered. "Kenna, seriously! Now is not the time — " I pushed my impulsive friend behind me, wedging myself between her and our jailer.

"Enough!" Jamie rumbled from his throne, a dangerous edge to his voice. "Gideon, stand down." The MacCrae had spoken. Immediately, Gideon took several steps back, but the feverish light didn't fade from his eyes.

I threw Kenna a death stare and then turned toward the throne. "Ja — ah ... Laird, please excuse my friend's behavior. She's tired and hungry and greatly distressed from being taken at knifepoint to a dungeon and — "

"Be silent." Jamie's disdain blazed at me across the room, causing heat to rush up my neck and into my cheeks. If I needed further confirmation that he didn't know me, this was it.

"What say you to the charge of conspiring with the witch to breech the boundaries of Doon?" he asked evenly, his words hacking into my heart.

Too humiliated to speak, I stood trembling before him. Was this how I wanted to go down? Accused and convicted without a word in my own defense? The answer was a resounding *NO*.

Clenching my hands into fists, I took a step forward. But an iron grip on my arm halted my progress. I stopped, never taking my eyes off Jamie's face. "Since you're obviously the only one whose opinion matters" — I made a sweeping gesture with my free hand — "why do you believe we're here, *Your Highness?*"

His ebony gaze narrowed and his hands gripped the armrests of his throne as if he struggled to hold himself in his seat. "Are you challenging my authority?"

"I wouldn't *dream* of it." The barb flew out of my mouth before I could think better of it.

Jamie blinked, and for a moment the mask of authority fell from his face. His white-knuckled grip loosened, his eyes softened, and his jaw unclenched. My heart stuttered as *my* Jamie appeared before me. Did he remember after all? Or was it on the edge of his consciousness like a dream — the harder you tried to recall the details the faster they slipped away?

With a deep, shuddering breath, he closed his eyes. When he opened them, he focused on some point behind my head. The monarch was back, his perfect face void of expression. Straightening his spine, he addressed Gideon decisively. "Take 'em back to the dungeon."

"What?" Kenna exclaimed from behind me. "That's the extent of our hearing?"

"Please ..." I almost added "Jamie," but stopped myself just in time. "Kenna's aunt — "

"Silence, witch!" Gideon hissed, grabbing my other arm with a painful twist.

"Let go! You're hurting me." Trying to pull out of Gideon's rough grasp, I looked to Jamie for help, but he showed all the emotion of a statue.

"Take them now, Gideon," the boy on the throne ordered impassively.

"A word, brother." A voice called from the back of the room. I turned to see Jamie's tall, dark-haired brother, moving toward us.

"Not now, Duncan." Jamie's regard shifted to his brother, but his expression didn't change.

Undeterred, Duncan barreled forward, "These wee lasses are —"

The crown prince's face turned as dark as a thundercloud. He shot to his feet, grabbed Duncan by the arm, and led him out the side door.

From my limited vantage point, I watched the princes whispering in heated conversation. After a moment, Jamie returned and stood before the throne, his arms crossed over his chest, his face a granite mask. Duncan stood beside him, a triumphant grin lifting one side of his mouth.

When Jamie spoke, there was no inflection in his voice. "I'm releasing you both into the custody of Fergus and my brother, Prince Duncan, until such time that yer trial can be conducted."

Gideon's hold tightened painfully on my arms and he sputtered, "But laird!"

Jamie's cutting gaze shifted to my jailor. "Gideon, I require your assistance with the king."

"Yes, sire."

Gideon released me, and as I rubbed the feeling back into my aching arms Jamie stalked from the room without so much as a glance in my direction. Gideon followed close on his heels. Great. Just what we didn't need — our fanatical accuser having the opportunity to fill Jamie's head with more lies.

Duncan approached with a smug twinkle in his eye. He extended one arm to me and then turned to Kenna. "Fear not, m' ladies. You are under the protection of Duncan Rhys Finnean MacCrae, Prince o' Doon, and no harm will come to you. I swear it on m' life."

CHAPTER 10

Mackenna

Huffing and puffing like the big bad wolf, I staggered to the top of the tower and paused to revel in my accomplishment. I felt like I'd scaled the Statue of Liberty or the Eiffel Tower. One-hundred and seventeen steps — this place really needed to invest in some elevators.

Ahead of me, our rescuer paused to open a heavy wooden door. With a formal bow and a flourish of his hand, Prince Duncan MacCrae waited for us to precede him into the room. "After you, m' ladies."

With a murmur of thanks, Vee hurried across the threshold. All that climbing and she wasn't even winded. I lumbered behind her, doing my best not to sound like a mouth-breathing phone stalker. Panting through my nose only made it worse, so I pretended to admire a painting on the wall until I could recover.

While I feigned an interest in bovine landscapes, Vee paced across the room, busying herself with our new surroundings. Despite the polite smile on her face, the corners of her mouth pinched in tight lines, as if she were holding herself together by sheer determination. Her eyes slid across mine, threatening to storm as she bit her lower lip. Hastily fixing her focus on the opposite end of the room, she exclaimed, "Oh, wow!"

Tearing myself away from the riveting oil canvas of cows, I walked over to where Vee had paused in front of a wall of glass. Floor to ceiling diamond-cut panes sparkled in the sun. Vee pointed beyond them to the tranquil rolling hills. "I'll bet you can see the whole kingdom from here."

"Aye, that ye can."

Sweet Baby Sondheim! I nearly jumped out of my skin as Duncan's words assaulted the back of my neck. While we'd been gawking at the sights, the sneaky prince had crept up behind us. Or, more specifically, me. He was light on his toes for a big guy. And a little too close for comfort.

With effort, Vee turned her attention away from the view. She flashed the prince a thousand-watt smile that didn't quite reach her eyes. "It's spectacular—like being suspended in the clouds. Isn't it, Kenna?"

Still trying to recover from being scared half to death, I managed a shrug. Which apparently wasn't good enough for my friend, because she suddenly dug her stiletto elbow into my ribcage. "*Gaphf*—I'm breathless with admiration."

Duncan chuckled. "So I noticed."

"Would you look at this?" Vee spun me around so the ogre and I were nose to nose as she gracefully slipped between us. "This room is *amazing!*"

I supposed I'd have to take her word for it, since my vision was blocked by the Medieval Hulk. Didn't this creep know about personal space? Up close and intimate with the prince, tiny details jumped out at me. His short dark hair contained some sort of styling product, giving his unruly waves an effortlessly tousled look. The golden flecks sparkling in his brown eyes created an effect that reminded me of melted caramel. Laugh lines creased the corners of his eyes. And he smelled ... like sun-warmed saddles.

His eyes widened at the same moment I realized that I'd sniffed him. *Fabulous.* Now he would think I was some deranged girl who went around smelling people. Before I could come up with some sort of plausible explanation, Vee made yet another comment about the decor. "Everything works together so well."

With a silent smirk, Duncan retreated enough to give me an unobstructed view of the roaring fire opposite the windows and sitting area in between. But not enough space to pass without brushing against him.

Trapped, I watched Vee flit about the room like an over-stimulated hummingbird, flapping her wings just to survive. "Check out this massive hearth. It's like staring into the mouth of a fire-breathing dragon." Despite her admirable performance, her tone betrayed her.

Vee coped with life's crap by smiling through it. Between the dungeon and high-and-mighty Jamie MacCrae, she'd faced more than her daily quota. And we hadn't even gotten to the ominous and looming trial we were meant to face. She'd fall apart when she was ready. The most I could do was be prepared — which usually involved obscene amounts of Ben & Jerry's Chunky Monkey and the Harry Potter saga on DVD. I doubted I'd find either at the local farmer's market.

She turned to survey the rest of the room, gliding across the plush navy and sage rugs that covered the polished wood floor. As she moved, she paused to manhandle pieces of elegant yet comfortable-looking furniture that captured her interest. Her path made me notice gleaming tables and overstuffed chairs in shades of walnut and gold, artfully arranged into conversation groups for an effect that was both intimate and feng shui.

"This space is so inviting and — you have a library!" Like a magnet, she drifted toward the collection of books lining the back wall. Her fingertips explored the spines with growing enthusiasm.

"Look at this, Ken. Shakespeare. Dickens. Chaucer. And Jane Austen." That was my girl. Despite the hellish day — and the threat of more to come — she couldn't resist the siren song of literature. She pulled a red, gilded volume from the shelf and delicately opened it. "This — this is a first edition!"

"They're all first editions." Finally, the prince moved toward Vee, his face beaming with pride. "And there's a hundredfold in the castle library."

With faintly trembling hands, Vee slipped the priceless book back into its rightful place before turning her questioning countenance toward the prince. "These books have got to be worth thousands of dollars. Why aren't they in the library with the rest?"

"Because these particular volumes are mine. This is my personal collection. All my favorites."

That didn't make sense. I charged across the room to join them. "Why would you keep your favorite books in the guest room?"

"Guest room?" The prince blinked at me for a moment, his brown eyes puzzled. Like the proverbial lightbulb, something clicked into place, and his gut-busting laugh filled the room. "These aren't guest rooms, lass. These're my chambers."

His chambers?

Besides being surprisingly refined for the lair of an ogre, the rooms were *occupied*. Did he really have the audacity to think we'd bunk with him? Not on his pampered royal life!

"We're not staying in your rooms."

"Relax, woman. It's not as if I'm asking ye to share my bed." He paused a second too long, peering at me from beneath half-lowered lids. "I'll be stayin' across the way."

Before I could respond, Vee lightly touched my arm, her cue that my mouth needed to stay shut while she diffused the situation. "While we're honored by your hospitality, your — eh — highness, we couldn't possibly put you out of your own chambers."

"Oh, but I insist." He leveled his gaze at me. "This is the safest place in the castle. I'll have one of my men stationed just beyond the door, and Fergus and I will be close by."

A man stationed just outside the door. Like what? A jailer. "Now, look," I began.

Duncan cut me off. "If ye won't think of your own safety, think of your friend's." As if in agreement, Vee shivered.

I couldn't argue with that. Gideon was skulking around somewhere — and the last thing I wanted was to wake with him standing over us. But that didn't mean I had to be all grateful about the accommodations. "Fine," I huffed. "As long as you have the servants change your sheets — *ugh!*"

Vee's elbow dug between my ribs to pummel my kidney. When we got home, I was going to duct tape a pair of elbow pads to her arms. With a toss of her shiny chestnut hair, she curtsied to the prince. "Thank you, Prince — eh — your highness, sir."

He reached for Vee's hand. When she gave it to him, he bent to brush a chaste kiss across her knuckles. He straightened with a grin, his bewitching eyes darting from Vee to me. "You needn't stand on formalities with me. Please, call me Duncan."

Faced with his smug, lopsided grin, I couldn't help but be contrary. "That's very kind, *your highness*, but I couldn't."

"I must insist." He offered me his hand, palm up. Then for good measure, he added, "If ye refuse me, I'll have ye thrown back into the dungeon."

"You wouldn't dare!"

"Is that a challenge?" The right corner of his top lip twitched in a way that made me almost completely certain he was bluffing.

The echoes of a long-forgotten incident floated up from my subconscious. Some kind of face off with a smug little boy — on the playground, maybe — but before I could capture it, Vee's elbow struck again and the thought vanished.

"Duncan," Vee interjected, all the while reprimanding me with her eyes. "You can call me Veronica. And she's Mackenna — Kenna for short. Isn't that right?"

And she accused me of being the bossy one.

"Fine. Call me whatever you want." Feigning indifference, I placed my hand in the prince's. His lips puckered as his head bent. Suddenly, I felt as breathless as when I'd stumbled into his room. I sensed the curse of the ginger — the blush of prickling heat — as it began to redden my neck and face. My only hope of controlling the affliction was cold water, and lots of it.

Giving his hand a firm single shake, I wrenched mine away before his mouth could make contact. In an overly loud voice, I heard myself babble, "Excuse me, but could you please direct me to the bath ... ah ... privy, the loo, whatever the heck you call it?"

He indicated a door along the back wall, next to his books. "Aye, it's through there and to the left."

"Come on, *Veronica*." I tugged her away from the rare editions. "I'm not facing this alone."

Duncan's bedroom was equally as dazzling as the sitting room. To the right, another roaring fireplace crackled like a mythical beast, and I had to admit the cozy window seat at the far end would make an excellent perch to contemplate the view of the mountains. I skimmed over an enormous four-poster bed that dominated the center of the room — refusing to consider what went on there — while in search of the bathroom. Just as our host promised, the door stood off to one side.

As I veered left, Vee broke from my grasp. She paused at the foot of the bed fit for a royal oaf and ogled the thick plaid-flannel comforter. Exhaustion accentuated the angles of her face, giving her purplish crescents under the hollows of her eyes. She teetered on her feet as she stifled a huge yawn. "I feel like I could sleep for a hundred years."

I agreed. Since coming to this crazy place, time had gotten skewed. I couldn't tell how long it'd been since we slept last, or how long until it was time to sleep again. But, unfortunately, some things were more important.

"No napping, Sleeping Beauty." When her gaze turned somber, I quietly asked, "Are you okay? Really?"

Her eyes closed on a deep sigh and then snapped open. "I'm going to be fine. We both are."

With images of the dungeon buckets still haunting me, I towed Vee toward the bathroom. How bad could it really be? I pushed through the doorway and froze in shock. "Whoa. Are you seeing this?"

"I would." Vee gave me a light shove, sounding more like her usual self. "If you'd get out of the way!"

As I regained my wits, I walked forward to the item that had astounded me, and pulled lightly on an overhead chain. *Ta-da!* Water whooshed from a high tank into the open toilet bowl below and swirled down the drain.

"Modern plumbing!" Vee exclaimed as she turned an ornate faucet and watched in fascination as fresh water flowed out. "I wasn't expecting this."

"Neither was I." I surveyed the rest of the spacious room. Blue and green ceramic tiling accented with little lion crests covered the floor and all four walls. While Vee turned her attention to the gold-plated mirror over the sink, I stepped farther into the room toward a sunken bath the size of a Jacuzzi. I tested the tap and hot water began to flow.

I couldn't help but clap my hands together in delight. "Houston, we have hot water. I wonder if the ogre has any bubble bath."

Rather than answer me, Vee made a small noise of alarm. Panicked, I spun away from the bathtub and toward my friend. But my alarm was unnecessary: She stared into the mirror, futilely rubbing a streak of dirt on her cheek. The wisps of hair that had escaped her high ponytail accented her face, giving her a sexy, windblown look. Attacking another smudge, this time on her forehead, she groaned, "I look disgusting!"

If by disgusting she meant flawless. It occurred to me for the umpteenth time in the course of our friendship that if I didn't love her so much, I'd be obligated to hate her on behalf of Plain Janes everywhere. I also knew, thanks to Vee, that even the prettiest of girls could be plagued by self-doubt about their looks. "Impossible. You would still be stunning even after dunking your head in a pig sty."

"Uh, thanks — I think."

I placed my hand on her shoulder, careful not to encounter my own undoubtedly revolting reflection. "I wouldn't worry about it, anyway. It's not like you need to impress these people."

As soon as I said it, I remembered the reason we were here. How stupid could I be? She thought she had some kind of cosmic connection with Kilt Boy.

Gently rubbing the streak on her cheek, I doubled back. "It's not anything a bath won't fix. Doesn't a soak sound heavenly right about now? Light some candles, maybe pour in a little lavender oil, just kick back with — *Duncan.*"

The slightly blushing prince filled the doorway. Clearly, he was uncomfortable being in the bathroom with members of the opposite sex. And since he'd caught me naked in my imagination . . . that made two of us.

"M' ladies?" His strangled voice sounded like he'd just hit puberty all over again. "Supper has — ehm — been brought up for ye. I wanted to let you — uh — know before it gets cold."

Before he could escape, Vee pointed to the sink. "Where did the modern plumbing come from?"

His demeanor instantly relaxed, and Duncan inclined his head toward me. "Contrary to what Mackenna may believe, we're no' barbarians." With a wink, he left the room.

"Arrg! What a total jerkwad!"

I waited for Vee's agreement, but she just laughed and said, "Let's go eat." Leave it to her to forgive any slight from brutes bearing casseroles.

In the main room, Fergus and a young woman with strawberry-blonde hair tucked into a white cap were busily arranging a feast. Gleaming platters overflowing with vegetables, fruit, bread, cheeses, and meat waited for us. My stomach growled in approval.

Duncan introduced the girl as Fiona Fairshaw and explained, "Fiona is at your service."

Resisting my baser impulses to dive face-first into the buffet, I waited impatiently as our self-appointed benefactor said his good-byes. Laughter colored Duncan's tone as he said, "I am needed elsewhere, m' ladies, so I will take my leave. But please, make yourselves at home in my quarters. Fiona can get you anything ye may have need of . . . including sheets."

Everyone turned their focus to the spread before us but I

continued to glare at the prince. In the space of a heartbeat, Duncan's mirth vanished. Calling Fergus aside, he said in a soft, bone-chilling voice, "Ye know what to do, man." Refusing to analyze the lethal look that passed between the two men, I turned my attention toward the food.

🜨 🜨 🜨

As Vee and I topped off our lamb and arugula sandwiches with blueberry puff pastries, Fergus beckoned Fiona to the opposite end of the room. I knew it was rude to eavesdrop, but I couldn't help myself. I'd watched enough BBC to know the help always had the best intel, and some scheme was definitely afoot.

Fergus cleared his throat, his voice projecting louder than a stage whisper in the confined space. "I think the lasses would do well with a wee nap."

"That they would, Fergus, but a summons is forthcoming. And they'd best be alert."

From the corner of my eye, I glanced at the girl who was our court-appointed babysitter. I figured she was about our age, or the Doonian equivalent. Maybe there was a way to calculate the difference — like you do with dog years?

Although taller than Vee, she looked like a child next to Fergus. Though a very attractive and strong-willed one. The reddish-blonde wisps of hair that had escaped her cap grazed the tops of her shoulders, and she had rosy cheeks and a dusting of pale freckles across her button nose. The young guard towered over her, but she stood her ground, hands clamped onto her hips, determined to get her way.

The rest of the exchange was lost, thanks to Vee murmuring into my ear, "What do you think she means by *summons*?"

"Shhh."

Whatever I'd missed caused Fergus to exclaim in a much louder voice, "Ye have no way o' knowin' that, wench."

"Fergus Lockhart! I'll no' have ye callin' me disrespectful names in front o' our guests." She jabbed her finger in Fergus's barrel-like chest. "Ye have no right ta tell me what I can and canna say or do!"

"Can I not?" Fergus searched her pretty face until her frown shifted. And as soon as she cracked, the big guy turned every imaginable shade of pink. Obviously, there was more to their relationship than met the eye.

Almost shyly, Fiona turned from the colossal guard and walked to the door. For a fraction of a second, we all stared in anticipation. Then three succinct knocks shattered the silence, causing Vee and I to gasp and jump up from the table. Fergus muttered a curse followed by a hasty apology for swearing.

Another round of knocks reverberated through the room. After receiving Fergus's go-ahead nod, Fiona opened the door to reveal a waiting messenger flanked by half a dozen heavily armed soldiers. Turning her grave face toward Fergus, she asked, "This proof enough for ye?"

Unable to contain her dismay, Vee scampered to Fiona's side. "Please. What did you mean by a summons?"

To me, the goon squad made it pretty clear. Vee's dream boy wanted to rake us over the coals again. I walked over and pointed to the soldiers, but lowered my voice as a precaution. "It means Prince Not-So-Charming wants to interrogate us some more."

Fiona laid a hand on each of us, her clear hazel eyes compassionate and sincere. "Well, I believe it be the auld laird ye'll have to face this time."

Vee cleared her throat. "Do you mean Jamie and Duncan's father?"

"Aye. He only involves himself in matters which impact the future o' the kingdom." Fiona paused, first searching my face and then Vee's before ushering us out the chamber door. "Remember ta speak the truth that's in your heart and all will finish right."

Easy for her to say. Since coming to Doon, everything from my mouth seemed to come from some place other than my heart — or my brain, for that matter. As I trailed Fergus down the one hundred and seventeen steps, I vowed to hold my tongue and play mute. From here on out I would reenact *The Miracle Worker* and leave all the talking to Vee.

CHAPTER 11

Veronica

Someday, I hoped I'd look back on this as a grand adventure. A tale of valor I could use to impress my kids. But right now I was having difficulty putting one foot in front of the other. Twenty hours of sleep deprivation tended to have that effect. Maybe after a good night's rest I'd be able to wrap my head around everything. Although it was pretty clear the fantasy of living happily ever after with the literal man of my dreams was a bust. At this point, I just hoped our trial wouldn't end with Kenna and me locked back in the *icky* dungeon for the rest of our natural lives.

Fergus half-carried me into a room that reminded me of a cross between the dining hall at Hogwarts and the throne room from Sleeping Beauty's castle. If I'd had the energy, I would've gawked over the three-story vaulted ceiling supported by stone columns, and marveled at the scalloped leaded glass windows. But in my diminished state, not even the vivid tapestries, larger than the giant man at my side, stirred more than a passing interest.

At our entrance, excited whispers rushed through the room. Hundreds of staring eyes strained to catch a glimpse as guards herded Kenna and me down the center aisle like circus freaks on display.

We approached a wide marble dais, where an elegant, aging man — who looked every bit a ruler — occupied the throne. My heart galloped ahead of me at the sight of Jamie standing beside his father, his hands clasped behind him, a lock of sandy blond hair across one eye. Duncan stood in a similar pose on the old laird's other side.

As we drew closer, and I could see the impassive set of Jamie's features, I reigned in my pulse, burying my emotions deep. If he could remain stoic, then so would I. When we stopped, I lifted my chin, locked my spine, and focused on the king. He looked incredibly regal, from the green and blue brocade robe that covered him from neck to feet to the simple gold crown. Even his thick, white hair, which hung down his back in a plaited braid, lent him an air of noble dignity. But it was his dark eyes that drew me in; they radiated with intelligence and life.

Scrutinizing the stalwart king, I couldn't help but wonder why Jamie had the duties of acting ruler.

"He totally has that King Lear vibe going for him, dontcha think?" Kenna whispered loudly in my ear.

"Shhh." I shot her a look of disbelief. Didn't she realize we were in serious trouble?

As King MacCrae opened his mouth to speak, he began to shake and appeared on the verge of pitching forward. Both princes tensed as if they were milliseconds away from lunging to catch him. As their father recovered, they both stiffened, their expressions identical masks of concern.

During the incident, the king's face remained passive, but his traitorous body betrayed him. Closer observation revealed red-rimmed eyes, a slight tremor in his knobby hands, and deep fatigue underlying his look of fierce concentration. My question regarding Jamie's role was answered.

As the royal family recovered, Gideon stepped forward and groveled before the king like the sycophant he was. "Sire, if I may, these two lassies before ye are about the witch's mischief. I apprehended them spying on the princes at the tournament."

Fear rippled through the crowd in a jumble of hysterical commotion. I turned to confront my jailer and froze. Gideon looked creepier than I remembered. The skin of his face stretched over his skull and his beady eyes protruded amphibiously from his head, like he'd been the victim of a terrible plastic surgeon. I steadied my breath and managed, "We're not working for any witch."

He wet his cracked, nearly nonexistent lips. "Why should we believe you?"

Before I could compose a persuasive reply, Kenna blurted out, "Because if we were, I'd have already turned you into a toad."

My friend wiggled her fingers ominously, inciting another round of outrage from the agitated crowd. I glanced behind her and met openly hostile stares. Many of the citizens seemed to have already made up their minds that we were guilty.

I turned back around and grabbed Kenna's elbow. "Not helping."

A single chuckle pulled at my attention. I turned toward the laughter and encountered Duncan's wide grin. My gaze flew to Jamie, daring to hope he shared his brother's lighthearted sentiment.

With an impatient gesture, he shoved the hair off his forehead and admonished, "Tis no laughing matter, Duncan."

Duncan shrugged one broad shoulder. "*'Tis* when someone's overreacting."

The king regarded the standoff between his offspring before settling a stern look of reproach on his eldest son. Speaking for the first time, his measured brogue oozed authority. "Just because yer brother laughs does no' mean he makes light o' the situation."

He shifted in his seat to favor Duncan with an indulgent smile. A glance of understanding — of preference even — passed between the king and his youngest son. Rather than react or defend himself, Jamie mutely turned away.

If I, an outside observer, could pick up so quickly that Duncan was the favorite son, what must it be like for Jamie? An overwhelming urge to comfort this beautiful golden boy with the dark, wounded eyes rose up inside me. But I dismissed the impulse as his deep scowl pinned me to the spot. Maybe I'd taken a knock to my head somewhere along the way, because I had far more important things to worry about — like, oh, I don't know, my imminent survival or imprisonment — than an arrogant boy who treated me worse than an ant he found crawling over his boot.

Clenching my jaw, I did my best to ignore his intense stare as King MacCrae addressed the crowd. "We shall hear the evidence against Miss Welling and Miss Reid."

Gideon once again approached the throne. "M' lairds, ye heard it with yer own ears. The one with hair the color o' devil's fire freely admits to witchery." His bulging eyes blazed like a zealot. "'Tis my belief the Witch o' Doon has built herself a new coven, and these two — her emissaries o' evil — are somehow impervious to the enchantment."

Nausea flooded my system as chaos exploded around us. Angry citizens pressed closer, shouting about witchcraft and malevolence. Kenna grabbed my hand, her voice quivering. "Enough of this Salem witch trial. I don't want to be hanged, or burned at the stake, or stoned — let's make a run for it."

I clasped her hand tighter and leaned in close. "Don't worry. We'll get out of this ... somehow." I chanced a glance at Jamie and prayed he wouldn't allow us to be carried down to the river by a mob of pitchfork-wielding villagers. In that moment, my prince commanded, "Silence!"

The clamor died instantly, replaced by a palpable and equally tense quiet. Jamie jumped down lightly from the dais and strode forward, his eyes never leaving my face. He stopped before me, and I met his catlike stare. Some indefinable emotion crossed his face and softened his rigid features, but before I could identify it the detached ruler was back. A vein pulsed in his throat as he demanded, "What have ye to say against the charges?"

My fear shifted into anger with a nearly audible snap. Letting go of Kenna's hand, I stepped forward. "What charges? So far, I haven't heard anything but conjecture from a raving lunatic. Shouldn't we be given the opportunity to defend ourselves?"

The prince moved into my personal space, forcing me to lift my chin to meet his gaze. Barely restrained energy radiated from his body, and against my will I trembled in response. His warm breath pulsed against my ear as he leaned in and hissed, "That 'tis precisely what I am doing. But if you have no explanation for yer presence here, we'll move on to the sentencing."

Gideon moved in and pulled Jamie back. "If ye continue to let her speak, sire, she'll beguile us all."

Jamie scowled at the guard's fingers, and Gideon snatched his hand back before continuing in a scornful tone, "Need I remind ye, they just appeared. By *magic*."

At this latest allegation, the crowd clucked in disapproval. Jamie stepped away from me, and the breath I hadn't realized I held whooshed from my lips. He nodded toward his father. "Gideon makes a sound point. We can't risk these alleged witches beguiling us."

On the second to last word, his voice cracked, but he turned to face the people and continued in an expressionless tone. "Any defense must be offered by a citizen of Doon."

For the first time in the proceedings, the room was as silent as a crypt. Jamie declared, "Is there no one willing to speak on their behalf?"

Duncan stepped down from the dais and winked in our direction. "Don't be daft, Jamie. You know I'll defend them."

Jamie's eyes narrowed slightly as his mouth quirked into a tight, shrewd smile. "You can't, little brother. As a member of the royal family, you sit in judgment on this hearing."

Duncan's expression mirrored his sibling's. "Then I renounce my royal claim. You must now be an only child and I an orphaned commoner."

I waited for the king to stop them, but he retained his Zen-like nonchalance. Either he was used to his sons' antics or his health was too compromised to intervene. Maybe a bit of both.

In an unexpected display of emotion, Jamie leaned toward his brother. Despite the quiet, I strained to catch his barely audible reproach. "Stop this madness. Ye know what's at stake here."

In an equally intimate tone, Duncan replied, "What happened to your heart, brother? What would Mother say if she were here to witness your callous behavior?"

Jamie's eyes widened as he turned away, dark color staining his cheekbones.

Duncan addressed his father. "If these girls held the power to bewitch us, they would've done it by now. As defense, I would like the lasses to give an account o' how they came to be in Doon."

When the king nodded in agreement, Duncan addressed Kenna and me. "Dinna be afraid. Speak whatever truth is in your hearts."

I glanced at Kenna, and she nodded for me to take the lead. Clearing my throat, I locked my knees against their shaking and focused on the king. "Respectfully, sire, we walked across the Bridge of Doon."

What I thought was a straightforward statement incited the mob, and Gideon had to shout to be heard. "Ye see, sire! The Brig o' Doon does no' open fer two more weeks — until the Centennial. Yet these lassies crossed it. 'Tis witchery, I say!"

"NOT — " Duncan paused until the roar died down. "Not if they possessed the Rings of Aontacht." Behind him, the assembly gasped.

"That is a bold claim, m' laird." Gideon scoffed and crossed his arms over his spindly chest.

Duncan smiled. "Is it?" Without taking his eyes off Gideon, he inquired, "Fergus Lockhart, what say you?"

The gentle giant stepped forward. His pale blue eyes met mine briefly before refocusing on his co-conspirator. Prompted by Duncan's nod, Fergus addressed the king. "Sire, we did remove rings from these lasses. One gold and ruby, the other silver with an emerald."

The king considered this for a moment then turned his attention back to Fergus. "If this is true, where are the rings now?"

"Gideon confiscated 'em, sire."

King MacCrae gestured for Gideon to approach the throne. Purple with indignation, Gideon reached into his vest. After a ridiculous amount of searching and patting, he produced the rings. Rather than hand them over immediately, he stammered, "M' laird, what if these trinkets be forgeries? Or cursed? They need ta be evaluated before — "

The king silenced him with an elegant flick of his wrist, then extended his hand and waited until Gideon surrendered the bands. They came to rest in the monarch's palm with a subdued clink.

King MacCrae took a ring in each hand and examined them. I watched mute, as he went into a trance-like state and held the rings reverently skyward. His lips moved in silent prayer. At long last, he proclaimed, "These are, indeed, the Rings of Aontacht. Where did ye get them?"

"They were left to me by my aunt Gracie and uncle Cameron." Kenna's voice rang through the hall.

"You're a relative of Cameron Lockhart?" As Kenna nodded, the auld laird favored her with a smile. "This explains much."

Jamie emerged from the crowd, apparently recovered from his moment of humiliation. "Father, just because these girls have the Rings of Aontacht does not mean they should be absolved. They could yet be aligned with the witch."

Without a trace of his characteristic smirk, Duncan interjected, "Or not."

Kenna sighed. "Just take us back to the bridge. We'll use the rings to go home. Problem solved."

My stomach bungee-jumped into my toes. Of course, leaving was preferable to death, but I wasn't ready to give up on this place ... or on *him*.

I ignored the impulse to glance at Jamie and instead focused on the one person who held our fate, King MacCrae. The same shrewd expression I'd seen on the faces of his sons now emerged on his. "I am afraid 'tis not so easily settled, lass. These rings belong to Doon. They will be locked safely in the chapel until Doon has need of them again."

"But — " Kenna sputtered. I knew she was thinking about her internship, life moving on without her in the modern world.

As if he could read her thoughts as well, the king elaborated. "Questions have been raised, Miss Reid, as to the purpose of your sudden arrival in our kingdom. You and Miss Welling will stay here in Doon for the next fortnight. At that time, the Brig o' Doon will open for the Centennial and ye will be able to leave without use of the rings. Until then, my kingdom is at your disposal. Fiona and Fergus will remain in your service."

Gideon's odious voice interrupted again. "But sire — "

"Gideon, it has been spoken. I will no' change my mind. M' ladies, ye have been granted a rare opportunity. Most travelers get only one day, but you have two weeks ta come to know Doon and its people. And for us to know you. At the Centennial, however, you must make the choice all outsiders are tasked with. Ye must choose whether to remain in Doon or leave us forever."

"Sire — " Gideon halted under the king's withering stare and dropped his beady eyes to the tip of his boot. The auld laird rose, and his sons each rushed to support him. As he leaned on his heirs, King MacCrae pronounced in a most wise and fatherly voice, "As Laird MacCrae, I welcome ye to Doon. Tomorrow my sons will present to you their kingdom. Ye must forgive my absence, but my health is not what it once was. Jamie will serve in my place."

Despite the distasteful grimace that moved across his face, I had to admit Jamie played the role of prince to perfection. With a deep, courtly bow, he said, "Miss Reid, Miss — uh — Welling, please permit me and m' brother, Duncan, to escort you about our kingdom tomorrow."

As he straightened, I nodded my acceptance. His eyes met mine briefly, before a furrow formed between his dark gold brows and he turned away.

In a low voice meant only for me, Kenna muttered, "Oh joy, a whole day with Prince Not-So-Charming and the overly flirtatious ogre."

I turned to face her, the fatigue I felt reflected in her face. Grabbing her hand, I smiled. "It's okay, Ken. Just think of it like a vacation."

Insinuating his gigantic form between Kenna and myself, Fergus wrapped an arm around each of our shoulders. "Uh, m' lairds? Your lady guests appear greatly fatigued. Please allow Fiona and I ta return them to their chambers."

With the king's leave and Fergus's assistance, we made our way through the mildly mollified crowd.

I had two whole weeks to explore this magical kingdom and convince the people of Doon we weren't witches. Fourteen days to try to find out why Jamie MacCrae had been visiting me in the modern world, and why he now looked at me like I might pull out an AK-47 and go *Call of Duty* on his beloved people. Three hundred and thirty-six hours to prove to my handsome prince that I wasn't evil incarnate.

Suddenly, two weeks didn't seem like nearly enough time.

CHAPTER 12

Veronica

In the shadow of the most spectacular castle I'd ever seen, I accepted Fergus's Frisbee-sized hand as he helped me into an open carriage. This place was straight off the pages of Cinderella. Surreal didn't begin to describe it.

Kenna settled next to me on the plush bench seat, humming show tunes under her breath as Fergus methodically checked the horses under Fiona's diligent scrutiny. Despite a full ten hours of blissful sleep, my shoulders ached with tension. The prospect of spending the entire day with Jamie MacCrae had me fighting the urge to hurl up my breakfast. Should I smile and be pleasant? Or stick my nose in the air and pretend he didn't exist? Playing hard to get didn't seem like the best strategy to win over a guy who'd done his darndest to keep me at arm's length.

"Stop squirming, Vee." I hadn't realized I'd been playing with the laces on the front of my bodice until Kenna's words stilled my restless hands. She looked at me with unmistakable admiration. "You look *amazing*—that sapphire-colored blouse makes your eyes pop."

"It does?" I glanced at Kenna. Her figure was perfectly suited for the moss-green, fitted bodice and the plaid skirt that was identical to mine. She looked curvy in all the right places. Me, on the other hand—not so much.

Kenna's penetrating stare raked over me and then she smiled. "Yeah, you look hot. Like a cross between a pirate wench and a Catholic school girl."

"Like Steph!" We said in unison, dissolving into peals of laughter at the thought of Stephanie Heartford, who'd worn a different naughty Halloween costume to school every year since junior high; each time she was justifiably sent home for flagrant violations of the school dress code.

"What's so amusing?" Duncan appeared out of nowhere on Kenna's side of the carriage. "See, Jamie, didn't I say we'd miss somethin' by being late?"

Duncan wore his perpetual grin, and Jamie—well, I assumed it was Jamie—stood next to him wearing dark pants and a black cloak with the hood pulled over his head, casting his entire face in shadow. He looked like a goth kid with a Jedi complex.

Choosing not to give him the satisfaction of gaping at him, I turned my attention to the normal brother and smiled. "Just an inside joke."

Duncan looked perplexed by my statement but didn't pursue it further; instead, he addressed the larger group. "Shall we be off then?"

"Aye. I'm driving." It was the first thing Jamie said since arriving. Not that I was counting.

As everyone settled into the carriage, I noticed we'd attracted the attention of various villagers going about their daily business in the courtyard. A man pushing a large wooden wagon overflowing with fruit stopped and stared at me. As I returned his gaze, his eyes widened and he hastily made the sign of the cross before rushing away, dumping half the contents of the cart in his wake. One of the overturned apples rolled past the feet of a guy our age wearing what looked to be a butcher's apron. He stopped to pick up the apple, and then turned toward me with a huge smile. Lifting the fruit as if in salute, he took a bite before continuing on his way.

Confused and a little saddened by what the men's behavior indicated, I glanced at the stiff set of Jamie's shoulders. Winning over the people seemed like the first logical step in earning the prince's confidence. What else could I do or say to change his mind about us when he didn't seem to believe anything I said?

Obsessing as I was over Jamie MacCrae, I couldn't help but overhear his low voice as he questioned Fergus. "Any news on Roddie MacPhee?"

"Naught a word. His wife hasn't seen him since yesterday eve. Search parties were dispatched this morn' per yer instruction."

Jamie nodded and then flicked the reigns, jolting the carriage into motion. Someone had gone missing? I hoped the man would be found soon — not only for his sake, but with many people in Doon believing the worst about us, I feared Kenna and I would become prime suspects.

Leaving the busy courtyard behind, we drove through the arched main gates and onto a cobblestone road. The views were breathtaking as we wound our way through the trees, catching glimpses of the sparkling lake — or *loch*, as Fiona called it — to our left and rolling green hills far off to the right.

Fiona served as our official Doon tour guide, sharing interesting facts and stories about the sights we passed.

Unfortunately, I just couldn't keep my mind focused on what she was saying. Being this close to Jamie, even with his back turned, was messing with my head. The deep sounds he made when directing the horses melted through me like rich hot chocolate on a cold day.

I rolled my shoulders, trying to dispel the viseral connection I seemed to share with the elder prince. What I really needed was a yoga class. Forcing myself to relax, I shut my eyes, tilted my head to the sky, and let the sun warm my face. Poses danced through my mind, *Warrior, the Bridge, Downward Dog...*

"I feel bad about taking you away from your dad when he's so sick," Kenna said, breaking the silence.

I cracked open an eye briefly and watched Duncan give Kenna a sweet smile before responding.

"Father's been ill for a very long time. He's requested that my brother and I live our lives as normally as possible. Not only for ourselves, but the health o' the kingdom."

It made sense that the royal family would set the tone for the people. If they walked around in a cloud of grief, everyone in Doon would feel it.

"Are we keeping you awake, Vee?"

Slowly, I opened my eyes fully and gave Kenna a serene smile. "Not at all."

Duncan's dark eyes sparkled with mischief. "I can tell ye a story guaranteed to keep sleep at bay."

"Please do," Kenna said with mock affront. "I'd hate for my friend to be sent to the gallows for falling asleep during the royal tour of the kingdom."

I straightened in my seat, too calm to be baited.

"A story it is, then," Duncan declared, hitching his thumb over his shoulder. "Through yon trees lies the ruin of an ancient witches' cottage." He deliberately deepened his voice, sounding like the voice-over for a Scottish horror movie trailer. "A hive of such pure evil that even the land is barren. To this very day not a single weed nor blade of grass dares to grow on that defiled ground."

"Wait," I interrupted. "How can there be evil here? Isn't Doon under an enchantment?"

"What you say is true … but ye see, the witches' dwelling isn't *in* Doon precisely."

We moved through a dense stretch of forest, the occupants of the carriage growing unnaturally quiet. Trees arched and met over the path, skeletal wood blocking out the late morning sun and stealing the heat from my skin. The rhythmic clomp of the horse's hooves and the squeak of the carriage wheels sounded magnified in the heavy silence.

I followed Duncan's and Fiona's stares through the screen of branches to a decaying ruin lurking just off the road. Leaning forward, I squinted into the unnatural darkness. The ground was grayish brown and bare, like winter. The crumbling stone structure, equally gloomy, appeared devoid of all life. It might have been my imagination, but the air seemed to move in a sluggish rhythm, punctuated by a steady throb like a heartbeat and carrying the slightest stench of rot.

Kenna wrinkled up her nose. "It stinks."

"Aye." Duncan nodded. "When my great-grandfather, King Angus Andrew Kellan MacCrae, made a covenant with the Protector o' Doon, a powerful blessing covered the kingdom. Our enemies, gathered in yonder cottage at the time, were instantly struck down and smitten from the land, except for one wee witch, a girl who managed to escape. But that land — the witches' land — was too defiled to be blessed."

I gripped the edge of the carriage and leaned back as Duncan continued, his voice quietly somber and devoid of theatrics.

"Therefore, the witches' land is not under our protection. No Doonian can set foot inside its malevolent boundaries — nor would they want to."

Only after the trees thinned, their patterns of dappled light and shade playing across my vision, did I have the courage to whisper, "What happened to her — the witch?"

"To this day, that wee witch still roams the hills outside of Doon in her eternal quest for revenge." At Duncan's words, icy fingers skittered down my spine, lodging an irrational fear into the pit of my stomach.

I looked over to Fiona as a shadow passed across her face. She made a hasty sign of the cross, her lips moving in what I assumed was a silent prayer. This was her heritage, and I could see she didn't take it lightly. As we left the forest behind and entered into the brilliant morning sun, she breathed more easily.

"You're trying to scare us." Kenna crossed her arms under her chest and shifted away from Duncan.

"Nay, but it does help to explain the suspicion of some of our people, does it not?"

Before I could ask Duncan how they knew the witch was still alive, Jamie bellowed "Whoa" and pulled the horses to a stop in front of an ancient stone chapel.

"This be the Auld Kirk," Fiona said with something akin to reverence in her lilting voice. She looked relieved to have moved on from evil witches to a more pleasant topic.

"The entire kingdom, if they so choose, attends services here Sunday morn," Duncan added.

"Even the royal family?" Kenna asked in surprise.

"Aye. We dinna stand on ceremony here." I looked up, startled to see that Jamie'd turned around to answer Kenna's question. "From the stable lads to the king himself, we each have a role to fulfill."

Even though his eyes where hidden in the deep cowl of his hood, I felt him watching me as he continued. "In Doon we are all equal parts of the greater whole. 'Tis our greatest strength."

After a pause, he turned, clucked to the horses, and drove on. His unassuming declarations about life in Doon struck me as remarkable — as if their idealistic existence was nothing out of the ordinary, as if there was no other way to live.

Having completely lost the tenuous calm I'd achieved earlier, I searched for something to focus on that wasn't our princely chauffer. Luckily, I was saved by the appearance of small gingerbread-like buildings in the distance.

"Is that the village?" I leaned out over the side of the carriage to get a better look.

Without even turning her head, Fiona said, "Aye," her face glowing with pride.

As we entered the gates of the thriving, picturesque town, its charm swept me away to another time. The winding cobblestone streets were lined with shops of various colors and shapes, all fitted together like perfectly matched puzzle pieces. A hundred fragrances swirled on the breeze, filling my nose with everything from savory grilled meat to fresh flowers. I smelled cinnamon and fresh baked bread, followed by the acrid tang of pitch. As we rounded a bend, the scent of something fried and salty made my mouth water.

Suddenly, I longed to experience this place at Christmastime; all lit up, gables coated in snow, doorways strung with garland, the scent of roasting chestnuts warming the icy breeze. It would be exactly like the miniature Christmas village I'd admired as a child in the window of Frank's Hardware Store. I'd spent cumulative hours of time over the years at that window making up stories in my head for the ceramic people living, shopping, and caroling in the tiny town. More times than I could count, I'd wished I could shrink myself down and live in that idyllic setting.

"It's like the Renaissance Festival," Kenna murmured. "Only cleaner. Look, there's a coffee stand!"

I had to smile at my friend's analogy — further proof of why we complemented each other so well.

We approached a lively area of town where people were bustling with noticeable abandon. Many paused in their interactions to wave at the princes as we passed. Duncan directed our attention to a smartly decorated store window. "There's Dinwiddie's leather shop; softest, most durable boots ye'll ever find. Doc Benoir's medical practice is next door. Oh, and that yellow building on the corner is Millie's Bakery. And this here's the local market. Villagers sell fresh produce and handcrafted goods — "

"Can we stop here?" My words ran over Duncan's, but I didn't care. Until Scotland, I'd never been outside of Bainbridge, Indiana. I wanted to live in this moment: sink my teeth into Doon's fresh fruits, feel the texture of the handwoven rugs, and slip my toes into Dinwiddie's soft leather boots. I would experience every bit of magic while I could, because if life had taught me anything, it was that the good things never lasted.

When he didn't answer right away, I begged, "Please?" He considered my question, which I didn't understand, as it seemed fairly straightforward to me. After several seconds, he reached around and tapped Jamie's shoulder.

Jamie pulled down a side street and parked the carriage, speaking to Duncan and Fergus in low tones. Then Duncan turned around and simply said, "Aye, lass. We can do that."

"Thank you!" Tiny wings of excitement fluttered in my stomach.

Duncan hopped from the carriage to assist Kenna and Fiona to the ground. Too impatient for chivalry, I unlatched the door on my side of the carriage. As I stood, yards of fabric pooled around my legs. The last thing I needed was to trip over my own feet. Cursing the heavy skirts, I gathered them in one hand and turned to make the short leap.

Too late, I saw the bent figure crouched on the ground directly below me, folding down a set of collapsible stairs. I teetered in mid-step with one foot on the edge of the platform. Frantically, I grabbed for the side of the carriage . . . and missed. Arms windmilling in the air, I pitched forward.

As if in slow motion, I watched helplessly as the bent figure in front of me began to straighten.

Oh, please, no — anyone but Jamie!

And then I flattened him. We landed on the ground, hard, Jamie on his back with my chest smashed uncomfortably into his face. It felt like I'd hit a concrete sidewalk. Worst of all, I couldn't breathe. Wriggling in panic, my vision began to darken. Then I gasped, sucking in a mouthful of air. Relief flowed through me, and I relaxed against the solid body beneath me. It was then I noticed the delicious scents of pine and soap mixed with . . . the charged air before a storm, a distinctive fragrance I suspected was coming from the boy whose body felt like fire against mine.

I tried to pull away from him, but strong arms held me in place as I stammered, "I'm so — so — sorry, please let me go and I'll get off you."

His warm breath pushed against my throat and a blush rushed up my neck as the truth washed through me — I'd tackled and was lying on top of Jamie MacCrae, boy of my dreams, future king of Doon. *Ugg!*

Just when I thought I couldn't handle the mortification any longer, his hold loosened. Quickly, I rolled to the side, landing in the grass beside him.

"I'm sorr—"

"Och, lass, I heard you the first time. Dinna apologize again." I caught a quick glimpse of his impossibly gorgeous face before he rose to his feet and tugged his idiotic hood back into place. Closing my eyes to shut out tears of humiliation, I lay as still as possible, hoping I would simply melt into the ground. This was *not* what I had in mind by living in the moment.

The distinct sound of someone clearing his throat caused me to open one eye. Jamie stood at my feet with his hand extended.

Slowly, fixing my eyes somewhere around the vicinity of his chest, I sat up and placed my hand in his large, warm fingers. The contact sent a delicious tingle all the way up my arm as he pulled me to my feet in one easy movement. I looked up into his face and our gazes crashed as forcibly as the recent impact of our bodies. His eyes, the color of rich coffee, flowed over my face, melting me like the first thaw of spring.

My eyes lowered to his strong lips. Would they be as soft as I imagined? I leaned toward him and—his face closed like a door slamming shut. He dropped my hand, practically flinging it back at me. Then he turned on his heels and strode away.

Stunned, I drew in a ragged breath and then busied myself with smoothing my hair and brushing bits of grass off my skirt. Kenna and Duncan were nowhere in sight. It appeared no one else in our group had witnessed my nosedive into the crown prince of Doon or the way he'd callously crushed my heart and then walked off.

Fiona fell into step beside me. "Are ye all right, Veronica?"

Except for Fiona, I corrected myself with a heavy sigh.

"I'll live," I said as lightly as I could, but one look at her knowing face made me realize I wasn't fooling her with my glib attitude. I shrugged, unwilling to replay Jamie's scathing rejection. "I feel like a fool. He was trying to put the steps down for me and I was in such a rush that I fell right on top of him!"

Fiona put her arm around my shoulders as we walked. "'Tis good for the lad ta have some sense knocked into him once in a while."

I smiled in relief at her irreverent comment, and we made our way toward the crowded marketplace. Fergus, Duncan, and Kenna waited for us at the edge of the crowd and Jamie — well, Jamie'd vanished . . . again.

Not that I cared. Just because I forgot to breathe when he looked at me didn't mean he had anything to do with my happiness. So he was the most gorgeous boy I'd ever seen. And yes, he was the prince of an enchanted kingdom . . . *So what* — he was a jerk! And he obviously didn't give a fig about me. I'd clearly misread his intentions when he was popping in and out of my world as if it were the local quickie mart.

Rushing ahead, I caught up with my new giant friend. "Fergus, where might I find the best strawberries in Doon?"

If I only had two weeks in this idyllic kingdom, I was determined to enjoy every moment of the experience.

"Right this way, little lass," Fergus answered, extending his elbow.

The market was a melting pot of cultures and beautiful handcrafted goods — colorful pottery, beeswax candles, flowing skirts, braided quilts, metal crafts — each item of such excellent quality, I couldn't believe the cheap prices. Fergus pointed toward the far end. "Strawberries are over yon, as are the bridies and pies . . . I recommend the steak and kidney and the lamb. A word of warning, you might want to stay away from the sushi — the fish is raw."

Doon has sushi? Before I could comment, Fergus resumed,

"Anything ye want, just direct the shopkeeper ta bill the royal family. I'm off to the haberdashery stall the next row over to purchase a new tam. I fancy one with a yellow toorie. Shout if ye have need of me."

I nodded to Fergus, content to wander on my own and ogle the amazing deals. A few stalls over, Kenna and Fiona inspected tartan plaids. Duncan drifted around the market shaking hands and speaking to every person in sight like a local politician … which to some extent he was. But no matter where he roamed, I noted he never strayed too far from my best friend's side.

As I continued my exploration, I began to notice something disturbing. The Doonians, both shoppers and salespeople alike, seemed hesitant to meet my gaze. I'd hoped with the king's blessing the people would give us the benefit of the doubt. To test my suspicion, I smiled at a merchant with russet skin, prominent cheekbones, and a jet-black braid, recognizing a fellow American, but as soon as I caught his eye his attention shifted back to the arrow he was fletching.

"Sushi! Are you kidding me?"

Ahead, Kenna's voice reverberated through the makeshift aisles. With Duncan and Fiona flanking her, they stopped to exchange pleasantries with an Asian family selling fresh sushi rolls and ale. I moved toward them until a booth glowing with all the colors of a summer sunset caught my eye. Altering my course, I moved through the crowd toward the magnificent display.

Paintings in radiant orange, red, deep purple, and gold decorated the booth. A tall, willowy woman with ebony skin inclined her turban-wrapped head to me as I approached. Pleased that she didn't appear to be afraid of me, I returned her greeting with a smile and then marveled at the vibrant watercolors of

African savannas, alongside landscapes of green hills carpeted with heather. Around the side of the booth, I found a display of painted sculptures, each one more remarkable than the next. In the center, a bit taller than the rest, was a perfect re-creation of the Castle MacCrae.

Mesmerized, I reached out and placed the miniature creation in the palm of my hand. It was perfect from every angle, each gray stone, blue turret, parapet wall, and arched doorway rendered in minute, flawless detail. It would make the ideal souvenir.

With a sigh, I set the castle back on its shelf. Although Fergus had said to charge anything I liked, I wasn't about to buy anything with Jamie's money. Continuing around the booth, I found a red-haired, freckled man minding two beautiful children with caramel-colored skin, the girl's braided hair a rich auburn and her younger brother a miniature of his regal mother.

The boy approached, extending a wilted flower clutched in his fist. "Yer pretty."

I squatted down to his level and smiled. "Is this for me?"

He nodded, his solemn chestnut eyes taking up half of his face, and my heart melted as I plucked the blossom from his hand. "What's your name?"

"Lachlan, miss."

"Thank you, Lachlan. I shall cherish this always." Maybe I didn't need money to have a remembrance of my time in Doon.

The boy's focus slid past me, his eyes widening in excite ment as a mischievous smile lit up his face. "Prince Jamie!"

I stood and spun on my heel to find a hooded figure hovering at the edge of the artist's booth. His face was angled away, but the set of broad shoulders beneath his cloak was unmistakable.

The boy slid a wooden sword from his belt and brandished it in front of him, rushing in Jamie's direction. "En garde, ye scoundrel!"

Jamie turned toward the boy, a tiny grin tilting his lips as he pushed his hood back and extended his empty hands in front of him. "I am unarmed, sir. Show mercy."

"No mercy for the weak. Choose your weapon!" Lachlan turned sideways, his little feet set in a fencer's pose, and poked Jamie's leg with the tip of his sword.

Jamie whirled and snatched a long baguette from the neighboring stall, wielding it in front of him like a weapon. "What be the stakes, Sir Lachlan?"

Clearly this wasn't their first mock sword fight. I glanced over at Lachlan's parents. His father grinned indulgently and his mother's eyes glinted with a kind of pride, perhaps because her son wasn't intimidated by the future king of Doon.

Lachlan inclined his head in my direction. "We'll fight for yon lady's favor."

A playful grin spread across Jamie's face and the heavy mantel of responsibility he carried disappeared before my eyes. "Yer on."

My heart twirled in a joyful pirouette as I watched the way Jamie engaged Lachlan, allowing the boy to gain the upper hand as they danced across the narrow space between stalls, their swords crossing again and again.

Lachlan advanced with wide sweeps, his little face set in concentration. Jamie retreated and then parried, taunting the boy. "Ah, Sir Lachlan, surely a champion of the crown can do better than that."

"Perhaps ye need to spend more time in the lists, ye nasty rogue!" The boy hefted his sword in both hands and chopped off the end of Jamie's baguette.

Laughter burst from my chest as Jamie stared in stunned indignation at his broken bread sword.

Pressing his advantage, Lachlan lunged. Jamie leaned into the blow allowing the toy sword to slide between his side and his arm. "Ugg! Ye got me!" The baguette dropped to the ground and Jamie staggered back, hunched over and clutching his gut with both hands.

Lachlan jumped up and down, cheering and waving his weapon in the air as the villainous prince fell to the ground. After a moment, Jamie's writhing and groaning stilled and Lachlan approached cautiously, leaning over his fallen advisory. Cupping his hand around his mouth, he whispered loudly, "Ye'll never win the pretty maiden's heart that way."

The prince's eyes popped open. "Ye dinna think?" He grabbed Lachlan around the waist and lifted him into the air, the boy's giggles echoing through the square as Jamie rolled him into the grass and tickled his ribs.

"Vee, you've got to check out this sushi." Kenna materialized out of nowhere and took my hand to pull me away, but not before Jamie sat up, his laughing eyes locking with mine in a shared, carefree moment. I smiled tentatively, hoping he didn't notice the blush heating my cheeks.

Jamie's lips quirked in a rueful grin and then he glanced away, hoisting himself to his feet just as Kenna gave my hand a yank. Reluctantly, I let her guide me away, but my mind lingered on the playful boy who happily indulged a child's fantasy without any ulterior motive.

Who was the real Jamie MacCrae? A ruthless ruler or a puckish prince? Perhaps he was a bit of both. And just like that, a tiny sprout of hope bloomed in my chest.

chapter 13

Mackenna

After the throne room, I'd commenced something I liked to call *Survivor: Brigadoon*. The bridge would open in a little less than two weeks. If Vee and I were going to escape with our lives and hearts intact, I couldn't afford to let my guard down for a second.

Despite the previous day's *Crucible* reenactment, Vee still felt this kingdom was her destiny. But when it came to my best friend, I was leaving no man — or in this case, no cheerleader — behind. So unless Prince Not-So-Charming came riding up on a golden unicorn and showered her with rainbows, she was coming home with me.

Vee'd been too busy ogling all the bright, shiny trinkets in the marketplace to notice Jamie shadowing us. Visions or not, he was far too bipolar to be a match for my best friend. She deserved a true prince — not some moody poseur with a crown. Yet, if I knew her, his conflicted Edward Cullen act would hook her faster than meth.

Duncan's sunny disposition, on the other hand, never faltered. Worlds apart from the golden-haired prince with the tortured soul, our dark-haired benefactor possessed an unwavering heart of gold and a quick sense of humor. Both of which, to my disconcertment, were growing on me.

The afternoon had passed quickly with Duncan shepherding us around the village. In his brother's absence, he'd even engaged Vee without being flirty. Duncan had also shared quirky little stories from his childhood and pointed out his most favorite places. No matter where he went, people greeted him like a beloved friend. He inquired after their families and promised to come round and help with various carpentry projects. Observing his interactions, I had no doubt every one of those promises would be kept.

If I'd met him on the stage, I would've instantly liked him. Heck, I'd have fallen like an avalanche of anvils — especially when he favored me with his smile. But in the not-so-real world, I did my best to keep a civil distance and not succumb to his charms. In two weeks, this would all be as distant a memory as a midsummer night's dream.

But like my opinion of Duncan, my impression of Doon had grown more favorable with each interaction. I was beginning to understand why Gracie loved this place. It was ideal for dreamers like my aunt and Vee.

The little tavern we were in was a perfect example. The place smelled like heaven — like rising yeast, spices, and roasting meat — yet part of me remained skeptical the dishes could live up to the olfactory tease.

Vee closed her eyes and inhaled appreciatively. For a skinny thing, she sure loved to eat. As she seated herself next to Fiona, she grinned maniacally at the prospect of another fabulous meal. "So, what's good here?"

Duncan and Fergus sat across from us, their faces mirroring Vee's food lust. Fergus, who looked like he'd never skipped a meal in his life, licked his lips in anticipation. Perched proudly on his head was a green and blue plaid beret-like cap with a yellow pom-pom. "I'd say just about everythin'."

As I opened my mouth to request a menu, Duncan interjected from across the table, "I shall order for us!" He caught my eye, his full lips quirking in a lopsided challenge.

"I've already taken the liberty of ordering, brother." Out of thin air, Jamie appeared. He pulled back his Prince of Darkness hood and sat in the empty chair next to Vee as easy as if they'd known one another their whole lives.

Duncan rolled his eyes. His fun-loving demeanor wavered as he regarded his MIA brother. "Decided to join us again, did ye?"

Jamie returned Duncan's stare with hard, defiant eyes and tightly set lips. "I had business to attend."

"Really? I struggle to see what could be more important than spending time with your people."

"I assure you, Duncan, my priorities were exactly where they needed to be."

Vee's hand flew to her mouth, her shoulders twitching with — laughter? Jamie's twinkling eyes darted to her and they shared a secret smile. I had no idea when they had time for an inside joke, since I'd been glued to Vee's side practically the entire day. Before I could ask what my bestie found so funny, a waitress with dark skin and a bright crimson sari approached bearing a suspiciously flat, round metal tray. Familiar garlic-scented wafts of steam trailed in her wake. I recognized that smell.

"Holy Hammerstein! Is that pizza?" My voice rang so loudly through the room that other diners stopped what they were doing and turned in our direction. But I didn't care. Doon had pizza!

As the platter containing what looked to be a large pepperoni was set before us, the occupants of our table relaxed. Vee slid Jamie a sidelong glance. "Is this really pizza?"

"Aye. Likely the best you'll ever eat." With a chuckle, he handed her a slice. Vee's thumb brushed Jamie's palm and he bobbled her food like a fourth-string quarterback. Hand off completed, he paused, his attention singularly focused on the area of her mouth while she bit into the triangle of meat and cheese.

After a moan of culinary bliss, she bit off a larger chunk and swallowed it whole. "Sooo good. I mean — thank you, m' laird."

Jamie tore his attention from Vee's lips with a slight grimace. "Glad ye approve. As I said, you need not stand on ceremony here. Call me Jamie."

Vee ignored his request as she dove into her meal like it was her last. I couldn't blame her … my own little slice of paradise beckoned. After several satisfying mouthfuls I asked, "How? I mean, where did you people get pizza?"

Jamie's eyes lit up as he explained with quiet pride, "Mario's an import from Italy, one of the Destined."

Unwilling to relinquish my slice for even a moment, I choked out between swallows of food, "Who's a what?"

Jamie laughed. "The restaurant owner's one of the Destined. Mario came to us during the last Centennial and decided to stay."

"As I told ye before, Mackenna, we're no' barbarians." Duncan's statement might have been more impactful if he hadn't been speaking with his mouth full, but I decided to let it slide on account of him being such a wonderful host.

The pride on Jamie's face deepened into quiet passion. "Each Centennial, while some Doonians are welcoming new arrivals, others will go out inta the modern world to gather up as much information as possible about the history and progress of that realm. With the help of the new imports, we implement changes that would best benefit Doon, like running water and modern plumbing, while preserving our culture."

Vee met Jamie's gaze with a hunger than had nothing to do with food. "Why not electricity?"

"Electricity was fairly new at the last Centennial." Jamie gestured around the tavern. "Doon has adequate sources of heat and light, so generating electricity wasn't deemed of enough benefit to implement. O' course, it will be evaluated again after the next gathering."

"How does the Centennial work, exactly?" Leave it to Vee to want to peek behind the curtain and discover the inner workings; it was our way out, which was enough for me.

"On the Centennial, the Brig o' Doon opens for twenty-four of your hours. In that time, Doonians and the Destined, those called from the outside world, are free to come and go as they please."

She digested the information, her pizza forgotten. "So the Outsiders could stay in Doon?"

"Aye. Most all do."

"And the Doonians?"

"Do not have to return, if they dinna want to — but that rarely happens."

Vee's train of thought furrowed her brow. Rather than look at Jamie, she picked at the checkered tablecloth. "So a Doonian could choose to stay in my world, if he — or she — wanted."

Jamie's eyes narrowed as if he were trying to read the thought behind her question. But rather than respond he indicated her neglected plate. "Ye best eat before your food gets cold."

Back to being Prince Not-So-Charming, Jamie turned to Duncan and began to discuss plans for the next gathering in a low voice. Duncan cast me a helpless glance that I took to mean he'd rather be socializing than talking official business. But it's not like he had much of a choice, as someday soon his brother would be in charge — Jamie was the heir and Duncan merely the number two. The spare.

A quarter hour later, Fergus leaned back in his chair and caressed his bulging belly with meaty hands. "I dinna think I can eat another morsel." Although I had not personally eaten two whole pizzas, like the big man, I still echoed his sentiments. *Best pizza ever!*

Fiona cast Fergus a teasingly stern look. "'Tis a good thing, Fergus Lockhart, because I don't think Mario has a morsel left ta spare." Through most of the meal, she'd remained silent. Observing. I doubted there was much of anything she failed to pick up on.

"Sì." Mario, the mustached restaurateur who'd been the benefactor of our incredible meal, joined us with a chuckle. *"Ma va bene se gli piaceva la mia cucina."*

Fergus looked blearily at Duncan, his brain likely struggling to process the conversation due to his food coma. "What'd he say?"

Trying to suppress his laughter enough to translate, Duncan replied, "He said, 'It's fine as long as you enjoyed his food.'"

"His *cooking*, Duncan," Jamie interjected with a hint of superiority. *"Cibo* is food. *Cucina* means cooking."

Duncan rolled his eyes. *"Cucina* also means kitchen, Jamie. My translation was contextual rather than literal." His impish wink at me made it clear Duncan was baiting his brother. Although I had no idea why. To me it seemed as advisable as poking a bear.

Jamie glared from across the table, his dark eyes narrowed

as a muscle in his jaw ticked. "Are you saying that your Italian is better than mine?"

Duncan nodded in the affirmative. "Sì, certo!"

The brothers jumped to their feet in unison, causing Mario to raise his hand to his forehead. In thickly accented English, he exclaimed, "Not again. *Ragazzi!*" Other than Mario's admonishment, no one else in the tavern appeared particularly alarmed that the princes were on the verge of coming to blows over a translation.

After a moment of testosterone-fueled opposition, Jamie's lips began to twitch and Duncan's shoulders started to quake. In a strangled voice, Jamie said, "Italian aside, can we not agree, brother, that Fergus's new tam is the ugliest hat in all the realm?"

Between heaves, Duncan replied, "Aye." Laughing too hard to say more, he collapsed back into his chair, tears leaking from the corner of his eyes.

Fergus looked from one prince to the other in astonishment, finally settling on his future leader. "Wha's wrong with m' tam, exactly?"

Besides the bright yellow pom-pom? In the marketplace, I'd seen lots of people wearing tams of the Doonian plaid — called the Auld MacCrae, which I'd learned thanks to Fiona — with a green or blue toorie on top. But nothing quite like Fergus's. To my left, I heard Vee muffling giggles behind her napkin and I couldn't help but cave.

Truth be told, he was a big man ... in a *little* hat.

With his pride at stake, the giant turned to Fiona. "You care for it, don't ye, Fee?"

Fiona blinked at him, her face deliberately placid despite widened eyes. After a moment she stood and smoothed her skirt. "I want ta pop round and see my mum before returning ta the castle. So if ye don't mind, I'll take my leave."

In a surprisingly lithe move, Fergus sprang to his feet. Before Fiona had taken a half dozen steps, he was at her side. She paused and lifted her lovely face toward her massive shadow. "What're ye doing, Fergus Lockhart?"

"Escorting ye." His face colored ten different shades of mottled pink, but he didn't back down.

"Because the streets o' Doon are so unsavory?" Undeterred by Fergus's size, Fiona placed a petite hand on his sternum and pushed. "Shove off! I can fend for m'self."

Fergus placed his bear claw of a hand over hers, trapping her palm against his chest. He leaned toward his captive and invaded her space while speaking in a low, even voice. "That may be, Fee, but the people are in a state of unease" — he glanced at us apologetically — "because o' our new arrivals. So I'm escorting ye."

Fiona's nostrils flared, but not from anger. Her pupils swallowed up her hazel eyes as she inclined her mouth toward Fergus's bright red ear. "Fine. But you better not eat all of Mum's biscuits again."

With that, she yanked her hand from the giant's grasp, spun on her heels, and stalked out the door. With a contrite "m' lairds" and a single nod, Fergus followed in her wake.

The moment the tavern door shut, Duncan and Jamie exploded with laughter. Duncan raked his hand through his already-chaotic hair so that it formed dark, spiky peaks. "Poor lad."

Jamie nodded in agreement. "Aye."

I failed to get the joke. "Why?"

"Why?" Jamie smiled, looking the most at ease he'd been all

evening. "Because he's totally besotted, that's why. He's been in love with Fiona since childhood."

A miniscule sigh slipped from my bestie. Out of the corner of my eye, I noted the devastating effect of Jamie's smile. In the aftermath, her eyes brimmed with stars that rivaled the Hollywood Walk of Fame's.

Not that I could claim to be completely unaffected. When he wasn't sulking, Jamie was one of the hottest guys I'd ever seen — aside from his brother. Staring at the two of them side by side was like stepping into a medieval Calvin Klein ad — only with more clothing. And when the both of them smiled, I felt the resulting swoon deep in my girly parts.

Speaking of swooning, Vee blinked dreamily up at Jamie. "And Fiona doesn't feel the same way."

"Nay, she's crazy about him too." Duncan pulled the focus back to himself, but not before I noticed Jamie's posture shift slightly away from Vee. "But he'll not have an easy time of winning her."

"Winning her?" While I wasn't a brainiac like Vee, I didn't typically need water wings in the shallow end. I was obviously missing something. "She's not a prize turkey. If they like each other, why don't they just talk it out? Honesty is the foundation of a healthy relationship."

"That's what I was saying to Jamie this very morning." Duncan propped his chin on his fist, batting his lashes and favoring me with a disarming smile. His twinkling eyes drew me in like a magnetic force field. Imaginary music swelled, filling the tavern with the sweet love ballad of Christine and Raoul from *Phantom*.

Unable to look away, I squirmed in my chair and sent Vee mental smoke signals. She reached across the table and lightly touched Duncan's forearm. "Is Fergus any relation to Kenna's uncle, Cameron Lockhart?"

For a moment, he appeared confused by Vee's touch. But he quickly recovered and favored her with a million-watt smile that abruptly silenced the romantic melody in my head. "Aye. Cameron Lockhart was Fergus's mother's cousin. But he and his bride left Doon the year before Fergus was born."

While Vee chewed thoughtfully at her lip, Jamie scowled at the juncture where her pale hand rested against his brother's coppery skin. A barely audible growl rumbled up from his chest. Vee glanced toward the noise, noticed the murderous expression on Jamie's face, and snatched her hand away as if stung.

Recognizing my cue to play rescuer, I quickly improvised. "But if Cameron left Doon more than fifty years ago and Fergus is — what, early twenties? — how does it work?" I was sooo not a math girl. On my best days, I struggled to add and subtract double digits.

Mario, the proprietor and import from Italy, paused in his task of clearing the table adjacent to ours. "If I may, *signori*? It is a *gigante* mystery." He illustrated his point by holding his hands wide apart and giving them a shake for emphasis. "As a young man, I was called to Doon from Napoli in 1915, during the last Centennial. I met *la mia moglie* — my future wife. Since then, I marry, make seven *bambinis* — babies — but I do not look over one hundred years old." He demonstrated by doing five quick jumping jacks. "I do not feel it either."

If I passed Mario on the street, I would've placed him in his late thirties or early forties — not in the hundreds. Yet he stood before us like the Italian cross between a Roman immortal and the old woman who lived in a shoe with all those kids.

Vee waved her hand, apparently unsatisfied with the breezy explanation. "But there must be some logical explanation."

"*Niente.*" Mario shrugged and then resumed busing tables.

Vee turned to Duncan who, in turn, gestured to his brother. Cautiously, Jamie turned toward her and answered, "There's no exact formula for matching the passage of time in Doon to the outside world, but it moves at approximately one-fourth the pace and can have a variable of eight years."

Nerd alert. Although Jamie MacCrac looked *GQ*, he had some serious IQ going on.

Plunging into the mental deep in the prince's wake, Vee hypothesized, "So, the Brig o' Doon opens once each hundred years in the outside world, but it happens approximately every twenty-one to twenty-nine years in this realm?"

"Tha's right. We call it the Centennial as a reminder of the passage of time in the world from whence we came."

Vee turned to me, her eyes shining with the power of knowledge. "That answers a lot of our questions, doesn't it?"

They'd been her questions, not mine, but the point wasn't important enough to debate. Instead, I swung my head back and forth and reveled in gleeful ignorance. "Nope. Afraid it's all Geek to me."

As patient as Mother Teresa, Vee explained, "It's like a sale where shoes normally cost $79.99 but are thirty percent off — you have to round up or down to get even sums. Because we're in an alternate realm, it doesn't match exactly. Like how we have leap year every four years to make time fit."

"So you're saying time *is* adjustable, just like I told you back in the cottage." This totally called for an I-told-you-so dance.

Before I could celebrate, Duncan leaned forward. His confidence had been replaced by an eagerness that made him seem as awkward as a freshman on his first date. "It's common that those who're led to Doon have visions or dreams about the kingdom prior to coming. Did either of you dream of Doon while ye were still in the modern world?"

Vee and I exchanged a cautionary look, wondering how much to divulge, when Jamie suddenly shoved his plate away and stood to tower over the rest of the table. While his words were meant for our conversation, there appeared to be some cryptic significance directed at Duncan. "Dreams have always played an important role for our people. We believe the Protector speaks to us through waking visions and dreams — *many* kinds of dreams. We must remain vigilant. It would be a mistake to let down our guard simply because we envisioned a pretty face and pair of fine eyes."

Duncan straightened in his chair, all traces of his easy-going disposition gone as he glared back at his older brother. "It would be a mistake not to trust the gift ye've been given."

"Agree to disagree then. 'Tis late. Fergus and Fiona will be waitin' for us." Jamie put an end to the discussion as he turned stiffly to Mario and thanked him for the hospitality.

Undeterred by Jamie's petulant mood, Mario kissed him on both cheeks. "Shall I send for the carriage, m' laird?"

"Nay." Duncan stood, pausing to roll the kinks out of his linebacker shoulders. "It's a beautiful night. We'll walk 'round. *Grazie*, Mario."

Throughout dinner, I'd noticed Duncan's flawless Italian. The way his lips moved, his easy cadence. When he rolled his *r*'s with wild abandon, it made me go all gooey inside.

Mario kissed my cheeks and then Vee's, saying, "*Signorine*, I hope next time you dine with us, you will be able to meet my beautiful wife. My Sharron and our seven *bellissimo bambini*." I thanked him profusely for the pizza before I took Vee's arm and we stepped out into the warm night.

Despite being summer, a light wind brushed over me, coaxing little goose bumps across my skin. I did my best to ignore the sudden chill and focus on my impression of the village after dark. The lit lampposts cast an amber glow over the cobbled street, like a set from *A Christmas Carol*. I half expected Ebenezer Scrooge to round the corner any moment and bellow "Bah humbug." The image was enough to remind me that despite the little pepperonied slice of home, we were trapped in another time and place.

Arm in arm, Vee and I strolled down the main street until Duncan stepped up to my free side. Giving my arm a quick squeeze, Vee veered away and picked up her pace. Jamie, back to his Emo Stalker routine, trailed several paces behind.

With a low sigh of contentment, Duncan matched his gait to mine. "Mario's a lucky man."

"He might be, but his poor wife ..."

Duncan stopped, his face hidden in shadow. "What's your meaning?"

As Vee moved farther ahead, I registered the increase in Jamie's stride as he silently skirted around Duncan. She rounded the corner and Jamie practically sprinted to catch up. With them out of sight, I returned to my own boy situation.

"I can't imagine having all those kids ... Actually, I can't imagine having any."

"Can't ye, woman?" Duncan's deep, soft brogue caressed me like the wind. "Not even for love?"

Someday I would probably want a couple of rugrats, but right now career came first. Well, career and getting home. I wasn't about to jeopardize either one by making a medieval love connection. Maybe telling that to Duncan would get him to back off. "What I want is to get back to America. I've got an amazing internship waiting for me in Chicago. It's a dream job, really."

Despite his dark vantage point, I could sense Duncan's scrutiny. "I'm not opposed to a career woman. I believe women and men should follow their passions."

"Exactly." I began walking so Duncan would have no choice but to move out of the obscurity of the shadows. "And my passion — my dreams — are back in the States."

He looked at me skeptically — like he knew more about my dreams than I did and was completely willing to argue the point. "My mum's dream was to be a weaver. She loved spinning wool inta yarn and creating beautiful fabrics." His eyes got a far off look as he continued, "When she fell in love with my father, the prince, she worried that she'd be forced ta sacrifice her dreams for the responsibilities o' the crown."

It was a valid worry. "Did she?"

"Nay. She realized her destiny was not to trade one dream for another, but to have both. A life more abundant than she could've possibly imagined. And she did ..."

My heart tugged, suspecting we shared the same wrenching loss. "What happened to her?"

"She passed a few years back. I miss her o' course, but it was even harder on my brother." Duncan shoved his hands in his pockets. "They shared a special connection."

I rounded the corner and bumped into Vee. Hard. "What the — "

Before I could get the words out, Duncan stepped in front of the both of us. Arms wide, he backed us up until we were flat against a wall. His hand moved automatically to his side, where his weapon should have been. But he was weaponless — both princes were. In an effort to be civilized, they'd left their daggers in the carriage.

An unfamiliar voice, thick and slightly slurred, curdled the half-digested meal in my stomach. "Just hand 'em over, yer highness, and we'll be on our way."

On my tiptoes, I peered around Duncan's shoulder. Jamie, his posture taut and coiled like an overwound spring, faced down a half dozen men. They ranged from young to middle-aged and, unfortunately, were not defenseless. Each man held some sort of improvised weapon — branches, rocks, and even a metal poker.

Utterly fearless, Jamie stood his ground against the mob. "You lads have been drinkin'. I suggest ye go home and sleep it off."

The bearded ringleader sported an official-looking blue tam, with a creased top and a bushy white feather that was identical to the one Gideon had worn in the throne room. He brandished a wooden club like he used it on a daily basis. "We dinna want any trouble, m' lairds. Just hand o'er the witch's emissaries."

Duncan, our human shield, took a nearly imperceptible step forward. "These lasses are under our protection."

Shouts of dissention assaulted us.

"But they're consorts o' the witch!"

"My son's got the croup!"

"And my livestock died!"

"'Tis witchcraft, I tell ye!"

"Hand 'em over!"

The ringleader advanced on Jamie, edging him back toward his brother. "I'm afraid we canna do what ye ask, yer highness. People are missing. Roddy MacPhee, and Robert Ennis's wife, Millie. The kingdom will no' be safe until the evil is cast out."

The princes could not prevail against six burly, drunk men. Under certain circumstances, they might've been able to handle three apiece, but without weapons — not to mention the burden of having to keep us away from the mob — it was impossible.

Then several things happened at once. The ringleader and Jamie leapt toward each other as a man my father's age charged Duncan, who braced for impact and then propelled the man through the air — like a rag doll. The old guy landed in the street with an overly loud thud and writhed with pain. He wouldn't be jumping anyone again for a long time.

Three others rushed Duncan so that he crashed between Vee and me. As one burly dude punched Duncan in the jaw while another guy kicked him in the gut, the third raised his club high into the air like a major league ballplayer. With a sneer, he swung squarely at Vee's head.

Her scream pierced the night.

In the final second before contact, Jamie lunged toward her and shoved. The blow meant for her cracked against the side of the prince's head, and he slumped to his knees.

An instant later, Duncan — still fighting two of the attackers — smashed into me. His elbow crushed my diaphragm, knocking me off balance as my vision blackened around the edges. The golden cobblestones rose to meet me as darkness swallowed them up.

I came to my senses on hard ground to the sound of running feet and the sight of Duncan standing over me like a grizzly bear. Four men, including the old guy, lay in a crumpled heap at his feet. Another took off as the first group of guards rounded the bend.

A short distance away, Jamie sat on his royal rump near the unconscious ringleader. A small trickle of blood flowed from behind his left ear and down his neck. Vee pushed herself away from the wall where she'd ended up and stepped toward Doon's future king. With a shaky hand, she reached down to assess his injuries.

"Don't." He snarled the word through clenched teeth. Irritation oozed from his every pore as he jerked away and lumbered to his feet. He pointed toward Vee, who regarded him with wide-eyed shock. "Duncan, get *her* back to the castle. The both of them. And do not let them out of your sight!"

"Aye."

As Duncan turned around, I forced myself into a sitting position. The throb in my shoulder informed me that I would have a wicked bruise in the morning. Catching my breath, I looked up and steadied myself once I met the young prince's eyes.

He knelt and smoothed a lock of hair from my cheek with the rough pad of his thumb. "Are ye all right, Mackenna?"

His concern stole the air from my lungs, so that all I could do was nod and try not to focus on what his touch was doing to my body. Before I could get to my feet, Duncan reached out and scooped me into his arms. Instead of protesting, I sagged against him and listened to his heart beating away like a massive jackhammer.

Since arriving in Doon yesterday, he'd saved me from Gideon, the icky dungeons, and now violent death at the hands of a lynch mob. Rescuing me was fast becoming "our thing." It would've been so much easier if "our thing" had been something normal and less life-threatening ... like karaoke.

CHAPTER 14

Veronica

Feathers floated around my head, landing on my eyelashes and sticking to my lips, but I didn't care. I hit the pillow again and again. Sure, Jamie'd pushed me out of the way and taken a club to the head in my place. But then the callous jerk had acted as if the attack were my fault. As if I'd begged for a bunch of drunk, tam-wearing thugs to jump us!

Why? Why did Jamie have to be such an incredible idiot? I pulled my arm back and punched with all my strength. My knuckles struck the solid wood of the headboard through the pillow. I leapt out of bed and danced in a tight circle, shaking out my aching hand.

"That's cute, Vee. New dance move?"

I stopped spinning and put my knuckles in my mouth. Kenna stood in the bathroom doorway, swimming in a green velvet XXL robe, her damp hair piled on top of her head. Pulling my tender fingers out of my mouth, I said, "Ha, ha. Nice robe, but I think the circus elephant might want it back."

Kenna giggled. *Giggled?* My best friend might hoot, snort,

or even cackle with the best of them, but she *never* giggled. It must've been a delayed stress reaction or something.

"It was hanging in the linen closet, and I was cold after my bath," Kenna said absently as she wandered around the room picking up random items and setting them back down, finally sinking into a chair in front of the fire with a heavy sigh. I watched her with narrowed eyes. She had the appearance of a girl who was completely smitten. And who could really blame her? Duncan was gallant and charming. Jamie, on the other hand, was a rude, egotistical pig!

Residual adrenaline coursed through my veins like a ricocheting pinball. Jamie's harsh rejection of my help, and even my touch, had me ready to punch something other than my pillow. Preferably a broad cheekbone or dimpled chin or — I cut my thoughts short.

Taking several deep, calming breaths, I swept my damp hair up behind my head, tied it in a knot, and then moved into a Warrior pose. I should have told that conceited jackwagon to go stuff himself. Instead, I'd let Duncan lead me back to the castle without saying a word.

Closing my eyes, I held the position and continued to breathe. I focused on my muscles elongating as I pushed negative thoughts out and drew in the positive.

Desperate to regain my freedom of movement, I'd shed my heavy skirts in favor of knee-length cotton bloomers and a silk cami. My ensemble would be considered scandalous by most Doonians, but ironically covered more than my old cheer uniform.

"What are you doing?"

Without opening my eyes, I answered, "Yoga." I brought my hands together and slowly arched back into a Half Moon.

"Well, when you're done communing with Yoda or whatever, I need to ask you something."

I returned to neutral and opened my eyes. "Yes, young one? Assist you how may I?"

A small cylindrical pillow hurtled across the room toward my face. I ducked at the last second, narrowly avoiding the projectile.

"I'm four months older than you, and don't you forget it!" Kenna teased.

My equilibrium renewed, I skipped over and dropped down cross-legged on the hearthrug in front of Kenna's chair. Sinking my fingers into the plush texture, I realized, with mild revulsion, that it was some kind of dead animal fur.

"Is that Duncan's robe?"

"Where's the journal?"

We spoke over each other, voicing our questions at exactly the same time.

"I asked first," Kenna declared.

"Okay. It's in the toilet."

"It's in the ... *What*?" Kenna uncurled from her chair, leaning forward.

Realizing more than an explanation was in order, I popped back up and grabbed Kenna's hand so I could tow her along behind me. We'd agreed earlier that since the rings were confiscated on sight, we'd better hide Aunt Gracie's treasure trove of information about this magical place, at least until we'd read it from cover to cover.

"They may have the newfangled plumbing here" — I looked over my shoulder and winked — "but I'm willing to bet they don't know this trick." Climbing onto the toilet seat, I raised myself onto my tiptoes and slid the lid of the antique tank to one side and withdrew a dripping plastic baggie containing Aunt Gracie's small leather journal.

"You're a genius! But where did you get a baggie?"

"The rings were in it." I shrugged. "I'd stuffed it in my pocket."

"I mean it, you're brilliant. But you could have come up with a slightly less disgusting hiding place." Kenna took the edge of the toilet water-covered baggie between her thumb and forefinger and shoved it toward me. "You've been dying to burrow into this thing since we found it. Now's our chance."

I took the soggy bag and placed it on a towel, slowly removing the leather-bound book. A moment of panic caused me to consider putting it back into its hiding place unread. The more I found out about this place, the more I worried I'd discover Jamie had every right to hate me.

&#127; &#127; &#127;

Unable to shut my brain down despite my weariness, I read the journal long into the night. Kenna had lost patience almost immediately, insisting first on the CliffsNotes before she gave up entirely and snuck off to bed. But I didn't mind the privacy, especially if Gracie's diary was going to crush any hopes of a future with Jamie. Turning another page, I continued to read.

As far as we can tell, there is no way for the Witch o' Doon to breech its enchanted borders — not even on the Centennial. However, if an object were to be enspelled by the witch and brought into the kingdom, the defenses of Doon could be compromised.

I was told that before Cam's time, the witch found one of the Rings of Aontacht and bribed a young man to enter the kingdom and do her bidding. When he was caught in the witch's cottage searching for something, his treachery was uncovered.

Maybe this could be a clue as to why Jamie didn't trust me. Perhaps he thought we'd brought some curse into the kingdom with us. But if that was the case, why wasn't he belligerent toward Mackenna as well?

A twinge of pain shot up my jaw, reminding me to unclench my teeth. What I really needed was to go for a run. Except the thought of running in heavy skirts didn't sound the least bit appealing, nor did the possibility of harassment by drunken Doonians. Not that the guards outside our door would let me leave anyway. So I determined to stay safely ensconced in the turret room like a good little girl, no matter how tense the imprisonment was making me.

It was well past two o'clock when I tiptoed into the bedroom. I crawled under the covers, doing my best not to disturb Kenna, who snored lightly on the other side of the massive bed. Taking a deep breath, I let my eyes flutter shut. But the images wouldn't stop.

I stared up at the shadowy ceiling, my mind wandering back to the pizzeria. Duncan said people often dream of Doon before coming here, but what if they saw a specific person — when they were awake? What did *that* mean?

"You might as well spill. You obviously want to."

I jumped at the sound of Kenna's sleep-scratchy voice.

"Sorry, I didn't mean to scare you. It's just something's obviously bothering you, and neither one of us are going to get any sleep if you don't stop flopping around like a fish."

The strike of a match prompted me to push the covers back and sit up. As Kenna lit the oil lamp on the nightstand, I focused on the soft light flickering behind her instead of the questions running through my head. Because as soon as I opened my mouth, I might have to face answers I wasn't ready to hear.

"Veeee…" Kenna's voice took on the whiny, nasal tone she knew I hated.

"Okay, okay." I let out a slow breath. "Duncan likes you. And you like him, right?"

Kenna frowned. "I thought we were going to talk about you."

"Just answer the question, please. Do you like Duncan?"

"Well, uh, sure." Her eyes darted away, focusing on everything but my face. After several moments of silence, she faced me and shrugged a shoulder. "Who wouldn't? He's yummier than triple-chocolate ice cream — and you know how I love my chocolate ice cream."

That said a lot, but unfortunately didn't answer the million-dollar question. "Did you see or dream about Duncan before we came here?"

"Nope."

"Okay, but if you and Duncan started dating…" When she glanced at me, I arched an eyebrow and quirked the corner of my mouth. "Would it be so bad to end up living in paradise with a tall, handsome prince?"

"One girl's paradise is another girl's purgatory." She released a heavy breath. "I mean, he's fabulous and all. But I won't give up my dreams of the stage to have a litter of *bambinis* and become some Doonian Stepford princess. And besides, I'm not the one who's been dreaming about snogging the king wannabe."

Laughing, I picked up a pillow and lobbed it at her head.

"Hey, ow!"

"He happens to be the crown prince of Doon. He's not a wannabe anything. And I absolutely have not been dreaming about snogging him!" *Much.* I swallowed a sigh at the thought of Jamie's hauntingly beautiful face and cleared my throat, sweeping the image out of my mind before continuing.

"So what if I saw him a few times before we came here." I tried to smile, but a deep grief pulled at the corners of my mouth and caused my words to tremble. "Since he hates me, it must not mean anything." I shrugged and climbed back under the covers.

"Why don't you just ask him?"

"Ask him if he hates me?"

"No, dummy. Ask him if he saw you too."

"It's not worth the risk." I'd spoken without thinking, but now that I said it I knew it was true. "I don't need another guy to let me down." I was done handing my heart to people who used it as a doormat as they walked out of my life.

"Oh, Vee." Kenna said as she turned the wick down, extinguishing the lamp. "Sweetie, your dad was a loser. You're better off without him in your life. And Eric, well, he was just a Neanderthal. He'll most likely end up impregnating Steph and having half a dozen blond babies before he's twenty-five."

"Yeah, I know." I turned my face to the moonlit window. The mountains of Doon loomed in the distance like giant sentinels. "I just wish there was some way I could erase the memories of Jamie from my head … forget the way he made me feel before we came here."

"How did he make you feel?" Kenna whispered into the dark.

Like he cared enough to pursue me, like I was more important than his own plans and desires. Like I wasn't alone. But I said, "Wanted."

Snuggling into the plush down comforter, I squeezed my eyes closed and attempted to count sheep.

"He doesn't hate you, by the way," Kenna said almost clairvoyantly. When I didn't respond, she continued. "Jamie, I mean. One of the first things we learned in acting class is that there's a very fine line between love and hate. It's obvious to anyone who's been around the two of you that Jamie MacCrae *does not* hate you."

I didn't answer. Instead I rolled away, unwilling to talk about it anymore — afraid to hope she could be right and even more afraid she was wrong.

CHAPTER 15

Veronica

At the tiny table in our sitting room, I speared my last bite of pancake. The fluffy morsel oozed with sweet blueberries and dripped with fresh-churned butter. I'd never tasted anything so heavenly in all my eighteen years. Dredging the cakes through a puddle of warm maple syrup, I popped the bite in my mouth and closed my eyes in bliss. "Mmm ..." Sorry, Aunt Jemima, but there is no substitute for just-tapped syrup.

"Geez, is that your sixth or seventh pancake?"

I opened my eyes to find Kenna scrutinizing me like I was some kind of science experiment. "I lost count at five."

"I'd give my left boob for your metabolism."

"Yeah? Well, I'd give my right butt cheek for one of your knockers."

She barked out a laugh and spewed a mouthful of tea back into her cup. "I'm thinking we'd both look pretty funny after that exchange."

With a giggle, I leaned back and patted my full stomach, surprised to find it still flat. "I think I need a nap."

After recovering her ability to breathe, Kenna poured me another cup of coffee. "Drink up, Buttercup. I can't stay locked in this tower all day."

My gaze wandered to the breathtaking view of rolling moors and stately mountains; all of Doon spread out before us just waiting to be explored. After a solid five hours of sleep and a belly full of the best pancakes in the universe, I felt my optimism returning.

Jamie'd used his body to protect me, taking a major-league smack to the head that'd been meant for me. Which, I had to admit, was pretty darn heroic. Regardless of the reasons he'd lashed out afterward, he'd saved my life without concern for his own, which meant that on some level he cared.

The possibility made me sit straight in my chair. I took a gulp of coffee and shook off my food coma. "You're so right. What should we do today?"

A light tap sounded on the door, announcing Fiona before she swept into the room. "Good morn', m' ladies."

"Morning, Fiona."

"Hey, girl," Kenna replied, our greetings overlapping.

"Prince Jamie and Prince Duncan send their regrets tha' they canna accompany you today, as they've urgent business to attend."

A wave of disappointment rolled through me as she added, "However, they ask that ye stay inside the protective walls o' the castle. For yer own safety, o' course." No surprise that the girl knew about the attack; it seemed nothing happened in this mystic microcosm without her knowledge.

"And ..." A brilliant smile lit Fiona's whole face, causing her hazel eyes to shimmer. "The MacCrae asked me ta give you this, Veronica."

She removed a small giftwrapped package from her pocket.

My hand froze in midair, and then dropped, my coffee mug hitting the table with a thump. *The MacCrae, as in Jamie?*

Fiona brought the package over to our table and set it in front of me with great care. I stared at the small box wrapped in heavy cream-colored parchment. There was a folded piece of paper tucked beneath a golden raffia bow.

"Well, are you going to open it or should I?" Kenna reached across the table, but I snatched the package away from her grasp. I longed to take it into the bedroom where I could open it in peace without the heavy expectation radiating from Kenna and Fiona. But if I knew my best friend, she would only follow me.

Unhurriedly, I slid the note from under the tie and opened it. I scanned the strong, bold strokes of Jamie's handwriting as I propped my trembling hands on the edge of the table and read the note aloud.

Dear Miss Welling,

I must apologize for my abruptness last evening. My brother assured me that you were unharmed during the attack, for which I am grateful.

I saw you admiring this trinket in the village yesterday and felt it an appropriate moment to give it to you. Please accept my apology and this gift as a token of my eternal esteem. I hope that you will cherish this small piece of Doon, always.

Jamie MacCrae

Eternal esteem? What the heck did that mean? *I hope that you will cherish this small piece of Doon, always.* What the . . . ? I read the note again in silence.

"Well, tha' was verra nice," Fiona said cheerfully. "So thoughtful of the MacCrae."

"Nice?" I glanced up, but her encouraging smile didn't reach her eyes. I read the note again. It was like he was patting me on the head and sending me on my way. *Sorry ye couldna be with me Verranica, but here's a little somethin' to remember me by.* The medieval version of a text breakup!

Not that we were ever really together. I slumped in my chair and threw the note on the table. Kenna placed her hand over mine and squeezed supportively. "Vee, sweetie. Aren't you going to open the gift?"

My mouth pulled down in a pout, and I shrugged. "You can if you want." Not caring what consolation prize was inside the box, I stared out the window as sounds of ripping paper filled the room.

"Oh . . . wow."

Kenna's reverent observation prompted me to look in her direction. My heart did a tiny *jeté* as I stared at the detailed miniature of the Castle MacCrae I'd fallen in love with at the marketplace. How did he know? Then a startling realization hit me. He'd been there — maybe the entire time — watching me.

I met Kenna's smirk as she handed me the perfect little statue. "I think Kilt Boy likes you."

Holding the castle in my hand, I couldn't deny the thoughtfulness of the gift, but that cryptic note was another story. "I'm not so sure."

Kenna's scrutiny narrowed in on my face, and in BFF solidarity she changed the subject. "So if we're on house arrest, what is there to do in this pile of bricks?"

Mentally cringing at her choice of words, I tried for a little counterbalance. "Since you're stuck with us, what would you like to do today, Fiona?"

"I typically help make baskets fer the community on morns like this. Would ye care to lend a hand?"

"Definitely. If you think we'll be welcome." As supposed witches, I knew we couldn't take anything for granted, including our acceptance by those inside the castle.

"Extra hands are always welcome." Fiona fluffed her strawberry-blonde hair and smoothed her skirt. "Let's go see Mags."

🌀 🌀 🌀

A half hour later, we were in the castle kitchens, being inspected by a thin, elderly woman wearing a pristine chef's hat and apron. She possessed the slightest trace of a French accent.

"I am Margaret Benoir, though you may call me Mags. In case you wonder — newcomers often do — I am originally from Geneva, but I came to Doon during the last Centennial by way of the Paris Culinary Academy."

I couldn't help but blurt, "Are you the one who made our pancakes? It was the most amazing breakfast ... ever!"

The chef gave me a small grin. "Thank you. I will be sure to make them for you again."

We then followed Mags through the bustling kitchen and into a cavernous room where several dozen women of all ages and a handful of men were busy at work. As we entered, activity ceased and smiles melted from what had been carefree faces.

I heard *Roddie MacPhee* and *Millicent Ennis* move through the room in a swirl of whispers, and several of the workers crossed themselves superstitiously.

Mags cleared her throat and overlooked the less than welcoming reaction. "This is the Great Hall. It is also where volunteers assemble weekly provisions for the sick and elderly, or anyone else who has need. We can always use extra hands."

As Mags escorted us across the room, I wondered what the

infirmed would say about our hands. Would they care that their basket had been assembled by girls allegedly in league with the Witch o' Doon? Right on cue, the girl who could read my mind leaned in so that no one would overhear. "Maybe we should curse their cucumbers."

"Be serious, Ken." I gently touched her shoulder, just below the deep purple reminder of what some Doonians were capable of.

"These are Mackenna and Veronica — and they have come to help." Although Mags addressed the table where we'd stopped, she clearly spoke for the benefit of everyone present. She turned to us once more and tilted her head in approval. "On behalf of the castle, I thank you for your service."

As Mags retreated, a few of the more petrified volunteers slipped away as well. But for every worker that left, two more nodded their approval to remind me that, although the kingdom was divided, our accusers were the minority.

Fiona picked up Mags' role as our tour guide/goodwill ambassador. She paused to return the wave of a grinning red-cheeked blonde. "That's Mario's wife, Sharron, and next ta her are their daughters, Sofia and Gabriella. I expect they're most anxious ta meet you."

Then, like an anxious hostess, Fiona rushed us over and introduced the family. Sharron, with her fair skin, golden hair, and emerald eyes, epitomized Scottish beauty. And Gabriella was a breathtaking sixteen-year-old miniature of her mother. But Sofia captured my attention. She had a riotous mass of black curls and huge ebony eyes, which peered at us curiously through long, silky lashes. She was so tiny that I nearly mistook her for a child, but on closer examination I realized she was my age — which in Doon years was probably somewhere closer to sixty.

As we settled across from Mario's family, the younger girl, Gabriella — who insisted we call her Gabby — pointed first to Kenna and then me, excitedly. "You must be Mackenna and Veronica. My *papà* told me all about you."

Italian pronunciation interspersed her lovely Scottish accent to give her speech an exotic quality. "How nice of you to help assemble baskets for those too infirmed to join us tonight."

Kenna's eyebrows lifted toward her hairline as she reached for a basket. "What's tonight?"

"Tonight is the weekly feast," Sharron answered. "The evening before the Sabbath, we gather as a kingdom ta celebrate our blessings. 'Tis a great pleasure ta make yer acquaintance, by the way."

"There's dancing." Gabby's eyes sparkled with the look of one whose dance card was always full.

"And you girls will be most welcome to join us," Sharron said with a warm smile.

Focusing on the basket in front of me, I managed a casual shrug. "Maybe we should skip it this time."

"Nonsense." Fiona's firm voice told me the matter had already been decided. "Do not bend ta the will o' fear and ignorance. Are ye really going to let a couple o' small-minded bullies keep ye from joining us?"

Kenna's eyes met mine, letting me know this was my call to make. Fiona had a good point. I would never prove we weren't in league with the witch by hiding in my room. "No. We're not."

Gabby clapped her hands in delight. "Excellent! You'll have a wonderful time, I know. The festivities after the meal are the best part." She nudged her sister. "I predict that Prince Jamie will ask Sofie for the first dance." At the mention of Jamie's name, I fumbled a jar of pickled vegetables, and tried to ignore the fact my stomach had plummeted with it.

Mrs. Rosetti's proud eyes shone with enthusiasm as she explained, "Jamie's been paying particular attention ta our wee Sofia."

Sofia blushed a deep red and lowered her inky lashes until her expression became unreadable. "None of that matters, Mamma, if someone — He's received *a Calling*."

"A *Calling*?" Gabby gasped. Her eyes darted across my face to focus on Kenna. "Oh. Have either of you had a Calling then?"

From the conversation at the tavern, I knew I'd probably experienced a Calling, but I wasn't about to fess up to my crazy visitations. Instead, I blinked and feigned incomprehension. "Uh — I'm not sure what you're talking about."

Gabby might have inherited her mother's coloring, but she'd inherited her father's mannerisms. Her hands started to flail as she explained with great enthusiasm how hearts called across the Brig o' Doon. "*The Calling of true love.* The heart calls to its soul mate, who answers back. The lovers actually inhabit one another's dream space, or in rare cases share a waking vision." My ears pricked. "It's usually strongest in the weeks leading up to the Centennial, when the Brig o' Doon opens and the lovers can be united. My parents dreamt of one another in this way. It was the dreams that brought my *papà* to the bridge."

I gripped a loaf of bread so hard my fingers poked holes in its crust. Both Gracie and Cameron, and now Gabby's parents, had dreamed of each other. But what if the Calling was one sided? Did seeing Jamie in my world — without his apparent knowledge — constitute half a Calling? A predestined condemnation to live a life of unrequited love?

Gabby's inquisitive eyes shifted between us. "Is a Calling what brought you ta Doon?"

"Nope." Kenna shook her head and put extra enthusiasm into packing her basket with fresh fruit.

I, on the other hand, panicked. If I told a boldface lie, would they be able to tell? And if I didn't say something quick, would the hesitation give me away? Kenna gave me a small kick. "Ow! I mean — No! No dreams or anything. Kenna inherited the rings from her aunt. I'm just along for the ride."

Gabby deflated and reached for an orange, but her mother's attention only became more focused on me. "No one comes ta Doon unless it is the kingdom's will. I wouldna dismiss yourself so easily, dear."

It wasn't that I'd dismissed myself, but it was hard to believe in your destiny when the boy you thought was in it was intent on dismissing you. I shot Kenna a mental SOS.

She nodded slightly and shifted into Kindly Kenna mode. "Sofia, did you say something about dancing?"

Sofia shook her head. "Yes, there will be some dancing, but with Laird MacCrae being so ill . . . he will not be able to attend as usual." She trailed off uncomfortably.

Sharron paused in her work to regard us gravely. "He's taken a turn for the worse. Doc Benoir does no' think he will last 'til the Centennial."

Before we could lapse into another silence, Gabby spoke in a lowered voice for our benefit. "If Laird MacCrae passes before the Centennial, his successor must be crowned before the Brig o' Doon opens."

"So Jamie could be king by next week?" The revelation was shocking. I swallowed my reaction, burying it deep down until I could get away.

"Aye." Gabby leaned in like a conspirator. "And my sister, Sofie, could be our new queen."

CHAPTER 16

Veronica

I sat staring at my own empty eyes while Kenna played Extreme Storybook Princess Makeover and curled my hair into dark ringlets with a twisted length of metal she'd heated over the fire — her make-do version of a curling iron. As she chatted about our "costumes" — the flowy calf-length skirts and embroidered peasant blouses Fiona'd brought for us to wear — all I could think about was what we'd learned from the Rosettis: Jamie was practically engaged.

We'd gotten a quick lesson on Doon's customs by the time we finished our care packages. When the Brig o' Doon opened for the Centennial, the king had to welcome all who'd been led to his kingdom. If the auld laird died, then Jamie would assume the throne. However, before he could be crowned he had to do this thing called *the Completing*.

In Doon-speak, he had to choose a fiancée in order to be king. Sharron had said something about the tradition being born from a need for balance and equality, but to me the reasons didn't justify the end result — Jamie choosing a bride in less than two weeks.

As we made our way down to the feast, I dropped back, only half-listening to Kenna and Fiona's plan to go shopping the following day. My head spun with dark emotions and I trailed farther and farther behind. Outside the wide double-doors, I stopped, poised to run back to the safety of the turret suite.

Lively music poured from the Great Hall, punctuated by the stomping of feet and the occasional hoot and holler. But for once in my life, I didn't feel like dancing.

Kenna got halfway into the room before realizing I wasn't beside her. She turned and pursued me as I backed away from the open door. "I don't think I can do this." I spun on my heel, but before I could take a step Ken looped her arm through mine and pulled me back toward the party.

"Relax, scaredy-cat." We moved through an arched doorway and into the assembly hall at a leisurely pace, though my heart was sprinting at full speed. "Vee, do you remember our first junior high dance?"

I nodded. "I was afraid no one would dance with me."

"And ..."

"And I ended up meeting my first boyfriend."

"And ..." She made a rolling gesture with her hand.

"And what? He forced his tongue into my mouth, which I accidentally bit because I didn't know what he was doing, and then he dumped me the following week."

Impatiently, Kenna finished the story. "And yet you've been popular ever since."

I shrugged. Popular and alone. Since that seventh-grade dance, every one of my relationships had been short-lived and lopsided — either the boy wanting more than I could give or being totally indifferent to my aching heart. Like Jamie.

Kenna squeezed my upper arm and sighed. "I know things aren't working out like you thought, but this is still the chance of a lifetime. Doon's a freakin' medieval kingdom — and we're stuck here for two weeks. We wanted an epic summer, and it doesn't get any more epic than this."

Before she could say anything else, Duncan came barreling across the room and skidded to a stop in front of my friend.

"You're a right vision, Mackenna Reid. Care to dance?"

"To this?" Kenna gestured to the revolving mass of people on the dance floor. Her eyebrows pinched together above her wrinkled nose to silently declare *Think again.*

At first glance, it was chaos; people spinning and stomping, couples twirling through the crowd in a vigorous two-step to the raucous tones of a fiddle. Then the sparkling notes of a flute joined in, cranking the tune up even more, and I could see the order in the chaos — the sublime composition in the movement. The beat of drums layered into the song, and my body began to move in time.

I gave Kenna an encouraging smile, which she answered with a head jiggle before answering the hot boy anxiously waiting before her. "Thanks, but I have two left feet."

Duncan looked vaguely appalled. "Ye have what?"

I chuckled while Kenna explained. "It's an expression. It means I can't dance."

I leaned in toward my friend, infusing fake innocence into my tone. "But you were in all those musicals, Kenna. The video clips you posted online had very complicated dance steps."

She rolled her eyes in my direction. "Just because you waltzed your way out of the womb doesn't mean the rest of the world did. Have you ever heard of choreography? I had to learn each step and practice it over and over. Even then, I still managed to mess up something at every performance."

Duncan raised his eyebrows in curiosity. "Performance?"

"Kenna's a stage actress."

"But Vee's a *dancer.*" As Kenna shifted the conversation away from herself, I felt as if we were caught in a game of verbal table tennis.

Duncan smiled politely at me. "Then perhaps you should join in the dancing, Veronica."

"So you're not dancing, Ken?"

"No!"

Thinking my BFF protested too much, I flashed Duncan my most irresistible grin. "How about you, handsome?"

"Not for the present. No." Immune to my charms, Duncan cast Kenna a sidelong glance while she raptly concentrated on appearing unaffected. His face was a mask of sincerity, but I sensed the mocking in what he left unsaid. "Perhaps I shall be more inclined later."

"Sure." I smirked at my best friend, enjoying the confusion that played across her face.

She rolled her eyes and then looked me up and down. "Go dance, Vee. Before you gyrate out of your stockings."

Ever gallant, Duncan took my arm and propelled me to the edge of the dance floor. "Feel free to join in. We have many fine dancers in Doon. Even my brother is most accomplished in this area."

"Really?" I paused to watch Jamie in the middle of an animated group of young women, including the lovely Sofia.

Suddenly the music was replaced by the pulse beating a tattoo in my ears, and my whole body stiffened. I couldn't do it. Couldn't go out there and lose myself in the music, like I longed to do. What if *he* didn't want me there?

Then Jamie vanished in the revolving mass of bodies, and I forced myself to relax. Did I want to spend the rest of my time in Doon as a spectator? I'd spent too many years locked inside myself, catering to others. It was time to live. With a deep breath, I swallowed my insecurities and let the music flow back into my veins. Ken was right; this was *my* epic summer, and if I wanted to dance, I wouldn't let *anyone* stop me. "If you will excuse me, Duncan, the music calls and I must obey."

With a lithe skip, I wove my way into the crowd. The music swirled around me as I high-stepped into melee, my feet flying into the tempo with a life of their own. My sadness and doubts melted away as I lifted my arms in abandon, clapping to the beat, time disappearing. I spun and shimmied with the escalating rhythm, the faces around me blurring into a kaleidoscope.

When the music slowed, I swiveled and almost collided with a handsome red-haired boy with sparkling green eyes. He extended his hand toward me and bowed with a wide grin. Accepting the unspoken invitation, I placed my hand in his. But as I stepped toward him, another hand clasped the boy's forearm. My gaze traveled from the sun-darkened fingers to a sapphire sleeve, across a black leather vest, and up to a familiar face.

Jamie.

He nodded once to the red-haired boy, who dropped my hand like it was covered in warts.

Jamie stepped in front of me. "May I have this dance?"

Not waiting for my response, he took my hand and pulled. I crashed against his hard chest, and blinked up at him. When he began to move, my body fell effortlessly into step with his. I'd imagined dancing in his arms multiple times — the reality was better than I'd imagined.

"I shall take that as a yes." He raised a tawny eyebrow, his mouth quirking to the side as if to say, "Was there ever any doubt?"

Seriously? His cocky expression was the reality check I needed. He was not the boy I thought he was — or hoped he'd be. Stepping back out of his arms, I lifted my chin and looked him in the eyes. "I'm sorry, but I'm not inclined to accept your invitation."

As I turned away, he grabbed my arm and spun me back into his arms. All traces of amusement were gone, and the intensity radiating from his face stole the air from my lungs as he growled, "No' so fast, lass."

Decisively, he took my right hand in his large fingers, the heat of his palm pressed firmly against my lower back, guiding me, once again, into the dance. As we began to move, I was conscious of every muscle, every movement of his body against mine. He leaned close, his warm breath stirring the tiny hairs by my ear, sending a jolt down my spine. "If you're no' inclined to accept my invitation, then I'll rescind it and make it a command, since you clearly dinna understand what you are refusing."

His words splashed over me like ice water, cooling my overzealous hormones. I'd had just about enough of his arrogant attitude — prince or no. Leaning back in his viselike arms, I watched a muscle in his jaw clench. Well, he wasn't the only one who could get angry. Heat ran up my neck, flooding my cheeks. How dare he treat me like some scantily clad wench from a romance novel!

"Oh, I think I know exactly what I'm turning down," I bit out.

As we turned in a waltz-like series of steps, I picked up my foot and slammed my heel down on top of his boot. He stumbled but recovered quickly. I had to admit I was impressed. Duncan was right; his brother was a strong dancer.

Jamie's eyes widened in surprise. "You did that on purpose!" He looked so dumbfounded — and so darned condescending — I couldn't help sticking my tongue out at him in childish defiance.

To my great satisfaction, he stumbled again. Not wanting to go down with my partner, I grabbed onto his upper arms and gasped. The power I'd seen him wield in the tournament couldn't compare to holding that strength beneath my hands. Giddy tingles pulled at my belly. In a desperate attempt to keep myself from turning into a spineless puddle of goo, I started talking.

"My good prince, what makes you think I'd ever bait you on purpose? I have the highest respect for you and your position, after all." I batted my eyelashes up at him, smiling innocently. With a flash of white teeth, a long dimple appeared in his cheek. Momentarily staggered by the force of his blinding smile, it was my turn to stumble.

"You be a fair dancer, Verranica, but I might recommend a lesson or two to help with your ungainliness."

It was a good comeback. I tried to stop the giggle rising up in my chest, but it was no use. Spinning and whirling, our bodies moving as one to the music, I felt lighter than air, and my laughter bubbled out.

Distracted by my own glee, I didn't at first notice Jamie's laugh — a deep infectious sound that lit up my heart. We smiled into each other's eyes, and for a moment the room and everyone in it fell away.

Realizing that we'd stopped moving, the smile slipped from my face. The song ended but I remained sheltered in his arms. Hyperaware of the proximity of his body to mine, I became shivery and hot all at once. The heart-stoppingly beautiful boy from my visions had returned and as he searched my face, it felt as if we were having a conversation without uttering a single word. Feeling sure he could hear my heart as it hammered away in my chest, I took a steadying breath and caught my lower lip between my teeth. Slowly his gaze moved to my mouth. As he tilted his head, I leaned into the heat of his body, releasing my lip.

In the space of a heartbeat, Jamie's eyes narrowed and he shook his head. He released me, stepping fluidly back into an elegant bow. When his eyes met mine again, they'd regained their aloof derision. "Thank you for the dance, m' lady."

I lowered into a brief curtsy as he turned away and walked back into the crowd. Immediately, he focused his blinding smile on Sofia Rosetti. Any hopes I had disappeared as I watched him escort her onto the floor.

Mentally kicking myself for thinking I could have been anything other than one of the masses to such an egotistical jerk, I inched my way into the crowd. From in between bodies, I watched my BFF in the arms of Jamie's younger brother. Smiling and talking animatedly, Kenna seemed unaware that, despite her "two left feet," she was dancing in perfect step with her partner. I wondered if Kenna would ever acknowledge Duncan was falling in love with her, or admit she had feelings in return. For anyone with eyes, it was more than obvious, but Kenna would most likely ignore the issue until it was forced upon her. Which, by the adoring look on Duncan's face, might prove to be sooner rather than later.

A slow, soft song began, and Jamie continued to dance with Sofia. An infinite ache filled my chest as I noticed the tender way they looked at one another; the soft smiles, her huge eyes filled with open admiration. Soon the crowd fell back to form a ring around the perfectly matched couple.

As the dance ended, Kenna and Duncan made their way toward me. The sympathetic expression on my friend's face was more than I could bear, and I spun away. She meant well, but any kindness would send me straight over the edge.

I picked my way through the endless crowd, intent on reaching fresh air. Once outside I found a spot along the battlement wall and gripped the cool stone, trying to calm my ragged breathing. Several feet away, a couple deep in conversation stopped to stare at me. It wasn't long before the man grabbed the woman's arm and they scurried away, casting nervous glances over their shoulders. Apparently being considered a sorceress's minion had its advantages, because now I was blessedly alone.

Tears burned my throat, but I refused to allow them to escape my eyes. I swallowed hard and concentrated instead on the beauty of the moon reflecting on the clear surface of the lake, as well as the geese swimming lazily in and out of the incandescent-streaked water. A breeze began to cool my blazing skin, and I felt my raging emotions ebb away.

Jamie's hot and cold act was draining. Every time he started to warm, to let me in the tiniest bit, he'd turn around and shut me out even harder. And why? What had I done? Except be nice to him and adore his kingdom. Even if he didn't return my feelings — which I couldn't determine one way or another — it didn't explain why he treated me like I had a communicable disease.

Because he's in love with someone else.

The thought dropped into my mind like a hand grenade without the pin, the reverberations shaking me straight to my toes.

Jamie's in love with Sofia and thinks I'm some deranged witch's minion bent on destroying his kingdom.

I lowered my face into my hands. So why was it when I looked at him, my heart said *Mine?*

"Vee? Sweetie, are you okay?"

I straightened at the sound of Kenna's voice and wiped the wetness from my cheeks with my palms. "I'm fine." I tried to smile, but the effort came out as a sob. She wrapped me in a hug, and I buried my face against her shoulder.

"I can see that you're fine. Just tell me who I need to kill." Kenna patted my back with enough force to pull me out of my self-centered musings. "I could put some serious hurt on Prince Not-So-Charming if I need to."

In danger of being crushed, I extricated myself from her not-so-comforting embrace. Smiling for real this time, I shook my head at her, my voice not steady enough yet to explain.

"It's not a big deal. Jamie can't help it if I got the wrong idea simply because he showed up in my life." I shrugged, turning back to look at the lake.

"The wrong idea? Wasn't he asking you to come to the bridge?"

"Sort of ..."

"Well, he obviously wanted you to come here. Why else would he have done the whole, 'Come ta me, Verranica' bit?" Kenna's imitation of Jamie's accent was so dead-on that I chuckled.

"Maybe he didn't know he was doing it. Haven't you ever had a dream that when you woke up, you had no idea where it came from?"

"Like the time I dreamt I was in Greg-the-stage-tech's bed, naked?"

"Exactly!" I chuckled and wiped the residual tears from under my eyes.

"But as much as I don't believe in the preordained destiny thing, you have to admit a *Calling* works a little differently than your normal relationship."

"Yeah, if it's mutual, but we have no proof Jamie shared my visions." Kenna opened her mouth to object, but I cut her off. "And even if he did, does that mean he has to pick me just because I somehow pulled him into my head?"

"No. That's as stupid as picking Sofia just because his mommy liked her."

"What did you say?" I spun on my friend, whose eyes had become as big as silver dollars.

"Ah, well it's no biggie." Kenna turned to lean heavily on the stone wall, avoiding my probing gaze.

"Who told you that?"

"Duncan might have mentioned that —" Kenna sighed and then rushed on. "That their mother favored Sofia."

And Jamie loves her. Perfect.

I turned to stare out at the lake, the natural beauty had lost its powers. Sofia being Jamie's sainted mother's favorite was just another confirmation that he and I weren't meant to be together. "What else did Duncan say?"

Before Kenna could answer, Fiona joined us by the battlement wall. "M'ladies, ye are not supposed ta be wandering alone."

"We're perfectly fine ..." Kenna's words dropped off as we turned toward Fiona, who tilted her head to the side, gesturing toward the dark outline of a man concealed in the opposite corner of the stone terrace.

"'Tis Gideon," Fiona stated matter-of-factly.

As the captain of the guard stepped out into the moonlight, I almost didn't recognize him. Dark purple bruises shadowed his sunken eyes. His normally ruddy complexion appeared pale, almost translucent. "Is something wrong with him?"

"I'm beginning to wonder," Fiona replied, her brows gathering in concern.

"Well, Gideon can go take a flying leap off a turret! In fact — " Kenna turned toward the skulking shadow.

"Nay, Mackenna." Fiona's voice was firm as she grabbed Kenna's upper arm to stop her. "'Tis clear he is only watching ye. Dinna provoke him."

Kenna stared angrily at Fiona for a brief moment before her irritation melted from her face and she shrugged. "Sorry, Fiona, I'm just not used to my every move being stalked, and it's putting me on edge."

I knew the feeling. I was beginning to see my time in Doon as one big test of patience. Glancing at the shadowy corner, I could no longer see Gideon but knew in my gut he still lingered.

"Gideon has a lot on his mind. We've just received reports that black petunias have sprouted around the witches' cottage." Fiona wrung her fingers, her eyes darting around the open area of the battlements furtively. The contrast between her current demeanor and her usual ultra-calm manner was a bit disconcerting.

"Didn't Duncan say nothing has grown there since the witches were destroyed?" I asked.

"Aye. But the black flowers are spreading in waves as if — " She trailed off, swallowing the rest of her words.

"As if what?" Kenna prompted.

"Nothin' you need to worry about." A too-bright smile chased away the trepidation on Fiona's face. "I've had the kitchen prepare a tray of hot cocoa and cookies ta be sent to yer rooms. Would ye fancy some girl time?"

I hesitated, debating whether or not to pursue the questions spinning in my head. *Black* flowers growing where nothing has grown for hundreds of years? *As if . . .* As if the witches were back. As if the witches were us. No wonder Jamie treated me with suspicion; on the surface I looked guilty as sin. I would have to find a way to prove my innocence, starting tomorrow. Tonight I needed to take a break from the drama that was or wasn't going on between me and the future ruler of Doon.

Linking arms with my new friend, I said, "Girl time sounds like heaven to me." Kenna took Fiona's other arm and we moved toward a doorway to the side of the Great Hall. I had no interest in returning to the festivities to watch Jamie romance half the kingdom, especially not a certain petite Italian.

chapter 17

Veronica

The girl time and hot chocolate didn't relax me as I'd hoped. Quietly, I slipped from the oversized bed I shared with Kenna and grabbed the enormous green robe she'd left on the chair. Duncan's suite sometimes made me feel like I was a dwarf co-existing with giants.

Moving into the sitting room, I slipped my arms into the robe and rolled the sleeves up several times. A profound quiet filled the air as I stared into the glowing embers of the banked fire. The peaceful hush was in such discordance with my restless spirit, it filled me with the insane urge to run screaming through the castle. Well, maybe not the crazy-screaming part. But with nothing to wear besides heavy skirts or a nightdress, I couldn't even go for a run to calm my nerves.

Hoping a bit of reading would do the trick, I found the leather-bound book Fiona had brought me from the library earlier that day; *Doon: An Esteemed Legacy*. I ran my fingers over the embossed letters. The MacCrae family crest — two lions back to back, one with an arrow clamped in its teeth, the other holding a sword — filled the center of the cover, and written below in looping script: *In Unity There Is Great Power.* Hefting the Bible-sized tome to the window seat, I cracked it open and scanned the table of contents by moonlight.

The Miracle
The Centennial
The Gathering
A Calling
Ancient Symbols

A Calling. Perfect!

Maybe I could find some clue as to why the visions that'd rocked my entire world had no effect on the one I shared the visions with. Finding the correct page, I leaned forward and drank in every word.

> A Calling is a sacred bond that draws an individual to Doon through dreams or waking visions. The Calling may be between two hearts or one individual who is called to Doon for a preordained purpose. The visions act as a beacon, guiding the called individual to the kingdom of Doon, typically at the time of the Centennial.
>
> It is believed the Calling was established by our divine Protector to sustain our culture.

Skimming over the information about those being called to Doon for a vocational purpose, I ran my finger quickly down the paragraphs to a passage that appeared to jump off the page:

> When the Calling is between two individuals, the outsider must choose Doon over their own world in order to complete the union. When this choice is made, the two souls become inextricably intertwined until death.

If I chose to stay in Doon, would Jamie no longer have a choice? His feelings for Sofia would . . . what? Simply disappear? Taking a deep breath, I continued to read:

> However, as with soul mates in the mortal world, individuals can forsake their Calling. The Calling relationship does not supersede free will.

I slammed the book closed, pushed the giant tome away, and shot to my feet. I couldn't breathe. The room began to shrink around me.

Rushing to the door, I tugged it open just enough to see that the guard on duty was fast asleep. I slipped into the hallway, and pulled the door closed behind me, tiptoeing down the corridor. The flannel robe dragged on the stones and made a subtle *whooshing* noise I prayed was too soft to detect. After rounding the corner, I leaned against the wall and struggled to control my breathing.

I couldn't think, couldn't still my mind. So I could choose to stay and accept the Calling, but Jamie could still choose Sofia? If so, I'd be stranded in Doon and bound to Jamie for a lifetime; an aging spinster, living for a brief glimpse of his beautiful face as he swept through the village, his lovely queen at his side. Screw that.

Needing to move, but having no plan of where to go next, I hurried along the circular hallway toward an open window. If I couldn't get outside, this would have to do. I stood on my toes and leaned on the thick ledge, pulling in a deep breath of the crisp night air. The full moon illuminated a panorama of pristine mountains and forest. The kingdom's unspoiled beauty quieted my soul. It was truly a marvel.

"I wouldna jump if I were you."

With a squeak, my heart accelerated like a stampede of

wild horses as I spun around to find Jamie leaning on the wall directly behind me. His arms were crossed in front of his broad chest, one knee bent, his booted foot propped on the rough stones behind him. The bored look on his face made it appear as if he'd been standing there for hours.

"I wasn't planning to, Your Highness." Sarcasm seemed to be my best defense. I needed to keep him at a distance until I could work through my jumbled feelings.

Jamie answered with a disdainful smile and pushed himself off the wall. Arms still crossed, he moved to stand in front of me, stopping so close I had to tilt my head back to see his face.

"What are ye doing out of bed?"

"Why are you such a close talker?"

"Pardon?" He narrowed his eyes and took another step forward. "I asked why yer out of bed?"

"I ... ah." My sarcasm shield dissolved on the spot. I gulped down the nervousness his nearness brought out in me and summoned the image of him gliding across the dance floor with Sofia in his arms. I cocked my head to one side and continued in a calm voice, "I couldn't sleep, so I decided to get some air. Is that a crime?"

Turning my back on him, I moved back to lean against the windowsill.

The opening was wide, but when he leaned down next to me, resting his forearms on the ledge, our shoulders touched. His heat reached me through the thick fabric of the robe, causing my nerve endings to tingle, but I couldn't move away. I glanced at his left ear where he'd taken a club to the head for me the day before, but there was no sign of the injury beneath the golden layers of hair. I jerked my gaze away; no way would I ask him about that again.

After several seconds of silence, my attention shifted from

the moon-washed landscape to his large, well-formed hands as he played with a ring on his right index finger. The thick gold band had an intricately carved lion head in the center, its onyx eyes glinting in the moonlight.

As if there'd been no break in the conversation, Jamie said, "Of course being out of bed is no' a crime. As long as you dinna leave the tower."

I opened my mouth to tell him exactly what he could do with his tower when he said, "Why can't ye sleep?" His voice sounded strained, as if it took a herculean effort for him to form a polite question.

Choosing to accept his peace offering, I answered truthfully, "I feel antsy." Out of the corner of my eye, I saw his head angle in my direction.

"What do ye mean by antsy?"

I glanced at Jamie, and turned back to the view so I could think rationally. "You know, restless. I'm used to physical activity, which I haven't gotten much of since we've been here."

"Aye. That I can understand." I got the feeling he could relate to more than just the physical nature of my restlessness. "We've been cooped up in meetings to plan the Gathering and the Centennial for weeks." He cleared his throat. "Speaking of the Gathering — the committee was wondering if you or your friend have anythin' that would be of benefit to examine. Such as inventions, devices, or footwear."

"They want to see my shoes?" I stared at his profile, the strong nose and the high slope of his cheekbone shaded by dark gold stubble.

"You can tell a lot about a civilization by the construction of their garments." He turned and met my stare, coffee-colored eyes raking over my face. "But anything ye brought with you from the mortal world would be helpful."

"Okay ... I did bring a cell phone, and —" I choked on my next words, my stomach jumping into my throat. I'd been about to tell him about Gracie's journal, but something — some instinctive warning — stopped me.

"Are you all right?"

Gasping for breath, I muttered, "Yes" and looked away from his searching eyes. I'd finished reading the journal, so what was my deal? I had no good reason for keeping it a secret. All I knew was I needed to keep it to myself for the time being.

"What is a cell phone?"

Grateful for the change of subject, I said, "Oh, it's a tiny communication device. But the battery —" His brows drew together over his nose. "I mean, the energy source died, so it doesn't work."

"I would love to take a look at this cell phone. It seems we will learn much through this Gathering."

We both turned back to the view, a sudden silence stretched between us and I became very aware of his large body so close to mine.

Abruptly, Jamie stood up, and I turned to see him drag his fingers through his gold hair. As he lowered his hand, his bangs fell over his forehead, softening the strong angles of his face. In that moment he looked exactly like the boy I'd first seen in the parking lot.

"Why are ye smiling, lass?" I hadn't realized my lips were curved until he spoke. Jamie smiled back, looking sheepish.

"Ah ... nothing." The smile dropped from my face. I wasn't ready to have that conversation yet.

His eyes narrowed, and a muscle began to flex in his jaw. Clearly, something was on his mind, but I was oddly content to drink in the sight of him as he worked it out. What was it about this boy that I couldn't resist? It was more than his appearance.

The pull felt natural, like gravity or thirst — an inevitable force drawing me toward him. A force I needed to find the strength to fight ... or did I?

"Shall we plan to get some exercise on the morrow?" Jamie asked, his dark eyes lighting up with boyish excitement. "We could take a hike to Muir Lea and then have a bit of archery practice?"

Finding my knees unexpectedly weak, I was grateful for the steady wall behind my back. Was Jamie MacCrae asking me on a date? Should I say no? Ask him what Sofia would think? Or maybe I needed to see this thing through, get to know him as a person, find out if he'd been envisioning me too. How could it hurt to spend a single afternoon with him?

Pushing off the wall, the question that popped out of my mouth surprised even me. "I thought you believed me to be in league with the witch."

He arched a brow and considered for a moment before answering. "That remains to be seen."

"But aren't you afraid to be alone with me?" My pulse accelerated as he moved closer again, his eyes traveling from my bare toes up my body and finally resting on my face.

His lips slid into a slow grin. "Not in the way ye might think."

Unwilling to analyze what he meant by that, I focused on answering his original question. "Okay, I'll go. Sounds like fun." I shrugged, trying to appear calm even though my pulse accelered with every heartbeat.

"Excellent." He took a step closer, his eyes never leaving mine. I crossed my arms in front of my chest. Feeling the voluminous folds of fabric under my arms reminded me that I must look like a drowning rat in the huge robe. Jamie stopped so close I could smell the warm sweetness of his breath. "After chapel, then?"

I nodded, my eyes wandering to the adorable dimple in the center of his scruffy chin.

"Verranica?" I jerked slightly, wondering how the sound of my name on his lips could rock me every single time. Raising my eyes to his, the intensity of his stare took me by surprise. "Is that my brother's robe yer wearing?"

"Uh-huh," I answered distractedly as he reached out and tucked a strand of hair behind my ear. The gentle touch of his fingers sent a wave of something like magma all the way to my core. Quickly, he jerked his hand away from my face and clenched his fingers into a tight fist. A vein pulsed in his throat, but his expression had gone stony again.

"See that Fiona gets you your own." And with that parting order, he was gone.

Even as the echo of his footsteps faded, I questioned the sanity of agreeing to go anywhere with this boy. His presence lingered in my blood like a drug, making my head spin. What would a whole afternoon spent with him do to me? I took a deep, steadying breath. Regardless, I had to find out if he was the reason I was here. And more importantly, if he wanted me to stay.

CHAPTER 18

Mackenna

More provincial costumes, more petrified villagers on the verge of a hate crime, and more of creepy, bulge-eyed Gideon. *Ugh.* Top that off with religious conformity and the Centennial could not arrive soon enough.

I stood outside the old stone church, *Ye Auld Kirk o' Doon*, determined not to let my intimidation get the best of me. My folks had never been churchgoers, so the whole worship concept — from the unnatural dressy clothes to the organized rites that everyone seemed to perform by osmosis — felt foreign and forced. Like doing a mash-up of *Spring Awakening* and *Spam-a-lot*.

I'd wanted to ditch, but Fiona had insisted it would appear worse if Vee and I didn't attend. So I'd let her dress me in yet another Girl-Scout-meets-pirate-wench ensemble: a calf-length skirt — dove gray — and a white cap-sleeved top that laced at the neckline. Vee, my mirror twin, wore a matching top and a pale turquoise skirt. We both sported plaid sashes bearing the

Doon colors, but I drew the line at the matching hats. I would never be that desperate to blend in.

Fiona sensed my unease and placed a reassuring hand on my shoulder. "Be at peace, Mackenna. This house is come as ye are."

"Yeah, don't sweat it, Ken." Vee meant to be helpful, so I resisted the urge to reach over and flick the royal blue pom-pom on the top of her head. Of course, she looked fabulous in her tam — all native and confident. I, on the other hand, felt conspicuously out of place ... and time, for that matter.

Rather than voice my feelings, I managed a somewhat sincere smile. "Let's do this, then."

As we entered the ancient structure of hewn rock and stained glass, I couldn't help but search for Duncan's gorgeous face. His velvet-brown eyes fastened on mine and his mouth widened into a lopsided grin. Across the distance, he sent a message meant only for me, a wink of reassurance even more intimate than our dancing the previous evening. My cheeks began to burn with the curse of the ginger and I dropped my head, annoyed that the charming ogre could make me blush with the merest facial tick. To my immense relief, rather than join him we took seats about halfway back.

From directly behind the princes, Gabby waved and flashed an impatient smile. I had no doubt she was anticipating a dance-by-dance recap of the previous evening. The kid meant well, but I wanted to spare Vee the agony of reliving the night at all costs.

As the service started, Gabby reluctantly turned around to face front alongside her parents and multitude of siblings, including the breathtaking Sofia. Gabby whispered something in Sofia's ear, which caused her to glance over her shoulder in our direction before giving her full attention to the proceedings. Teeny-weeny Sofia was not smiling.

Commotion up front indicated the start of the service. The minister, an elderly man with thick, gray sideburns, whom we'd already met a handful of times since our arrival, cleared his throat and pronounced, "Let us commence by remembering *the Miracle*." His strong rolling brogue echoed through the space.

"When Wise King Angus Andrew Kellan MacCrae retreated ta the castle chapel ta pray for deliverance for his people, those that weren't in battle wi' the witch and her minions gathered in ye Auld Kirk ta pray for guidance for their king."

The preacher was a natural storyteller. Despite myself, I leaned forward and hung on his every word. "'Twas not jus' the king who won favor that blessed day but *all* the people o' Doon with their selfless petitions. It was the kingdom's unity which invoked *the Miracle*. The people pledged never ta forsake their kingdom. In return, they were granted protection from evil, a bountiful land, and new citizens ta multiply their population. That is the great covenant between the people o' Doon and their Protector.

"Now let us recite the Prayer of Unity in preparation of the Centennial."

A single child, a girl of about nine or ten with pale hair and freckles across the bridge of her upturned nose, stood and began to sing in a high soprano. After the first verse, Jamie MacCrae — of all people — echoed her, his strong tenor pitch perfect. By the chorus, the entire congregation had joined in. Italian, French, and several languages I couldn't readily identify melded together in a melodic petition.

The prayer was so beautiful — even more moving than "You'll Never Walk Alone" from *Carousel* — that I wanted to cry. A sniffle from Vee on my right and the outright sobbing of Fiona on my left reassured me that I was not the only one.

As the service concluded, the congregation began to stir and break the spell. Doonians clumped together peering at us with trepidation; I heard several murmurs about black petunias, and yet again the names Roddie MacPhee and Millie Ennis. Across the sanctuary, Gideon appeared ready to burn us at the stake.

In sudden need of air, I strode toward the door. Before I made it outside, someone grabbed my elbow. My free hand balled into a fist as I swung around and nearly punched Duncan MacCrae in the jaw.

"We're ready to set off for Muir Lea." He slipped his arm through mine, oblivious to the ripple of gossip he created by doing so.

One look at his candid expression confirmed not all Doonians were hypocrites.

◉ ◉ ◉

The road bumped and thumped so that my teeth rattled continuously. As the royal carriage jostled its way up the mountain, I gained new insight into the turnip I'd played in first grade. Vee, of course, had been a cute little strawberry with an adorable lisp while I had the honor of being drab, hugely round produce.

If I ever portrayed a turnip again, I would tap into the impatience to get somewhere — anywhere — where I wasn't constantly knocking knees with the other turnips, the expectant, searching glances of one smokin' hot turnip in particular, and the uncertainty of what was coming next. Yep, in the future I'd make one Oscar-worthy root vegetable.

After an eternity plodding uphill, Fergus halted the carriage. "This is as far as I go," he announced cheerfully.

It appeared to be the end of the path — the cart path, at least. I looked about me in confusion. We'd stopped on the side of a steep mountain at a dead end. Aside from the road, which was just wide enough for the carriage to turn around, the ground sloped sharply in either direction — one way steeply down, the other sharply upward. This was their highnesses' fabulous picnic spot?

"Wow." Unable to keep the sarcasm from my voice, I gestured to our unremarkable surroundings. "This is amazing."

"We're not there yet, woman." Duncan flashed me a conspiratorial smile. "Fiona? Would ye mind staying here and keepin' Fergus company?"

I looked back to see Fergus unhitching the horses. He considered Fiona shyly, already turning a patchwork of pink. Unfazed, Fiona unloaded wicker baskets from the trunk of the carriage. "Aye. I packed an extra basket just in case."

Jamie gave the girl a rare grin, handed a picnic basket to his brother, and took another for himself. "Thanks, to the both of you. We'll be back before sunset." His eyes were full of mischief and adventure as he turned to Vee. "Ready, then?"

My bestie had mentioned bumping into him during the previous night ... and based on the sparks zinging between them, it must've been one heck of a bump. Without so much as a glance my direction, Vee nodded and they were off. Straight up the side of the mountain like poster children for extreme sports.

Skeptically, I examined the path they'd just taken. "Where exactly is this place?"

"Not far." Duncan's boyish, lopsided smile inspired confidence. "Muir Lea's just a wee bit up the hill."

Just a wee bit up the hill turned out to be a grueling hike. A hike that, if I'd known just how arduous, would've tempted me to stay in the carriage. Apparently, we were going to the top of the mountain peak. That, or Duncan was trying to kill me.

About thirty feet from the top I collapsed on a boulder and

chugged from the water pouch Duncan handed me. When I showed no inclination to get back up, Duncan towered over me, his arms crossed over his chest. He tilted his head teasingly. "We're nearly there now. You need me ta carry you the rest of the way?"

The idea of Duncan MacCrae throwing me over his shoulder like a sack of, well, turnips got me on my feet again. I began to climb, stubbornly ignoring his quiet chuckles and the idea that I'd played right into his hands. Whatever this place was, I doubted anything could be worth the hassle.

The top of the rise opened up into a craterlike field, emerald green and lush, dotted with wildflowers and majestic trees. A clear stream bisected the meadow down the middle, and at the far end, just out of sight, I could hear the trickling of a waterfall. The warm air was fragrant and alive with butterflies of every imaginable hue. If Doon was Utopia, Muir Lea was its Eden.

"Wow!" Okay, so maybe it was worth it.

"Did I not tell ye?"

I ignored his "I told you so" and drank in the wild, unexpected beauty of this secret field. A view-inspired soundtrack — mostly *The Sound of Music* — played in my head.

At the far end of the meadow, I spotted Vee and her very nice prince slipping into the woods. Fabulous! Just what I wanted — more hiking. In hopes of convincing Duncan that we'd gone far enough, I turned to catch him staring at the other half of our little group. The wistful, unguarded expression on his face caused my heart to wrench.

When he caught me staring, he flashed me a sheepish grin. "I think my brother likes your friend."

And my friend loved his brother. But that wasn't my secret to tell, so instead I answered with a casual shrug. "Could've fooled me."

"He's just reserved. What lad has confidence enough to go after what he wants without a little encouragement?"

"If you say so."

"What say you to giving them a bit o' alone time?"

I was for anything that didn't involve traipsing through the forest like a Sondheim character. When I agreed, Duncan spread a green and blue plaid quilt in the shade of a giant tree and bade — there was no other word that quite captured the courtliness of his action — me sit. After our grueling hike, I eagerly complied, collapsing next to him on the soft blanket with a sigh of relief.

"Comfy now?" As he set the picnic basket off to one side, his cheeks pulled the corners of his mouth in a lopsided tug-of-war.

"I guess." I ignored his self-satisfied smirk and straightened my skirt. "I'd feel better if I were wearing pants."

Duncan reacted to my words as if he'd swallowed a nest of bees. "You're — not — wearin' — any pants?"

"No, I'm not. I'm wearing this skirty thingy."

He made a croaking noise. His eyes looked about to pop out of his head as his eyebrows shot up into his hairline. "And what about underneath?"

"That's none of your business!" The words came out with a squeak as I smoothed my skirt protectively over my thighs. What a perv! Did he really just march me all the way up here in the hopes of getting lucky?

Expression still aghast, he pointed at me. "You made it my business, just now, with your little announcement. Didn't you?"

Prince or no prince, this was going too far. Duncan crossed a line and I wasn't about to let him get away with it. "I don't see why you feel entitled to have a say in whether a girl prefers pants or a skirt. Is there some royal decree I'm missing?"

"Hold up for a moment." He furrowed his features, thinking hard. "When you say 'pants,' what exactly are ye talking about?"

With a frustrated roll of my eyes, I explained as patronizingly as possible. "Cloth that covers up your legs. It goes from your hips to your ankles. Like what you're wearing." I indicated the form-fitting clothing Duncan seemed to prefer over the traditional Scottish kilt. Not that I had any complaints.

"Oh." His wide eyes blinked rapidly as he processed my description. Then he looked at me with a broad smile that dissolved into gut-wrenching laughter. "Tha's a relief. I thought you were talking about not wearing any knickers."

Knickers, pants — same thing. I failed to see what was so hilarious. "So?"

"Do me a favor — " He paused as he shook back and forth, not even bothering to wipe away the tears that rolled from the corners of his eyes. "Next time you have the urge to talk about your 'pants,' please use the word 'trousers' instead. Even 'breeches' would serve. Here in Doon, your pants are what's worn under your trousers."

Translating in my head, I tracked my way back to Duncan's overblown reaction and the origin of our misunderstanding. If pants were the Doonian equivalent of underwear, and I'd just insisted — loudly and repeatedly — I wasn't wearing any ...

"You thought that I ...? *Agwk!*"

I flopped face first onto the blanket and willed a gaping hole to swallow me up. It didn't matter where I ended up — China, Wonderland, a turnip truck — anywhere was better than being forced to stay here and wallow in humiliation.

"It's okay, woman. In Doon, any conversation about one's knickers is strictly confidential. I wouldna betray your confidence." Duncan tried to sound sincere, but tiny guffaws punctuated his speech.

Hyper aware of the blush creeping over my skin, I burrowed deeper into the quilt. Soon I would resemble a sunburned lobster. "I'm not talking to you anymore."

"Suit yourself." Duncan reclined on his side until his head was level with mine.

I tried to shut him out and focus on the quiet peacefulness of the glen: dappled sunlight caressing my skin, the soft musical chimes of the distant waterfall, birds calling back and forth in cheery chirps. But I couldn't ignore the warm air that tickled my hairline each time he exhaled. Heat coaxed the clean scent of leather from his skin. Vibrancy rolled off him in waves and bathed me in undeniable awareness ... so much so that I began to tremble.

I turned onto my side and opened my eyes to find him considering me with a half-smile. Determined not to be intimidated by his unwavering gaze, I stared back ... for all of ten seconds. I'd always sucked at staring contests, undone by the urge to blink or laugh, or in this case the desire to kiss my opponent. Instead, I looked everywhere but his sincere brown eyes, and tried to pick apart his nearly flawless features.

Were his ears too big, and his slightly stubbled chin too square? Maybe his lips were too full, too perfectly shaped? And his eyes, were they too expressive? The only true imperfection I could find was a slight crook in his nose, a tiny defect that, unfortunately, only enhanced his appearance by proving he was, indeed, human.

Captivated by his striking features, I didn't realize how long I'd been looking until he squirmed. "Och, you're makin' me uncomfortable with your staring."

He chuckled self-consciously, and that little bit of vulnerability made me bold — that and the memory of how it felt to be in his arms at the dance. So many times the previous evening,

I'd ignored the urge to touch his beautiful face. Unable to resist now, I reached out and traced the line of his nose from between his brows to the tip.

"How'd you break your nose?"

Duncan nipped at my finger and I pulled away. His voice when he spoke was so quiet that I leaned toward him to hear. "I'll give ye one guess."

"Jamie?" I had a hard time believing his brother would hurt him so deliberately, until I remembered the sword fight the morning Vee and I'd arrived.

"Aye."

"Do you and your brother often try to kill each other?"

It took a moment for him to grasp my implication, and when he did his eyes widened in shock. "No. My nose was an accident." He rubbed the crooked bump thoughtfully. "At least I think it was an accident. 'Twas a long time ago."

Propping myself on my elbows once more, I challenged, "What about the tournament? The day I arrived?"

Duncan shrugged, a masculine yet elegant gesture that threatened to derail my train of thought. "What about it?"

"Jamie cut you — more than once. You looked like something out of a horror movie."

His dark brows lifted in confusion. "Horror movie?"

I tried a different analogy. "You were bleeding like a stuck pig."

In the face of my genuine concern, Duncan MacCrae tipped his head skyward and let loose a gut-busting laugh. It was so infuriating that I wanted to tackle him and — and — *Bad idea!* So I waited for him to get over his hilarity, doing my best to hold on to my indignation and hold back the rising heat that'd started at the mental image of me on top of him.

Once he could manage to talk again, he grinned. "I wouldna go so far as to call me a stuck pig."

"Well, I would. It was like you were trying to get him to kill you."

Duncan reached out and captured my chin. "Look at me, Mackenna."

Instead, I clamped my eyes shut out of spite.

"Look at me, please." He waited quietly until I complied. When I did open my eyes, the soft look on his face made my insides go gooey. "It was just a bit o' blood. I'm fine. My brother would never intentionally hurt me. He loves me."

I struggled to reconcile Duncan's words with the images burned into my brain. As we stared at one another, his pupils expanded to become deep, dark wells. The intensity of those fathomless eyes reached into the secret places in my soul. Unable to stand the magnetism of his gaze, I pulled my face away and traced the plaid pattern of the blanket with my eyes.

He continued as if our conversation had been going on the whole time. "Jamie has a lot of pressure on him. He'll be our king — soon — and combat is the only way he seems to be able to blow off steam. That's why I provoke him sometimes. I'd rather he take his aggression out on me than one of the other lads. And he means no harm. Truly."

"It must be a lot — having to become king and settle on a bride in such a short time."

"Aye."

"And he plans on marrying Sofia?"

Clearly surprised by my knowledge, he blinked several times. "You're better informed than I thought."

I shrugged and risked a peek in his direction. "What else is there to do but talk?"

"Aye, 'tis true. The village expects his engagement to Sofia." His eyes turned suddenly soulful, and he flopped on his back to stare at plump clouds marring the perfect summer sky.

"The truth is, I envy my brother. He struggles over the simple things — things I've always wanted. To carve out a life here. And ..."

His dramatic pause irritated me. "And ..."

"To have a Calling."

It appeared that here in Doon, receiving a Calling was like winning the romance lottery. For a medieval land, they appeared surprisingly enlightened. So why was everyone absorbed with getting hitched? "What's so great about a Calling, anyway?"

Duncan turned his attention back to me. His eyes blazed with a light that matched his impassioned words. "It's divine confirmation of your partner — that you've found your perfect match in every way. No uncertainty. And that love will only grow. It will never fade, never die. It lasts forever."

"You believe Jamie's had a Calling?"

"Aye."

"What does he think?"

"He thinks it's complicated. He's confused. But in my opinion, the problem is he's busy thinking when he should just trust his heart."

Somehow Duncan and I had drifted closer together during the last bit of conversation, and my face was now inches from his. When I glanced at his mouth, he angled his head and parted his lips in an unmistakable invitation.

What were the implications of kissing in Doon? Did they have such a thing as hooking up? Or would a little lip locking send Duncan scurrying to the imperial jewelers for a diamond ring?

Uncertainty caused me to roll away from him and sit up. "Aside from finding true love, don't you have things you want to do with your life?"

He pulled himself up beside me and rested his forearms on his knees. "All I've ever wanted since I was a wee lad was to serve the citizens of Doon, my kingdom and my king."

"Even if that king is Jamie?"

"Aye. He needs me." I sensed Duncan would be satisfied to play second fiddle. His loyalties ran deep — he'd have no problem seeing Jamie as a king first and a brother second. As if he read my thoughts, he smiled impishly. "Though he still might need takin' down a notch now and then."

I imagined the big ogre beating the new king of Doon playfully across the butt with the flat of his sword and the royal outrage it would cause. That would *nearly* be worth staying for.

A flock of birds shot from the canopy of the forest like they were bent on avenging their stolen eggs. Duncan pointed to them. "Crossbills. They're a type of finch."

We watched as they disappeared into the thick gray clouds rolling our direction. I wondered how much time we had until the rain came.

After an eternity, Duncan cast me a sidelong look. "What about you? What do you want to do with your life?"

Resisting the urge to lose myself in his brown eyes, I struggled to put my aspirations into a context he would understand. "It's always been my dream to become a professional actress. I have this amazing theater internship in Chicago."

"And then what?"

"Then I conquer Broadway and win a Tony." Duncan's brows pinched together and I clarified, "Tony's not a person. It's an award — an accolade. It's like the Calling of the theater world."

He nodded in understanding. "And after Broad Way?"

"I die happy?" That was such a long way off. I always imagined I'd be like Betty Buckley, performing way into the sunset of my life.

With a hint of frustration, Duncan demanded, "What about love and a family?"

"Maybe ... someday. But neither one is at the top of my to-do list. Your culture might be fixated on Callings, but for me, true love is one of the worst things that could happen. I can't have my heart getting in the way of my dreams."

Duncan regarded me impassively. "I see. Thank you for clarifying your position."

As he began unpacking our picnic basket, I told myself it was better this way. The last thing I needed was to let some romantic entanglement get in the way of me leaving at the Centennial. And if flirting was the first step on the Doonian path to matrimony, better not to venture down that road at all. Perhaps if I were really lucky, Duncan Rhys Finnean MacCrae would get his Calling and turn his charms toward some nice local lass. Then I'd barely even regret not kissing him when I had the chance.

CHAPTER 19

Veronica

It felt good to stretch my muscles as I followed Jamie up the mountain path. But I couldn't get the morning's chapel service out of my mind. I hadn't been to church since before — that is, before Dad went off the drug-induced deep end.

It wasn't that I didn't believe. I'd always believed in the existence of God. It'd just been too painful to go back to the place where I'd sat sheltered between both my parents, listening to my dad's smooth, tenor voice singing beside me. But seeing the Doonians' — and Jamie's — united faith sparked a longing inside me to be part of something bigger than myself.

At the close of the service, Jamie had stood in for his father and led the kingdom in song, his rich voice flowing into the darkest corners of my spirit. Then he'd smiled that smile of his, and I'd sensed half the population of Doon, young and old, swooning along with me. And how could they not be affected by someone possessing such internal and external beauty?

Pebbles dislodged under Jamie's boots and my focus shifted to the view directly in front of me — powerful legs, agile as a mountain lion, dashing up the path. Jamie was wearing a kilt. For the ten-thousandth time, I doubted the wisdom of this little outing. Really, I was setting myself up for an epic fall.

As if in fateful confirmation, I stubbed my toe hard and fell to my knees in the dirt. "Mother cusser!"

Dusting my hands off, I looked up, blew the hair out of my eyes, and saw Jamie hovering above me, one eyebrow arched, his lips wobbling with suppressed laughter.

"Do ye need to turn back?"

I glared up at him, refused the hand he extended to help me up, and attempted to get back on my feet. But as I moved to stand, my foot anchored the edge of my skirt to the ground and I pitched forward, right into him. My momentum pushed him back a step as he caught me under my arms.

"I'm starting to think you throw yourself at me on purpose, lass."

The joke struck far too close to home. Getting my feet underneath me, I tried to pull away but his hands tightened around my sides, locking me in place.

"Let go!" I grabbed his solid forearms, pushing back in a futile attempt to extricate my ribcage from his strong fingers. But he just stood there, unmoving, a sort of dazed half-grin on his face.

Gradually, I became aware of the steady pressure of his warm palms against the sides of my chest. Unwilling to acknowledge how our intimate contact affected me, I opened my mouth and said the first thing that came to mind. "Do you maul all the females in your kingdom? Or just those that will be gone in two weeks?"

Jamie's face turned to stone, and his hands dropped to his sides. Immediately filled with regret for my unkind words and the loss of his touch, I reached out and grabbed his hand as he turned away.

"Jamie, I'm sorry … I didn't mean it."

Slowly, he turned back toward me, his face an unreadable mask. I returned his stare for several long seconds, and then he squeezed my hand, his mouth tilting into a thoughtful closed-lipped smile before he replied, "Do you realize that's the first time ye've used my given name?"

"No, I hadn't realized that." I shrugged and stared at the toe of my boot as I made circles in the dirt.

He was right, of course. I hadn't once, since arriving in Doon, addressed him by his first name, even though he'd invited me to do so and I'd thought of him as Jamie all the time. But after having said it, I felt as if my two images of him, the unattainable dream guy and the real-life Jamie, were inexplicably merging into one.

"I liked it," he said, lifting my chin with his thumb and forefinger. His warm brown eyes swept over my face, lingering on each individual feature. Would he kiss me? Blood rushed in my ears —

A thrashing sound behind us drew Jamie's attention. Looking over my head, he dropped his hand from my face, his posture alert.

I turned to see a fawn, its liquid eyes wide and unblinking, a cluster of leaves forgotten in its mouth. Half expecting it to trot over to us like an animal in a fairy tale, I held very still.

"'Tis but a wee babe," Jamie whispered close to my ear. "When I was a lad, I tried to keep one as a pet."

In a blink, the fawn whipped around, showing us the cottony underside of its tail as it leapt back into the forest.

Turning, I asked, "What happened with your deer?"

He grinned, and I could see him as a little blond boy, dirt smudged on his dimpled cheeks.

"I lured it into the castle with a trail of raspberries. But my ma wouldna have any of it. Said deer droppings were not an appropriate addition to the castle motif."

I burst out laughing at the image of the spoiled princeling thwarted by his mother, the pragmatic queen.

"Come. We're almost there." He tugged my hand and we set off together up the path.

The rocky trail opened onto a plateau, surrounded by forest and guarded on three sides by soaring mountains.

"Oh." It was an inadequate response, but the beauty of the glen that lay before us stole my breath — and apparently my ability to form words.

Jamie squeezed my hand in understanding. "Worth the hike, eh?"

"Absolutely."

Hand in hand, we stepped off the path and into a rainbow of prairie grass and wildflowers, our movement releasing a fusion of bright, sweet perfume that I wished I could bottle and save for a rainy day.

"I've taken the liberty of selectin' a spot for us on the far side o' the glade. Are you hungry?"

I tore my gaze away from the deep-red poppies, golden buttercups, and delicate bluebells brushing my skirt to glance at the impossibly gorgeous guy gazing down at me, and felt a little faint. Whatever happened in the future, I had to stop analyzing Jamie's every move and seize this moment. Taste it, touch it, smell it, feel it — etch the memory forever in my heart.

A smile burst from deep inside me. "Yes, ravenous, and thirsty too."

With an amused grin, he hefted the basket in his hand like a dumbbell. "Well, ye're in luck then. By the weight of this thing, I'd say Fiona packed us a right feast!"

Down a short hill and across a gurgling stream, we found Jamie's perfect spot and spread out a tartan blanket under the trees.

I stepped onto the fluttering plaid cloth and sat with my legs crossed under my skirt. "So, how did you find this place?"

"As lads, Duncan and I made it our life's goal to explore every inch of Doon."

Jamie moved to the opposite side of the blanket, lowered himself to one knee, and began unpacking our lunch. "As large as Doon is, it is finite, and what adventure is to be found ..." He glanced up, mischief dancing in his eyes. "Well, two lads such as m' brother and I were determined to find it."

"Did you accomplish your goal then? Have you seen every inch of the kingdom?" I asked before popping a grape into my mouth.

A cloud passed over his eyes as he looked at me. "Aye. Every glade, forest glen, and mountain peak."

As he spread out the amazing selection of food, the tension in his shoulders lessened, but he remained pensive. I wanted to say something cute to distract him, but nothing came to mind, so I busied myself filling my plate with cheeses, fresh rye bread, fruit, and a variety of salads. A feast fit for a king, I thought as a tense giggle slipped from my lips.

"Lemonade?"

"Yes, please." I punctuated the two words by another giggle. Now that we'd stopped moving, my nerves were catching up to me.

Like a predator sensing fear, he fixed his gaze on my face, a hungry smile curling his lips. I froze, the laughter dying in my throat. Our eyes locked as he leaned forward with feral grace.

In the shadow of the trees, his eyes took on the hue of a midnight sky. My mouth opened, and I suppressed the urge to bite my lip as he moved closer.

Never breaking eye contact, Jamie reached toward me and carefully took the glass out of my hand. Then he sat back on his haunches, and picked up the carafe of lemonade. When he handed me the filled glass, I avoided touching his fingers.

"Thanks," I said, pleased my voice didn't squeak.

"You're quite welcome."

He smiled and I had to look away. Get a grip, Veronica! What was is it about this guy? I mean, besides the fact that he resembled a male model with the build of a professional athlete, his accent consistently melted the bones from my body, and, last but not least, he was a real-life freakin' prince? Really, what did I have to be nervous about? That ridiculous conclusion made me giggle again.

"I like that."

Startled out of my private thoughts, I looked up at Jamie, who during my preoccupation had devoured his first plate of food and was now loading up his second.

"What?"

"That ye dinna care what other people think of you." He bit into a slice of turkey, grinning as he chewed.

"What do you mean?" I was sure he was making fun of me, but I hadn't yet figured out how.

"You just start laughing at somethin' you thought about in your head." He took a huge bite of bread and kept talking. "Has anyone ever accused you of being a wee bit mad?" He twirled his finger in a circle near his ear in the universal gesture for crazy.

"No!" I pursed my lips in mock offense. "Has anyone ever told you that you have appalling table manners?"

He quirked an eyebrow.

I tilted my nose in the air in my best imitation of Mrs. Francis, Bainbridge High's ever-pretentious Home Ec teacher. "'One should never speak with one's mouth full.' Didn't they teach you that in Prince School?"

Jamie flashed a wicked grin before stuffing half a slice of bread into his mouth, "Well, as the soon-to-be ruler o' Doon, I declare speaking with one's mouth full an edict. From this day forth, no one is to speak unless their mouth be stuffed full!"

At least that's what I thought he said around the chunk of bread in his mouth. Mentally adding 'great sense of humor' to my growing list of his desirable traits, I sat up, jammed half an oatmeal cookie into my mouth, and raised my glass in the air. "Here, Here!" I cried, or rather, garbled around my stuffed mouth.

His loud laughter rang through the glen as he rocked back, catching himself just before he fell flat on his back. The dimple appeared along the side of his mouth, and I thought my heart might burst. This boy-king-to-be desperately needed a little fun in his life, and if I could play any part in that, then whatever time I had here in Doon would be well served.

"I never thanked you for the miniature castle." I focused on a string that had frayed from the hem of my skirt before glancing up with a small smile. "I love it. Thank you."

"You're verra welcome." Jamie beamed, set his plate down, and stood. "Come on," he said, cocking his head in the direction of the trees.

"Archery?" I asked as I got to my feet and brushed crumbs from my skirt.

"Later. I have a mind to show you something special."

We wound our way through the forest for at least fifteen minutes before he turned to me, extending his hand. I couldn't read his expression clearly in the shadow of the dense trees, but as I put my fingers in his I felt the excitement buzzing through him.

Pushing through a line of dense brush, we came out of the forest to face a sheer rock wall rising into the sky farther than I could see. Up ahead, a boulder protruded from the mountain appearing to block the path. A deep roar vibrated through my chest, and I tightened my grip on his hand.

As we approached the boulder, the roaring grew louder, and a new scent permeated the forest — a refreshing, briny aroma that cut straight through the pine and cedar. Glancing over his shoulder, Jamie smiled broadly and then turned left into a narrow rocky passage. I couldn't see around him, but an invigorating breeze flowed around us, the rhythmic roaring becoming almost deafening.

The ocean. The realization hit me just as he pulled me out onto a ledge, and the whole world opened up before us.

"Oh, Jamie." Squeezing his hand, I leaned into his arm.

Cobalt-blue water met the cerulean sky, stretching infinitely into the horizon. Jagged moss-covered rocks broke the waves crashing along the coastline far below. It was the most spectacular thing I'd ever seen. Of course, the only other time I'd seen the ocean I'd been careening down a crooked Scottish road in the rain, Kenna driving like an escaped NASCAR lunatic. That first day in Scotland seemed a lifetime ago now.

"'Tis the northernmost boundary of Doon," Jamie said reverently.

We were standing on an outcropping protruding from the side of a cliff, the narrow beach two hundred feet below us.

"It's breathtaking."

"Aye. I come here often to think. When I feel ... auntsee."

His pronunciation threw me for a moment, but when I realized he was saying *antsy*, I grinned up at him. He returned my smile but it didn't reach his eyes.

"Do you feel that way often?" I asked.

"From time to time…" He trailed off, but I sensed there was more he was not saying. "Shall we sit?"

"Sure."

Jamie lowered himself on the ledge, leaned back against the rock face, and pulled me down beside him.

I let go of his hand to situate myself. The cool stone cut through the thin cotton of my shirt as I leaned back. Arranging the fabric around my bent legs, I realized I was sitting over a foot away from him. I stared back out at the ocean, and contemplated scooting closer but decided it would be too obvious.

"Come here."

Although it was what I wanted, I bristled at the direct order. This boy was a little too accustomed to getting his every whim fulfilled without question.

Looking over at him, I lifted my brows in challenge. "No." Then I turned my attention back to the view.

"Dinna be stubborn, lass," he practically growled.

"You're the stubborn one. I'm fine where I am." I shrugged and stared straight ahead.

"Please, come sit with me," he said, forced sincerity dripping from every word.

I glanced at him, fighting the smile curving up the corners of my mouth, and said, "Better."

Scooting across the smooth rock, I closed about half the distance between us. A slow smirk spread across Jamie's face, causing his eyes to narrow. I tensed, wondering if he would pounce.

"I would like it verra much if you would come sit next to me." He patted the ground next to his thigh, indicating where he wanted me to sit. Then he stared directly into my eyes, leaned forward, and picked up a lock of my hair, brushing the ends across the pad of his thumb. "Please, Verranica?"

Something warm settled in the pit of my stomach, my limbs going all rubbery. With a sigh, I closed the remaining distance between us. A girl could only take so much.

Promptly, Jamie wrapped his muscled arm around me and tucked me close to his side. His delicious scent enveloped me — clean pine and the wind before a storm, a combination that smelled perfect to me. Although I couldn't remember ever being so glad to comply in my life, I threw out one last jab. "Happy now?"

"Aye." There was a smile in his voice.

"Have you ever gone swimming in the ocean?" I asked, desperate to diffuse the sparks his knuckles created as they brushed rhythmically against my arm.

"I canna."

I stared at our legs stretched out in front of us, side by side, trying to focus my thoughts on something other than throwing myself into his lap and kissing him until neither of us could breathe.

"So you can't swim?"

"Nay, I can swim." His voice sounded slightly higher than usual.

"Didn't I see a path in the rock over there?" I pointed to our left to indicate the steep trail leading down and out of sight.

"When I say this is the northernmost border o' Doon, I mean this cliff. We can see the ocean but never touch it. Except for the Centennial, o' course. But during the last Centennial I hadna yet been born."

"What would happen if you tried to go down to the beach?" Gray clouds were gathering, darkening the sky. The wind picked up, whipping the waves below us into a frenzy. Jamie's hand stopped moving against my skin.

"'Tis complicated, but if I were able to cross the border, the kingdom and everyone in it would cease to exist. They would all vanish into the mist as if they never lived." The timbre of his voice had turned low and anguished.

His words confirmed the legend, but there was something I didn't quite understand. "What do you mean, 'if you were able to cross the border'?"

"Why are ye asking me this?"

"I'm just trying to understand how it all works." The intensity of his expression sent shivers of apprehension up my spine.

"Why — " He cut himself off, his body going still beside me as he whispered, "The price."

"The price of what?" I searched his face, but he just stared at me, a furrow between his brows.

"My mother always said there was a price for everythin'." He looked out at the water and said something under his breath that sounded like, "the price of true love."

"What did you say?" I breathed, afraid to move or break the spell.

"I shouldna have brought you — " He stopped. With a blink of his eyes and a clench of his jaw, my Jamie was gone, and the heir to the throne was back. "We need to return."

"But — " He was slipping away from me. I was watching it happen but didn't know how to stop it.

Standing, he turned and helped me to my feet, promptly releasing my hand afterward. "Ye need not worry about it, Verranica. It is my responsibility alone to bear." His reply was terse, almost accusing.

And in that instant, the fragile peace between us shattered.

The reality of my situation — the choice I needed to make — crashed down around me.

As he turned to go through the rock passage, I clutched his bicep and dug my fingernails into the granite muscle, not willing to let him walk away from me. I needed answers. "Don't you dare shut me out! What about the Calling?"

He turned, the strength of his gaze piercing my very soul. "What Calling?"

My heart plummeted to my feet and I removed my hand from his arm. When I spoke, it was a whisper. "Did you see me before I came here?" I held my breath for any sign of emotion but his eyes were hard as obsidian.

"Aye, I saw you in my dreams. But it doesna matter."

"How can you say that?" I shook my head. "Isn't the Calling sacred in Doon?"

His eyes locked on mine and something stirred there, something volatile that sent fear rushing though my body.

"Aye, but that's not what we have." His jaw clenched, his posture going rigid. "Not all dreams are sacred."

Cold rushed down my spine, I swallowed hard. "What are you talking about? Jamie, you can trust me."

He moved so fast, I was unprepared when he grabbed me. His strong fingers wrapped around my upper arms, and he pulled me onto my toes, bringing my face to within inches of his.

"Really? I can trust you? You have no idea what yer saying! The very fate of Doon rests on me. And you ..." His face contorted with torment. "You touch me and I'm ready to throw it all away!" He shook me as if the violent movement would make me understand. "What I feel doesna matter. If yer truly connected to the witch ... there will be no mercy. I have to remain strong. Don't you see? I dinna have a choice!"

"Strong, how?" I whispered as tears stung the back of my eyes. I already knew the answer — strong because he had to deny what was between us, so he could objectively sentence me to death or whatever punishment Doonians reserved for conspiracy to commit witchcraft.

He abruptly loosened his hold on my arms, and I stumbled back several steps. He reached out and steadied me but stepped away quickly. "This" — he gestured toward me and then back at his chest — "canna go on." His voice was strong and sure, but his eyes filled with regrets.

Thunder bellowed across the sky. All the blood seemed to drain out of my body as I took a step toward him. "Jamie, please believe — "

"M' laird!" A shout in the distance cut me off. The male voice was familiar, but too distorted with agitation for me to place.

Jamie turned toward the passage without a backward glance and began to run. Cursing my stupid skirts, I yanked up the material to my thighs and followed.

Ahead, Fergus burst through the trees, his face mottled crimson. Leaning over to catch his breath, he watched us approach with anxious eyes. "M' laird," he gasped, "'tis yer father. There are horses waitin' for ye on the low path. Duncan's already gone ahead. Ye must make haste."

Jamie put his hand on Fergus's massive shoulder. "Stay with the lasses. See them safely back to the castle."

"Aye."

Then without so much as a word, or even a glance in my direction, Jamie MacCrae was gone.

chapter 20

Veronica

I plodded along behind Fergus through the forest and back toward the glen, dragging my battered heart behind me. Not even Eric had emotionally sucker punched me like the future king of Doon. Guys were idiots. Plain and simple.

I knew the connection between Jamie and me was real — more real than anything I'd felt in my life — so why did he think he had to resist it? Did he really believe I was in league with the witch? Or maybe his history with Sofia trumped anything he felt for me. I kicked a pebble, sending it shooting through the underbrush. I still didn't know if we'd shared the same visions, or dreams — whatever they were.

And why did I care? Obviously, he didn't.

Fergus stopped so abruptly I almost smacked into his arm. Quick as lightning, he drew his weapon and maneuvered me behind him. "Gideon, man, ye better start talkin'."

"I arrived and found the girl standing over them." Gideon's voice sounded strange, even for him — agitated, almost frantic. "I subdued her for my own protection."

Peeking around the giant guard, I had to blink several times before I comprehended what I was seeing. Kenna sat rubbing the back of her head, looking dazed, surrounded by bodies. Dead bodies — soldiers I recognized from the castle guard — with faces frozen in various stages of terror.

"Lass, do ye know how this happened?" Fergus asked Kenna, his tone carefully modulated. These soldiers could've been his friends, men he'd worked alongside every day.

Kenna seemed on the verge of tears. "I ... I don't remember how I got here."

"She's killed them wi' her evil magic. The witch must die!" Gideon proclaimed, his skeletal face emanating zealous triumph. Gideon held a broadsword in one hand and a wicked-looking dagger in the other.

Like a scene from a movie, Gideon charged at Kenna, his face contorted in rage as she let out a strangled cry. Racing against Gideon, who was just a dark blur in my peripheral vision, I leapt forward and tackled Kenna. We both slammed into the ground. The air whooshed from my lungs as I gripped her shoulders and braced for the impact of a sword in my back.

But it never came.

Jerking my head toward where the guard should be, I sucked in a sharp breath. Fergus and Gideon were engaged in battle not two feet away. The tension left my body in a surge of relief, and I thanked God for Fergus Lockhart — our guardian angel.

Gideon shouted a jumble of accusations and curses. Flecks of froth appeared at the corners of his thin mouth as he swung his weapon with the appearance of superhuman strength. But the raving madman was no match for Fergus, who disarmed his captain with a deft movement and a great heave, then finished him off with a swift uppercut. Gideon crumpled to the ground, out cold.

"Kenna, are you okay?" I asked, rolling onto the grass.

"I'm fine, but you've been holding out on me."

As we both sat up, I blinked at her in confusion. "What?"

A small smile formed on her lips. "I thought you said you were a cheerleader, not a ninja." Her voice hitched, betraying the feelings behind her words.

I smiled, tears filling my eyes as she threw her arms around me. "Thank you," she whispered.

"Och, lass! Were ye trying to get both of you killed?" Fergus scolded as he squatted down beside us. "Next time, wait for my signal."

"Yes, sir," I answered as Kenna and I broke apart.

"Mackenna, are ye hurt?"

"I'll be fine. No permanent damage — at least to me." She absently rubbed the back of her head as she looked around.

"And you, Veronica?"

Meeting Fergus's pale blue eyes, I searched for answers I knew he didn't have. "I'm fine."

"Go on and get back ta the trail. I'll be right behind ye." He picked up Gideon's rag doll body and effortlessly hoisted it over his shoulder.

I picked my way down the rocky trail with care. How had those poor men died? The Doonians were certain the witch had no power here — but I was beginning to wonder. A conversation I'd had with Fiona after the tavern incident circled through my mind. There had been no crime in Doon before we came. No violent acts, no unexplained disappearances, no black petunias growing on dead ground, and certainly no murders — aside from the time long ago when the witch had bewitched a man into doing her bidding. What were the odds of Doon having a sudden crime wave at the same time the two American girls showed up?

My heart squeezed in my chest — everything Jamie thought of me could be true. It was possible that when we crossed the Brig o' Doon we made the kingdom vulnerable to the witch's influence. And if we didn't find a way to stop it, more people could die.

⚜ ⚜ ⚜

The next morning, I sat curled in the alcove of the window seat and stared into the crackling fire, picking out patterns in the flames. It was hard work keeping my mind blank, but everything that'd happened in the last twenty-four hours hurt too much to contemplate. Kenna and I had been ordered to stay in the turret room — for our own protection, according to Fiona. But with a guard inside the suite, as well as outside the door, the confinement felt more like a prison sentence.

Kenna paced the other side of the bedroom, mumbling to herself. The occasional word reached my ears: "mob," "pitchforks," "dungeon," "beheading."

We'd both fallen into bed after dinner the night before, too exhausted to speak. Now, listening to my friend babble, I realized I couldn't put it off any longer.

"Ken, please stop. We need to talk." I patted the cushion next to me.

She flopped down, her arms crossed under her chest and her lip jutting out like a kid who didn't get the last pink balloon at the fair.

"Yesterday in the meadow, what happened before I got there?"

"One minute I was urging Duncan to go to his father ... and the next, I was lying on the ground surrounded by a bunch of dead guys." Her eyes were silver with tears. "I have no idea what happened to those poor men."

I nodded and took her hand. "It's not your fault, you know."

She shrugged and then wiped her cheeks. "I can't find a single box of Puffs in this joint."

I bit my lip against a chuckle, popped up, and jogged into the bathroom. Thankfully, Doon was progressive enough to have toilet paper. As I wrapped a few pieces around my hand, I stopped and stared up at the toilet tank above me. Maybe the tiny book hidden there contained some clue that I'd missed. What I'd said to Kenna was true; the deaths weren't her fault. But I couldn't absolve myself so easily. I'd been the one obsessed — the one Kenna followed to the bridge.

Jamie'd said there was a price for everything. It seemed as if the price I'd paid to enter this paradise was costing my best friend as well as innocent Doonians. After delivering the tissue to Kenna, I sank down at the table. I cradled the journal in my hands, knowing it was too late to turn back the clock, but praying there was a way to stop what I'd inadvertently set into motion.

Hours later, I closed the journal with a sigh and picked up the page of notes I'd taken. The pieces were here; I could feel it. But for some reason I couldn't fit them together. I ran my finger across the last paragraph of my notes.

The Rings of Aontacht are purported to do different things depending on the Protector's will. Page 47 says that their purpose is to enable individuals to cross the Brig o' Doon at times other than the Centennial. This seems consistent with pages 73 and 109. But on page 148 Gracie says the symbols on the Rings indicate they can be used for the purposes of protection and substitution. The prominent symbol indicates that someone can take the place of another at a spiritual level. Sacrificial substitution.

Opening *Doon: An Esteemed Legacy*, I flipped to the chapter on ancient symbols.

Kenna, fresh from a nap, flitted around the room, singing snippets of show tunes and lighting lamps to push back the growing darkness of the stormy afternoon. When she stopped to light the lantern on the table in front of me, I lightly touched her hand. She paused mid-song, her brows pinched together.

I pointed to the open page at a three-looped knot labeled Unity. "Does this look like the first symbol on your aunt's rings?"

"I think so." She sat across from me. "Why?"

I ran my finger down the drawings, to another one that looked familiar. "And this one?"

She leaned over and studied the triple spiral. "I do remember that one. What does it mean?"

I read the tiny script beside the picture aloud. "The Triskele is the symbol of substitution or rebirth." I moved to the next symbol I recognized. "And this one represents sacrifice or an exchange offering."

"It's pretty, but I wouldn't get it tattooed on my lower back or anything." I glanced up to find Kenna's scrutiny on me rather than the symbol. "What're you doing, anyway? As soon as the bridge opens, we're gone. We'll probably never see those rings again."

"Has it occurred to you that all the horrible stuff going on in Doon started after we got here?"

"I guess, but I figured that was just a coincidence. I mean, Glinda and Elphaba we're not." She leaned forward, her eyes sparkling. "But I could totally get my Glinda on if you think it'll get us out of here faster."

Not in the mood for one of her *Wicked* sing-alongs, I shot my best friend a dirty look as a succession of knocks sounded.

Our eyes darted toward the door and then back toward one another for reassurance. After so much time in isolation, the implications of that knock felt ominous.

At the guard's signal, Kenna and I moved to the bedroom and waited for him to answer the door and then sound the all clear.

When we returned to the living quarters, Fiona stood beside a flushed Fergus, whose bright red nose and eyes told me he'd been crying. The giant guard turned to me, lifting his chin in an attempt to hide his anguish. "Our good king seeks an audience with Miss Veronica."

My heart stuttered, my eyes darting to Fiona and then back to Fergus. "Why?"

Fiona lifted her pursed lips and exchanged a meaningful glance with Fergus, then said, "The Laird MacCrae doesn't have long for this world."

I'd figured as much, but that didn't explain why the king wanted to see me. Unless it was to punish me for what I'd allowed into his kingdom. I fastened my concentration on Fergus, hoping he was gifted in cryptic conversation. "Does the laird — uh — know about the meadow?"

Fergus cleared his throat, a sheepish look on his mottled face. "Ye kin speak plainly in front of Fiona. She knows about the guard's deaths, as does Duncan. But we're keeping it from Jamie and the Laird MacCrae, fer now."

"What about Gideon?" Kenna asked. "I figured he'd be screaming my guilt from the rooftops by now."

"Hard to do when he's locked in the dungeon." The corner of Fergus's mouth lifted in a hint of a smile. "Everyone thinks he and his men are on a border mission for Centennial preparations."

Fiona's pretty mouth in turn twisted into an expression that was equal parts smile and frown. "Veronica, you should go. I'll stay with Mackenna until ye return."

Fergus placed a meaty hand on my bicep, his voice both reassuring and urgent as he guided me toward the door. "That's true. We need ta hurry, m' lady."

As I moved with the giant, I glanced over my shoulder and met Kenna's guilt-ridden face. Without exchanging a word, I could tell she was relieved she wasn't going with me and at the same time ashamed she felt that way. "Don't worry," I said, fostering confidence I didn't feel. "I'm sure it's nothing. I'll be fine."

Right.

Knees shaking like an arthritic granny as I descended the stairs, I tried to reassure myself with worst-case scenarios. When visions of public execution and slow torture brought on by Jamie's orders didn't do the trick, I focused on the only positive I could find — I could protect Kenna. I would shoulder any blame if it meant getting my best friend across the bridge at the Centennial. That way, at least one of us would live to see our dreams come true.

Chapter 21

Veronica

The dim corridor grew longer with every step Fergus and I took. Torch-like sconces diffused our path in flickering light as we hurried past the rich tapestries, distinguished portraits, and burnished suits of armor that lined the austere passageway. Like living creatures, deep shadows set up residence along every angle.

I rubbed the goose bumps along my arms. This part of the castle felt ancient, almost like an entirely different structure than the bright and airy palace I'd come to love.

We approached a set of arched wooden doors, iron hinges, and ringed door pulls lending authenticity to the gothic atmosphere. Fergus lifted a lion-head knocker and tapped lightly while I lingered a few feet behind. Waiting, I glanced up at my protector. I must've looked as scared as I felt because he broke his stoic façade to give me a tiny smile of reassurance. His usually flushed skin appeared colorless, his bright eyes dim and shadowed.

The depth of his sorrow pulled me out of my selfish preoccupation. The people of Doon were suffering along with their beloved laird. I caught Fergus's meaty hand in mine and gave it a brief squeeze. Knowing if one of the other guards saw our exchange, my new friend would suffer for it, I let go quickly. Fergus acknowledged the gesture with a slight nod of his head.

The door opened a crack and Fergus spoke in hushed tones to someone inside. The only word I could make out was my own name. As the door closed again, I clenched my teeth. The waiting was the worst. I just couldn't fathom why the king would want to speak to me, of all people. I wasn't even a Doonian. *Yet*, my heart whispered before I could stop it.

The door opened again, and Duncan slipped out into the corridor, followed by Jamie.

A lock of golden hair fell over Jamie's forehead, partially obscuring his red-rimmed eyes. It had been only a day since I'd last seen him, but it felt like a thousand years of miserable separation. I had to fight back the urge to run and embrace him.

"Lairds, I will escort the lassie. No need ta concern yerselves." Fergus's posture was rigid, his words uncharacteristically formal.

"Thank you, Fergus," Jamie said, his voice sounding strained. "I have need to see to a few judicial matters. Duncan shall attend Father after h — " Jamie's voice cut off, and he cleared his throat with a rough cough before continuing. "His meeting."

Jamie's eyes darted to mine and then away so fast, the supportive smile I started to give him died on my lips. But I couldn't leave things like this — not after what had happened between us on the cliffs.

As he turned to go, I followed on his heels. "Jamie, wait!"

Stopping abruptly, he turned. His pale face void of emotion, he stared down at me. And I had no idea what to say.

"Are you okay?" Mentally kicking myself for being an insensitive jerk, I watched every feature of his face tighten. Of course he wasn't okay; his dad was dying. "I mean … Is there anything I can do?"

A sardonic smile twisted the corner of his mouth as his eyes shifted to hard ebony. "Aye. You can leave me alone."

Without waiting for my reply, he turned and walked away, his swift footsteps echoing through the corridor. Feeling as if I'd just taken a blow to the gut, I wrapped my arms around my waist in an attempt to keep myself from collapsing onto the stone floor.

Catching my eye, Duncan flashed an apologetic smile before turning and following his brother.

"We should no' keep the laird waitin'," Fergus said gently.

Hoping I could keep myself together, I turned to follow him, clasping my hands tightly in front of me as we entered the dark chamber. A single candle on the nightstand illuminated a massive bed draped in burgundy velvet and shadow.

"My laird, I have brought Miss Veronica Welling, as ye requested." Fergus stood in front of me, his large frame blocking my view of the king. I checked the urge to twist my hair behind my head, knowing Fiona'd spent considerable time that morning braiding the sides and neatly tying them back with a ribbon that matched my royal blue skirt.

"Well, let me see her then, man." The voice sounded stronger than I'd expected for a dying man.

"Aye, sire." Fergus stepped out of my way.

The king sat propped up by large pillows behind his back and under his arms. His long silver hair rested loose on his shoulders.

"Have a seat, my dear." His kind, dark eyes helped relax the knots in my chest.

Fergus moved a chair to the side of the bed and I sat. The king tilted his head, studying me for several seconds. Then he focused his regard on Fergus, whom I could feel hovering close behind. "Tha' shall be all, Fergus."

With a furtive glance in my direction, Fergus let himself out of the room.

I turned back to face the king, and he appeared to shrink before my eyes. Falling back into the pillows, he closed his eyes. Just when I started to ask him if I could get him anything, he said, "Authority can be quite exhausting." His eyes opened then and he stared at me intently.

Sitting straight, my hands folded in my lap, I wasn't sure if I should agree or remain silent. But before I could make up my mind, the king continued, "Veronica — may I call ye Veronica?"

"Of course."

"Veronica, dear, why have ye come ta Doon?"

I jumped a little, startled by the question no one had yet bothered to ask. But now that it had been put to me, it seemed the most obvious question of all.

What had led me to Doon? Had I manipulated Kenna to the bridge, knowing she would force me to cross? Or had I done it to help my best friend find what her aunt had so desperately wanted for her? Or had my own personal mission to find the boy who'd haunted my days and nights influenced my every action? I was pretty sure I knew the answer. I glanced up at the patiently waiting king.

"I ... began having visions shortly before I came to Scotland. When I first put on the Ring of Aontacht and heard the legend of Doon, I felt in my spirit it was all true. Gracie Lockhart believed Kenna had a reason to come here, but Ken had a hard time believing it and well, I ..." I hesitated, not sure what I wanted to say.

The king nodded in encouragement.

"I knew the kingdom existed, and that no matter what it took I had to find it."

"Because of the dreams ye were having?"

"They weren't dreams exactly, since I was awake, but in any case ... it seems I misinterpreted them."

The king sputtered as coughs began to rack his frail body. I scrambled to the pitcher I'd seen sitting on a nearby table. Returning with a glass of water, I helped the king sit up straighter and held the glass to his lips. After a moment, his hands were steady enough to hold the cup on his own.

"Sir, should I get Fergus?"

He waved his hand and shook his head dismissively. "Sit, lass. I'm fine now."

I perched on the edge of the chair, wondering if I should cut the audience short. The conversation was clearly taking its toll, but my heart urged me to continue on the chance it could shed some light on Jamie's behavior.

"Could ye indulge an auld man and tell me what ye had visions of before coming here?"

My shoulders slumped. The moment of truth had come. I didn't want to give him false hope, considering the strong implications of the Calling in Doon's culture. But I couldn't lie to this honorable man, the king of Doon, and, most importantly, Jamie's father.

"It was your son ... Jamie." Inexplicably, tears filled my eyes.

"Ahh, yes. 'Tis as I suspected then." There was a gentle smile on his face, and as his dark eyes crinkled at the edges I could see why this man held a special place in the hearts of everyone in the kingdom. He reached out his hand for mine. I held his large, bony fingers, wondering what I'd just done.

"I'm sorry." I wiped the tears from my eyes and stiffened my spine in determination. "I had no right."

The king looked directly into my eyes, a shrewd expression on his face. "No right ta what?"

"No right to fall in love with your son." Having said it — actually admitting it for the first time — a breath whooshed out from deep within my chest.

"Veronica, ye are here fer a reason. Our Protector does no' make mistakes." Coughs began to shake his body once more. I refilled his empty glass, and then helped him hold it as he took short sips between ragged breaths. When he spoke again, his voice sounded strained. "But there is something in your way ..." His eyes watered in his effort to continue. "Someone."

The king's face turned crimson as he valiantly fought for breath. "You alone can save the kingdom." He began coughing again. "When the time comes, ye must be willing ta sacrifice ... for Jamie's sake."

"Sir, I don't understand." Someone? Was he talking about Sofia? Did he mean I should sacrifice my feelings so Jamie could be with Sofia? And how could I save the kingdom?

He swallowed, seeming to struggle for breath.

"I'm going to get Fergus." I started to rise.

He shook his head, "Nay," he croaked. "I need ta tell ye ..."

"Yes, sir, I'm listening." I leaned in close.

"Doon did no' call ye here ta become its queen by marrying my son." The king sunk back into his pillows then, a coughing fit consuming him.

I stood frozen and stared at him for several seconds, trying to comprehend his words. Was he saying what I thought he was saying? I wasn't meant to be with Jamie?

I stood on weak legs to fetch Fergus. But before I could move away, the king sat up, his cold hand clutched my arm, and he gasped out one chilling word. "Witch."

Suddenly, the room spun away from me in a vortex of sights, sounds, and emotions. The dizzying effect sent me to my knees as the whirl of images flashed before my eyes and then ground to a sudden stop on a single hazy figure.

Waves of asymmetric blonde hair shifted over the figure's shoulder as she turned toward me — Adelaide Dell, the caretaker of Dunbrae Cottage. What the — ?

The vision grew sharper, like the lens of a camera coming into focus. Addie's flawless skin thinned, becoming lined with age, her mouth turning down slightly at the corners. Her pencil skirt and twin sweater set morphed into an old-fashioned black dress that covered her from neck to ankle. Her pale hair turned white, twisting into a tight bun as she clutched a small leatherbound book to her chest.

The vision fell away, leaving me in a crumpled, boneless heap on the floor. Addie Dell is the Witch of Doon! Working to focus my eyes, I lifted my head and saw the king's arm hanging limply over the edge of the bed above me. Gripping the mattress, I struggled to my feet and found him still and silent. His eyes half-closed, his head lolled listless on his shoulder. Oh no! Was he gone?

"Laird MacCrae?" I whispered into the dead silence of the room. Leaning forward, I placed my fingers on the side of his neck and counted to thirty before I found a pulse. It was weak, but steady. I turned to get help.

Raised voices greeted me as I neared the chamber door. "Father thinks you've misread the dreams. Tell her, Jamie, perhaps — "

"I can't risk it."

"If you care for her at all, give her a chance."

"I care for this kingdom. As should you, brother!"

"If you dinna tell Veronica, I swear to you I will!"

My stomach did a sickening backflip, and I burst out of the room to find Jamie and Duncan nose to nose. "Your father passed out!"

The brothers turned to me, their faces twin masks of stone as I added, "I checked his pulse. It's weak but steady."

"I will attend him." Duncan strode through the open door. "Veronica, Jamie has something to discuss with you."

Jamie sighed heavily and shoved a hand into his disheveled hair. When he turned to me, his perfect lips twisted in a scowl. "You've wanted to know if I was dreaming about you?" he snapped.

I nodded, not trusting my voice.

His face softened. "I did dream of you ... You were crying the first time I saw you. Then I couldn't walk down the street without seeing your haunting face. And that day in the bedroom window ..." He swallowed convulsively.

My pulse stuttered as I waited for him to continue.

"At first the dreams were ... amazing. You were more than I could've dared hope for." He glared at his feet, shoved his hands in his pants pockets, brows drawing together. When he looked up, his eyes were misty as if tears — no, it had to be a trick of the torchlight. "But then the dreams changed. I couldna get close ... an evil surrounded you, moved with you, contaminating everything, until ..." He paused, a muscle jumping in his jaw as he stared at the wall.

I desperately wished he would stop, but I couldn't make a sound, couldn't move.

His eyes sliced back to mine, his entire face drawn, almost haggard. When he spoke, his voice was thick with grief.

"Until everythin' was destroyed. The entire kingdom ... gone forever ... because of you."

Like a blow to the chest, his words stopped my heart.

I stared at him and shook my head. My mouth moved for several seconds before I could whisper, "No. You're wrong."

His eyes burned into mine, begging me — to what? Believe him? Prove my innocence? There was nothing I could say.

I wanted to shout that even if he'd dreamt that I'd harmed the kingdom, it didn't mean anything. It was just a nightmare. But that wasn't true. A bubble of panic pushed against my ribs, and I pulled in a ragged breath. Dreams meant everything here.

Jamie took a step and reached for me. I stumbled out of his reach. Turning on my heel, I ran blindly down the opposite corridor. He called my name but I didn't stop. Consumed by tears, I ran aimlessly through the maze-like castle until I found a dark, quite hallway and sank to the floor, my head in my hands.

The worst part was that I'd begun to let myself hope. As hard as I tried to deny it, there'd been a secret part of me that wished, prayed even, that the visions meant this amazing boy was my soul mate — the destiny that'd brought me here. But instead, I was his nightmare and my destiny his ultimate destruction.

🔮 🔮 🔮

Help me!

Every time I tried to surface, another hideous dream tugged me under. I was strapped to a chair, forced to watch Jamie and Sofia twirl across the dance floor while the benevolent king repeatedly told me I wasn't meant to be with his son. Addie appeared, as real as if she were standing before me, her eyes glowing an unearthly purple. She handed me a small book and moments later Jamie walked toward me, tall and solid. I held the familiar leather volume out to him as warnings shrieked through my brain. He took what I offered and crumpled at my feet, gasping for breath. Abruptly, he stopped struggling, his beautiful face frozen in death. The witch cackled gleefully, "Thank you Veronica. You've done well!"

I jerked awake and swallowed a scream.

The journal!

I lay rigid under the covers, my heart pounding to the beat of my cascading thoughts. Aunt Gracie's notes said an object cursed by the witch and brought into the kingdom could compromise Doon's protection. I thought that Kenna and I had found the journal by accident. But it was entirely possible that Addie had planted it. Who knows what she'd done in the cottage before we arrived. She'd have had plenty of time to place a spell on the book. The more I thought about it, and how easily we'd found everything, the more it made sense.

No, no, no! I dug my fingernails into my palms, squeezing my eyes tightly closed. What had I done?

My first instinct was to tell someone. But who? If I told Jamie, I'd not only be confirming his worst fears about me, but likely put him in grave danger. The image of him falling dead at my feet, the book in his hands, wouldn't leave my mind.

I glanced at Kenna sleeping peacefully beside me. I longed to wake her and tell her everything, but then I remembered the king's words: I alone could save the kingdom. Did that mean if I involved my best friend, I'd fail to save Doon? Or that it was best if I acted alone? I had no idea how the curse on the journal worked. But why endanger others if I didn't have to? I was the one who brought the journal across the bridge in the first place — the one who'd put the people of Doon in danger.

Picturing the dead guard's faces, frozen in agony, tears leaked out of the corners of my closed eyes. My fault. The king had given me the vision for a reason. And Jamie's dreams had nothing to do with Kenna. This was my responsibility, my problem to fix. But the bridge was closed until the Centennial, and the king had taken the rings.

Suddenly the walls closed in around me. I had to get out, had to come up with a plan — guards or no guards. Careful not to wake Kenna, I pushed the coverlet back and slid to my feet. After tugging on my skirt and blouse, I retrieved the journal from its soggy hiding place and tucked the tiny book in my skirt pocket.

I knew what I had to do — how I could save the kingdom. Grabbing an apple out of the bowl on the coffee table, I moved to the door and flung it open — only to stop just short of barreling into a teary-eyed Fiona. Before she even spoke the words, I knew what she would say. I didn't want to hear it, but like so many other things in Doon, I had no choice in the matter.

"The Laird MacCrae has passed on."

My throat tightened as I moved to embrace Fiona. There was one choice still left to me. I would not let the king's vision, the effort it'd cost him to warn me, go to waste. I'd get the cursed journal out of Doon before it was too late.

🔹 🔹 🔹

The rest of the morning passed in a blur of dark, drab clothing and Kenna's cryptic references to *Our Town*. I numbly went through the motions of getting ready for the funeral while also looking for my chance to escape. Despite my resolve, I both dreaded and longed for that moment; alternating between the desires to speed time up and freeze it in place.

After what felt like an eternity, we arrived at the Auld Kirk. From my vantage point in the middle of the church, I let my eyes slide over the sea of mourners, searching for the face of my prince. He and his bother sat alone in front, opposite, yet the same; one dark, one light, their broad shoulders squared in an almost identical steely bulwark against their anguish — stoic islands of grief. I wished I was sitting next to him, if only to hold his hand.

Pain shot up my jaw and I unclenched my teeth. Jamie wouldn't want reassurance from me. He'd made his feelings abundantly clear, and after what I'd done, it was for the best. I shifted in my seat, the impulse to duck out the back door, to grab the journal and go, almost overwhelming. Fearful to bring the witch's evil into the Doonians' place of worship, I'd stashed the book outside the doors of the chapel, in the pot of a tall fern.

A deep silence pulled my focus back to the front of the church where Jamie made his way to the center of the altar. Stopping behind the podium, he stood tall and strong, sincerity shining from his face. As he began to speak, his words filled the chapel with an almost visible peace, his internal strength comforting and encouraging his grieving kinsmen.

Kenna shifted beside me. She slipped her warm hand into mine and squeezed. If she chose to stay in Doon, this could be the last moment I spent with her. I squeezed back, hoping she knew how much she meant to me.

"You okay?" she whispered.

Afraid she would read my thoughts, I nodded but kept my focus on the eulogy. As I listened, something inside of me shifted. The resentment I'd felt since discovering it was my responsibility to save the kingdom transformed into quiet acceptance. Jamie MacCrae would make a wonderful king, and it was my duty — no, my destiny — to give him that chance.

Even if it meant leaving the two people I loved most in the world ... forever.

Chapter 22

Mackenna

As I followed the funeral crowd around the side of the Auld Kirk to the pavilion behind, I asked myself WWSSD: What Would Stephen Sondheim Do?

I thought about the two gladiator princes who, despite all their strength and cunning, were powerless to stop the death of their beloved father — even in an enchanted kingdom. Bittersweet, coming-of-age melodies swirled in my head. If only Stephen were here to give them a musical silver lining to cling to in their time of need.

Instead, they had a whole community of loved ones who grieved in harmony with them. And the discord of two alleged witches, causing unease in their realm at a time when they needed it least.

Make that one witch.

Vee had wandered away from the masses at the first opportunity. Ever since the picnic at Muir Lea, she'd been a ghost girl, barely here. Considering the whole Sofia thing, I figured she just needed some space.

But this morning had been different. Whatever happened between Vee and the auld laird before he passed had seriously messed her up. In our entire friendship, I'd never seen her so devastated — or withdrawn. Not even when her dad went MIA.

It was time for a Kennavention ... just as soon as she returned.

Moments after Vee slipped away, I watched Jamie follow. From what little she'd told me, Prince Not-So-Charming had a lot of sucking up to do. Maybe after some alone time they'd be able to reach an understanding.

To take my mind off my bestie's drama, I focused on the scene before me. Wooden tables, laden with food and drinks, bordered the length of the space closest to the church. At the far end, a band — complete with bagpipes and drums — began to set up just in front of the Doonian crest. The opposite side of the tent opened to reveal the spectacular shoreline of the Loch o' Doon. In the middle of the shore, a small wooden ramp sloped into the gently lapping waters of the lake. A rectangular pyre of twigs sat on the makeshift dock in preparation of the king's final journey.

As the good citizens of Doon gathered in the pavilion, the musicians took up their instruments. Accompanied by the sad, slow strains of the fiddlers, the bagpipes began to weave their haunting tale of sorrow. Perhaps Sondheim's spirit was present after all.

Fiona wove her way through the crowd to check on me. Her swollen eyes spoke of a grief I wasn't entitled to share. Feeling like an intruder, I picked the first safe topic I could come up with. "I think it might rain."

At my seemingly benign statement, Fiona stifled a sob. "Aye. I've no doubt that it will. The weather and the kingdom share a distinct connection. Although we have seasons, the weather is always harshest when we Doonians are — struggling." Her voice broke on the last word, and I decided my curiosity was better left unsatisfied. As she moved on, the first fat drops of moisture began to fall, giving the impression that the sky cried along with the people.

Or maybe these were the tears of God?

I'd heard someone say that about rain once, and the thought sent a shiver trembling up my spine. Would God cry at the death of one king? Or any single Doonian for that matter? What about my world? Had he cried over my mother? Would he cry for me?

He would cry for Duncan — that I was certain of. The younger prince of Doon had a simple faith that resonated from his being. He was kind and loyal, and ... good. Everything nobility ought to be.

My gaze roamed restlessly through the crowded pavilion, seeking the face of Duncan MacCrae. Over the past few days he'd been absent, busy with the Centennial and grieving over his dad. His playful banter seemed to have died along with the soldiers in the meadow. Now the unsettling feeling of missing him, if only as a friend, tugged at me.

He was easy to spot — a dark-haired hulk standing a full head above his peers. Well, not peers exactly ... In this case, he held court with a half dozen girls, each one prettier than the next. A dozen lashes batted in unison, as mouths of all shapes and sizes curved in empathy. Large doe eyes of every hue imaginable gazed up at Duncan with invitations of solace.

Thinking of him taking consolation in one of their arms made me feel like going postal. Stupid, stupid me. I'd had my shot ... and blew it. I could've kissed him in the meadow, but I'd taken the high road. Or the low, slinking road of cowardice, depending on how you looked at it. My heart twisted sharply with that observation, and I had to remind myself that it was better this way. I was leaving at the first opportunity.

Unable to continue watching the macabre flirtfest, I drifted along the edges of the pavilion until I came to the lake. Heavy rain caused a symphony of ripples on the water's surface. Little clusters of ducks and geese, reveling in the downpour, swam in jubilant pursuit of each another. At times, one or another would stop to dive for an underwater morsel, their duck butts quivering and bobbing along the water's surface.

In the midst of such aquatic frivolity, a single swan glided in complete isolation. The graceful black and white bird cast such a somber contrast to the reckless ducklings that I felt drawn to it. Wasn't it a bird like the others? Yet unaffected by the ducks' infectious play, it floated among them as an entity apart.

"Swans mate for life, ye know."

In my distraction, I hadn't heard Duncan approach. His smooth brogue caused me to jump in surprise and set my girl parts to tingling. "No, I didn't know." Intrigued by the noble swan, I returned to my contemplation of the lake and conveniently away from an even more captivating view.

"His name's Romeo," Duncan supplied. The words rolled softly from his tongue, making me long to hear him recite the soliloquy of Shakespeare's iconic hero. *O that I were a glove upon that hand . . .*

Pulling myself back to present, I asked, "Where's his Juliet?"

"Died."

The poignancy in that single word caused my chest to contract as I faced the prince. Grief etched deep lines around his eyes and the corners of his mouth. As I stared at him, Duncan continued to regard the lake with luminous eyes. "Five winters ago . . . Not a day goes by that he does not miss her terribly."

"How do you know?"

He turned to me with his weary, honest gaze and a tight smile. "Because they were inseparable. If ye were to watch them, you could feel how happy they were. Romeo's not been the same since his Juliet left him."

"What if you found him a new mate at the Centennial, maybe — "

"No. He wouldna take to her."

His face held more than a deep empathy for the bird, something honest but unfathomable. The golden flecks in his chocolate eyes shimmered as he leaned slightly forward and reduced the distance between us. Caught in his magnetic pull, I struggled to recall our dialogue — oh, yeah, swans, and mating for life.

I swallowed down the egg-sized lump that'd materialized in my throat. "It must be difficult to be a swan."

"But amazin' too. Swans are nature's true soul mates."

Duncan and I were not swans. Or Romeo and Juliet for that matter, and we hadn't — uh — mated. We were humans — plenty of fish in the sea, and all that.

Duncan cleared his throat. When he spoke, his voice cracked awkwardly. "Have you — uh — ever been to a funeral before?"

Okay, that was a random, personal segue. As I pondered my answer, I looked into his guileless eyes and the world slipped away. I felt myself nod without any conscious decision to open up. "My mom's — but I don't remember much. And then when my aunt passed ... I was twelve."

Quiet as a whisper, he said, "Tell me about it."

Under his hypnotic spell, I began to share. "I remember feeling devastated, lost. Everyone was telling me how sorry they were, but all I wanted was to be left alone. When I finally slipped away, I went to see an old friend. A boy, actually."

"And?" Despite the heaviness of the word, his face remained impassive.

"He kissed me." Never mind that Finn was imaginary — so the factualness of the kiss was questionable. Duncan didn't need to hear that part. "It was the last time I ever saw him."

"Have you been kissed since?"

"Oh, sure." I'd had my share of lip locks and tongue tangles, both on stage and off, though none had come even close to Finn. Made up or not, it was hands down the best kiss I'd ever had.

Following my unspoken thoughts, a deep sigh slipped from Duncan's mouth. "But there's nothing like your first."

"Exactly."

His dark, luminous eyes continued to work their magic, pulling me toward him like an invisible tether. As his lips came within striking range of mine, his long lashes fluttered closed. "Except, perhaps, kissing your soul mate."

Suddenly, I felt like I'd swallowed a mouthful of wriggling bugs. Pulling away, I tried to cover my panic by looking at the crowd. "When will the Coronation happen?"

That stopped him. His eyes snapped open and he blinked his confusion away before straightening himself. "Day after tomorrow."

So Saturday, right before the Centennial. "And the Brig o' Doon will open when?"

Between one heartbeat and the next, Duncan flinched as if I'd slapped him and quickly recovered. "Day after tomorrow at midnight."

And Jamie will name his betrothed ...? My mind flipped the sentence around trying to come up with a way of asking that wasn't totally obvious. When I couldn't work the question out, I gave up. Instead, I lowered my voice to just above a whisper. "And Gideon?"

He matched my volume. "Still contained. With everything going on, he won't be missed."

We just had to get through the next two days. "You've got a lot to do before the Centennial."

"Aye." Duncan raked his hand through his hair to create those brown, spiky peaks that were both chaotic and modern. "You've got something to do too."

Figure out your feelings.

He didn't need to say it aloud. It was scripted in the yearning on his ridiculously gorgeous face. But my choice had already been made.

I would have plenty of opportunity for romantic leads in my life. Once I returned to the real world. And Duncan would eventually marry one of the locals from his fan club. In time, we would be nothing more to each other than a bittersweet ballad of remembrance.

Which was what I wanted. Right?

"M' laird." A man from the village placed a sympathetic hand on Duncan's shoulder. He nodded somberly. "It's time."

With a final, sad smile in my direction, Duncan left to lay his father to rest.

🌀 🌀 🌀

As mournful bagpipes underscored the fiery bier floating toward the center of the lake, I thought about the beauty and savagery of the ritual I'd just witnessed. The voracious fire that consumed the pyre seemed jarring juxtaposed against the gentle motion of the water. Yet somehow, together, the pervasive impression was one of peace.

"Shall we return ta the castle?" Fergus, with Fiona clutched at his side, smiled down at me. Despite their obvious grief, they looked mighty cozy.

As my gaze darted from one to the other, Fiona intercepted my train of thought. For the first time since I'd met her, she blushed, a pretty pink that accentuated her wide cheekbones. She held a thick shawl in her outstretched hand. "Take this, Mackenna."

Mesmerized by the funeral ritual, I hadn't noticed how chilly it had gotten. Until now. The rain had finally stopped, but the cold front that followed in its wake seemed more like November than August.

As I wrapped the thick woolen shawl around my shoulders, Duncan and Jamie drifted our way. Hopefully, Vee and Doon's future king had been able to work some things out. I looked beyond the princes for some indication of her mood. But she wasn't there.

Doing a slow three-sixty, I examined the clusters of mourners to confirm what I already suspected. She wasn't anywhere in the pavilion. The irrational concern I felt at her absence rocked me to my core. It'd been hours since she'd crept back toward the church with Jamie in pursuit. Was that the last time I'd seen her?

"Jamie, where's Veronica?"

The tight smile on his face melted into alarm that mirrored my own. "Isn't she with you?"

"No. I haven't seen her all afternoon." In an effort to stay calm, I over-enunciated each word. Accusation flashed across his features and I clarified somewhat defensively, "She was upset and I was trying to give her some space."

Jamie's dark eyes grew as round as saucers as he, too, began to scour the crowd. "You let her leave?"

I began to doubt the assumptions that seemed so reasonable at the time. "I didn't let her do anything. She left. I was going to go after her — but then I saw you follow, so — I thought — "

Jamie's lack of recognition made me want to hurl. "Why'd you go back toward the church if you weren't following Vee?"

"To pray for my father's soul. 'Tis customary before the final rites." His voice was thick with condemnation, as if my being an outsider didn't excuse my ignorance.

Vee'd been missing for hours.

I sagged onto a nearby bench. Duncan's arms caught me just before my backside hit the wood and he eased me the rest of the way down. My chest tightened. The air squeezed from my lungs and made it difficult to speak around my fear. "You really didn't see her?"

Equal measures of rage and concern mingled in Jamie's scowl. He looked capable of flaying someone alive. "Nay."

Fergus cast a sheepish glance over the group. "She's not been with Fiona since the service. I woulda noticed."

Duncan still held me loosely from behind, the soft, reassuring brush of his fingertips as he stroked my back at odds with the steel in his voice. "How long has she been missing?"

I did some hasty mental gymnastics. "Three hours, at least. Maybe more."

Jamie swore and whirled around to bark at Fergus. "Where's Gideon?"

The gentle giant shot Duncan a guilty look while clearing his throat before answering his new king. Little beads of sweat appeared on his pink brow. Apparently lying was not one of his strong suits. "Gideon and his men are still in the eastern paddocks following a lead on the disappearances. But we've no' heard from him since yesterday."

"Bloody hell!" Jamie addressed me without apology. "Mackenna, are ye sure she didna return to the castle on foot?"

"It's possible." I negated the words with a shake of my head.

"But I don't think so. We've been stuck in the castle for days. She'd be too stir-crazy to go back."

Fergus's lips formed a grim line of resolve as he towered over us. I could see the self-recrimination on his face. He'd been focused on Fiona when his job had been to watch us — watch Vee. Now, he felt responsible. "I'll have one of the lads organize a search o' the castle. But we should search the village and the woods at the same time, m' lairds."

Jamie's response was practically a snarl. "Get it done, man."

Fiona put a gentle hand on my shoulder and spoke over my head to Duncan. "I'll get Mackenna back ta the castle, m' laird."

As I watched Fergus hurry away, my attention shifted to a single white speck floating downward from the sky. In slow motion, I reached out my hand and wondered as the tiny object came to a rest in my palm. A nearly perfect snowflake.

"It snows in summer here?"

Duncan, Fiona, and Jamie stopped mid-discussion to stare into my cupped hand. They watched the already melting snowflake dissolve into a speck of water. Duncan gaped in wide-eyed shock as Fiona pronounced, "Veronica's tryin' ta cross through the mountains."

Already on the move, Jamie growled at us from over his shoulder. "I'll get Fergus to stop the search parties."

Totally confused by Jamie and Duncan's reaction to the wintery weather, I twisted first toward Duncan and then Fiona. "Why is he calling off the search parties? And how do you know where she is? And what — "

Duncan gently, but firmly, cut me off. "We've no time for this right now."

"Time for what?" I struggled free of Duncan's arms and back onto my feet as Jamie and Fergus barreled toward us at a full run. Obviously, I was missing something. Something huge. "What the hell is going on?"

"Hell is right." Jamie skidded to a halt. His nostrils flared like a bull and his fisted hands jerked as if seeking something to hit.

Fiona looked at me, sympathy radiating from her kind face. I knew that look — it was the one people gave before breaking terrible news. "Your friend's tryin' ta leave the kingdom."

"No, she's not. She loves it here." If anything, I'd have to hog-tie and carry her back to Alloway when the bridge opened for the Centennial. "And she'd never leave without me."

But the panic on the faces of the three guys before me made me ask, "Why do you think Vee's trying to leave?"

"Because — " Jamie harshly snatched another errant snowflake and held it before me as evidence. "The borders are tryin' to stop her any way they can."

Fergus cleared his throat. "We must hurry, m' lairds. The mountain range is vast. We'll need ta split up."

I grabbed at Duncan's arm in desperation. "I'm going with you."

"Nay. If your friend doesna turn back, there's to be a full-on blizzard comin'. We'll not risk any more lives than is necessary. Fergus and I will go." Duncan stepped in front of Jamie and angled his body to block him. "You're our king now. You should stay behind as well."

"Not a chance." Jamie's eyes were hard slits providing no context to his granite features or his flat voice.

Duncan pulled free of my grasp and crowded his brother's personal space. "So you'd risk the crown then?"

Just as forcefully, Jamie leaned forward until their chests were less than an inch apart. "This isn't just about Verranica. If she makes it across the mountains and through ta the other side, we're all doomed."

"Whoa!" I appealed to Fiona and Fergus. "Would someone please explain?"

As the brothers glared at one another, Fiona tersely elaborated for my benefit. "Doon's borders are enchanted. Impassable. If anyone tries ta breach them, the kingdom itself'll stop them."

I thought of Vee — of how stubborn she could be when she got an idea in her head. I had no idea what motivated her to leave, but she would not give up easily. "What if she succeeds?"

"If she succeeds, the pact between Doon and our Protector will be broken," Jamie ground out.

As much as I dreaded what he'd left unsaid, I needed to hear it. "And?"

He ran a trembling hand through his snow-coated hair, combing the wet, blond strands away from his face. "If she doesn't get herself killed in her attempt to reach the border, the Covenant will be destroyed, and Doon will vanish into the mists. Don't you see? If she succeeds, it will be the end of us all."

The end? Numerous questions flitted through my head, but now was not the time. The snowfall was thicker, making it difficult to look at Jamie without shielding my eyes. "What do you need me to do?"

"Just get out of my way. I'm going after her. Alone." He growled as I scrambled out of his way. But Duncan didn't move. Coiled and ready to strike, Jamie angled himself closer to his baby brother. "You too."

When Duncan still didn't budge, Jamie raged, "Thas' an order from your king! Stand down!"

A muscle ticked in Duncan's jaw as he mutely took a half-step to the side. Without the slightest hint of remorse, Jamie continued, "Don't let that one" — he jerked his head my direction — "out of your sight until I return. That, too, is an order."

As Jamie shouldered his brother the rest of the way out of

his path, Fergus pleaded with him. "But, m' laird, how will you know where to look for the lass?"

Jamie tensed, but didn't turn around. In a voice thick with condemnation and colder than the winter storm, he answered, "Because I willingly gave her everything she needed, including her escape route. If Verranica succeeds, it will be me who's destroyed Doon."

CHAPTER 23

Veronica

Relentless, icy snow pelted my face, sticking to my eyelashes and obscuring my vision. The hood of my thin cloak had long ago soaked through and lay like a wet second skin on my head. Covered by the saturated fabric, my ears felt as if stakes were being driven into them with a giant hammer.

"Verrannica!"

Clearly, I was hallucinating.

I stumbled forward, my toes and fingers burning with a cold, penetrating fire. I'd almost turned back dozens of times, realizing the futility of getting anywhere in this raging blizzard. But despite the pitch-black night and the blinding snow, turning back wasn't an option.

The wind screamed through the mountain valley like an angry beast, pushing me to my knees. I sank down on my haunches in the snow and found I didn't have the energy to get back up. As I slumped forward, my eyes drifted closed and I lay my head on my legs. I'll just rest here for a moment, I promised myself.

I had to get the journal out of Doon. No matter what the cost.

That morning, while Kenna was in the bath, I'd thrown the book into the fireplace and watched the flames leap around it like it wasn't even there. After twenty minutes, I'd pulled the unblemished journal out of the blaze with a pair of iron tongs — it's flawless condition confirming my suspicion that getting the cursed object out of Doon was the only solution.

Since the bridge was impassible until the Centennial, I'd snuck away from the funeral, headed for Muir Lea. If I'd read Jamie correctly, very few people knew about the secret cliff path that lead down to the beach and out of Doon. But none of my plans or calculations had included this freakish blizzard.

The roaring in my ears clued me in to the fact I was not only hallucinating, frostbitten, and lost — but most likely dying. I should have confided in Kenna or even Fiona. If I perished now, the knowledge of the cursed journal would die with me and the witch would win.

No freaking way was I letting that happen.

Drawing together my last reserves of strength, I began to uncurl and get to my feet when a strange warming sensation permeated the hood of my cloak. I opened my ice-crusted eyelids and lifted my head. But instead of finding the endless snow-covered landscape, I stared directly into the eyes of the biggest animal I'd ever seen — a giant brown bear crouched so close, I could smell its rotten breath.

I choked on a scream and fell back onto my behind, the movement startling the animal into action. It took a step back and let out a furious, ear-splitting roar. I scrambled back on my arms and legs like a crab, cursing my snow-encrusted skirts. The angry beast stalked toward me, a deep growl vibrating from its massive chest.

Heart hammering, I continued to move backward on all fours until my shoulder slammed into what I assumed was a tree. Unable to take my eyes from the advancing monster, I pushed myself to my feet. Big mistake. Apparently, the bear saw this as a challenge, and rose to its full height. As it lumbered toward me on its hind legs, I swallowed a scream, afraid the noise would trigger the animal to charge.

If a bear attacked, you were supposed to poke it in the eye — or was that for a shark? I searched for a stick or rock, anything that I could use as a weapon. Nothing. Not that I had any delusions of defending myself against the eight hundred pound mass of muscle looming over me.

The next raging roar shook snow from the leaves above my head. Wicked-sharp claws and huge jagged teeth flashed in my face. I sent up a quick prayer and balled my hands into fists, bracing for the first strike.

Thwack!

The bear stumbled back, roaring furiously into the sky with a red-feathered arrow lodged neatly in its chest. Then it charged, its razor claws slashing toward me. I ducked as another arrow whizzed close by my ear, landing in the animal's muzzle. Dropping to all fours, it whined and swiped at the arrow with its paws.

"Let's go!" A tall hooded figure appeared beside me. He jerked me by the arm and we set off at a quick walk into the dark forest. The wind howled, whipping through the trees with an almost human anger. I leaned forward as my protector pulled me directly into its raging strength.

The unidentified archer wore a heavy fur-lined cloak, a scarf around his face, and a bow and quiver of arrows slung over his shoulder. Letting go of my arm, he looked back the way we'd come. I followed the direction of his hooded stare, and saw that the bear was no longer in view.

"Can ye run?" he yelled, his words barely reaching me over the wind.

Nodding, I picked up my pace. He stayed beside me even though it was clear he could've outdistanced me easily. We reached the other side of the glen and stopped at the base of a mountain path. As I pulled in deep breaths of icy air, the archer took the bow and quiver off his shoulder and lowered his scarf.

"Jamie!" I flew into his arms, clinging to his neck as if my life depended on it. If I hadn't been frozen from the inside out, I would've cried at the sight of the face I thought I'd never see again. He pulled my arms from around his neck and set me away from him. Oh, right; he hated me. But at least he was here.

He unfastened his cloak and shrugged it off. Swinging it around my shoulders, he lowered his face to within inches of mine — his cheekbones stained bright red and his lips pressed into a dangerous line.

"What the devil were you thinking!" he shouted as he fastened me into his cloak.

"I ... I ..." My teeth were chattering so hard speech was difficult. Not that I really knew what to say anyway.

"Never mind! Come on." Slinging his weapons back onto his shoulder, he took off up the path. I stood watching his long strides eating up the trail, shaking with cold and aftershocks of fear. The luxurious fur-lined cloak seemed only to trap the cold closer to my wet skin. When Jamie glanced over his shoulder and saw I hadn't moved, he came back for me, a mask of rage distorting his features.

"Dinna just stand there. We need to go now!" Grabbing my upper arm, he turned and guided me up the path. Although he'd nearly wrenched my arm from its socket, I was grateful for the support as my knees kept giving way on the steep, slippery trail.

Long, agonizing minutes blurred together as I forced my frozen, exhausted body to keep moving. Finally, we turned right onto a narrow path sheltered by giant evergreen trees. Here, there was only a light coating of snow, the trees a barrier to the harsh wind.

Then Jamie cut left and a door appeared as if set into the mountain. Pushing me through the entrance, he followed closely on my heels. He pushed the door shut and we were plunged into complete blackness. I blinked, blind and disoriented, with no choice but to trust him as he took my hand.

"There's a staircase in front o' you. Step up and hold on to the railing on yer right."

I followed his instructions like a robot. My fingers and toes stung with tiny needle pricks as my blood warmed. The soaked dress I wore hung on my shoulders like a thousand-pound weight. More than once, I tripped up the steps, with Jamie pulling me to my feet each time. After what felt like an eternity, we made it to a landing where he opened another door.

Moonlight flooded into the room through a wall of floor-to-ceiling windows, bisected by a massive stone fireplace. He led me to a sheet-covered sofa in front of an empty hearth. Judging by the animal heads hanging lifeless on the walls, I figured we were in some sort of hunting lodge.

"Sit." Jamie's voice was void of emotion as he pushed my shoulder, and I fell onto the cushions behind me. He stacked logs and kindling in the fireplace while I shook so hard I had to clench my jaw to keep my teeth from chattering like a battery-powered Halloween skeleton.

A tiny fire began to grow as Jamie knelt, blowing patiently into the flames.

"Ye need to get out of that wet dress."

I stared into the fire, and standing on shaky legs made my way toward the heat.

"Verranica."

My teeth clicked together uncontrollably, making words impossible. When I failed to answer, Jamie turned me by the shoulders to face him. His jaw clenched and his brows scrunched over his eyes.

"I'll be back." He let go of me, and I swayed but managed to stay on my feet. My brain felt like it was shutting down. Maybe I was in shock.

Jamie returned with a pile of clothing. "Can ye change or do I need to undress you myself?" Despite the small act of kindness, his mouth remained hard.

"I ... I ... cccann ... mmanange," I stammered between shakes.

"Fine. I shall be changing in the other room."

Several uncomfortable moments later, I wore a shirt that went down to my knees and huge trousers rolled and hanging on my hips. I wiggled my toes inside large wool socks, relieved that the feeling began to return. I'd stashed the journal under the cushions of the sofa — not an ideal hiding place, but since I didn't have a plastic bag it would have to do.

Sitting on the stone hearth, my arms wrapped around my bent knees, I was as close to the fire as I could get without burning my skin — and I'd finally stopped shaking. What was going on? Did summer blizzards occur often in Doon?

Jamie returned with two steaming mugs. As I watched him approach, my insides thawed, quickly reaching the molten state that was fast becoming a constant when he was around. He wore a dark cable-knit sweater, a casual pair of trousers, and his feet were bare. His golden hair was damp and curling against his neck. He handed me a mug as he sat on the stone hearth. Facing me, he kept one foot on the floor and bent one knee in front of him, resting the crook of his arm casually on top.

Not taking my eyes off him, I took a sip of the hot tea, the liquid sliding down my throat to warm my belly. He appeared to have calmed himself, except for a muscle that still ticked in the square line of his jaw. Several moments passed, the crackle of the fire and occasional howl of wind the only sounds in the room. I felt a compulsive need to fill the silence, but I wanted him to say what was on his mind first, so I distracted myself by shifting my attention to his large hands. His fingers, wrapped around his mug, were long and blunt, his nails almost perfectly square.

"Why? Why did ye do it, Verranica?" His eyes were narrow, his lips tight. I could see despite his casual posture, his anger was barely in check.

Turning away from his penetrating gaze, I stared into the dancing flames, unsure how much to tell him. "After you told me about your nightmares, I knew I needed to leave."

"Tell me why," he demanded harshly.

What was so hard for him to understand? "I figured it was the best way to protect ... everyone."

"You mean everyone, or yerself?"

"That's not fair," I said evenly, determined not to fuel his anger with my own. I set my tea down, straightened my legs, and put my feet on the floor. None of this was his fault.

"So destroying Doon was for the good of everyone?" He asked in a rough whisper, setting his mug on the hearth with a loud clunk.

"What?" My voice raised several octaves. "What are you talking about?"

I stood unsteadily and I stared down at him. "You're the

one who told me I was" — I made air quotes with my fingers — "contaminating the kingdom with my presence." His expression didn't change. "I was trying to save Doon, you pig-headed jerk!"

Jamie stood and grabbed my shoulders, his eyes burning into mine. "You stupid lass! I told ye if anyone crosses the borders o' Doon it would break the Covenant!"

"No! You said if you crossed the border."

"Don't tell me what I said or didna say."

I shook my head in denial. "I'm not even a citizen of Doon. You said I shouldn't concern — "

His hands tightened painfully on my arms, cutting off my words. "I meant that the rules were my burden to bear. I dinna say they wouldn't apply to you. If you've accepted Doon as yer home in your heart, yer a citizen."

"You're hurting me." I shrugged my shoulders and his hands dropped instantly.

He turned and began to pace, his every move punctuated by frustration. When he finally spoke, his words were as curt as his movements. "What did ye think caused the blizzard?" He took a step closer, his hands clenched into fists. "And the bear attack?"

I stepped back and stumbled over my own feet. Grabbing the sofa to steady myself, my stomach did a nauseating flip. He couldn't be saying what I thought he was saying — that I'd almost fulfilled his dreams by destroying Doon and everyone in it.

He advanced on me, his every move feral. I scrambled backward, shaking my head in denial of the awful truth.

"It was the kingdom, the enchantment trying to stop ye from reaching the border — and obliterating us all."

My knees gave out and I landed hard on the stone hearth.

How could I have been so colossally stupid? I buried my head in my hands so Jamie couldn't see my shame.

He grabbed my shoulders again and pulled me to my feet. I kept my arms locked, my hands on my face. Should I tell him about Addie and the journal? Show him proof of why I was trying to leave before the Centennial? Some deeply seeded instinct warned me against it. Without knowing how the witch's dark magic worked through the book, I might be putting Jamie in more danger.

"Verranica, look at me," Jamie barked.

Slowly, I lowered my hands and he released my arms.

"Tell me ye didna know," he demanded. His eyes bore into me, searching. "Tell me ye didna think leaving would destroy the kingdom!"

"Jamie, I promise. I didn't know. I didn't understand," I implored. "I was trying to protect you—by leaving."

Unable to face his condemnation, I tore my eyes away and focused on his chest. He thought I was in league with the witch and deliberately trying to destroy Doon and everyone he loved along with it. "No wonder you hate me."

A heated silence crackled between us. Had I spoken that last part aloud? It didn't matter. Nothing mattered. All I wanted to do was get away from him, but there was nowhere for me to go.

"Hate you? Is that what ye think?" he spoke in a hushed tone. His silence stretched on until I raised my eyes to his.

His body was wound so tight he looked like he might snap into pieces. When he spoke, his voice was deep and raw. "Do you have any idea what it was like when you walked into that throne room—my every dream and fantasy come to life?"

That, I could understand. Afraid to breathe, I nodded my head, remembering that first day I saw him at the tournament;

the sensation of all the blood draining from my body and my knees going weak.

"But all the while knowing you were the embodiment of my every fear?" He stepped back, raking a shaky hand through his hair. "Like seeing what ye want most in the world on the other side of an impossibly deep chasm, knowing you can never touch her or hold her …"

His eyes churned like dark waves in a storm. "Being near you is like being on a torture rack — my duty pulling me away from what my heart and body crave."

My stomach fluttered at his words, but questions tumbled through my mind, tangling my thoughts into knots. "But, if you believed the nightmares … why didn't you just make me leave as soon as I got here?"

"My da thought I'd misinterpreted them, missed some vital part that exonerated you … and I longed to believe him. But with my father so weak, the kingdom was at its most vulnerable. I couldna afford to think with my heart." He reached toward me, but stopped then lowered his hand and shoved it into his pocket. "Do you know before you came to Doon, I considered coming after you?"

I shook my head, speechless while my heart took up acrobatics in my chest.

"I begged my father to find a way for me to cross the bridge so I could find you in the modern world."

"Why?" I croaked, picturing my kilt-wearing, sword-wielding prince showing up at Bainbridge High — for real.

"I couldna wait round for the Centennial. Doing nothing was killing me. I had to know if you were real, if you were everythin' I'd dreamed … angel or devil." He stepped closer and tucked a strand of hair behind my ear. I shuddered under his fingertips. "But without the rings, there was nothing for me to do but wait for you ... to come to me."

Tears began to leak out of my eyes. With a half curse, half groan, Jamie gathered me into his arms. "So, no. I dinna hate you."

I slumped against him, unable to resist the comfort he offered. Resting my head on his strong chest, I sobbed. "I'm so sorry, Jamie. I'm sorry, for everything."

"Shh ... shh. Luv, stop," he whispered as he stroked my hair, resting his cheek against my head. I wanted to stay there in his arms forever. After a long moment, he guided me over to the sofa. "Here, sit."

I curled up with my feet under me, trying to regain control as Jamie gently wiped the tears that continued to stream from my eyes away with the pad of this thumb. The sweet, familiar gesture made my stomach tighten.

"Hush now, lass. I believe that ye didna purposefully seek to harm us."

"What about the warning dreams?"

His smile gone, he wiped my cheeks again, staring into my eyes. "Perhaps since I stopped ye from leaving, the danger has been averted."

But the true danger hadn't been averted — it was tucked under me in the sofa at that very moment. I hadn't yet completed my mission to get the journal out of Doon.

Jamie lowered his face toward mine. But as desperately as I wanted him to kiss me, I didn't know if I could survive the repercussions. "I thought you said to leave you alone?"

His face stopped a hairsbreadth away. "Tha' I did." His husky voice slid through me like hot, spiced cider on a crisp autumn day. I licked my lips, tasting salt, and watched in fascination as Jamie's pupils darkened, his gaze shifting to my mouth. "But I canna hold myself to the same standard."

The kiss was soft at first, his lips warm and firm on mine. Then his hand cupped my head and he increased the pressure, opening my mouth with his. Sparks shot from the base of my spine, setting all my nerve endings on fire. I lifted my hand to his face, the stubble on his cheek alluringly rough against my fingers. As the kiss deepened, his other hand caressed my neck, his thumb sweeping along my jawline.

I'd been kissed before, but never like this. Any illusions I still held of him as a picture-perfect fairy tale prince vanished in that moment. This boy knew exactly what he was doing.

When he slowly pulled his lips from mine, he was breathing hard. I stared up into his dark eyes knowing my emotions were written all over my face but unable to look away.

"Verranica, did ye dream about me?"

Did he know the power he held over me at that moment? That I would have done anything he asked?

Except tell him the truth. His dreams had warned him for good reason; I'd brought the witch's evil into his kingdom. I couldn't let him get too close. I still had to leave — get the journal out of Doon and make sure Jamie ended up with the right girl. So I told him a half-truth. "I had some visions, but they weren't really significant." I straightened, moving slightly away from the magnetic heat of his body.

"Indeed." His brows lowered over his eyes.

I turned away and swallowed the lump in my throat. Could I really do this? Push him away for his own good? Follow my head and not my heart?

"Vee, look at me." It was the first time he'd shortened my name, but it sounded so right on his lips. I turned back to face him. "Why are ye lying to me about the dreams?"

Staring into his impossibly beautiful face, I knew what I had to do. No matter how much it killed me. "Because I know you need to choose Sofia ... not me."

He jerked back as if I'd slapped him.

I rushed to explain. "It's okay though. I know she's the right one for you. But it still ... hurts." I stared down at my hands, wishing I could take back the last part.

"What makes ye think you know what's best for me?"

Doon did no' call ye here ta become its queen by marrying my son.

The king's words were perfectly clear. I wasn't meant to be with Jamie and I knew Sofia would make an outstanding queen. "I wasn't called —"

"Nay, let me finish. My whole life my father has told me what to do. My mother always wanted to shelter me. Everyone in the kingdom has tried to protect me. Do they fail to notice that I'm no longer a child?"

I certainly hadn't failed to notice, but I remained silent.

"Verranica, I've verra few choices that are mine. But this" — he grabbed my arm, his eyes drilling into mine as he crushed my body against his — "is still one of them!"

chapter 24

Veronica

As if to prove he could take whatever he wanted, Jamie surrounded me, his mouth crushing my swollen lips. A powerful rush of longing swept away the last threads of my self-control when the slant of his lips crossed mine, compelling me to return his kiss with all the love I felt for him. I wrapped my arms around him and moved my fingers into the silky hair at the base of his broad neck as I pushed closer to the solid heat of his body.

Our mouths broke apart, and a growl came from deep within his throat. "Mine."

He pushed me back on the sofa, following with his upper body, hesitating for a fraction of a second before his eyes glazed over and he lowered his head. His lips possessing mine again.

Out of nowhere, thoughts of Sofia in his arms and the king's final words swirled in my mind, warring with the need coursing through my veins. I really had to stop. But if I could have this one moment with the boy I loved, shouldn't I take it?

I closed off my conflicted conscience, melting into the glorious feel of his lips on mine.

With a start, I realized his fingers were moving against the buttons on my shirt. His rough knuckles brushed urgently against the flesh below my throat. The tug and slide of the first button was amplified against my hypersensitive skin. When he arched back to reach the rest, a warning bell began to sound, growing louder by the second. With effort, I stilled his hand with mine.

"Please," I said against his mouth. "Stop."

"Did I hurt ye?" he whispered.

I shook my head silently, afraid if I spoke again I might beg him to keep going. Our eyes locked in a soul-piercing gaze as his warm, intoxicating breath mingled with mine. Then his jaw tightened and he squeezed his lids shut.

In the next instant, he was gone.

With a deep, steadying breath, I sat up and adjusted my clothes while Jamie moved to the other side of the room. His fisted hands braced against the window casing as he rested his forehead against the icy windowpane and stared at the wintery landscape. The tension in his posture caused reality to infiltrate my fuzzy brain, and shame washed through me. I was supposed to convince him to be with Sofia. Not make this harder on both of us.

"Jamie?" I whispered as I rebuttoned my shirt.

"Just give me a moment," he ground out through clenched teeth.

Was he struggling to gain control? Or was he angry that he'd let it happen at all?

He began to pace, running his fingers through the top layers of his hair, causing it to fall in a tangle over his forehead. Even distraught and rumpled, he resembled a Greek statue come to life.

Forcefully ignoring the ache of longing the sight of him stirred within me, I focused on restarting the necessary, but painful, conversation I'd begun earlier. "Jamie —"

I stood, clutching the ridiculously large pants before they fell down around my knees. "I'm not trying to make any decisions for you, but it's obvious you have feelings for Sofia and have for some time. You've only known me a few days." I couldn't bring myself to tell him what the king had said to me; it would only make him feel as if his father were controlling his destiny from the grave.

He stopped pacing and stared down at me like I imagined Heathcliff had with Catherine. And look how their romance turned out.

"You've known her your whole life. The people of Doon trust and care for her." Then, before I lost the courage, I rushed on. "How could anything you feel for me compete with that?"

As I stared into his expressive eyes, the emotions warring across his face convinced me I'd made my point. I may be the shiny new toy that'd momentarily attracted his attention, but his relationship with Sofia had history and substance. And a future . . .

He took my hand and led me to the hearth, where we sat facing each other. Jamie searched my face. "Will ye deny the Calling then?"

I pulled my hand from his, realizing with a sinking heart that the more we touched, the harder our ultimate separation would become. "Considering the direction your dreams took, I don't know if we can ever be sure it was a real Calling."

I broke eye contact, unable to bear the expectation burning in his gaze. "Besides, you would always be watching me, waiting for me to prove your nightmares true. There wouldn't be any trust between us."

"I admit it would be much easier if I could put the dreams out of my mind ... put you out of my mind." He cupped my cheek, urging me to return his tortured stare. "But I canna. Can you?"

Ignoring his question, I turned away from him and unwound my damp hair. The mundane task of fanning the strands out in front of the fire helped to distract me from the temptation sitting way too close.

"Has anyone ever told you that yer so beautiful you glow?"

Chills raised the hair on the back of my neck. Trying to act as if his words didn't affect me, I shrugged. "No."

I felt him close the distance between us and stifled a groan of frustration.

"Let me do that for ye, love."

My arms dropped into my lap as if they had a will of their own. Jamie pulled his fingers smoothly through the strands of my hair, and I wondered if this was part of his strategy to win me over. But as he repeated the motion, his fingers brushing the nape of my neck and massaging my scalp, I forgot to care. Melting into a puddle of spineless goo, I was ready to curl up on his lap and purr like a contented kitten.

Seriously, how much more could a girl take?

"Do ye not care for me, Verranica? If no', then tell me to leave ye be." His deep voice was hypnotic. And calculating ... and controlling. At least that's what I tried to believe as I steeled myself to say the words that would turn him away from me forever: I don't care for you a bit, Jamie MacCrae ... I could never love you.

But when I opened my eyes to his beautifully noble face only inches from mine — looking as if I were the only thing that mattered in his world — the lie died on my lips.

His mouth shifted into a lazy grin. The hand that'd been

stroking my hair cupped my jaw. His thumb rested on my chin as he tilted my face and lowered his mouth toward mine, his tempestuous scent weaving its spell around me.

He watched me under heavy lids as the pad of his thumb swept over my bottom lip. "I canna resist you."

Oh no! I turned into a mindless lemming when he kissed me. I could not let it happen again. My mission repeated in my head. It was my only defense. Get the journal out of Doon and make sure Jamie ends up with the right girl — which, heartbreakingly, wasn't me.

"No!" I practically yelled the word as I jumped up, my exhausted body betraying me when I stumbled back several steps.

Jamie was up in a heartbeat, his powerful arms steadying me.

"Please don't," I whispered, trying to twist away from him. He loosened his hold but didn't let me go. Afraid if I met his eyes he would try to kiss me again — and this time, I wouldn't have the strength to resist — I stared at the spot where the edge of his sweater met his neck. It was such a nice neck: smooth, tan skin, the slightest bit of stubble leading up to his square jaw, and — the delectable dimple in his chin. Then my hand was on his face, my thumb sweeping across the indentation that'd fascinated me from the first moment I saw him.

Apparently, I had no willpower whatsoever.

I lifted my eyes to his and felt dizzy, like gazing into an endless midnight sky sprinkled with stars. Gently, he took my hand away from his face and held it between us, his expression becoming uncertain.

"I'm not myself around you, Verranica. When you look at me with those captivating sea-green eyes, I canna even think straight." He swallowed, hard. "I canna fight what I feel for you any longer ... I dinna want to."

My voice stuck in my throat. As I searched his face, a gust of wind blew down the chimney, fanning the flames and causing sparks to sputter onto the hearth. I couldn't let him say any more; I had to find a way to convince him I wasn't the right choice for him or his kingdom.

Pulling out of his arms, I pursed my lips. "Do you want to know what I think?" Before he could respond, I continued, "I think the Divine Protector of Doon would be gravely disappointed that his new king was being so selfish. If your faith was strong, you would know the warning dreams were for good reason." I watched him turn steely, but I rushed on.

"We aren't meant to be together, Jamie." I swiped at my tears. Now was not a time for crying. There would be time enough for that later. "You asked me if I care for you, but my feelings are irrelevant. So are yours. Don't you see? It's not about us. It's about what's best for the people of Doon. Your people."

"Don't I get a say in what's best for my people?" he asked as he stalked toward me. I held up my hands to warn him off, as I could see by the hardening of his expression his patience had come to an end.

"You don't even know me, Jamie. How could you know if I'm good for the kingdom or not? You know nothing about my life before I came here." On shaky legs, I slumped down on the couch, and cleared my throat before continuing. "I'm just a momentary distraction. You'll forget about me once I cross over the bridge."

"Never." His jaw was set in rigid determination, but it was his dark, imploring eyes that sucked the fight right out of me. "Vee, you dinna — "

"Just stop." I shook my head. This conversation was getting us nowhere. "Can we talk about this later? I'm so tired." It wasn't a lie. As I curled my legs beneath me, I yawned and my eyelids fluttered closed for several seconds. Emotionally and physically drained, I didn't have the strength left to argue.

Despite my best efforts to stay upright, my head lowered to the arm of the couch, and exhaustion washed over me like a corporeal force.

Several moments later, I blinked to discover Jamie as he squatted down in front of me, concern shining from his face. He reached out and tenderly brushed my hair off my cheek.

"Do the right thing ..." I wasn't sure if I spoke the words aloud or said them in my head. "Make Sofia your queen."

"Dinna worry, I will ... Sleep now, love. We have the morrow."

I think I smiled at him — my beautiful prince, I thought dreamily, before sleep swept me away.

🌰 🌰 🌰

I awoke to the harsh light of day and the knowledge I had a little over forty-eight hours left in Doon. I just prayed that the Covenant would protect all of us from the witch's malice until I could get the journal out of the kingdom. Now that I knew I couldn't leave until the portal opened at the Centennial, each minute felt like a ticking time bomb.

In vain, I searched for a clock. How much time had I wasted sleeping?

Jamie must have covered me during the night because I was buried under a mountain of thick wool blankets. Rolling over and sitting up, I became aware that the sun was high in the sky, filling the cozy room with early afternoon light.

Make that less than forty-eight hours left in Doon.

With a sigh of resignation, I pushed off the covers and stood with a yawn. A sleepy-eyed Jamie emerged from the other room in the pants he'd been wearing the night before — and no shirt.

Oh no.

His broad shoulders and perfectly sculpted torso would've put the models on the giant Abercrombie and Fitch posters to shame. He was all bronze skin and smooth muscle.

"Good mornin'." His voice sounded rough from sleep. Rubbing his open hand against his eight-pack abs, his eyes crinkled against the sun and a languid grin spread across his face. He'd never looked hotter — correction, I'd never seen anyone look hotter. As my pulse skyrocketed out of control, I acknowledged that I'd made a huge mistake. I should've demanded he take me back to the castle the night before, no matter how exhausted I'd been.

"Good morning," I mumbled as I self-consciously smoothed my hair and straightened the huge shirt he'd loaned me.

"Oh!" Startled, I glanced down at my bare legs. I was fairly sure I'd been wearing pants the night before. I tugged the shirt down to cover my thighs and wondered why I felt so embarrassed. My cheer-skirt barely covered my behind, and I'd practically lived in it during football season. Maybe it was all the long skirts and stockings I'd worn for the last two weeks.

"What are ye — Och!" Jamie cut off as he noticed my missing clothes.

"I must have kicked them off during the night," I explained as I sat next to the mound of blankets and began searching for my pants.

"I have seen legs before, ye know," Jamie said with studied casualness.

I glanced up to find him staring at me with a boyish grin, his eyes fixed on my one bare leg visible between the disarray of blankets. I was pretty sure viewing a woman's naked legs — especially the length that was currently visible below my shirt — would be considered taboo in his culture. Something about the situation made me feel giddy — and a little powerful.

Without taking my eyes off him, I experimentally removed the blanket covering my right leg and watched in satisfaction as his eyes widened. Slowly, I stood, allowing the shirt to fall into place just above my knees. Jamie cleared his throat but his eyes stayed locked in the downward position. Knowing I was playing with fire but unable to resist, I lifted my arms above my head with a great yawn. As I stretched onto my toes, the hem of the shirt rose to the top of my thighs.

"By the saints," Jamie muttered, shoving a hand through his sleep-tousled hair.

Fluidly, I lowered my arms and brought my feet to rest flat on the floor. The knowledge that I could beat him at his own game filled me with wicked satisfaction. Then I caught his eye, and the forceful heat of his stare hit me like a wave, almost knocking me back onto the sofa. With great deliberation, he moved in my direction. And I knew I was in way over my head.

"Ah … Jamie? I ah … need to … Is there a privy I can use?"

"Aye, it's through that door." His voice low, he pointed in the general direction of the room he'd slept in. But with a mountain of blankets blocking my most direct path and Jamie advancing toward me, I was trapped.

Teasing this particular boy had been a bad idea — especially in light of the lecture I'd given him the night before. I pivoted to my left, leapt over a small pile of blankets, and ran around the back of the sofa. Feeling like the worst kind of coward, I stopped and faced him with the large piece of furniture between us. The corners of his mouth turned down in a disappointed frown.

"Um … I'm sorry?" It came out as a question because I didn't have any idea how to diffuse the situation. I offered him a small smile. He stared at me blankly for several seconds and then grinned.

"No, I'm sorry. I suppose I have no' seen legs — ah — like yours before." He shrugged ruefully. "For future reference, lass, dangling bait in front of a hungry shark is a bad idea."

The laughter bubbled out of me. "Really? Thanks for the advice."

Jamie picked up a clump of brown cloth and threw it at my chest. "I think ye better put these on. Before I do somethin' verra un-princelike."

My eyes widened at the implication of his words. Quickly tugging on the pants, I sprinted from the room.

Safely ensconced in the small — but to my immense relief, well-equipped — bathroom, I leaned against the door, sucking in ragged breaths. I had to remember my goal — get the journal out of Doon and, in the process, get myself out of the way, so Jamie could marry Sofia and live happily ever after.

Less than forty-eight hours, Veronica. You can do this!

I walked over to the sink, splashed cold water on my face, and then left the room in search of Jamie. Following the scent of eggs frying in butter, I found him in the kitchen. Thankfully, he was wearing a shirt and ... cooking?

"You're making breakfast?" I asked in disbelief.

"Aye, I'm no' an invalid, you know." He gestured with his spatula. "Take a moment to enjoy the view."

The kitchen jutted out over the treetops at a right angle. Wood framed windows lined three of the walls, giving an unobstructed view of the valley below; a sea of verdant trees made even more vibrant by sunshine glistening off the melting snow.

Jamie set two plates of over-easy eggs, bread, and cheese on a small table. "After you, m' lady," he insisted, holding a chair out for me.

I took the seat he offered and breathed in the savory aroma of hot eggs. My mouth watered and I realized I hadn't eaten since yesterday morning. Jamie brought two mugs of steaming tea to the table and sat down.

"Thank you," I said, genuinely impressed.

"Yer quite welcome."

A small smile lifted the corner of his mouth and I couldn't look away. I searched his face, longing to find some fault with him, some desperate flaw that I could cling to, so when I compared guys to him in my future — as I inevitably would — they wouldn't fall miserably short in every way.

Ah, crud, I might as well become a cat lady!

I tore my eyes away from him and stabbed my eggs with such force that my fork clinked against the plate. I refused to think about the gaping black hole that was my future. Instead, I focused on filling my belly.

"So, what part of America are ye from?" he asked as he chewed — talking with his mouth full, per usual.

"Indiana. A small town in the midwest called Bainbridge."

"And yer parents? How are they?" His expression was indecipherable and so fascinating I had to force my attention away from him and back to my food.

Gathering a bite of cheese and eggs on my fork, I contemplated the best way to answer his question. "My parents split up when I was twelve and ..." I swallowed, but the food stuck in my throat. I gulped a mouthful of scalding tea and then stared out the window. Maybe telling him I lived in the shoddiest part of town in a run-down two-bedroom rental house with my chronically absent mom, or that my dad chose drugs over me, wasn't the best idea. I didn't want him to see me as some charity case, or worse, someone who needed rescuing — well, more rescuing.

I turned back to the table and found Jamie watching me contemplatively. "And?"

"And I haven't seen my dad since." I shrugged. "It's no big deal, it was a long time ago."

Jamie set his fork down with exaggerated slowness. "Tell me about him." He paused. "Please."

I stared at the boy of my dreams, his golden hair falling in wavy locks across his forehead, his brown eyes brimming with warmth and encouragement, and the words began pouring out of me.

"He was a great dad, never missed a single dance recital, bedtime story, or family dinner, but then both his parents died within months of each other. He couldn't handle it, I guess. He began disappearing for days at a time, coming home strung out — on drugs, I mean." Jamie nodded his understanding, so I continued. "After awhile, he barely remembered my name." Jamie took my hand in his large, rough fingers.

"On my twelfth birthday, I woke to find the dad I used to know, his face open, his eyes clear, and I knew it was going to be a good day." I stared out the window, but all I could see was my dad's face as it had been that day, asking me what I wanted for my first "big girl" birthday. "I told him I wanted a strawberry-flavored cake with pink frosting, and a surprise."

My gaze shifted back to Jamie, he was leaning forward in his seat, sheltering my hand in both of his. "Daddy said, 'Okay, Sweet Pea, one pink cake and a special surprise coming up!' He hugged me and said he'd be back before dinner."

I swallowed, my words coming out in a whisper. "That was the last time I ever saw him."

Jamie was out of his seat in a blur and pulled me into his arms before I could blink the gathering tears out of my eyes. He stroked my hair from the top of my head, down to the middle of my back, making soothing noises. I rested my head on his chest, feeling the strong steady beat of his heart resonate inside me.

"Verranica, I'm so sorry."

I blinked rapidly and clenched my teeth against the memories of my past life, trying not to dwell on what little I had to go back to, or how being in this boy's arms made me feel like I was home for the first time in a long time.

"He has no idea what he's missing."

I leaned back and stared at him, my brows scrunched over my eyes. "What did you say?"

He smiled a sad, sweet smile. "I said, he's an idiot and he has no idea what an amazing daughter he has." He said the words simply and with such sincerity that they washed over me like absolution. I closed my eyes, but the tears flowed hot over my cheeks anyway. How was it possible he knew the exact right thing to say? The words I'd secretly longed to hear, but hadn't realized it until they came out of his mouth?

I smiled at him through my tears. "You have no clue how perfect you are, do you?"

"Well ... ah." He scratched his head and looked away, his cheeks turning pink.

I couldn't believe it — I'd made Jamie MacCrae blush. Absurdly pleased with myself, I moved out of his arms and danced away from him. He laughed softly before sitting to finish the last of his meal.

Unfortunately, this happiness couldn't last.

I stiffened my back and began to clear away the dishes. "I think it's time we head back to the castle. You have the Coronation to prepare for, right?"

"That I have," he stated as he stretched his arms over his head and then hooked his elbow around the chair spindle, fixing his dark eyes on my face. "I do have one request of you, before we head back."

I nodded my head, indicating he should continue, afraid to trust my voice.

"Since I believe we can both agree that I saved yer life last night ..." His smile was confident and a little bit wicked. "I would ask something of you in return."

My stomach clenched into knots. He had rescued me from the bear, it was true, and a part of me felt willing to give him anything he asked for, as long as it didn't derail me from my goal. "Go on," I said flatly.

He wiped his mouth and stood. "Come to the Coronation and the Centennial Ball."

"I don't know ..." The thought of watching him and Sofia become engaged, although I knew it was the right course, could very well push me over the edge.

"It would give me strength to see ye there."

I swallowed hard, his statement moving me more than I cared to admit. "I'll think about it."

"Fair enough. Let me just do one thing, then we can go." And with that, he grabbed the back of my head and kissed me full on the mouth before stalking out of the room.

Affected beyond reason by the simple kiss, I forced myself to refocus. All I had to do was prevent the witch from hurting anyone else before I could remove her evil vessel from Doon. And watch the boy I loved be crowned king and announce his engagement to a mini Italian goddess. While I was at it, maybe I would schedule some time to have my heart cut out of my chest.

Chapter 25

Veronica

The journey back to the castle alternated between tortuous bliss and blissful torture. I didn't know which I wanted more: for our time to be over quickly or to drag it out as long as possible. In the end, the beauty of the day tipped the scales toward procrastination. Well, that and the company — Jamie hadn't left my side all morning, taking my hand to help me across a fallen log, lifting me over puddles, brushing tendrils of hair off my cheek, all of which made maintaining a comfortable emotional distance next to impossible.

We made our way out of the forest and through the lush hills, past rushing streams, flowing clear and pure, around fields of golden gorse and wild heather, and along meadows populated with grazing stags. In the light of the lovely summer countryside, it was almost as if the hellish blizzard of the night before never happened.

"Not far now, Vee. Come, I wish to show ye something." He grabbed my hand.

Walking so close beside him, I felt small — in a delicious,

protected kind of way. I squeezed his hand, smiling as he led me off the path to the edge of a steep drop-off.

"Oh my —" The entire kingdom of Doon stretched before us. Slate-blue castle turrets soared into the sky, replicated in the sparkling mirror of the lake. The steeple of the Auld Kirk towered above the trees, standing sentinel to the winding cobblestone streets of the village. My Christmas village, I thought, wishing I could stay here forever. My stomach twisted in longing.

Shaking off my melancholy, I pointed west and asked, "Are those the flags of the tournament stadium?"

"Aye." The single word contained all the pride and adoration he felt for his kingdom.

"This is the most beautiful thing I've ever seen."

"Not me."

I met his eyes as they moved possessively over my face, and my pulse soared like a hummingbird taking flight. Desperate to divert his attention I blurted, "Someone should build a house here. This view is amazing!"

"That is an excellent idea. Maybe I shall."

"You?" I stared at him in mock horror. "Don't you think an enormous castle and a hunting lodge are enough for one young monarch?" But I couldn't stop the impish grin from spreading across my face.

"Dear Miss Welling," he teased, the long dimple appearing in his cheek, "the castle is a public building and the lodge is used by many. Maybe I long for a place o' my own." He pulled lightly on the end of my braid, his eyes full of insinuation. "Or maybe a retreat to share with another. I imagine it shall be advantageous to have a wee bit o' privacy once I" — he winked — "take a queen."

"Oh, don't be a perv!" I smacked his arm and immediately

clutched my stinging fingers with my other hand. The guy's biceps were ridiculous.

Jamie just laughed and hopped away from me.

Turning around, I headed back down the trail, leaving him to follow me or not. The image of him building a house on this hill to share with Sofia made me almost blind with jealousy.

After a few moments, I heard him jog up behind me. "What is a perv?"

I glanced at him. "You know, a pervert ... a sexually depraved lunatic."

"You think I'm some kind o' crazy sex fiend?"

With satisfaction, I saw his eyes widen in shock while I managed a nonchalant shrug. "If the shoe fits ..."

"Well, what would that make you then, little miss dance-around-the-room-wi'-no-trousers-on? Hmm?"

I stopped and he kept walking.

There was no way he could know I did that on purpose — could he? "I didn't — you don't think I — "

He turned to face me, and crossed his arms over his chest, goading me with a single raised eyebrow.

"Well — I certainly did not dance!" I insisted with a huff.

"A pity, that." He took a large step closer, his eyes narrowing with intent.

I stepped back and he advanced. I turned around to run, but he grabbed my arm from behind and spun me around with enough force that I hit his chest with a loud "Umpf!"

"Who taught you manners anyway? Geez!"

"I'm sorry but I couldna resist. You're just so adorable when you're bein' self-righteous."

His smiling eyes shone into mine, then something shifted, and the dark power of his gaze caused me to panic. "Verranica, I ..." He hesitated, clearing his throat.

I pulled back, but his arms tightened around me.

"No, please dinna pull away. Touching ye is like breathin' …
I canna seem to stop myself." I wanted to shut him down, keep
him from breaking the spell of the idyllic afternoon, but against
my better judgment I kept silent.

"I've never known anyone like you. Ye challenge me and
make me see things in ways I couldna on my own. I heard every
word you said last night. Ye shamed me a bit."

He paused, favoring me with a brief flash of straight, white
teeth. But the gravity in every line of his face stopped my breath
as I anticipated his next words. "Nevertheless, ye made it clear
to me what was right — what the Protector's will is for the kingdom and what I must do for the realm."

My heart beat painfully in my chest, full to the point of
bursting with the conflicting emotions inside of me. Being with
him felt so right — so perfect — that I opened my mouth to tell
him everything about Addie and the journal. And beg him not
to marry Sofia.

But just as the words formed on my tongue, I stopped. The
journal, tucked into the tightly rolled waistband of my pants,
seemed to burn against the flesh of my stomach. A terrifying
image of Jamie taking the tiny book and falling dead at my
feet flashed through my mind. As much as I wanted to tell
him everything, I couldn't dismiss the warning in both of our
dreams or the counsel of the dying king. My purpose was not to
stay in Doon, but to get the witch's evil out of the kingdom, so
Jamie and Sofia could fulfill their destinies as king and queen.

So, I swallowed my heart and said, "I'm glad. Thank you
for telling me."

He searched my face, his eyes churning like the ocean before
a storm. Without warning, tears tracked down my cheeks.

"Ah, Vee," he whispered before his mouth took mine, his

hands cradling both sides of my face. I pressed against him, tasting the salt of my tears on his lips. Knowing this would be the last time I felt the heat of his body surrounding me, the bliss of his lips on mine, I returned his kiss with everything I couldn't say.

"Ho, laird! Is that you up there? Lad, where have ye been?" A disembodied voice shattered our last private moment before I was ready to let go.

Jamie pulled his mouth from mine with a violent curse, but kept his hand on my cheek, forcing me to meet his eyes. "Can you trust me? That I'll make the right decision?"

I nodded, wiping the tears from my face. "Of course," I whispered. I was crazy, head-over-heels in love with Jamie MacCrae; trusting him was easy. The question was, did I love him enough to let him go?

As we entered the cool stone interior of the castle, a young man I recognized as a royal steward walked quickly in our direction.

"Sire, we must go immediately." The man stopped in front of us with military precision, his hazel eyes focusing somewhere over Jamie's left shoulder. "I've taken the liberty o' assembling the coronation team in yer office suite. The tailors have just arrived and must get a final fitting fer your ceremonial ensemble. There's also been another dispute over the east highland property—"

"Whoa, man." Jamie cut the austere young man short with a lift of his hand. "Excuse me for one moment, Verranica."

They walked a short distance away as Duncan and Kenna entered the vestibule. A wave of relief swept through me—swiftly followed by a sinking dread. Would they forgive me for putting them in danger—almost destroying us all?

I turned in Kenna's direction, but Jamie's words stopped me in my tracks. "And send a note to Sofia Rosetti and request she meet me in my suite as soon as possible. Give me ten minutes to greet my brother, then I'll join ye."

Reality smacked me upside the head like an icy ball of snow. Dragging in a deep, ragged breath, I reminded myself it was better this way, better that he'd chosen the right girl—just as I'd urged him to do. So why did it feel like the world had just dropped out from under my feet?

Kenna rushed forward, her wide gray eyes shimmering with unshed tears as she threw her arms around me.

"I'm so sorry!" I cried, hugging her with all my might.

"I'm just glad you're safe," she whispered fiercely in my ear. Duncan grinned at me over her shoulder and then headed to his brother. Ken leaned back and gripped my arms. "But if you ever pull a stunt like that again, I'll kill you with my bare hands!"

"No worries." I shook my head and bit my bottom lip to keep it from quivering.

"Hey, it's okay, Vee. You didn't know what would happen."

Not wanting to get into my sad tale in front of everyone, I let her misunderstanding of my teetering emotions stand. Unable to stop myself, I glanced over at Jamie.

"Hey, did you just get back? Who found you?" she asked in a Kenna-whisper.

"Jamie," I muttered with a tiny shake of my head, trying to signal for her to shut it.

"Wait. You spent the entire night with him?" Every head in the courtyard swiveled our way.

Heat crept up my face, as my eyes locked with Jamie's. His lips curved into a slow, wicked smile, stealing the pulse from my body. Funny how he could do that without even touching me.

"Okaayy. What's going on?"

"Later," I ground out between clenched teeth as I grabbed her arm and tugged her toward the arched castle doorway.

But before we could make our escape, Duncan strode over to us. "Glad you're back safe and sound, Veronica." With uncharacteristic awkwardness, he turned to Kenna and cleared his throat. "May I speak with you on the morrow?"

As if awkwardness were catching, Kenna shifted on her feet, suddenly unsure what to do with her arms. "Sure. I guess."

Duncan captured her flailing hand, and bent down to give it a hasty kiss. "Until the morrow then."

As he walked away, my friend lit up like a firefly, and I knew her heart was opening to him — whether she was willing to admit it or not. And unlike his brother, Duncan came with no baggage: no warning dreams, no almost-fiancée, and no mixed signals about wanting her in his life. It gave me hope that despite my own tear-jerker romance, her love story could still have a happy ending.

CHAPTER 26

Mackenna

Near-death experiences … Broadway would have us believe that they serve a greater purpose, like bringing reluctant lovers together. In some instances, it might be true. But for other relationships, it's the trigger that shatters them apart like glass. What these events don't do is significantly change the game. After the danger passes, the obstacles from before are still there, patiently waiting for the opportunity to dominate our lives once again.

Apparently, the other thing near death caused was fatigue. After a brief account of the blizzard and the hunting lodge, Vee crashed. By the time Fiona brought tea, she was sawing logs.

Not wanting to spend the evening alone, I invited Fiona to stay. I wasn't sure she would, since my bestie had instigated Snowmageddon. But I liked to think that Fiona had become the kind of friend who would stand by us, mistakes and all.

Just to be sure, I decided to attack the elephant in the room head on. "You're probably counting the seconds until the bridge opens tomorrow night, huh?"

Fiona placed the tea service on the little table in front of the settee and began to prepare our cups. "Far from it. I'll be quite sad ta see you and Veronica go."

"After we nearly destroyed your kingdom? Doubtful."

The girl pushed a lock of strawberry-blonde hair behind her ear and made a noise that sounded like *piffttt*. "It's good ta be reminded of our own mortality now and again. Reminds us what's really important in the final moments."

"And what would that be — for you?" The moment the question fell from my lips, I couldn't help but answer for myself. The image of the dark-haired prince with an easy smile and a fierce love of his realm filled my thoughts.

Fiona paused thoughtfully. "If it were truly the end, I'd want ta be with the person I loved best in all the world."

Her expression was so strange — so astute and knowing — that I couldn't help but worry she could read minds. Specifically mine. Averting my gaze, I folded a plaid blanket I'd left in a heap on the floor. "But you never thought the kingdom was coming to an end, did you?"

"Nay. I've faith you and Vee were both brought to Doon for a purpose. Ye couldna undo the Covenant unless it was the Protector's will." Finished preparing tea, she uncovered a tray of delicious-looking pastries. "My mum says I've a divine gift. Sight o' the supernatural."

"Isn't that like demons and zombies and stuff? I thought Doonians didn't believe in magic."

"The supernatural is about good and evil. The working of spiritual things beyond our understanding." She gestured I should sit with her. As I settled, she handed me a porcelain cup and saucer. "My gift merely gives me an insight into the eternal realm."

Her transparency encouraged me to show her the same

measure of honesty. As I helped myself to a strawberry and chocolate puff, I admitted, "I'm not sure I buy all that."

"Fair enough." She smiled and took a dainty sip from her cup before asking, "Do you mind if I give ye something to ponder?"

"Not at all." No one had ever asked me before if I minded them sharing their beliefs. I found myself surprisingly interested in what she would say.

"Would ye admit that the Protector o' Doon has dominion over our kingdom?" I nodded, which prompted her to continue while I nibbled on my treat. "So our enchantment comes from the eternal realm. And yet it seems the Rings of Aontacht brought ye across the Brig o' Doon by magic."

She paused to look at me sagely, before asking, "So which do you think it was — the Protector's will or magic which brought ye here?"

This felt like one of those baffling logic questions my dad was so fond of ... If a plane traveling from Spain to South America crashes in the Alaskan tundra, how many licks does it take the survivors to get to the center of a Tootsie Pop? I always hated those things; I mean, why worry about random events that could never happen? With no good answer to her question, I shrugged and waited for her to continue.

"Sometimes the Protector's will and the means he uses ta bring it about seem like magic. I can't say for certain that magic doesn't exist, since the witch would tell you her evil power comes from magic. But I'm of the opinion that she possesses no power in and of herself, that 'tis the Deceiver working through her."

My comprehension of her words was profound. "That's why Gideon and his followers are out to get us. They think we're pawns of the dark side?"

"Aye. They've forgotten the evil one isn't the only one with power. The physical laws of nature do not apply to the one who created them."

We were roughly the same age, and yet in that moment she seemed like a wise old soul. I couldn't help but wonder if that was a result of the slower aging process or something unique to Fiona.

"There's something I don't get ..." I set down my plate and began to pace about the room to work out my thoughts. "If the Protector shields Doon from evil, why are people so freaked out about the witch?"

Fiona tipped her head. "Freaked out?"

"It means panicked — agitated. Why do they think the witch could have any influence here?"

Fiona looked at me kindly. "Because she kin. When Doon was blessed, the witch was cursed fer her evil ways. She's forever connected ta us. As long as Doon prospers, she suffers terribly — her power is unsteady and weak. The only way the witch kin be free o' the curse is fer her ta destroy Doon and all the inhabitants along with it."

At the far end of the chamber, I pivoted, stage style, and retraced my steps. "But can she really do that? I mean, she was banished, right?"

"Aye, but even in banishment she's still connected to us. Everything is a balance, Mackenna. Without the witch, we would not exist — at least no' like this. There are times — windows — when Doon is verra vulnerable. This is one of them. And when Doon's weak, the witch grows strong ... as evidenced by the black petunias blossoming 'round her cottage. And she'll use any means she kin to get stronger. Even good people."

"I'm sorry." What else could I say? When the kingdom was most vulnerable, two American girls appear and everything goes sideways. They were right not to trust us.

She appraised me with her astute hazel eyes. "Dinna apologize. Ye've brought the Rings of Aontacht back ta Doon. And I suspect we're going ta have need o' them before this chapter in our history's done. Trust me when I tell ye, there's a purpose in all this."

⊛ ⊛ ⊛

"I didn't do it on purpose."

Tired of Vee's apologies, I launched a pillow at her head as evidence of my forgiveness. We both knew she was sorry and that she'd never intentionally do anything to harm Doon. Enough end-of-the-world angst already; I was ready to move on to the juicy stuff. Like the details Vee had so obviously omitted from her account the previous afternoon.

"Sooo — " I casually lounged on Duncan's giant bed, swaddled in his massive robe. At discreet intervals, I sniffed the flannel fabric, drawing Duncan's scent deep into my lungs. "Anything interesting happen between you and Jamie at the hunting lodge?"

Things had definitely changed between them. The king-to-be looked at her with a fierce possessiveness that did not make me want to do somersaults of joy for several reasons — the least of which was his very public entanglement with a teeny-weeny Italian.

Vee struggled for a moment. Her cheeks turned scarlet as a hint of a smile appeared and then melted from her face. "He kissed me."

Underneath her neutrality, I could see she was on the verge of an emotional breakdown. "Let me guess. The kiss was awful, like making out with a lizard."

"It was a little more than a kiss actually, and it was — um —

good." Her tongue swiped across her upper lip as if she could still taste him.

"Even better than Eric?"

"Who?" For a minute, my best friend drew a blank. Her impending breakdown dissipated as she thought harder and then laughed. "Oh, him. No comparison."

I feigned disappointment. "So Jamie couldn't even compare with Eric's superior skills? Now I'm wishing I'd made out with your ex when I had the chance."

In response, Vee lobbed the pillow-missile back at me. "Ow!" And then because I couldn't resist ... "Such a shame Eric's ruined you for all other guys."

"I am ruined — but not by him." The emotions started to gather again, fueled by her admission. I didn't need her to say *the Completing* or recount Jamie's summons to Sofia to know where her mind was. A moment later, she shook her head. "I'm being a self-centered shrew. Enough with my pity party — what did you do while I was gone?"

When I told her about spending the evening with Duncan in his chambers, she pursed her lips and said, "Oh, really?"

"It's not like you think. Duncan mostly read, and I did what I always do when I'm stressed."

She nodded sympathetically. "Show tunes?"

"My entire repertoire."

Although she tried to mask her disappointment, it wasn't her best performance. "You must've talked some, right?"

I thought about the degradation Duncan experienced when his brother had ordered him to stay behind and babysit like he was hired help. It was as if a light had been snuffed from his spirit. In the two weeks I'd known him, I'd never seen his features so tight and lifeless. He'd closed himself off and bordered on total jerk all evening.

But Vee didn't need to hear that. I wasn't about to tack any more mileage on to her guilt trip. "We were a little freaked out. I wish I could tell you we sat around singing end-of-the-world duets. But we didn't. We kind of went our separate ways — while occupying the same space. If that makes any sense."

"Oh." Vee frowned. She seemed genuinely upset that I hadn't shared the same kind of cataclysmic love connection with my prince as she had with hers. But in the great scheme of things, neither event changed anything. Closeness with Duncan would not deter me from leaving the moment the bridge opened any more than her closeness with Jamie would enable her to stay. The only true difference is I would leave by my own decision.

Not wanting to let her down entirely, I added, "We did sleep together — I mean in the literal sense — in the same room, together. Well, not together together. He slept on the floor and I slept in his bed. But with him just a few feet away, I slept hardly at all. And then when I finally dozed off, I had this crazy dream where he was Spider-Man and we were building an ark with — " I realized I was rambling and abruptly stopped talking.

Vee waggled her eyebrows with significance. "But you slept with Duncan?"

"Pretty much. I mean, he slept. I just lay near him and swooned all night."

A noise in the doorway, specifically the masculine clearing of a throat, announced the object of said swoonification present and well within earshot of my last comment. Completely mortified, I stared at Vee with huge eyes. With a grimace over my unlucky timing, my best friend dove into the bathroom. The only word I caught in her hasty retreat was "shower."

"Sorry to intrude." Duncan held a small silver tray in his big hands, embarrassment evident on his face. "I brought ye your breakfast, Mackenna."

The tray contained a mug of coffee, a covered plate, and a small green vase bursting with lavender. As I leaned over the arrangement and inhaled, my childhood came rushing back. All my happy summers spent in Alloway. Even the vase was a miniature version of Aunt Gracie's, right down to the design and shade — which made total sense, if hers had originally also come from Doon.

I breathed in again, pulling the calming scent deep into my being. "Not that you'd have any way of knowing, but lavender is my favorite flower. Thank you."

Duncan's gaze traveled from my face down the length of my body and slowly back up. "'Tis customary, I hear, when a girl sleeps with you."

"But we didn't — " His lopsided smirk stopped me midsentence. He was teasing me — at least I thought that's what he was doing. His light demeanor carried an undercurrent of something more serious that I couldn't completely define.

"Funny," I drawled, as Duncan set the tray on the end of the bed. "I was under the impression that if a maiden slept with an ogre, she'd wake up with a prince."

"And didn't ye?"

I slowly shook my head. "Sadly, no. Just the same smelly old ogre."

"Tha's too bad." His intoxicating brogue dropped a full octave. "Because I woke up with a vision o' loveliness."

The sparkle in his eyes confirmed he'd slain whatever demons he'd been battling the night of the blizzard. Just to be sure, I asked, "So you're, um, feeling better?"

"Aye. And I owe you an apology for my unconscionable behavior. Please allow me to make it up to you by escorting you to the ball tonight."

Step, kick, kick, leap, kick touch . . . Butterflies commenced an impromptu chorus line in my stomach at the thought of spending an entire evening decked out and on Duncan MacCrae's arm. I'd skipped prom — but didn't every girl deserve one night to be a princess? While my brain ranted about romantic entanglements and leaving as soon as the bridge opened tonight, my hasty heart ignored common sense and answered, "Okay."

Duncan's resulting smile put an end to any lingering objections. He removed the top off the silver tray with a flourish. "This is the other part of my apology. I made it myself in Mag's kitchen."

I leaned over the dish of fruit blobs and a plate of unidentifiable brown stuff. "What is it?"

With mock affront, he set the cover down heavily. "Melon balls and crepes. They're French."

I stared dubiously at Duncan's attempted cuisine. "I know what crepes are, but someone forgot to tell that stuff on the plate."

"You're a right hilarious lass, Mackenna Reid." He gave me a playful shove that would've knocked me onto my breakfast had I not tensed for it. The playful gleam in his eyes faded into something more responsible as he bounced impatiently on the balls of his feet. "Unfortunately, I canna stay. I've much to do before the coronation."

Disappointment burned through my chest. By tomorrow, I would be gone. Did he really want to waste the time we had left? Feeling reckless, I picked up a piece of melon and slowly slid it into my mouth with a throaty murmur of delight.

Duncan's gaze riveted to my lips as he eliminated the space between us in two strides.

His large hands settled firmly, yet gently, on my hips. I angled my head to the right in feigned surprise and his tipped left in a hormonally charged game of chicken.

Batting my lashes, I whispered, "Sure I can't tempt you to stay?"

"Nay." A muscled ticked in his set jaw as his dark head managed a nearly imperceptible shake.

He was trying to beat me at my own game. But my acting skills gave me an advantage, both in discernment and one-upsmanship. I pressed my palms flat against his chiseled abdomen — low — and had the satisfaction of seeing his nostrils flare as I gave him a light shove. "Then you'd better go, Ogre."

He overpowered my feeble attempt to repel him as if I were a paper doll. My heart thrummed against his body like an overexcited bird as he closed the gap between us. My eyelids drifted closed, as Duncan ... kissed the tip of my nose?

I sensed him straighten up, while I waited idiotically with my eyes shut and my lips puckered. I might as well have worn a neon sign around my neck that said, "Desperate." My lids snapped opened to find Duncan grinning at me. He appeared quite pleased with himself.

"Good-bye, Vision." With a light chuckle, he released me and walked away.

The pompous jerk had won our little match. But the knowledge that he could and would walk away from me left a bitter taste in my mouth. Yes, I wanted him to get on with his life, but I didn't want it to be easy. It wouldn't be easy for me.

Listening to Duncan's retreating footsteps, I felt like the unfortunate recipient of one of those cheesy vacation T-shirts: I slept with a Scottish prince and all I got was this lousy breakfast. Nauseated, I put the lid back on his sweet attempt at a homemade meal.

As soon as the front door closed, the bathroom opened behind me. Certain Vee'd been eavesdropping on my encounter with Duncan, I braced for her unsolicited opinion. Rather than comment about the tray of misshapen breakfast food, she tossed Aunt Gracie's journal on the nightstand and turned to challenge me. "Maybe you should think about staying."

"Not gonna happen."

Her big turquoise eyes pleaded with me to be reasonable. Well, her version of reasonable. "At least think about it."

"I have — and if I don't leave, I'll be trapped here. With no Broadway, and no guarantee that it would work out with Duncan. What if I stay for him and then he imprints or something?"

"Imprints? Uh, he's not a werewolf."

"You know what I mean. What if he has a Calling? Then I'll be forced to spend my very long life watching him make googly eyes at some skank that I've sworn to hate on sight."

Vee's eyes turned fierce as angry tears gathered in the corners. "Love is a risk. Even with a Calling, nothing is sure. But if you want him, you need to fight for him!"

Holy segue, Marvin Hamlisch! We were no longer talking about the absurd challenges of my love life. "So Jamie admitted that you guys have a Calling?"

She flopped onto the bed as if her bone structure was no longer capable of supporting the crushing weight of her disappointment. "Pretty much. But he's also got a duty to his kingdom, and a fiancée."

"Alleged fiancée," I countered as I sat beside her. "I haven't seen a ring on that freakishly tiny finger, have you?"

Vee propped herself up on her elbows so that I had the benefit of seeing the determined expression fueling her counterargument. "No. But Jamie's an honorable guy. If he's got an understanding with Sofia, he'll keep it."

"What about the honor in obeying his Calling?"

"Please, just stop." She rolled away from me onto her side,

signaling I had pushed enough for the moment. Vee didn't buckle easily, so I took the cue and backed off. She was afraid of getting hurt. I got that. People had been letting her down her whole life. But if she wanted this bad enough, she still had time to make it happen.

Changing tactics, I stood and walked around to sit on the other side of the bed. "Fine. You can make like Cinderella and disappear at the stroke of twelve. But until then, I'm acting as your FG."

"FG?"

"Fairy Godmother." I took Vee's hands and gently pulled her up until we were eye to eye. "I'm going to make you all fancy, then you're going to go to the ball and party like a rock star to ensure Jamie MacCrae regrets letting you go for the rest of his very long life."

Vee chewed her lip as she thought over my proposal. "Okay. I'll be your cinder girl, if you do something for me."

"Shoot."

"Pretend you're not turning into a pumpkin at midnight." When I started to protest, she cut me off. "Give Duncan a real chance. Let yourself be in love with him — just until we leave."

Could I pretend to love him? Vee gave me a slight nod of encouragement and I read her thoughts as easily as if they were my own. Even if Duncan and I hadn't shared a Calling, I was somewhat crazy about him. I didn't need to pretend I had feelings.

If I didn't make the most of our last night, I would most likely regret it for the rest of my life. Giving me the final push I needed, she extended her hand. "Deal?"

"Deal."

We shook on it and then Vee clasped me in a bear hug. When she pulled back, her face was troubled. "I've got to tell you something else. Another reason why I can't stay ..."

She hesitated long enough to take one of her deep yoga breaths. "I don't want to tell you, and I'd even convinced myself to keep it from you for your own good. But then I started to think about the situation being reversed and how I would feel in your shoes."

"Whatever it is — just say it."

Her grave eyes seemed far too old for her innocent face. "I know who the witch is."

"What?" Blindsided by her confession, my mind swirled with questions. "Who? And when? I meant how? And why didn't you — "

Vee held up her hand to stop my barrage and then paced away. "When I went to see the king, I had a vision ... or something. The journal's cursed. I wanted to tell you, but then the king died and all I could think about was getting it out of Doon. And — well — you saw how well that plan worked."

Deliberately, I stepped into her path and blocked her ramble. "Who is it?"

"It's Adelaide Dell — Addie, Dunbrae's caretaker."

I thought about the modern, stylish woman with her no-nonsense demeanor. "Addie's the old hag who's been after Doon for centuries?"

Her gaze narrowed and I could see her mind replaying events I couldn't see. "I read that the witch who attacked Doon was named Adelaide Blackmore Cadell. But in my vision, it was Addie."

"Do you think Ally knows?" I considered the sweet girl who'd shown us around Alloway.

"I don't think so. That's why she didn't bring Ally with her when she came to the cottage. She acted ... odd, remember? I'm certain she did something to your aunt's journal and then planted it for us to find — "

"Manipulating us into crossing the bridge." I didn't doubt Vee for an instant, remembering the way Addie fawned over Gracie's journal and calling my bestie a "clever" girl. She'd been the one to pack my aunt's things away in the first place. "That witch played us!"

"Yep. And I carried the journal into the kingdom for her." Vee squeezed her eyes shut in recrimination. "I'm responsible for everything that's happening. If she destroys Doon, it'll be my fault."

Fiona's words about the witch growing strong in Doon's weakness filled me with dread. Could the journal tip the scales in her evil favor? I indicated the book sitting benignly on the nightstand. "We need to destroy that thing, now!"

"We can't. I tried burning it, and when that didn't work ... well, you know what happened next." She tucked the small book protectively to her chest and walked to the window. "As soon as the Brig o' Doon opens for the Centennial, I'm taking the journal out. I've got to make things right."

I slung my arm around her shoulder, careful not to touch the cursed journal. Although she abandoned me, she'd been trying to protect us. I would not let her carry this burden alone any longer. "*We* are going to make this right."

For a moment, we stood in silence and contemplated the gorgeous view. The dazzling morning sun had eradicated the last icy reminders of the blizzard so that the idyllic countryside looked just like it had on our first day. Heather dotted the hills. Birds called back and forth. Doonians went about their lives. Ironically, it was as if the witch hadn't nearly succeeded in bringing about the end of their existence. For most living beings in Doon, everything was exactly the same as before.

CHAPTER 27

Veronica

A wise man once said love is a temporary madness. It was the temporary part I clung to like a life raft as I watched Jamie, strong and confident, go through the rituals that would make him a king.

He looked magnificent. His dress kilt, complete with formal jacket, was ornamented by his jeweled sword and the rich blue and green tartan of Clan MacCrae draped over his left shoulder — closest to his heart. I sat among the adoring masses, a silent participant while the emotions boiling through me threatened to erupt and rip the world in half. Was this the madness part?

The mirror told me I looked like a princess, with a burgundy fairy-tale gown and fantastical silver and garnet circlet woven into my hair as proof, but inside I was a quivering mess. I'd never felt more like a fraud. Everything inside me wanted to storm the stage and beg Jamie to ignore his destiny with Sofia. Beseech him to abandon his duty and run away with me, the king's vision be damned! But in the end, I would remain seated with a smile pasted on my face, pretending to be in control — just as I'd done most of my life.

Placing his hand on the Bible, Jamie took the oaths that bound him to his kingdom. With every word he spoke, the chasm between us grew more insurmountable. His fate more tightly linked to the girl he would claim as his queen.

Unable to watch another moment, I glanced up at the stone columns and vaults arching over my head. Fiona had explained that the first king of Doon commissioned this chapel as a spiritual retreat for the royal family. Now it was only used for the most significant ceremonial occasions.

Next to me, Kenna's soft sigh drew my attention away from the flawless architecture. I followed her stare toward the altar. Duncan mounted the steps two at a time and joined his brother with a squeeze on the shoulder and a heartening smile. As the clergyman announced the Oath of Fealty, Duncan solemnly lowered to one knee before Jamie and raised his right hand.

"I, Duncan Rhys Finnean MacCrae, promise on my faith that I will, now and always, remain loyal to my laird and king, my brother. Will never cause him harm and will, in all things, observe my homage to the kingdom o' Doon. I pledge my devoted counsel in all situations and vow to protect the laird with my life, against all persons and in all circumstances in loyalty and without deceit."

Every word of his commitment rang strong and true throughout the cathedral, his love for his kingdom and his brother clear to all. But it occurred to me that Duncan seemed to weigh his vow of protection above his declaration of honesty. Was withholding Gideon's true whereabouts and the mysterious deaths of his soldiers a violation of loyalty? I couldn't judge Duncan, because like me he must know the terrible secret he held would hurt more than it helped. We both had our reasons for keeping information from the new ruler of Doon.

Finished with his pledge, Duncan tipped his head and

kissed his sovereign's ring. In a touching display of humility, Jamie clasped his brother's hand and helped him to his feet, pulling him into a brief hug, their locked fists between them.

The haunting music of unseen bagpipes wove through the room as every citizen filed into the aisle, patiently waiting their turn to step in front of their new laird and repeat an abbreviated version of the oath Duncan had just confessed.

As the Rosetti sisters made their way toward to the platform, I watched Sofia, mesmerized by her glowing countenance and the dazzling sapphire gown trailing gracefully behind her. Her smile seemed brighter than the sun as she faced Jamie. With a sickening lurch in the pit of my belly, I watched them exchange a meaningful glance before she sank to her knees and made her pledge. I tore my gaze away from the touching scene and let my eyes wander over the crowd.

It seemed the Doonians were trying to ignore Kenna and me. Aside from a few nervous glances, they seemed determined to enjoy the festivities. I turned to ask Ken if she'd noticed their indifference when tingles skittered up my spine. Searching the room for the source of my discomfort, I spotted a middle-aged woman — tall, wafer thin, caramel-colored skin — staring at me. I recognized Roddie MacPhee's wife from the marketplace.

Her mocha-colored eyes pleaded with me, silently begging me to do something to return her loved one. My throat tightened as she turned away. I didn't understand exactly how the witch's magic worked, but the disappearances were partly my fault for bringing the cursed book into the kingdom in the first place. I just prayed taking the journal across the bridge would restore the missing people to their families . . . unharmed.

The minister's reverent voice shifted my attention away from Mrs. MacPhee and back to the ceremony. "The Completing affirmation shall now commence."

The announcement echoed through the chapel, every word like a nail in my heart. My eyes darted to Sofia seated several rows in front of us with the rest of the Rosetti clan. Gabby, practically bouncing out of her seat with excitement, leaned over to whisper in her sister's ear.

The ever-poised Sofia smiled indulgently and then whispered something back that caused the younger girl's eyes to widen, an irrepressible grin lighting her up from within. Sofia glanced over her shoulder and scanned the crowd. When her eyes landed on me, she lifted her chin, a small smile sliding across her lovely lips. And I could almost read her thoughts: You may have had him for one night, but he's mine for eternity.

"Nice," I mumbled under my breath as I broke eye contact with the gloating queen-to-be. My spine crumbled and I slumped in my seat, focusing every ounce of energy I possessed on not falling apart. Jamie was supposed to be mine! For a brief second, I fantasized that I'd met him in Alloway that day I saw him on the street, and that he was an ordinary boy. He would've smiled at me and said hello, maybe inviting me to get a coffee.

The image popped like a soap bubble. Jamie was nothing close to ordinary and no amount of wishing would change him — not that I really wanted to.

"Did you say something?" Kenna asked belatedly, her eyes glued to Duncan as he took his place beside his brother.

"Nothing," I mumbled, hoping she was preoccupied enough to let it drop.

A young steward walked up the center aisle carrying an elaborately carved wooden box. He ascended the stairs to the platform and set the box on a table to Jamie's right. The chamber was silent enough to hear a pin drop.

The clergyman's voice rang through the crowd. "Man is not meant ta be alone, nor in Doon shall he rule alone. James

Thomas Kellan MacCrae, have ye chosen a suitable partner that will help ye rule the kingdom in wisdom and in truth?"

"Aye," Jamie answered with certainty, a tiny smile curving one side of his mouth — the smile I'd always imagined was just for me. My stomach clenched, bile clawing its way up my throat.

"Laird, please record yer selection for our future queen on this slip o' parchment." The vicar handed Jamie a feathered quill with one hand, while gesturing toward the table and the wooden box with the other.

What did he mean, "record yer selection?" All the muscles in my body stiffened.

"What the — ?" Kenna exclaimed.

"Shhh." I pressed my elbow into her side as she scooted out of my reach.

"Seriously, Vee, could they draw this out any more? Is he trying to torture you?"

I smiled gratefully at my friend — my sister — who voiced the words I felt but couldn't let myself say. Coming clean with Kenna had not only lifted a huge weight from me, but also united us in a common cause.

Squeezing her hand, I lied for her sake. "I'll be okay, Ken."

After Jamie placed the folded paper into a cream-colored envelope, the steward pressed the hot wax seal onto the flap, closing it with a quick flourish. Applause filled the room as Jamie turned toward the crowd and executed a deep, graceful bow, a huge grin revealing the long dimple in his right cheek. "All will be revealed in due time, but ye must attend the ball this evening." Cheers echoed through the room at Jamie's teasing announcement.

"What an idiot!" Kenna muttered beside me. I knew she wanted me to agree, but I didn't have any anger left. It didn't matter anyway. The name he'd written on that slip of paper wasn't mine. A blessed numbness descended, buffering me like a cloak against a cold night. I just hoped this odd detachment would stick around long enough to get me through the ball and then over the bridge.

"We have one more order o' business ta attend to, friends," the clergyman said, obviously joyful while attempting to keep the ceremony on track. He indicated a rough slab of sandstone at the center of the altar. "Prince James, I ask that ye take a knee on the Liath Fàil."

A reverent silence descended on the room as Jamie lowered to one knee, his golden head bowed. Analytically, I noticed the slight curl of his hair where it lay against the tan skin of his neck, the strength of his calf muscles defined beneath woolen hose, and the humble set of his broad shoulders as the simple gold and diamond circlet was placed on his head — it was like a page ripped out of a storybook.

"Rise, new laird of Doon, and take your rightful place before your people."

Fluidly, Jamie stood to the responsive roar of the crowd as they shot to their feet while I remained frozen to my seat. Despite my newfound aloofness, a lump filled my throat, my volatile emotions threatening to pull me into the frenzied adoration surrounding me. The rustling of multicolored silks and plaid kilts encircled me, and I grasped for the protective cloak that was already slipping through my fingers.

Less than five hours. You can do this.

Rising slowly, I joined the crowd, bringing my hands together in polite, respectful applause — just another person in the crowd, not someone whose heart and soul was, and always would be, irrevocably intertwined with the young King of Doon.

CHAPTER 28

Veronica

Loser was not a word I liked to use to describe myself, but I was pretty sure only a pathetic loser — or a complete moron — would subject herself to this torture. And yet here I was walking into a ballroom that looked like it had been decorated by Jane Austen and Tinker Bell. As I stepped through the doorway, I drew a deep cleansing breath, resolving to relax and enjoy the otherworldly brilliance before me.

Kenna, Fiona, and I were among the first to arrive, so the displays of tantalizing edible art — including a dessert table anchored on both sides by confectionary sculptures resembling the Castle MacCrae — remained untouched. When I ran into Mags, I would be sure to tell her how amazing everything looked. She and her kitchen staff had certainly outdone themselves for the occasion.

Beyond the tables of food, a row of french doors opened to reveal a harvest moon lighting the elaborate gardens and lake beyond. The vast ballroom itself, adorned in garlands of flowers and greenery, glowed with hundreds of candles, their warm light casting a golden sheen on every surface like a coating of pixie dust.

The room oozed romance.

I had a sudden desire to knock over the nearest candelabra and burn the whole place down. Instead, I pressed my fingernails into my palms and took another deep breath.

Three more hours, Veronica. You can do this.

My dark emotions firmly in hand, I turned toward my best friend, determined to focus on her possibility for love. "When do you think Duncan will get here?" I asked, snagging a glistening melon ball from a table as we passed.

Kenna spun around, fire in her eyes. "I've no idea. And it doesn't really matter at this moment. Fiona, explain that whole envelope thing."

So much for turning the focus away from my own crappy life. But when Fiona's eyes flickered to mine, I nodded for her to continue. I needed to hear this.

"When the new king is crowned, he must record his selection fer his queen and coruler, but he does no' have ta declare his betrothal right then. If he feels he needs more time ta prepare, or ta court the girl, he kin write her name down and open it at a time of his choosing."

"So it could be years before Jamie opens that thing?" Kenna demanded.

"Usually, yes. But the timing of the Completing this year is ... unorthodox. The king has ta be betrothed before the Centennial. When the Brig o' Doon opens, his intended must stand by his side and welcome the Destined — all those who've been led ta our great kingdom."

At the far end of the hall, I could see another entrance and a mass of people approaching from the corridor beyond. I hoped

Duncan was among them. Ken meant well, but this conversation was chipping away at the little strength I had left.

Kenna's eyes flickered toward the crowd and back to Fiona as she lowered her voice conspiratorially. "What does that mean, exactly?"

"It means that he'll have ta open the envelope before midnight tonight."

Awesome. Why had I let Jamie convince me to be here again?

"Fiona, Kenna, Vee!"

I recognized the rolling, exotic voice of Gabby Rosetti. It figured — nothing like the queen-to-be's little sister adding salt to the wound.

"Your dresses are bea-u-tifulll." She elongated the final consonant as she slipped in front of us to twirl in an excited circle, the rich green fabric of her skirt belling out around her.

Since we shared a brain and Kenna had always been more demonstrative with her feelings, the glare she shot Gabby was completely unfiltered. Luckily, Gabby didn't seem to notice.

Fiona's eyes darted from Kenna, to me, then back to Gabby and she rushed to return the girl's complement. "Ye look lovely as well, Gabriella."

"Sure do — so does your sister." Fake enthusiasm dripped from Kenna's every word. "Where is Sofia, anyway? She must be sooo relieved."

"Ken — " I pinched the back of her arm in warning. When she set her mind, she was like a runaway car — reckless and unable to stop short of smashing into a solid object.

Gabriella Rosetti regarded us with large, trusting doe eyes. "Over what?"

"The betrothal, silly." Kenna's shark-like smile rivaled Cinderella's wicked stepmother as she leaned toward Gabby and gave her a wide wink. "I know she and Jamie spoke in confidence yesterday."

Surprise moved across the girl's lovely features and she nodded in confirmation. She searched our faces for reassurance that she was among friends. Satisfied, she leaned in to share her secret. "I've been awfully concerned about her lately. But after she and Jamie talked last night, she's been so very happy."

Ken lowered her voice to indicate this juicy bit of gossip was just between us girls. "Is that so? What did he say, exactly?"

Gabby paused to draw in a breath, her eyes shifting from Kenna's eager face to Fiona's deep frown, and then warily back to me. "I think I've already said too much. If ye will please excuse me, I should go in search of my sister."

As soon as Gabby turned her back to us, I smacked Kenna across the arm while Fiona admonished her with, "That wasn't verra nice."

"Well — " She crossed her arms contentiously. "I didn't feel verra nice."

"Excuse us for one minute." I grabbed my friend by the sleeve and hauled her away from Fiona. Just short of the doors, I whirled on her. "What do you think you're doing?"

"He's not going to get away with it!"

My eyes widened. "Who's not getting away with what?"

"Jamie's not getting away with marrying Sofia when he loves you."

I shook my head, a sad smile creeping onto my lips. She wanted to fix everything for me and I loved her for that, but she needed to accept that it was over. "I appreciate what you're trying to do, I really do. But did I ask you to fight my battles?"

"No — "

"Don't you think after everything we've been through, if I needed help I'd come to you?"

"Yes, but — "

"No buts! This is a royal ball." I pointed beyond her left shoulder. "And you've got a real-life prince over there working so hard to get your attention that he looks like he's trying to land a plane. Go dance with him! Have fun!"

Kenna glanced behind her and Duncan made another broad beckoning gesture, his face lighting up with enthusiasm when he saw he'd gained her attention.

"He looks like he's provoking a bull." A small chuckle slipped from her mouth before she turned back around. "I don't think I should leave you."

Wrapping my arms around her in a bear hug, I whispered, "If I need you, I'll come find you."

"Are you sure?"

I pulled back and in a sing-song voice attempted the words to one of her favorite songs. "There's only this. Only tonight. So let go. Find out if it's right."

She burst out laughing. "Before you go all *Rent* on me, it goes both ways."

My smile faltered. "Kenna, there comes a time when admitting defeat becomes the logical choice — "

She waved her hand in a dismissive motion. "Is there a wedding ring on his finger?"

"No, but — "

"No buts. Fight for him!"

My best friend had always been a fighter. She single-mindedly pursued her dreams, whether they were the right ones or not. But that wasn't me. Whenever things got messy, I preferred to paste on a smile and walk — or run — the other way. It's how I'd protected myself all my life. Between fight or flight, I definitely preferred flight. Just like Dad.

The realization hit me like a sledgehammer, causing me to

slump against the edge of the table behind me. I resisted the urge to grab my aching chest as I pretended to consider my friend's call to action. My father was a weak, selfish coward. Did that make me one too?

With effort, I focused on Kenna's searching gaze. "Okay, I'll try," I conceded to shut her up. "But we had a deal, remember?"

Kenna glanced at Duncan, then back at me, my fearless friend's eyes full of uncertainty. "I only promised for tonight."

"Fine. Now go enjoy it!" I accented my words with a sharp shove that sent her stumbling in Duncan's general direction. If I couldn't face my own fears, at least I could help my friend face hers.

Duncan rushed forward with a grin and took her hand — and she let him keep it. As they walked away, I hoped she would keep other things, like her promise to give him a fair chance. I felt sure that if she did, she'd change her mind about leaving.

A wave of panic rose within me at the thought of a future without her, but I forced it down. Wrapping my arms around my waist against a sudden chill, I walked over to the french doors and leaned against the frame to contemplate the moonlit garden. Tonight at midnight, the bridge would open and I would be there, journal in hand, with or without my best friend.

Sometimes running away was the brave thing to do.

CHAPTER 29

Mackenna

Sometimes running away like a coward was the only thing to do. Especially where dancing — the gateway drug to love — was concerned. *Footloose, Hairspray, The King and I, My Fair Lady*, and even *Hello, Dolly* leapt to my mind as cautionary tales. These musical public service announcements warned us about the dangers incited by something as innocuous as a hip wiggle or waltz.

As the heart takes flight and your daydreams appear, any kind of thing can happen. A yes leads to hands and cheeks pressed, the brush of bodies as they sway. It would lead to sweating, and kissing. And romance. Which was to be avoided like the plague.

Duncan's velvet gaze searched my face as he waited for my answer. Would I care to dance? He might as well have asked me if I wanted to flush my dreams down the toilet. No thank you. Duncan's eyes widened slightly, cluing me in that I'd spoken aloud. His eagerness vanished as I quickly pointed toward my toes. "Two left feet — remember? How about we go outside and ... talk?"

Doing his best to recover from his disappointment, Duncan nodded and offered me his arm. "Verra well. 'Tis a beautiful night. Almost as beautiful as you."

Before we could slip between the open doors, Fergus blocked our path. He cast me an apologetic glance, and then spoke in a low, urgent voice. "M' laird, I'm verra sorry to bother ye, but I need ta speak ta you on a matter of great importance."

With Fergus close behind, Duncan guided me outside and into a remote corner of the patio. He looked about to gauge our privacy then nodded for Fergus to continue. The large man's pale face grew mottled with agitation as he explained, "It's Gideon, m' laird. He's gone. His guards are gone as well. I've had yer men scour the village but there's no sign of him. It's as if he's vanished."

Duncan cursed under his breath. His lips pressed into a thin slash as his square jaw set determinedly. "Then we canna' wait much longer to tell Jamie about the deaths at Muir Lea."

Fergus's pale brows puckered as he surveyed the multitudes enjoying the party. "In the middle of the coronation ball, m' laird?"

"Nay. As soon as the celebration has finished. But we need to speak to him before Gideon does. Please go tell the king his brother wishes a word with him in private after the ball."

"Aye m' laird."

As the gentle giant hurried away, Duncan offered me his arm once again. "Dinna worry, Mackenna. Everything will turn out right in the end."

"Really?" Because from where I was standing, he was covering for me by imprisoning his fellow countryman and lying about it to his own brother, who also happens to be the supreme ruler of the kingdom. "I don't see how."

He offered me a lopsided smile that radiated assurance. "There are lots of ways of lookin' at things."

"Okay. So how do you see this turning out?"

"It's not about only this, Mackenna. It's about how I see everything. My world. Your world. And everything beyond. I believe you and your friend were both brought here for a specific purpose. And if it's your destiny to be here, who am I to be doubtin' that?"

"You make it sound so simple."

Duncan raked his hand through his hair creating those dark, spiky peaks that I loved so. "Faith is hard. Especially when your mind and maybe even your heart might be sayin' otherwise. But when things seem difficult and we're tempted to doubt, we need to trust in what we can't see."

His faith did little to fill the hollow place created by Fergus's news. Doing my best to shake off the feeling of doom, I slipped my hand into the crook of his arm and let him lead me into the perfect summer night. After a few minutes of quiet rambling along the hedgerow, we approached a huge stone archway. Duncan turned to look back the way we'd come. His face shone with quiet pride as he instructed me to turn around.

At the far end of the lawn, the most beautiful castle I could ever imagine glowed against the indigo sky. Although the sounds of celebration had become hushed, I could still see much of the action through the open doors. It was like watching an elaborate pantomime.

I spotted Vee — a vision in burgundy, near the buffet. As she watched the Doonians celebrating, her angst-ridden face declared all the yearning she refused to vocalize. If her feelings had only been about Jamie, I would've insisted we skip the stupid ball and camp on the bridge until it opened. But Vee loved this place. She'd longed for this paradoxical kingdom her entire life. And she belonged here.

If there was even the slightest chance Vee could have her dream, I would not aid and abet her fugitive intentions. Although I didn't want to go to Chicago without her, I was perfectly capable of carrying Aunt Gracie's journal out of Doon by myself. And dealing with the witch — honestly, I'd yet to figure that part out, but having Vee by my side didn't change my odds. I mean, what could she do — cheer Addie to death?

Deep in my heart, I knew she was supposed to stay, the same way I knew I had to go. Unfortunately, I suspected it was already too late. I had little hope that fate would allow Jamie to get unengaged to Sofia and confess his undying love for Vee all in the span of one royal ball.

"We've time yet." Duncan's voice brought me back to the garden with a start. For a moment, I thought he'd answered my unspoken thoughts. But that was impossible. Only Vee and I shared a brain. As I frowned up at him, he smoothed a tendril of hair from my cheek and clarified, "The Brig o' Doon doesn't open for hours."

His freakishly gorgeous face held such hope that the rational part of my brain urged me to bail — on him, the ball, my promise to Vee, all of it. But my fanciful heart, overcome by the possibilities of the night, compelled me to ask, "What do you want from me?"

"Just be here. Tonight. Dinna leave me yet."

Had Duncan and Vee conspired ahead of time? If he started singing *Rent* songs, every last one of my barriers would come crashing down. His hand slid from my cheek to cup my neck. The heat of his touch counteracted the chill wafting off the lake.

When I shivered, his other hand skimmed across my collarbone. The pad of his thumb blazed a trail down my shoulder to my elbow. "It's just one evening. What are ye afraid of Mackenna?"

I wasn't afraid. I just didn't see the sense in indulging in something that wouldn't — that couldn't — last. His dark gaze crackled with heat and the edges of my argument began to blister, melting my resistance to reveal the devastating truth. I couldn't walk away — not without knowing what I was giving up.

On pure instinct, I grabbed Duncan's lapel and pulled him toward me. My lips crushed his in a hard, closed-mouth kiss. He felt firm, yet gentle — and so warm. His eyes went wide and then fluttered closed, his lips parting. I opened mine in response.

Duncan froze, his hands digging into my upper arms as he tried to be a gentleman. He trembled and I could sense the war waging inside of him. Unwilling to let him go, I wound my fingers around his neck and into his soft hair.

The remainder of his willpower broke apart. Sharp angles of rock pressed into my back as he pinned me against the stone arch. But I barely felt it. I closed my eyes and gave myself over to the sensations of being kissed by Duncan MacCrae.

Sometime later, Duncan lifted his head to gaze at me like a man enchanted. His husky voice was thick with relief. "Finally, ye've accepted your destiny. I wasn't sure tha' you would."

Geez — didn't he know when to keep his mouth shut?

I gave him a light shove. His rock-solid chest was immovable, but I pushed anyway. I needed to get some space between us. And air — boy, did I need some air.

Duncan straightened, but his hands remained anchored to my hips. "Are ye mad at me for kissin' you?"

"No." Actually I had kissed first, but now wasn't the time to point that out. I inhaled deeply in an attempt to clear my head. His clean warrior scent, leather saddles and sunshine, filled my senses and attempted to undermine my resolve. "But we need to talk."

"Talking's for later."

His crooked grin upended rational thought. Hypnotized by the motion of his tantalizing lips, I leaned toward them for another taste. "Later ..."

Instantly, his mouth was on mine. After another searing kiss, he pulled back just enough to speak. Against my lips, he breathed, "Tell me you'll stay."

What? In a delayed reaction, my head shook back and forth mid-kiss. "No."

Duncan's mouth hesitated over mine. His full lips parted in anticipation as they paused. His body went still. Finally, he straightened so that we could properly see one another. "Won't ye have me?"

"You're asking me to choose. To give up one dream for another." It didn't help that a part of me — and I wasn't willing to examine how large a part — wanted Duncan MacCrae as much, if not more, than the stage.

I stared into his compelling brown eyes and willed him to understand. "It's always been my dream to become a professional actress. I have this fabulous theater internship in Chicago, with a phenomenal director — " Weston Ballard flitted across my mind, but compared with the amazing boy in front of me, the young director held zero appeal.

Duncan took my hands in his and tipped his forehead down until it rested against mine. "I'll build ye a theatre here. Anything your heart desires."

Anything? The temptation to stay — for him — suddenly

overwhelmed me. "What if I stay and it doesn't work out between us? I don't want to grow to regret that decision or you."

"I'll spend every day making sure you don't."

"What if you experience a Calling? Then I'd be stuck here —"

"Shhh." Gently, he touched his finger to my lips. "You're worrying over things that may never come to pass. If you stay, I'll give you my heart and never ask for it back."

It was the most beautiful thing I'd ever heard. Just when I thought my feelings for Duncan couldn't get any deeper, he rocked me to a whole new level. I kissed him again, like the world was coming to an end, but it wasn't enough. Nothing would ever be enough.

The realization hit me like an avalanche, freezing me to my core. I wrenched myself out of Duncan's arms and scrambled away before he could change my mind. No amount of lip locking could change the fact we lived in two different worlds.

As Duncan came up behind me, I fixed my eyes on the palace as if for the very last time. Although he didn't touch me, he stood close enough to ward off the chill. "You're not staying, are ye?"

Unshed tears caused the image of Castle MacCrae to swim in front of me. If I stayed, I would always be afraid of losing him to a Calling and to regrets of choosing him over my ambition. Not trusting my voice, I shook my head back and forth.

"Then take me with you." Duncan bridged the distance between us by wrapping his arms around me. He pressed his lips against my shoulder and proceeded to kiss a trail up the sensitive skin on my neck. His teeth softly nipped at my earlobe and then he whispered, "Promise you won't leave without me."

My world shifted yet again. Was he asking what I thought he was asking? To leave Doon for me like Uncle Cameron had eventually done for Aunt Gracie? I twisted in his arms to search his face. "What about Doon?"

"It doesn't matter." As if sensing my skepticism, he placed his hand over his heart. "I promise."

Could that be true? Could I really have both — the boy I cared for and my dreams of glory? It almost seemed too good to be true. With a flutter of his lashes and a flash of crooked smile, Duncan banished any lingering doubts. "I'm in agony, here. Please say yes to me, woman."

Seizing the moment, I took his hands in mine. I made my promise and sealed the pledge with a perfect kiss. Standing under the stone archway, the gesture felt monumental, like making a sacred vow.

As I basked in Duncan's adoration, everything felt right for the first time since coming to Doon. His guileless smile warmed places in my heart that had never known summer. In the face of such beautiful sincerity, I wanted more. Surprising both of us, I said, "I've changed my mind. Shall we dance?"

CHAPTER 30

Veronica

Sinking my teeth into my third chocolate éclair, I tried to disregard the silence that swept through the room like a wave. The new king of Doon had arrived at the ball. But I refused to give him the satisfaction of staring and twittering behind my hands, like every other female in the room. Instead, I'd drown my sorrows with as much fancy French junk food as a girl of my small stature could consume without puking.

Raising a flute of champagne to the light, I watched tiny bits of strawberries bob in the iridescent bubbles. It tasted so delicious that I drained the entire glass, strawberries and all, in very short order. Blissfully, I popped the remainder of the éclair into my mouth, set the empty flute on a nearby table, and turned in search of more bubbly. Overflowing dessert plate in hand, I came face-to-face with the newly crowned king and his exquisite future queen.

"Oh, hi," I said through a mouthful of pastry, so it sounded more like, "Ow, hho."

Sofia gave me a sweet, sympathetic smile as if to say, "Poor, ill-mannered girl. I feel embarrassed for you."

Jamie smirked, shaking his head. "I dinna think ye would take it so literally when I said this would be my first edict." He waved his hand toward my overstuffed mouth.

With one gulp, I swallowed the lump of sugary goo that now tasted bitter on my tongue. Under different circumstances, his comment would've made me laugh — but not tonight. Since I was out of here at midnight anyway and had nothing to lose, I replied, "Appalling manners seem to be one of your special talents, your majesty. I was only trying to make you feel more comfortable."

Sofia made a choking sound and covered her mouth with a delicate hand.

"I see," Jamie remarked with an imperiously arched brow. "And what would some o' my other special talents be, Miss Welling?"

Uncontrollable heat rushed up my neck at the implication in his words. No way was I letting him get away with embarrassing me, especially in front of the too-perfect Sofia. I tapped my index finger on my chin, pretending to think.

"Hmm ... let's see. Bossiness comes to mind." I held up one finger and began counting off his faults. "Arrogance, extreme stubbornness, an ugly temper ... Shall I go on?"

"Nay." His eyes narrowed. "Sofia, would you please excuse us for a moment? I wouldna want to expose you to anymore o' Miss Welling's drunken accusations."

"I. Am. Not. Drunk. You ... conceited pig!" I didn't think this was the kind of "fighting" Kenna had been talking about, but I'd never intended to follow her advice anyway.

"Och, lass, I could have ye thrown in the stockades for callin' me that."

I stepped toward him and glared up into his insolent face. "I'd like to see you try, your highness!"

Jamie stiffened his spine, taking full advantage of his height. "And I saw ye down a whole glass of champagne with my own eyes."

We glared at each other for several seconds. Disconcerted by his unwavering stare, I broke eye contact. But then I was staring at his delectable mouth. Vivid memories of those scorching lips on mine sparked a flutter low in my stomach. Desperate to diffuse the tension building between us, I started babbling, "I wasn't trying to get drunk, the champagne tasted good and … and I like strawberries," I finished lamely, glancing away from him. "Now look what you've done. Sofia's gone."

"I asked her to leave. Unlike some people, she knows how to listen," he snarled between clenched teeth, taking my plate and setting it on the table behind me.

"An important trait if she's going to get along with you for the rest of her life," I spat, just as I realized he was reaching for my hand.

"What're you doing?" I asked, my muscles stiffening in rebellion.

"Dancing. I thought that was obvious." With a show of teeth, he ordered, "Smile."

Sweeping me into his arms, I could tell he was still angry, but clearly didn't want everyone in the kingdom to know it. So I complied with a pasted-on smile as my body began moving effortlessly in time with his.

"I think you should know, my dance card is full, your eminence," I said with undisguised sarcasm. Despite the glittering circlet on his head, I couldn't think of him as a king. He was still the beautiful boy from my visions, who laughingly spoke with his mouth full and kissed me with so much passion I felt it all the way to my toes.

"Dance card, eh?"

"Yes, as we speak you're stealing me from some poor soul who asked for my first dance hours ago."

Something dark flared in his eyes, his smile fading. "Let me see it."

"See what?"

"Yer dance card."

There was no dance card and we both knew it.

"I lost it?" I said, glancing up at him hopefully.

His loud laughter drew the attention of everyone around us. "Verranica, ye never cease to amaze me."

Longing and sorrow swirled in my chest, threatening to erupt. I knew this was the end — the last moments I would spend with the boy I loved more than my own life. I tried to console myself with the fact that even if he did choose me, he'd leave me eventually, like every other man in my life. But the thought was petty and I knew it.

"Hey, where did ye go?" Jamie asked, squeezing my hand and trying to catch my eye.

Afraid to meet his gaze and reveal the ache burning inside me, I concentrated on the slope of his shoulder. "I'm still here." For the moment, I thought, noting the late hour on the grandfather clock as we twirled past.

Two more hours, Veronica. You can do this.

"Jamie, I'm glad you made the right decision." I glanced at his face but he fixed me with a deeply penetrating stare, and I quickly refocused back to his shoulder. "About the Completing, I mean."

"Vee, look at me." He pressed the flat of his palm into the

curve of my lower back and electric sparks shot up my spine. "Please, love."

Slowly, I lifted my head.

"My ma would've been so happy tonight," he whispered, his whole face lighting up.

"Why?" Our feet had stilled until we stood swaying, our bodies pressed close.

"She was the one who groomed me, since I could walk, for the role of king. Teaching me to think with the right balance between head and heart." A small smile tilted his lips and he touched his temple, then the left side of his chest with two fingers, before taking my hand again. "She also never let me forget that as a leader there is a price for every decision, not just for me but for others. That the right choice could sometimes contradict my own wishes or those of the people, but that a strong ruler will make the choice that is best for all."

"I remember what you said on the cliffs. I get it Jamie — the price of being with me is too high." My voice broke and I shook my head, his face blurry through the veil of my unshed tears.

"That's no — "

"It's okay." I cut him off. I didn't want to hear the words that would confirm I was the second choice of someone I loved — yet again. "You have to put the safety of your people first. It's very noble — "

"Och, no," he ground out with determination, his midnight eyes boring into mine. "If ye willna listen to me, then maybe you'll listen to this."

With those cryptic words, he pulled out of my arms and left the dance floor.

Couples twirled around me, my head spinning along with them as I tried to make sense of Jamie's sudden desertion. Kenna waltzed by, spotted me, and stopped so suddenly that

Duncan tripped forward. She grabbed his arm to steady him and then without so much as an explanation, headed in my direction still clutching his sleeve. The poor guy appeared completely dumfounded as he stumbled along behind her.

Just as abruptly, the music came to an unceremonious halt. Jamie stepped up on the bandstand, followed by a young steward carrying the wooden box.

My heart began beating so hard it hurt. Had Jamie been trying to tell me he didn't choose Sofia? I searched the faces gathered around the stage and found Sofia standing with her sister and a group of friends. She met my eyes across the room and smiled broadly. Was she gloating? Or was there a hint of relief in her grin? I couldn't be sure.

Jamie cleared his throat and the crowd stilled in anticipation. "Thank you all for comin' tonight to celebrate this momentous occasion." Applause erupted, but Jamie raised his hand for silence.

"Never before in Doon's history have a Coronation and the Centennial occurred on the same day. In an attempt to keep with the tradition o' the Completing, I will declare my choice of bride this evening. So if she'll consent to have me" — he quirked an adorable grin amidst laughter and shouts — "this ball will be the celebration of our new queen." The audience erupted in approval.

He couldn't mean me.

On the verge of hyperventilating, I began to back my way through the crowd. The old king had been right; the people would never accept an outsider suspected of witchcraft as their queen, especially if they learned I was responsible for bringing the witch's evil into their land. Before I got far, Kenna squeezed my arm in a death grip. "Where are you going?" she hissed.

I met her eyes and shook my head in denial. Terrified to let myself hope.

"Vee, you need to hear this." She didn't let go of me as we both turned back to the stage.

Jamie took an ancient key from his jacket pocket and motioned for the steward to bring the box forward. Silence once again descended as he carefully removed the wax-sealed envelope from the box. "Shall I open it now?"

"Aye!" all of Doon cried in unison.

Pulling a small, jeweled knife from somewhere on his person, Jamie cut the wax seal.

"Sire! Wait!" The cry from the back of the crowd caused Jamie to stop and glance up. To my right, people parted like the Red Sea as a cadaverous Gideon pushed his way to the front. Fear caused the fancy pastries I'd consumed to claw their way back up my throat. I swallowed hard as Kenna squeezed my hand, a slight tremble running through her fingers to mine.

"M' laird." Gideon stopped at the edge of the platform to catch his breath. "I have proof!"

Jamie's face darkened. "Proof o' what, exactly?"

Duncan and Fergus closed in on either side of Gideon, Duncan's hand on his sword. But before either of them could stop the captain of the guard, he cried out, "Witchery, kidnapping, and murder."

The crowd's reaction was sharp and immediate.

"Silence!" Jamie held up his hand. Although muted, the tension in the room felt palpable. "Gideon, now is no' the time."

"I found Roddie and the other missing villagers. I've left them in the infirmary," Gideon said hastily as a collective gasp ripped through the room. "They were near death . . . bound and gagged near the witch's cottage."

Chaos erupted. Shouts of fear and demands for justice mingled with weeping. The people closest to us began to shrink away.

Jamie leaned over and whispered urgently to the steward, who sprinted out of the ballroom. I imagined he wanted to confirm that the missing individuals were safe as Gideon claimed. Fergus lifted two fingers to his mouth and a piercing whistle cut through the pandemonium, bringing all but a few to silence.

"Thank you, Fergus." Jamie nodded his head to the big guard before continuing. "Now listen to me well, all of you. There is a time and place for these accusations. Gideon's claims shall be heard but I willna be making any decisions without proper proof."

"This book contains all the proof ye need, sire." Gideon pushed a tiny weathered volume in Jamie's direction.

He had found Aunt Gracie's journal. Although I didn't understand the full implications of the curse on the small book, I knew deep in my bones I had to stop Jamie from touching it. Blindly, I began pushing my way toward the stage.

I couldn't move through the people fast enough. Jamie reached out to take the journal from Gideon's outstretched hand.

"Wait!" I screamed and every head in the room swiveled in my direction. Startled, Jamie searched the crowd, his hand suspended in midair.

Reaching the edge of the dais, I caught his eye. "Don't touch that!" His normally confident-yet-relaxed posture stiffened visibly as he glanced at the book still in Gideon's extended hand. Slowly, he lowered his arm.

Thank God. "Jamie, I can explain everyth — "

"M' laird, I found this evil tome hidden in the American girls' suite." Gideon pushed the book toward Jamie again.

Jamie glanced at me, his eyes masked. "Verranica, you'll have your chance to explain."

I reached up to intercept the book, but hands on my arms and shoulders restrained me. The air whooshed from my lungs as I watched Jamie take the book and open the cover. When he didn't collapse or show any sign of harm, I allowed myself to breathe again.

He leafed through the journal, stopping to study a particular page for several seconds in silence. When he glanced up, his soft voice carried across the room, his expression neutral. "Miss Welling, is this your book?"

"Yes," I responded, feeling it was critical to be as honest as possible. "It's Kenna's Aunt Gracie's journal. We brought it with us as a guide to the kingdom."

"Indeed. And have you read it?"

On the surface, the journal was Aunt Gracie's loving record of Doon — nothing more, so I didn't think there was any harm in admitting to having read it. "Yes, I've read every page ... several times," I finished, my voice trembling.

He stared down at me with flat eyes. "How do ye explain this?"

A frown turned down the corners of his mouth as he held the book open for me to see. I gasped, along with a few others around me who could see the page in question. It was a sketch that I knew had not been there before ... a portrait of the witch of Doon.

"Addie ..." I whispered in stunned disbelief. What was going on? I'd memorized every word, every page in that book, and there had never been any reference to Addie, let alone a lifelike portrait. Gideon must have planted it.

"And how, pray tell, would ye know who she is?"

I noticed too late that there was no caption on the picture. I panicked, the words rushing out of me like nails hammered into my own coffin. "She's the caretaker at Aunt Gracie's cottage. I met her in Alloway. I'd known her for less than twenty-four hours when — "

"And yet ye know her as the witch o' Doon." His hard voice sliced through the chaos, quieting the building hysteria.

"No. I mean — I didn't — "

"Silence! You're a liar and I dinna want to hear another word." Jamie snapped the journal shut in front of my face.

"That's not all, sire!" Gideon's voice rang over the crowd, two octaves higher than normal. "The devil-haired one killed my men in Muir Lea and yer own brother locked me up to protect her."

Jamie's gaze flicked dispassionately to Kenna and Duncan before returning to me. Looking into his stony face, I realized the prince I loved had been replaced by a cold, condemning king. "Fergus, escort Miss Welling and Miss Reid to the dungeon. Bind and gag them if ye have to. Take my lying brother with them."

Duncan stepped forward, "Jamie, I — "

"Your king commands you to be silent!"

Duncan's whole body stiffened. Sure that he would protest his brother's irrational behavior, I watched him expectantly. But the brash prince hung his head, his congenial face transformed by guilt as he allowed himself to be restrained and led away.

Fergus faced me with an apologetic grimace, and I noticed he was holding my arm in his meaty hand. "Come, Miss Veronica."

"Please wait!" As he led me away, I dug in my heels and twisted back toward the dais. I had to at least try to get through to my Jamie. "You know I would never do anything to harm Doon or its people! You know me."

"Take the witches away." Jamie's emotionless words chilled my soul. His hollow stare passed right though me, as if I no longer mattered. Still holding the journal in his hands, he turned to Gideon. "I'm going to the chapel. See that I'm no' disturbed."

Catching a glimpse of Kenna's terrified face as a guard forced her out of the ballroom, her arms behind her back like some kind of criminal, I set my jaw in determination. I may not have a choice about going to the dungeon, but I wasn't giving up that easily. Urgently, I whispered, "Fergus, let one of the other guards take me. Follow Jamie and get your hands on that journal. Then get it out of the kingdom, no matter what you have to do!"

The giant's steps slowed and he stared at me in bewilderment.

"Fergus, if you've ever trusted me, trust me now. The journal is cursed. We have to get it out of Doon. That's what I was trying to do when I caused the blizzard."

He stopped walking and stared at me for several seconds. His face hardened and I was sure he would refuse. But then he said, "Not sure why, but I've always believed in ye, and I'm not goin' to stop now."

Tears of relief filled my eyes as he motioned for another guard.

With Kenna and I locked in the dungeon and the bridge opening in less than two hours, Fergus could be our last chance to get the witch's evil influence out of the kingdom. I hated to think about what would happen if he failed.

Was it too much to ask for another miracle?

CHAPTER 31

Veronica

The more I thought about his actions at the ball, the more convinced I became that something was wrong with Jamie. He was nothing if not logical, and yet he'd jumped to an unjustified conclusion in less than ten seconds. He'd just finished telling me how his mom had taught him to think with the right balance, yet neither his heart nor his head appeared to be in control.

I paced the length of our cell struggling to maintain control and think rationally. I still had hope that Fergus would get the journal from Jamie and get it across the bridge. But just in case, I needed to come up with a plan B.

The echo of footsteps in the corridor caused me to rush to the dungeon door. Fiona hurried toward us, but not fast enough for me. I pushed my face between the bars and called out, "Something's not right."

Fiona stopped in front of me, remorse and a trace of my own panic in her eyes. "Something? Try everything. The Brig o' Doon will be openin' soon."

"No, I mean with Jamie."

"Aye." Fiona's soft lilt of reassurance was edged with doubt as she added, "Don't ye fret, Veronica. Fergus will talk some sense inta him."

"Fergus has failed." Fergus's ragged voice reached us through the void, followed by a scuffle, a moan, and a soft thump. "I didna even get to see him."

Slumping against the bars, I grasped them for support as I banged my head against the metal. Behind me, Kenna stirred for the first time in over an hour. She'd been uncharacteristically despondent since the guards had locked us up, staring into space as if the slimy stone walls were the last thing she'd ever see.

Fergus emitted a humorless chuckle and continued to address himself in the third person. "So now as second-highest commander of the royal guard, Fergus is committing treason."

The unmistakable click of the locking mechanism caused me to step back as the heavy iron door creaked open. Duncan rushed in and gathered Kenna into his arms. His disheveled hair stuck out at odd angles, and a purpling bruise darkened his right cheekbone.

Kissing the top of her head, he asked, "Are ye all right, Mackenna?"

Kenna buried her head in his chest, her words muted. "I know how it must look, but we're innocent. We found out about the witch but we were trying to stop her. You have to believe m—"

"Shhh." Duncan smoothed her hair. "How many times are ye going to put me through this? Doncha think I know yer innocent?"

"Uh, guys?" Their reunion was touching, but I didn't have time for romance at the moment. "Sorry to interrupt, but I've got to see him. Now."

With a great sigh, Fergus turned his doleful face toward me. "Jamie'll not see you, lass. Ye'll not make it past Gideon's men any more than I did. They got the jump on me." His black eye and swollen lip were evidence that he'd given it his best shot.

"I'm not giving up." There had to be another way. Stiffening my spine, I met each of my friend's eyes in turn, landing on Kenna's last. "I'll go by myself if I have to."

Ken pulled out of Duncan's arms. The hardening of her features echoed my own determination. "I'm coming with you."

Next to me, Fiona squared her shoulders. "Me too."

Already half a dozen shades of pink, Fergus emitted another grave chuckle. "Seeing how I'm already slated for the dungeon m'self, count me in. Where Fiona goes, I go." They shared a quick smile that filled me with optimism. They were good people — and good always prevailed ... didn't it?

I turned to the only one of us yet to speak. Other than me, Duncan had the most to lose. If he chose not to go against his sovereign's orders, I wouldn't blame him. "Duncan?"

His dark-brown eyes, so like Jamie's, turned and focused on my best friend. "Aye. I'm in."

We stepped from the cell into the corridor. To our left, the dungeon guards sprawled lifelessly on the ground. As I stifled my reaction, Kenna gasped. "Are they dead?"

Duncan shook his head "Nay. Just unconscious."

Of course, the scuffle and moan made sense now. They had to knock out the guards in order to rescue us. It wasn't just Fergus who'd committed treason, but the king's own brother. Unfortunately, I had a sinking feeling if we didn't get to Jamie soon, facing treason charges would be the least of our worries.

Following Duncan's lead, we crept through the back passages until we arrived at the main corridor to the castle chapel unnoticed. At the entrance, Gideon barred our way, flanked by a half dozen guards. Although he stood at attention, tremors racked his emaciated body. His visible skin was a patchwork of flakes and sores. "No one is ta disturb the king." His bluish lips twisted in a sneer aimed at Duncan. "Not even you, m' laird."

Duncan squared his linebacker shoulders. "You've caused enough mischief for one night, Gideon. Stand down!"

"I'm verra sorry, sire. I canna. I have my orders. And so do my men."

"Oh, fer Heaven's sake!" Fergus reared back and delivered a knockout punch to Gideon's nose.

As the misguided guard crumpled to the ground, his men surged toward us. Half grabbed Fergus, who growled and lashed out, his fists and boots directed at his attackers. The others moved toward Duncan, who held them off with his sword. "Stand down, men! Your prince commands it!"

Indecision, thick and palpable, charged the air, making the guards' attack disorganized and sluggish. Duncan easily fought two guards at once, and projected his voice over the clang of their swords. "Graham, you know Gideon is not in his right mind. He's obviously ill."

The guard I assumed was Graham glanced back at Gideon's prone form and lowered his sword. His comrade continued to fight until Duncan lowered his weapon and pleaded, "Patrick, I've known ye since we were lads. I must speak to my brother. It's a matter of life and death."

After several agonizing seconds, Patrick lowered his sword and called for his cohorts to release Fergus. Duncan regarded the men with a steely nod. "Go home to your families. Tha's an order."

The resounding "Yes, m' laird!" filled the tight corridor. Then the guards turned and scattered, their footsteps echoing noisily off the cobbled stones as they ran.

Gideon lay unconscious as rivulets of sweat trickled across his twitching body. Duncan unfastened a key ring from the guard's belt and rushed the massive chapel door. At my feet, Gideon convulsed, causing his fist to unclench, and with a soft clink the Rings of Aontacht rolled from his hand.

"What's he doing with the rings?" I asked as Fiona stooped to pick them up.

"I don't know why I didn't consider it before. My mum told me that many years ago a servant of the witch used one of the Rings of Aontach to enter Doon. The ring was enspelled with a curse."

"A curse?" Kenna asked, the last part of her question drowned out by Duncan swearing as he tried various keys in the lock.

Bouncing on my toes in impatience, I heard Fiona reply, "Aye. Wrapped around it — like a parasite and attaching itself to the first Doonian it touched."

Kenna's eyes widened. "Could the curse have caused Gideon to kill his own men?"

Fiona's fair head dipped in terrible confirmation. "Aye. With a spell this strong, 'tis verra likely the witch's been in control of him. Gideon could've done terrible things and no' had any recollection after the deed was done."

Her words cut through me like an icy wind, stealing my breath. The journal held a curse and when Jamie touched it he hadn't been harmed as I feared, but he had changed. For the first time since I'd arrived in Doon, he'd looked through me as if I wasn't even there.

With a loud creak, Duncan pushed open the chapel door. "Got it!"

I shoved past him while calling Jamie's name. Halfway down the aisle, I stopped, searching the cavernous space. "I don't see him."

Duncan pointed to a closed door off the main altar. "He'd be in the annex."

I ran. Jamie'd had the journal for hours — plenty of time for him to turn into a possessed monster like Gideon. I slammed my shoulder against the door and shoved the handle, but it didn't move. "Duncan, do you have a key?"

"Nay, it only locks from the inside."

I rushed backward and then ran forward, flinging myself against the door with all my strength. But I bounced back, struggling to keep my footing. "It won't budge."

"Step back." Duncan waved me a safe distance away. With the count of three, Duncan and Fergus hit the door together. Their combined strength splintered the wood into kindling.

Impatiently, I shoved my way between them. "Jamie!"

The small room was empty. Fear balled in the pit of my stomach. I whirled around to Kenna, my voice thick in my own ears. "Ken, he's not here."

Duncan stepped to one side, allowing Fiona access to the deserted chamber. "What do you make of this?" he asked.

She passed in front of me, her eyes locked straight ahead. Across the small, dim room, Aunt Gracie's journal sat open on the altar railing. It flickered with a strange violet light. The dancing purple flames reminded me of burning copper, but without the heat. Even from a distance, I could feel the chill emanating from the flame.

Fiona drew in a deep, controlled breath. After a moment, her eyes widened with alarm. She turned toward Kenna and me. "Remember how I said there's good and bad power beyond our comprehension? This is the worst kind. Verra old — verra potent evil."

My stomach clenched into a knot. Dreading the answer, I

asked, "If it's that powerful, does it mean she's been controlling me? Using me to hurt the kingdom and Jamie in some way?"

A sob hitched in my throat, and rendered me unable to continue. Large, hot tears rolled down my cheeks. Had I been the witch's pawn all along, just as Jamie's dreams had predicted?

Gently, Fiona placed her hand on my shoulder. "There's an energy ta everything, Veronica, and yours is not evil. I kin find no trace of the witch on you. And this spell was only meant for one."

I sniffed, fighting against my useless tears. "But I brought the journal into Doon."

"And Doon's Protector brought ye here … for a purpose. Don't doubt that now when yer faith is ta be tested."

Faith? It wasn't that I didn't believe in a higher power, but I had never put my faith in anyone besides myself — until coming here.

"I agree with Fiona." Duncan attempted a reassuring smile that didn't reach his eyes, before redirecting his comments to his fellow countrywoman. "But what of my brother? What are ye able to discern?"

Fiona's countenance shone with gentle empathy. "I'm sorry, but I believe the witch has enthralled him."

Although it was what I'd expected myself, her words were not a theory, but a statement. "Wait! How could you possibly know that?" Fear and confusion made my voice sharp.

Fergus placed a calming hand on my shoulder. "Fiona has the gift o' discernment. She can see beyond the natural realm."

That explained a lot about my new friend's propensity for the prophetic. A million questions about her ability swirled in my head, but I pushed them aside. "Fiona, what else can you see?"

Rather than reply, Fiona held up her hand in a gesture I

took to mean *wait*. From around her neck she unclasped a simple golden cross. It dangled from her hand like a rosary as she cautiously stepped toward the journal. With her approach, the diary burned brighter and colder.

Her voice sounded fluid and far away. "This journal is not evil. 'Tis been misused. It belonged to a Keeper — one who's been called from Doon to protect it from the outside."

Softly, Kenna said, "But Aunt Gracie was an outsider."

Fiona raised her hands tentatively over the violet flames. "Aye. But she took Doon inta her heart and made it her home."

Her eyes closed in concentration and her lips moved noiselessly. In a trancelike state, she continued to share her revelations. "After she died, it fell into the clutches of evil. 'Tis a seeking spell the witch's working from the other side o' the bridge. This one's meant specifically for the king. Once Jamie touched the journal, the witch's spell was set inta motion."

Shivers racked my body as I admitted, "I knew it. In my dreams I saw him touch the journal and die. So I kept the book a secret for his protection. Fiona, is he ..." My throat closed, but I choked out the last word. "Alive?"

"Aye."

I grasped the back of the nearest pew as bittersweet relief swept over me. It wasn't too late. But we still had to save him.

Duncan began to walk the length of the tiny room. He paced like a caged animal whose only wish was to run free. "Where do we find my brother?"

Fiona made a few more silent petitions. "The witch compelled him ta come ta her. He crossed the Brig o' Doon on horseback as soon as it opened. But — I canna see beyond the bridge."

Impatient for action, Duncan gripped the hilt of his weapon. "Please, lass. Try."

With a small nod, Fiona reached toward me. "Will ye help me, please, Veronica?"

"Me?" I squeaked. "What can I do?"

Fiona gravely met my eyes as she reached for my hand. "Ye've experienced waking visions of Jamie and dreams regarding our kingdom, have ye not?"

I nodded, the vision of the witch in the king's chamber flashing in my mind as she placed the gold and ruby ring in my palm. "Ye'll need this."

Regardless of the things I'd seen, I was skeptical, but I'd do anything to help Jamie. So I let Fiona lead me toward the flickering light of the journal.

"Dinna be afraid." The violet flames reflected in Fiona's eyes, turning them an eerie purple. "Put the ring on and focus with all yer heart on overcoming the witch's evil — and finding yer true love."

I slipped on the ring, and squeezed my eyes closed as Fiona raised our joined hands over the burning book. My terror morphed into a living thing breathing down my neck, my thoughts ricocheting between Jamie's blank stare after he took the journal to Addie's gloating face to Jamie lying dead at my feet. Clenching my teeth, I squeezed Fiona's fingers. My pulse accelerated, forcing rapid breaths from my lungs. I would not allow the witch to win.

I lowered my hand and peeked at the burning book; the flames danced before me, taunting me. Nothing had changed. In desperation, I turned to Fiona. "It's not working! I can't do this."

Fiona's calm voice urged me on. "Ye have ta let go of yer fear and be a vessel. Let yourself believe, Veronica."

Believe. I stopped focusing on the witch. Instead I focused on my love for Jamie ... the joy I felt every time he laughed, the warmth in his eyes meant exclusively for me, how his unguarded smile refreshed my battered soul. No matter what happened in the future, whether we ended up together or not, I would do everything within my power to save him now.

I believe.

The pages of Aunt Gracie's journal began to flip wildly as the violet blaze turned to ice and shattered with a heart-stopping explosion. Shards of frozen flames blanketed Fiona and I with frigid purple debris as we rocked backward. Fiona's wide eyes radiated shock as she steadied herself. "The witch's curse has shattered. It's broken."

Instead of feeling relief and a sense of accomplishment as I leaned over the book and examined the unmarred pages, dread bloomed in my chest.

"That's a good thing, right?" Kenna moved closer to stand beside me.

My hand trembled as I reached out and touched the journal. In a flash, I could see Jamie — bound, his face slack in unconsciousness, blood dripping from the corner of his mouth. The vision faded, but the image stayed imprinted on my mind's eye.

I blinked away the horrifying picture and answered Kenna's question. "I don't think so. It means she doesn't need it anymore ... because she has something better. She has Jamie."

Duncan swore and rubbed the bridge of his nose. "All she has to do is keep him until the Brig o' Doon closes. If the ruler o' Doon fails to return by the end of the Centennial ..." His words faded out.

Fiona finished the terrible truth as Fergus reached for her hand. "... the Covenant will be broken, and Doon will vanish inta the mists of oblivion forever."

"And she wins." Rage pumped through my veins, screaming for an outlet. I closed the journal with a bang. "But we're not going to let that happen. Are we?"

On cue, they snapped out of their collective despair. "Nay!"
"Of course, not!"

"We fight — to the death if need be!"

"For Doon!"

As they spoke over one another, their actions became focused and decisive. Fiona said a short prayer, Duncan and Fergus quickly inventoried their weapons, and Kenna met my gaze, resolution blazing in her eyes.

"Let's go!" I grabbed the journal and led our ragtag rescue team back down the aisle of the chapel.

"Where, exactly, are we going?" Kenna touched my arm as we moved into the dim corridor.

"Alloway." Practically running, I turned the corner toward the stables. The fastest way to the bridge was on horseback.

"What's the plan?" Kenna asked, keeping pace with me.

"Rescue Jamie. Save Doon. Take Addie down."

That was it. My master plan boiled down to seven little words. It sounded so simple, so straightforward. But how to accomplish it was a different matter. I had no idea how to find Jamie or win against a wicked witch with supernatural powers. But I did know that I would fight for the people I loved, no matter the cost. If ever in my life I'd needed to stand and fight, it was now.

I was done running.

CHAPTER 32

Veronica

The bridge should've been open. I blinked again and willed my burning eyes to see something different. But it was no use. The Brig o' Doon remained a ruin surrounded by impenetrable walls of swirling mist, as if the Centennial hadn't happened.

Upon our arrival, Fiona had discerned a powerful curse that kept the portal to Alloway from opening. But I refused to believe the Protector of Doon would bring us all this way and then let evil win. There had to be another way.

Fergus and Duncan had gone in separate directions, to search the borders for any opening that might get us to Alloway. Fiona and Kenna, meanwhile, sat huddled in their elaborate gowns on the cold stone ground, the former engaged in supernatural introspection while the later dozed with her head slumped against her knees. Both girls appeared to twitch in the flickering light of the torches at the base of the bridge.

All too aware of the minutes ticking away, I turned to Fiona. "Any idea what time it is out there?" I tipped my head in the direction of where Alloway should have been. Wherever Jamie was, time was passing differently, more quickly but in a way I didn't have enough data to quantify.

Fiona's hazel eyes brimmed with fear not only for her king but for all those she loved. Her voice, when she spoke, sounded thick with despair. "Nay. I wasna born at the last Centennial."

Her anguish mirrored my own. I wanted to ask her if she sensed anything that could help us, but I didn't want to add to her misery. I knew if she had, she'd have said so. She was pushing herself nearly as hard as I was.

Instead, I paced the cobbled stones at the mouth of the Brig o' Doon. Each pass caused my legs to ache a bit more. Without a clear focus for my energy, fatigue started to set in. After an indeterminable amount of time, Duncan's sputtering lamp materialized in the heavily wooded forest. A moment later shadows leapt in the opposite direction announcing Fergus had returned as well.

Duncan, slightly out of breath as if he'd been sprinting, spoke first. "This side is impassible."

"Aye," Fergus confirmed as he approached. "My way as well."

At the sound of voices, Kenna sat up, blinking against the artificial light. "Did they find a way across?"

"No." My single word came out harsher than intended as frustration threatened to consume me from the inside out. Any problem could be solved under the right circumstances. Usually I could step outside of myself and examine different perspectives, but at the moment all I could feel was hopeless. We would never find the right solution in the time we had left.

"This is useless." The girl who shared my brain spoke my exact thoughts. "I say we go back to the castle."

Duncan and Fergus nodded in agreement as Fiona said, "Aye. It's time to accept what's ta be."

Yes, we should go back. Wait! What was happening? Kenna wanting to go back to Castle MacCrae? Duncan and Fergus meekly accepting the inevitable destruction of their kingdom? And Fiona's reaction was most telling of all. She wanted to give up? She was the most tenacious person I'd ever met, besides myself.

With a sinking feeling I shouted for everyone to get off the bridge. Despite some grumbling, my friends complied. When we reconvened about thirty feet away, I asked, "Everybody still want to give up?"

Overlapping exclamations of disgust and determination punctuated the quiet.

"Give up?"

"Never!"

"Death first!"

Only Fiona remained silent. After a moment she announced gravely, "It was an attack. I should have sensed it. Despair is the Deceiver's weapon."

I opened my mouth to ask the group what we should do next, but before I could speak Muir Lea filled my senses. A flash of snowy peaks, a sandy beach, and an ocean crashing against rock told me the impossible. "I know how we get to Alloway."

Like a good lieutenant, Duncan was instantly alert and at my side. "How, Veronica?"

"Through the mountains."

Fergus spoke first. "You've gone daft!"

Duncan's face mirrored the other boy's skepticism, and with good reason. The first time I'd tried it, I'd nearly destroyed Doon ... but that still, small voice that had been guiding me since Bainbridge insisted that this time was different. Unfortunately, persuading Fergus and Duncan would waste valuable time—time we didn't have. Turning to my best ally in the group, I said to Fiona, "With every fiber of my being, I know this will work—that the portal will be open for us."

Fiona voiced her agreement. "Veronica speaks the truth. We must cross through the mountains."

Kenna reached for Duncan's hand. "We're in."

"Me as well. With one condition." Fergus's gaze moved across our faces before looking up into the sky. "Fiona stays here. I'll not risk her life on the chance the mountain border is passable."

Spinning the giant around to face her, Fiona cried, "Ye don't get ta decide for me, Fergus Lockhart. If the mountain pass doesn't work, we're all goners anyway."

She gave him a shove but he captured her hands and held them over his heart. "Please, Fee. I will follow Veronica, but I need ta know yer safe." His eyes softened as his voice dropped. "I know I'm not the manliest of lads, but I still need ta protect my own. If anything happened ta you, I'd never be able ta live wi' myself."

As I watched, the girl's resolve melted. All her tumultuous affection poured from her hazel eyes, causing the object of her feelings to turn forty shades of pink.

Sensibly, Duncan added, "With Jamie and me gone, the people will be afraid and lookin' for someone to blame. We need someone who can speak the voice o' reason. And we'll be needin' a welcome party for the Destined who cross when we restore the bridge. We're depending on you, Fiona."

Tearing her eyes away from her love, Fiona gave Duncan a curt nod. "Dinna worry m' laird. I'll see ta the people."

She hugged him and then Kenna. As they parted, Fiona pressed Cameron's ring, the emerald one, into Kenna palm. The look on my BFF's face told me she didn't want it, until

Fiona slipped it on her finger and lightly admonished, "You didna choose the ring, it chose you. And it continues to have need o' you."

Next Fiona turned to me. "I know this has been hard for you, but when the time comes ye must be willing to sacrifice ... for Jamie's sake." As she hugged me good-bye she whispered, "Pure, unselfish love can break any spell."

While I appreciated the sentiment, I had no idea how it could apply to saving Jamie. This wasn't like one of those fairy tale movies where Love's True Kiss could break any curse. But since she'd never steered me wrong before, I tucked the information away.

Fergus, still mottled from their last encounter, cleared his throat shyly. "We may never see each other again. Won't ye kiss me, Fee?"

She leaned, doe-eyed with puckered lips, and whispered, "Come back ta me after ye help Veronica save the world. Then you kin have all the kisses ye like."

Abruptly, Fiona spun out of Fergus's reach and mounted her horse. Without a moment to lose, the rest of us followed her example. Together, we galloped to the fork in the trail where Fiona would take the low road back to Doon while we climbed the high road toward Muir Lea. Just after the split, before she disappeared from sight, Fiona looked back over her shoulder and bellowed, "Believe!"

CHAPTER 33

Mackenna

Thankfully, we encountered no bears or blizzards, which Vee had been worried about. But we'd had to abandon the horses at the end of the cart path and go the rest of the way on foot. It seemed a lifetime since I'd last hiked this hill carrying worries over whether or not the boy I liked wanted to kiss me. And if I'd let him. Now I fervently wished my cares were as trivial as kisses.

As we approached the mountain meadow the sky began to lighten to indigo and then fuchsia. Moments later, crimson, orange, and hot pink streaked across the heavens at an impossible rate as dawn became day. When we entered the woods on the far side of Muir Lea, the sun blazed down from high noon. By the time we finally crossed through the passage in the rocks that would lead us to the beach, the sun already hung low over the ocean, bathing the modern world in gold as it prepared to say good night. The whole day had lasted maybe thirty minutes.

The final descent into the real world had been murder in ballet flats. After Jamie's kidnapping, Vee'd been so singularly focused on getting him back that she refused to waste any time on inconsequential things like practical clothes or clean underwear. The dress code for this pursuit was strictly formal.

We stumbled onto the beach at sunset looking like something from a high school horror movie. My gorgeous teal ball gown had been shredded by thorns and low-lying branches, and my sagging hairdo, complete with twisted tiara, flopped annoyingly over my right eye. Deranged Homecoming Queen was not a good look on me.

Duncan and Fergus, in their ragged dress kilts, looked like they'd just survived the Scottish zombie apocalypse. And Vee, well, she'd ripped off the bottom foot and a half of her scarlet gown ages ago. What was left of her tattered dress, plus the leaves and other debris poking from her hair, made her look like a crazed pixie. It gave me new insights into the integrity of some of my favorite TV shows. Saving the world while looking fabulous *was* next to impossible.

Although the beach had looked deserted during the climb down, the minute we touched the sand clumps of vacationers materialized. Weaving through a touristy maze of plastic lounge chairs, striped blankets, and oversized umbrellas, Duncan and Fergus did their best to temper their reactions to the strange new surroundings as they followed our tiny fearless leader toward the parking lot.

Trading sand for asphalt, I glanced back at the beach just as the sun dipped beneath the horizon with a flash of green. Soon it would be night—only a few hours until the Centennial was over. A nearby sign announced Ayr Beach back the way we came, and Promenade, which I remembered, thanks to Ally, was the main oceanfront drive. Alloway was only a couple of miles away, but without a car, it might as well have been light-years. I placed my hand on Vee's shoulder, grateful for the momentary rest. "What now?"

"We need a cab." Without warning, she raced toward the promenade waving at a passing van. The cab slowed as the driver scrutinized our battered appearances. With a smile that didn't quite reach her eyes, Vee explained, "Bridal party. We were celebrating on the beach and must've passed out. We need a ride back to Alloway."

The cabbie nodded and Vee wrenched open the door. I climbed in first. Without a word, Duncan followed, elegantly tucking his large frame into the bucket seat. But when it was Fergus's turn, he began to backpedal like a cartoon elephant shrinking away from a mouse. "I'm not goin' near that thing," he declared.

"You promised Fiona you'd follow me." Vee balled up her fists, threatening the gentle giant with bodily harm, which under other circumstances would have been hilarious. But the frantic desperation that lurked just under her violent surface was no laughing matter.

Fergus shook his head from side to side. "Not in that thing. What is tha' foul beast?"

In no mood to humor him, she grabbed his hand and twisted. "A horseless metal carriage. It's not going to eat you. Now stop being such a big baby and get in!"

In a death-defying feat of agility, she wrenched Fergus forward, single-handedly catapulting him into the "horseless carriage" with *Taxi* scrawled on the side. Before he could protest, she'd slipped inside and shut the door, and we were speeding off to rescue a boy-king by defeating an evil witch. Perhaps she was part ninja after all.

CHAPTER 34

Veronica

Dunbrae Cottage loomed before us, dark and silent, appearing completely undisturbed. My chest tightened painfully. I'd had no tangible signs we were on the right track, but something in my gut had led me here. That same something made it impossible to be patient while Kenna searched for the spare key she'd hidden in the garden.

"It's near the door … somewhere around here, I'm sure of it," Kenna muttered to herself as she and Duncan lifted every leaf and rock within ten paces of the entrance.

About ready to break the cottage door down myself, I turned to Fergus. The gentle giant hopped up and down on the balls of his feet, his outward agitation a reflection of my own inner turmoil. "Can you open it?" I asked.

"Aye, m' lady." He took a giant step forward, almost knocking Duncan out of the way in his eagerness. "Watch out! I'm going in."

In the same moment, Kenna yelled, "I found it!"

Fergus stopped in mid-stride. Obviously annoyed to have

no physical outlet for his fear, he balled his massive hands into fists the size of melons and glowered fiercely.

"Thank the good Lord!" Duncan exclaimed as Kenna fit the key in the door and we all filed into the foyer. A stale smell of abandonment greeted us. Kenna flipped the light switch, but nothing happened. "Power's turned off."

My heart raced, beating so loudly in the eerie quiet that I glanced at my friends to see if they could hear it. But they were all looking around in distraction, frozen with indecision.

"Let's split up," I said. "Duncan, Kenna — you take upstairs. Fergus and I will search down here. Look for clues ... anything, no matter how small, that seems out of place." Three sets of eyes turned to me with undisguised skepticism.

"Vee, sweetie," Kenna said gently, "I don't think he's here. It doesn't feel like anyone's been here in a really long time." Duncan and Fergus nodded in agreement.

"Then the witch has done her job, hasn't she? Don't you see? She wants this place to appear deserted." They all stared back at me, doubt clear on their faces. "Fine! You go, but I know he's here."

He has to be, I thought as I pushed past them and into the entryway. I headed to the hall storage cupboard and rummaged until I found candles and matches. Holding the matchbox, I attempted to strike a stick across the flint, but my hands shook so badly I couldn't bring the two elements together.

"Let me help ye, lass." Fergus's voice, so close behind me, caused me to jump.

I handed off my task without a word. As the candlelight filled the space, I grabbed several candelabras on an upper shelf of the closet. Fergus inserted candles and lit the wicks one by one. In the shifting light, he appeared thoroughly chastised as he said, "I'm with ye, m' lady. There's a special connection between those who've received a Callin'."

"But I —" I started to deny his words, but Duncan interrupted me.

"No, lass. Whether ye or my brother choose to accept it, the link between you is undeniable and should no' be discounted. Hand me two o' those candelabras. Mackenna and I will search upstairs."

"Thank you," I breathed, swallowing the lump in my throat. No time for tears now.

🌀 🌀 🌀

Two hours later, we'd found nothing. Kenna and I searched everywhere, pausing only long enough to get out of our cumbersome gowns and into modern clothes before ripping the cottage apart.

I splashed cool water on my face and stared into the gilded bathroom mirror at my huge, haunted eyes. We were no closer to finding Jamie than we'd been when we arrived. None of us had found a single clue to indicate anyone had been in this house since Kenna and I left, let alone a sign that a witch harbored a young king here.

Jamie's image appeared before me, a cocky grin on his beautiful mouth, his dark eyes shining with love. With love? Did he love me? Or was I superimposing my own romanticized wishes on his memory? There was no point going there now ... or ever. For Doon, I would find their new king and bring him home. Safe. From there I would let my future unfold, however it was meant to be.

Taking several deep, cleansing breaths, I focused my heart and mind and prayed, *Please, God, show me the way.* In desperation, I waited, gripping the cool porcelain sink until my fingers went numb. What made me think the Protector of

Doon would hear me, the girl who'd started all this trouble in the first place?

Gradually, a pinkish light filtered in behind my closed lids. With a start, I opened my eyes and stared down at my hand. The Ring of Aontacht glowed, filling the small bathroom with a radiant light.

Jamie was here!

Grasping onto hope, I rushed from the bathroom. Kenna was nowhere in sight. I wanted to yell out for her, but as I opened my mouth some instinct warned me to remain quiet. If the witch was near, my shout would alert her to my presence.

With only the dull glow of the ring for a guide, I took a tentative step into the foyer. The glow became startlingly bright. Curiously, I took a step back, and it dulled again. I rushed forward, and as expected the ring flared as I hurried into the middle of the entryway. According to the ring's blazing light, I was on the right track.

I considered my options. Fergus and I had searched the library together, removing most of the books from the shelves, so I stepped toward the front door ... but the ring dimmed in response. Turning in a circle, I walked toward the stairway. The light within the ring remained unchanged. I backed off the stairs and moved toward the library, and to my relief the ring glowed brighter with every step.

I entered the room and shut the door behind me. The luminosity of the red stone eclipsed the candles we'd left burning on the coffee table, casting macabre shadows on the walls and cold stone hearth. I fought back a shiver as I threw open the curtains and allowed a beam of moonlight to slice through the room. With singular focus, I ran my fingers around the edge of the hearth stones, testing the seal of the mortar. It appeared solid. Concentrating on the walls, I turned a slow pirouette, searching for any inconsistency ... There!

In the corner to the left of the hearth there was a gap between the wall and the shelf, wider at the top than at the base. The flame in the red stone danced encouragingly as I moved forward, my stomach doing sickening backflips. Slipping my fingers around the gap, I pulled with all my strength.

With a great whoosh of musty air, the bookcase swung open to reveal an ancient stone staircase that curved down into blackness. Not wanting to risk the glow of the ring giving me away, I twisted the stone around and closed my fist over it. Saying a quick prayer, I stepped down into the unknown.

CHAPTER 35

Mackenna

On the stage, conflict never resolves until the third act — at the eleventh hour. I tried to comfort myself, but the words felt empty. The eleventh hour had passed, and we were no closer to finding Jamie than we'd been at eight — or nine — or ten. With less than an hour left to save Doon, each futile minute scraped through me as if I were the narrow center of a sand timer.

Throughout the day Addie had grown more Grimm-like in my mind, until she epitomized evil incarnate. Just like the storybook kingdom and fairy-tale princes come to life, the wicked witch lived in the flesh — and she was a mean, cunning old hag. Her magic had messed with Doon's enchantment. If she was powerful enough to prevent the Brig o' Doon from opening and fill us with such despair we were ready to roll over in defeat, what chance did our little Scooby Gang stand of defeating her?

Unfortunately, we had to find her first. Despite Vee's irrational insistence Jamie was here, we hadn't found any evidence that Addie or the king of Doon had ever been in Dunbrae Cottage. We'd investigated every inch.

With nowhere inside left to search, Fergus and Duncan had gone to inspect the riverbank while Vee and I reexamined the house. Exhausted and in desperate need of a timeout, I wandered upstairs to grab a few things. In the flickering candlelight, I hurriedly ransacked Vee's drawers, stuffing cotton undergarments, jeans, a couple of hoodies, her jogging gear, and a few of her favorite books into a canvas bag. None of her other possessions would be of much benefit for her new life in Doon. After everything she'd gone through today, I refused to accept she and Jamie wouldn't end up together.

When I finished with Vee's room, I headed to my own. I hastily searched for anything else that might be useful and added it to the bundle. Rifling through the closet, I grabbed my favorite jacket. As I shrugged it on, a crumpled rectangle of paper fell from the pocket to land faceup at my feet. My acceptance letter to the Adrenaline Theatre Company internship program, personally signed by Weston Ballard. Ever since I'd gotten it in the mail, I'd carried it around like a talisman, to ward off the spirits of an unremarkable life.

Although half dead with fatigue and fear, that letter caused something inside of me to break. What would happen if I failed to save the boy I cared about? My life — my goal of a successful career on the stage — wouldn't matter if Doon and all its inhabitants perished.

And if by some miracle they were saved, what then?

To his credit, Duncan had done his best not to gawk at his strange new surroundings, and he hadn't said one word as I crammed him into the taxi. Although he was desperate to find Jamie, I knew a little part of him had been trying to prove he belonged in my world.

But how? And as what? I suspected there weren't too many job openings for the position of prince. And no matter how hard I tried, I couldn't reconcile the idea of Duncan working in a random office, or worse yet flipping burgers at some greasy fast food joint, with the daring Scotsman I'd first seen trying to pummel his brother to death.

I guess he could always keep house. Shop at the local Walmart and cook misshapen meals while I pursued my career. Survive on misplaced infatuation while I embraced my dreams.

My legs gave way and I slumped to the floor, too numb to go on. Duncan's gorgeous yet tortured face appeared before me. His brown eyes held an unrelenting agony at the thought of his beloved home perishing. The hard set of his jaw conveyed his determination to save his world. His mouth clamped tight against unspoken fears that he might fail.

All he'd ever wanted was to serve his kingdom, his king, and his Protector. He'd told me so at Muir Lea. Yet for me, he would walk away from his heart's desires. How was that fair when I couldn't — no, I wouldn't — do the same for him? He deserved better: a long and happy life with someone who shared his ideals. Not some girl who insisted on putting herself first.

Grains of sand continued to drop and shred my insides as I prayed for Duncan and Fiona's Protector to work a miracle. Please save him, I begged. If you rescue him, along with his king and country, I'll give him back to you. I'll give him up forever. I promise!

A gentle whoosh resounded in the hall, followed by a blast of cool, dank air on my face. I blinked my eyes open to absolute black. The breeze that'd come out of nowhere had gutted the candles and left me in darkness.

Was this the universe's way of telling me to give up? Why

would the Protector of Doon extinguish what little light I had? Wasn't light synonymous with hope? And Divine promise?

Please ...

My hand began to tingle. I watched a shimmering green flame dance in the emerald of my ring as amazement stirred in my chest. With each passing moment, Uncle Cam's ring grew brighter. As the glow expanded to light the room, a great and terrible knowledge settled over me. The curtain had not closed on the final act. The plot still contained a few twists, and there was magic yet to do. In the grand scheme of the universe, my own dreams meant nothing; the only thing that mattered was saving those I loved.

CHAPTER 36

Veronica

The stone felt cold and slimy beneath my fingers as I made my way down the passageway. To calm my nerves, I counted steps as I went. Twelve ... thirteen ... fourteen. The stairs funneled down in a tight circle. Moving silently, I descended into complete darkness. Eighteen ... nineteen ... twenty.

I wouldn't allow my imagination to form pictures of what I would find. Instead, I concentrated on keeping my balance and counting — as if my life depended on it.

Twenty-six ... twenty-seven ... twenty-eight ... twenty-nine ... *Whack!*

I pitched forward, hitting something solid with my shoulder. Belatedly, I realized the steps had ended. My pulse pounded in my ears as I explored the barrier in front of me. It felt like wood, warmer than the stone but still slick with damp. Images of spindly legged spiders dropping on my head and rabid, hungry rats milling about my feet almost paralyzed me. I opened my fist, and the red light of my ring erupted, illuminating a crude wooden door — thankfully, no spiders or rats were in sight.

With trembling fingers, I lifted the heavy wrought-iron lever, cringing as a squeak echoed through the corridor followed by a soft, creaking moan. The door opened about a foot and stuck, forcing me to squeeze through the opening. Flickering torches lined the stone passageway that led to another window-less door at the far end. On tiptoes, I jogged toward the end of the hall as every instinct within me screamed in warning.

I put my ear to the wood, held my breath, and listened. Nothing. I braced for the screech of metal on metal, but this door didn't make a sound as I slowly inched it closer to me.

Pressing my spine against the gritty wall, I peered through the opening. A single candle flickered in the far corner of a small, cell-like room. I blinked against the shifting light, sifting through shadowy details. A bare cot ... a wooden table ... Jamie!

He was bound to a chair, his head resting on his chest. Was he unconscious, or was I too late? All thoughts of caution gone, I pushed into the room and ran toward him as his eyes rolled open.

"Stop. 'Tis a trap," he groaned.

Heedless of the warning, I ran forward. But just before I reached him, something slammed me back against the wall. I hit so hard, my legs collapsed, sending me to the floor.

"Vee!" Jamie cried.

I sucked air into my burning lungs and searched for the source of attack. Through the gloom, a slight figure with long, wavy blonde hair emerged. "Allyson?" She glanced up at me, her green eyes huge in her pale face, her diamond nose ring glittering in the candlelight. She wasn't bound like Jamie, but she was trembling. There was no one else in the room — it didn't make sense. "Ally, run and get help! My friends are upstairs." I pushed to my feet. "I'll untie him and meet you there."

Hyperaware of the time slipping away, I stumbled over to Jamie, who barely seemed to be able to lift his head. "Jamie?"

He turned toward my voice, his eyes unfocused. "It's her."

"What?" I began working on the rope binding his hands behind his back, but it was stuck tight.

"Veronica." It was Allyson's voice but — different. A chill rushed down my spine. I raised my eyes to find the girl walking steadily toward us, her edges strangely blurred. "You've done well."

Something was wrong with her face. Slowly, I straightened and placed my hands on Jamie's shoulders, my heart dropping to the floor. Impossibly, Ally's hair began to shrink, growing shorter and straighter before my eyes. Her rounded cheeks sharpened, the skin on her face pulling tighter over her cheekbones. As she drew closer, tiny lines spidered out from her eyes. The nose ring was gone and her mother, Addie Dell, stood before me.

Oh no. I shook my head in denial as my knees grew weak and I gripped Jamie's shoulders harder. Allyson and Addie were the same person? And they were both Adelaide Cadell — the Witch of Doon.

I couldn't tear my eyes away from the terrible excitement lighting her face as she purred in a silken voice, "I'm so glad to see you. Come here, my dear."

"Stay away from her!" Jamie growled. The wooden chair legs knocked against the floor as he struggled against his bonds.

It occurred to me that my hands should've been resting on his shoulders, but he was suddenly several feet away. I hesitated mid-step, unsure how I'd gotten halfway across the room.

"Be still and silent, young king o' Doon," Addie commanded.

She flicked her wrist in Jamie's direction and he froze, unable even to speak.

"Strong willed, that one," Addie said with a glow of appreciation in her eyes. "I've had ta enthrall him thrice now."

Focusing her full attention back to me, she announced, "Veronica, I wanted ta thank ye for delivering my spell inta the proper hands."

I stared in shock at Jamie's eerie, lifeless form across the room. "I didn't deliver anything for you."

"'Tis no matter, really. It got ta him somehow. I must admit, though, I was beginning ta despair that my plan had failed."

Blood rushed in my ears as I clenched my hands into fists. I already knew she'd manipulated me like an empty-headed marionette, but hearing her gloat about it made me dizzy with rage. I'd never wanted to punch someone more in my life. "And what plan would that be?"

"My plan to destroy Doon, o' course." Addie arched a golden brow. "It's just an added bonus that ye're here ta watch your sweetheart die at midnight along with his kingdom."

Something about her gloating statement caught me off guard. "Wait. What makes you think he's my sweetheart?"

Her laugh was musical, like the tinkling of breaking glass. "I knew from the moment I touched ye that you'd received a Calling. It was delicious, really. Though it negated all the effort I'd gone to in conjuring a vision o' the crown prince and planting the enspelled sketch in Grace Lockhart's journal for Mackenna to find. I no longer needed young James's beautiful face ta lure her to take the journal over the bridge. The power of the Calling did all that for me. *You* did all that for me." Her focus shifted back to Jamie as she stalked toward him. "And o' course Gideon's eyes were an invaluable tool. I just wish he'd been able to find the journal sooner. 'Twas a truly brilliant hiding place, Veronica. But 'tis no matter now." She laughed as she waved her hand in a dismissive motion.

My mind tumbled back to all the times I'd caught Gideon lurking in the shadows, and wondered how often the guard — or rather Addie — had been watching us over the past weeks.

The witch moved to Jamie's side and ran her fingers through the layers of his hair. "Your prince and I get on quite well. A pity we don't have more time."

Speaking of time, I knew the long-winded explanations were her way of trying to run out the game clock. I needed to make my move. As I glared at the lazy movement of her hand, a reflection on her finger caught the candlelight. She wore a ring almost identical to the Rings of Aontacht in size and shape but with a flat black stone. Was it a source of power, like Gracie and Cameron's rings? Or merely a benign piece of jewelry? I'd almost inched to Jamie's other side when I noticed his eyes following me.

"A pity one so lovely has ta be destroyed." She ran one long violet fingernail down the strong lines of Jamie's immobile face.

I ground my teeth together, my blood boiling hotter every time she touched him. "Maybe he doesn't."

The words slipped out before I could stop them. I had no plan. No reason for her to change her mind. But there had to be some way, some bargain I could make — in exchange for Jamie's life. "Have to be destroyed, I mean ... We could make a deal."

She threw her head back and laughed. "I'm the most power-ful witch in my line, fer generations! What could one little girl possibly have ta offer me?"

With a calming breath, I tried to place myself in her black soul, to figure out what dark thing the witch might crave — that I could provide in the next thirty minutes. Would she want the ring now that I'd brought it back across the bridge? Probably not. If Doon's sacred rings were any use to her, other than a host for her parasitic spells, she would've exploited them by now. Instead, she'd planted them for Kenna and me to find. But there had to be something else.

I watched as she stared at Jamie hungrily, like she might devour him to the bone. She ignored me, disregarding my presence as if I was no match for her power and therefore no threat. Her arrogance was a weakness that I might be able to use.

Adrenaline rolled through my body as I considered the odds of taking her out the old-fashioned way. She moved to light another candle, and I saw my chance. Clenching my fists, I hurtled toward her back.

With a mumbled word and a flick of her wrist, she propelled me through the air as if I were nothing more than a feather. But I landed like a boulder. My head bounced on the concrete floor and I struggled against the blackness that threatened to swallow me.

Addie's dark form knelt over me and she shook her head from side to side. The curtain of her loose hair cast her face in unearthly shadow, transforming her into a faceless specter.

Brushing my bangs almost lovingly off my face, she intoned, "You stupid, stupid girl. Did ye think you could best me that easily?"

Past Addie's crouched form, Jamie glared holes in the witch's back. With great effort he opened his mouth and called to me. "Vee — "

The witch's eyes widened in surprise before she stood and spun to face him. "I see our obstinate hero is back." Her entire body was coiled and tense as she walked to Jamie's bound, vulnerable form. Flipping back her sleeve, she glanced at her watch and smiled — a wide, maniacal leer that made my blood run cold.

"Not long now, young man. I canna wait to watch you disappear into the mist, along with your beloved kingdom. What would yer dear departed mother say if she knew her favored son was the cause of Doon's ultimate demise?" She shook her head and made a tsking sound with her tongue.

Barely a whisper, Jamie labored to contradict her. "She'd say Doon's blessing is yer curse ... and it always will be."

"Not for long —"

He shook his head feebly. "Aye. Forever."

Emboldened by Jamie's strength in the face of certain death, I scrambled to my feet. I knew only one thing: I couldn't watch him disintegrate before my eyes, or whatever horrific thing would happen to him at the stroke of midnight. I had to find a way to save him and Doon, no matter what the cost. The Ring of Aontacht had to be the key. Fiona had asked me to put it on in the chapel just before the spell around the journal shattered, and it had led me to Jamie. This was no benign piece of jewelry; it contained power, if I could just figure out how to use it.

I closed the ring in my fist and channeled my desperation into a question — How can I defeat the witch? Several seconds ticked by, and then I heard the auld laird's lilting brogue resonate in my mind. "When the time comes ye must be willing to sacrifice ... for Jamie's sake." Echoed by Fiona's parting advice: "Pure, unselfish love can break any spell."

Bits and pieces of information slipped into place, and a perfectly crazy plan took shape. Before I could put too much thought into where my scheme would lead, I stepped forward and said, "Maybe I have something to offer you after all, Addie."

Jamie's eyes pleaded with me, as if he knew what I was about to say. Clearly, he'd fought against the enthrallment to speak, and it had cost him. He no longer raged against his bonds, but sat hunched over in the chair, bruises of exhaustion under his eyes.

I took a deep breath, faced Addie, and announced with all the confidence I could muster, "I want to trade places with him."

Jamie groaned, "Vee, nooo."

Addie stilled. Now that I had her attention, I continued. "I know I can invoke some sort of exchange using this ring." I rotated the stone around on my finger and lifted my hand.

She stared at it as if examining it for flaws and then lifted her gaze to me, her eyes burning with something I couldn't identify. "Ye want ta offer yerself in sacrificial substitution?"

That sounded about right. I nodded. "My life for Jamie's."

"Why should I?" Addie's eyes narrowed with suspicion.

Searching for a compelling reason to give her, I dared a glance at my prince, and my heart contracted. His eyes glistened with unshed tears, and his muscles trembled as he strained to break his bonds.

"Adelaide, dinna listen to her. I'm the one you want." His voice was low, but his words were underscored with steel. "Leave Vee out of this."

The effort it took him to speak appeared to drain the last of his strength. His shoulders slumped and his eyes fell shut. I crossed to him and cupped his rough cheek in my hand. His eyes cracked open, blazing at me under heavy lids.

My true destiny clear for the first time in this journey, I quietly pleaded, "It has to be this way. Don't you see? This world would be much too dark a place without you in it."

Jamie's mom had said there was a price for everything, and now I finally understood. I placed a single lingering kiss on his warm lips and then leaned in close to his ear and whispered, "I would pay any price for you."

Addie clapped her hands in glee. "Aww, how verra sweet! I was going ta enjoy his death at midnight, but victory will be even sweeter witnessing his suffering as he watches you die along with his precious kingdom. Not to mention I get to keep the lovely young king as my plaything."

A sliver of fear shot through me as I met her wide, bone-chilling grin. I clenched my teeth tight to keep them from chattering and nodded. This was it, my last hope.

"Place your hand on yer prince's shoulder."

I complied and she lifted her ring to her lips, muttering secret words against the precious stone. Her eyes glowed neon green in the gloom as she declared, "So it shall be."

A light flashed and then a blinding blackness engulfed me, followed by a quick, intense pain, like fire shooting through my veins. Maybe her spell was too powerful. Was I dying?

Weightlessness pulled me toward oblivion. I struggled against the welcoming dark, and a flash of memory pierced the swirling abyss. "Veronica ... Doon did no' call ye here to become its queen by marrying my son. Ye are here for a reason. *Our Protector* does no' make mistakes ... by marrying my son ... its queen."

With a flutter, I opened my eyes. I was sitting in the wooden chair, Jamie standing between me and the Witch of Doon. All traces of Addie's enchantment over him had vanished.

"As a citizen o' Doon by blood," he spat, "ye must surrender to me." He had no weapon, but his fingers twitched as if ready to rip her apart with his bare hands.

Addie's laughter was as evil as any Wicked Witch of the West I'd ever heard in the movies. "Dinna test me, James."

Jamie took a menacing step forward, doing just that.

"I could kill you both without so much as a word." Then, as if to make her point, she lifted her hand and Jamie flew through the air, hitting the wall with a sickening thud. "But where would the fun be in that?"

Still weak, I stood on shaky legs and made my way to his side. His dazed eyes met mine as I crouched beside him and whispered, "Are you all right?"

He nodded and then closed his lids, grimacing in pain.

I sprang to my full height and spat, "Don't ever touch him again!"

Addie advanced, evil triumph radiating from her countenance. She flicked her wrist and suddenly I couldn't breathe. It was as if invisible hands were pressing on my windpipe. "Poor deluded Veronica. Just as you are nothing ta Jamie, yer irrelevant to me. Because you are nothing."

Stars were dancing before my eyes when she released me with a chuckle. I sucked in shallow, ragged breaths and clutched my burning throat as she turned to address Jamie. "See what a weak coward you've chosen? She's nothing but a child."

Weak coward — the exact phrase I'd used so many times to describe my father. Too cowardly to stick around when things got hard, too weak to face his problems and fight for the people he loved. But I wasn't like him, at least not anymore.

Suddenly, the Ring of Aontacht burned on my finger, each symbol branding my skin. I'd researched every rune until I knew them by heart. And yet I still felt like I was missing something — some greater significance that I sensed but couldn't see. I flipped the characters in my mind's eye, examining each one.

Jamie struggled to his feet, every line of his face etched in pain, but his voice was strong and clear. "As yer king, I command ye to release us at once!"

"I'm terribly sorry, young James, but since Veronica so selflessly took yer place, not only are ye no longer a citizen o' Doon but" — she narrowed her eyes, a malevolent smile twisting her lips — "Doon no longer has a king."

The ring's symbols tumbled in my mind until they were

one connected blur. Symbols became pictures, pictures became words, and then everything clicked into place.

Addie raised her fist, and the black stone on her ring glowed with an ethereal energy. I stepped toward her. With confidence born of a higher purpose, I lifted my hand, my own ring gleaming on my finger, and stared evil incarnate directly in her brilliant green eyes.

"No, but Doon has a queen."

CHAPTER 37

Veronica

Adelaide Dell let loose an unearthly wail—like a banshee going through a wood chipper—and leveled her ring at my chest.

"Vee! What've ye done?" Jamie stepped closer, intending to shield me with his body.

With a shout of warning, I wrenched him back as white-hot light shot out of my ring, slamming into the violet power blasting toward me. I had no idea how, but the ring on my finger was neutralizing the witch's spell. An explosion of white, purple, and fuchsia sparks filled the air, cascading around us like fireworks. I held my arm steady, spots dancing in front of my eyes as the embers of magic dissipated.

The fury in Addie's now violet irises rivaled something out of a monster movie. Her voice filled the hollow space, low and lethal as she growled, "How did ye know?"

Neither one of us lowered our arms as I lifted my chin and forced myself to meet her turbulent stare. "I finally saw it. The symbols on the rings have individual meanings, but *Aontacht* means *unity*. They work together like a sentence." I glanced at Jamie, who'd remained by my side despite my warning. "When I took Jamie's place, I could complete the spell by declaring myself the new ruler. Now I'm the one who's life is linked to the fate of Doon."

Addie clasped her hands behind her back. "I gravely underestimated you, Veronica."

Her relaxed posture tempted me to let down my guard, but I couldn't allow myself any weakness. This was no time for gloating. We still had to find a way to get out of here and back to the bridge in less than twenty minutes. Now that Jamie was free, all we had to do was get past one very angry witch.

"Yer a clever one, but you're still going ta die," Addie continued as I caught Jamie's eye and tilted my head toward the exit. He nodded once.

"Vee, watch out!" I turned toward Kenna's voice as she ran into the room, Duncan and Fergus barreling in behind her. Ken pointed over my shoulder at the witch and I spun toward the threat. Addie stared rapturously at her ring, watching it ooze black goo that coalesced on the floor like nightmarish Jell-O molds.

"Serpents!" Fergus shouted as he drew a large two-handed sword and charged. "Three o' them."

Duncan rushed into the fray, tossing Jamie his spare sword before unsheathing his own weapon.

Addie's serpents bore little resemblance to snakes or dragons; they were more like wriggling, ashy slugs. I stumbled backward as their gaping maws hissed, permeating the air with the stench of rotten meat. Black ooze dripped from between their rows of sharp teeth. In mere seconds, they quadrupled in size. Their ravenous mouths snapped hungrily as they writhed back and forth.

Jamie grabbed my arm and hauled me behind him. With a glance toward his fellow swordsmen, he yelled, "Now!"

Fergus, Jamie, and Duncan slashed at the serpents. They deftly sliced their way down the length of the creatures, but by the time they hacked the serpents' tails off the severed heads had begun to shimmy. Other disembodied pieces followed and grew like something from a science-fiction experiment gone wrong.

"They're like giant worms!" I exclaimed, grateful I'd paid attention in Honors Biology. "Every piece will grow into a new monster."

Kenna clutched my arm in a death grip. "We have to help them!"

Not only were our guys severely outnumbered, but they'd ended up on the opposite end of the chamber, separated from us by a live wall of voracious serpents. Despite the danger, they held their own, so I tried to focus on the source of the threat. If I could thwart the witch, the victory would hopefully put an end to her monstrous worms as well.

My head swiveled to find Addie lounging against the wall behind us, reveling in her work. I glanced at the seemingly lifeless ring on my finger. I'd used it in defense, but I'd no idea how I'd done it or how to activate its magic again.

Pushing off the wall, the witch strode toward us at a leisurely pace. "You girls think yer so smart. Yer just like them." She raised her angular chin to indicate Fergus and the MacCrae brothers. "So predictable. So easy ta control. Just like that feeble-minded captain of the guard — so afraid of the evil Witch o' Doon, and yet he fell instantly under my spell. My merest suggestion had him committing murder."

Although I didn't exactly care for Gideon, that didn't mean I approved of Addie using him like a hand puppet — I knew the feeling of being played all too well.

Kenna let go of my arm and faced the witch. "You're pretty proud of yourself ... for someone who used a rent-a-cop to do her dirty work. Can't handle things on your own?"

Addie chuckled and advanced like a hungry wolf stalking its prey. Suddenly, she stopped and shook her head. Her edges blurred once again. Long blonde tresses wound about her shoulders as the effects of twenty years of aging reversed. "I used you lasses too. And ye did everythin' perfectly. Thanks ta the two o' you, my plans are nearly complete."

"Ally?" Kenna gasped, stumbling back a step.

She was showing off, performing her tricks for my best friend. But why? Was she trying to distract us? Maybe if I could keep her talking, she'd give me a clue. "Why, Addie? Doon was your home once. Why would you want to destroy it?"

"Silly girl. 'Tis more than destroying Doon that I want. When Doon was ... blessed, I became cursed. As long as the kingdom thrives, my magic is unstable."

As if to underscore her point, she morphed back into her forty-something self. "But there's power in Doon. Once the kingdom has vanished, the enchantments it contains will be mine for the taking."

She turned to regard a mirror that I hadn't noticed before. Her reflection was the stuff of demented nightmares — cadaverous gray skin stretched too tightly over sharp bones; brittle yellow-white hair hung around her skeletal face in uneven tufts; thin, flaking white lips pulled back to reveal rotting brown teeth. Only her violet eyes remained unchanged.

Goose bumps prickled the back of my neck as Addie looked away from the hideous image. Hatred for her true appearance burned in her false, attractive face. "When Doon is destroyed, I'll finally be free. I'll take the kingdom's power and recover my true beauty. Once I'm restored, I'll rebuild my coven and the modern world will worship me."

Outrage poured through me. This hideous creature sought to gain power at the expense of hundreds of innocent souls. I stepped toward her. "People will never worship you."

The witch chuckled, an icy sound like claws scratching my brain. "We shall see, little queen."

Before I could react, Kenna shrieked and swung her duffel bag at Addie's head.

"Mackenna!" Duncan yelled in warning. The bag stopped mid swing, falling out of Kenna's stunned fingers and dropping to the floor.

Addie arched her perfect brows and flicked her hand in Kenna's direction. My best friend froze in place, unable to move a muscle — except, apparently, those around her mouth. She let go a string of profanities and threats that under any other circumstances would've been inspiring.

The witch emitted a humorless chuckle. "Now that the colorful sidekick is out o' the way, it's time to address the wee girl who would play the hero. For you, o' queen of Doon." She raised her hand, made a circular motion, and then a quick downward slash.

Reflexively, my arm jerked up, and I saw the ring on my finger was glowing again. But before the magic could form, a weight like a concrete wall crushed me to the floor. I couldn't move. Couldn't breathe. Panic ripped through me as I felt my body being crushed to nothing. As if from a great distance, I recognized my own hysterical voice screaming for help.

Wave after wave of crippling pain slammed down on me. Through it, I could just make out Jamie's voice. "Vee." His words were punctuated by blows of his sword. "I shoulda — told you. The monarch o' Doon's — meant to be the — counter balance to the witch. When the ruler's weak — the witch's evil grows — more — powerful. Ye must — be — strong — love."

His words bolstered me, giving me the strength to focus and mentally push against the crippling, invisible weight. I had an instant of relief before it slammed back doubly strong, the attack no longer just an external pressure but also a mental assault. The spell moved through me like jagged bits of glass, gouging my soul and draining my will.

A thousand insecurities bombarded my mind, urging me to give up. Telling me I couldn't win. That I was nothing but a powerless fraud. A pathetic loser. Unwanted. Stupid and weak. Never good enough ...

Tossed in a raging river, I was drowning in self-condemnation. Memories of my many failures flashed through my mind — Eric in Stephanie's arms, Mom's resentful gaze, Dad waving as he backed out of the driveway for the last time — draining my will with each recollection. Who was I to think I could make a difference? I was just a worthless girl from Podunk, Indiana who'd never done a noble thing in her life. I wasn't a warrior like Jamie. Tears leaked from my eyes and my lungs burned, ready to explode.

Darkness closed in on my vision, and I realized it was over. The substitution had been a mistake. Doon's new queen had failed.

CHAPTER 38

Mackenna

I would never look at a game of Scene Freeze the same way. In fact, if I ever got out of this I would never play it again. Being frozen was painful and humiliating, not to mention terrifying.

All I could do was watch my best friend being crushed to death. Gawk as the boy I cared for fought off a half-dozen hell worms alongside his brother and his friend. And stare at the Big Bad Witch strolling from one end of the room to the other inspecting her handiwork.

The only arsenal I had left was my words. I hurled them at her like a virtuoso, calling her every name I could think of and then making some up when Vee howled again in pain. If this was the end, I would not die quietly.

"What's the matter?" I goaded. "Did some prince ditch your skanky butt for a nice girl? Or were you just born a pathetic, monarchy-hating slag?"

Bull's-eye.

Addie's smile faltered as I earned her full attention. A vein under her eye twitched. As she sauntered in my direction, I worried that slag would be the last word I ever spoke.

Nah — I could do better. But just as I opened my mouth, Addie's hand made a grasping motion. Suddenly, I had no air. My chest seized, paralyzing my lungs as my eyes began to bulge.

"Slag," she mused. "Such an interesting colloquialism."

Although her attention was riveted on me, her fist opened to hurl a gust of air at Duncan. The blast knocked the sword from his hand. Helplessly, I watched as he ducked into a roll and dove after the weapon, narrowly avoiding a snapping serpent in the process.

Addie clapped her hands and my air returned. I wheezed like an asthmatic bullfrog while she studied me as if I were some kind of lower life-form. From the opposite end of the room, Fergus yelped in pain, causing the witch to chuckle. "Careful," she called in mock warning. "They bite."

She was toying with us — adding insult to our injuries and impending death. My body may've been a statue, but my insides seethed with rage. "One day you will rot in hell, you shriveled old troll."

With a shrug, Addie mused, "Perhaps. But not before her." She stepped around me to sneer down at my best friend. A wave of her hand and Vee shrieked like she was being skinned alive.

"Stop! Please . . ." I was no longer cursing, I was begging. For the sake of my loved ones, I'd go silently.

"Does the plucky sidekick want ta add anything else?" With a satisfied smile, Addie tipped her head as if to say, "I could keep this up all day, you incompetent slag."

But we didn't have all day — just minutes. A quarter hour at best. Once the clock struck twelve, her sick little game would come to an end along with Vee and the rest of Doon. Was it too much to ask for one final twist in the plot?

Vee moaned. Sweat coated her face while she struggled against an unbearable weight. As I watched my best friend whimper in pain, I decided to use my words in a way that I hoped would cause less of a backlash. "Vee, if you leave me again, I'll never forgive you. Doon is your destiny. Fight for it!"

"Can't — " With great effort, Vee's hand — the one bearing my aunt Gracie's ring — reached out to brush against my ankle. As the golden metal touched my skin, a live current raced up my leg and throughout my entire body. The sensation stung like thawing ice with flash fire, but I was free.

I was free!

My instincts screamed at me to stay still, to use my freedom to some advantage. But how? I couldn't fight the witch with my bare hands. And I would clearly lose any kind of verbal sparring match.

"You know — " Addie raked her nails softly down my cheek, her tone casual as I pretended to be too helpless to do anything other than submit. "I could freeze your internals, ta match yer exterior. All your bodily functions would cease, instantly. Painlessly. Or ..."

Or I could endure unspeakable agony.

Despite the crushing pain, Vee sputtered on my behalf, "Please let. Her go. Take me. But let Ken go."

"Perhaps — although she would make a lovely minion after the rest o' ye are dead." Addie's eyes narrowed into snakelike slits as she leaned over Vee. "Such a sad little queen. All alone ... in excruciating pain ... Are ye ready to meet yer destiny?"

But Vee wasn't alone. She had Jamie and a kingdom ... and she had me.

The truth I'd been so reluctant to face burned from Uncle Cameron's ring into my finger. The Rings of Aontacht had chosen us — both of us. I had a significant role as well.

As the metal seared my skin, my finger twitched. Luckily, that hand was hidden behind my back. Hidden from the witch, but not everyone.

"Vee! Look at me. As much as I've denied it, Doon is our destiny. We need to stick together. Are you paying attention?"

I prayed that even in her weakened state, the girl who shared my brain would be able to discern my unspoken meaning. I couldn't best the Witch of Doon with physical power or clever words. But I did have one skill that Addie would never see coming.

I was a damned good actress.

CHAPTER 39

Veronica

Through a haze of agonizing pain, I saw Kenna's finger wiggle behind her back. The emerald stone of her ring shimmered luminously in the shadows. A spark of life bloomed in my heart, and with it hope pushed against the darkness, driving back my growing despair. I may not have been able to defeat the witch on my own, but fortunately I wouldn't have to.

My own fingers twitched as I clenched my eyes and focused outside of myself, on my purpose — our purpose. Kenna and I had always been stronger as a team. Even the rings we wore symbolized unity. My ring had allowed me to neutralize the witch's earlier attack, so what if combining the rings made them even more powerful? Blood began to flow back into my knotted muscles as my strength returned. Addie may have won the battle, but she would not use me to harm the people I loved. She would not win this war.

Visualizing my purpose as a sledgehammer, I crashed through the pall that threatened to crush my will and lunged toward Kenna. "Now!"

Our hands locked and Ken pulled me to my feet. The witch's shriek of protest echoed in the small room as our rings' power fused. The red and green united, and energy crackled through me like a lightning storm. Instantly, the lingering weight of the witch's hex lifted.

"Yer going ta regret that, little queen!" Addie screeched.

Furtively, my eyes shifted to Jamie. He edged nearer, still battling the serpents — beating them with the flat of his sword. Even in the midst of fighting for his life, he was amazing.

Addie cackled, pulling my attention back to her. The hair at the back of my neck stood on end as her hands moved in a circle like she was caressing an imaginary ball. Words I couldn't understand spewed from her lips. A purple haze swirled between her palms, growing more solid by the second.

My chest tightened for the impending blow of magic as cold sweat trickled down my back. The glow of my ring began to dim. I'd broken free from her binding curse, but that was only half the battle. What was I supposed to do now? I met Kenna's frantic stare, searching for answers she didn't have.

And then Jamie was there. His dark eyes locked on mine, and something beyond reason, beyond even time, passed between us. His gaze surrounded me like a physical force and ran deep inside my soul. A slow, confident smile spread across his face. He didn't need to speak; faith shone from his eyes, filling me with strength. And I knew not even a maniacal, power-hungry witch would stop me from saving him.

Addie continued to chant, the violet mist between her palms growing stronger. The dark magic illuminated her face like a ghastly X-ray, revealing her jawbone and every tooth beneath the transparent veil of her skin. The ball knitted faster in her hands.

I turned and squeezed Kenna's fingers. "We have to do this together."

She nodded and we lifted our joined hands. The ring's combined power blazed, brilliant and sparkling like the sun reflecting on a fresh blanket of snow. We moved forward as one, and Addie froze in place, the midnight shine of her spell fading rapidly. The demonic sphere swirled faster and faster, until with a high-pitched squeal it imploded into nothingness.

As Kenna and I advanced, I chanced a quick glance in her direction. She arched her eyebrows in challenge. "Are you the queen or aren't you? Take that witch down!"

With a slight nod of my head, I turned back to Addie. She mumbled words that seemed to wilt in the wake of the divine power arching from our rings. Her magic faltered. But I needed to do something more, something that would keep her from hurting those I loved ever again.

Remembering how Fiona and I had broken the spell on the journal, I pictured Doon in my mind — the cobbled streets, castle turrets reaching into the sky, the old chapel emanating the glory of the souls within, and lastly, the faces: Jamie, Duncan, Fiona, Fergus, Mario and Sharron, the Rosetti sisters, and even poor, abused Gideon.

The people were the essence of Doon. I focused every ounce of my being on saving them and their enchanted kingdom, which I'd come to love with all my heart. Then I sent up a desperate plea to Doon's Protector.

Blinding beams shot from the rings, passing through the witch's torso. Addie twitched as if burning from the inside out, purged by fire and righteousness.

She screamed in outrage, "Nooo!"

A hellish shriek rent the air, and Addie slumped over, her body aging rapidly before my eyes. Her lush blonde hair grew stringy and gray. Her skin turned sallow and shriveled into a thousand wrinkles. Her gorgeous figure shrunk, bending into her drab medieval dress and cape. Behind her, the self-perpetuating serpents began to deflate like damaged tires, dissolving into putrid lumps of ebony slime and ash on the floor.

Pure, unadulterated shock crossed Addie's rapidly aging face. Her eyes became huge and buglike as she clutched at her throat. "What have ye done?"

"What someone should've done a long time ago." I released Kenna's fingers. This one I could handle on my own. Stepping forward, I balled my hand into a fist and punched the old woman smack in the face. "That's for hurting Jamie!"

"And for calling me a sidekick!" Kenna added as the hag dropped to her knees and crumpled into a heap on the floor. Stripped of her wickedness, she appeared nothing more than a pathetic old woman. Innocuous, if not benign.

I stared at the miraculous ring on my finger, wondering how such an innocent-looking object could harness the power of the Almighty Protector of Doon — who somewhere along the way had become my guardian as well. I harbored no delusions that Kenna and I possessed latent superpowers; it'd simply taken an unwavering belief in the light to extinguish the dark.

Jamie rushed to my side and gathered me in his strong arms. I gratefully leaned into his solid warmth, clinging to him as fatigue washed through me. Being a warrior was seriously exhausting!

"How did ye know?" His voice was as gentle as I'd ever heard it, filled with wonder and something more intimate, meant only for me.

Leaning back, I searched his dark eyes. "Know what?"

"How did you know that you had to be willing to die to invoke the power of the substitution?"

"It was something the king — your father — said to me. That when the time came I'd have to be willing to make a sacrifice for your sake." I lowered my head and then glanced at him from under my lashes, tapping the left side of my chest with two fingers. "It wasn't a hard decision. I just followed my heart."

CHAPTER 40

Mackenna

Just when I thought real life couldn't get more theatrical, hag-Addie started to cackle again. Her hateful, brittle laugh scraped over me like dead branches in February. Vee spun in Jamie's embrace just as Fergus and Duncan moved toward the witch with weapons drawn. But with a puff of wind, she . . . vanished.

The room went oddly silent as scenes flitted through my mind: the Phantom vanishing on Christine, Sondheim's witch disappearing into the woods, the Wicked Witch of the West shrieking, "I'm melting!" That was always the end, right? There ought to have been music underscoring the moment so we could rejoice it was over and that we'd won.

Fergus kicked Addie's empty cape with the tip of his boot. "She's gone."

When Vee started to frown, Jamie picked her up off her feet and twirled her in a circle. "Tha's a good thing. Ye did it! You beat her."

Over their whirling forms, I looked to Duncan for final

confirmation. As he watched his brother and my best friend, he grinned, his smile equal parts smirky and awestruck. He brushed his dark hair back from his forehead so that it stuck up in those fantastic damp spikes. There was something so familiar — so comfortable and endearing — in the gesture, as if my heart had known him a lifetime. Our eyes locked. His velvet brown gaze radiated with expectancy that tugged at my soul.

The gossamer strands of a long-forgotten memory floated across my consciousness. Sunshine and summer heat. Someone standing on the Brig o' Doon waiting for me. As I struggled to remember, a clock chimed from somewhere in the house. The melody of the bells pierced the thought and snapped me back to the present.

Duncan's face grew pale, his smile slack. Heavy with shock, he murmured, "Midnight."

With a gasp, Vee pushed out of Jamie's arms to face me with round eyes. "Please tell me you set the clocks ahead."

A couple of minutes. "Not enough."

In my head, I could imagine Addie still cackling from wherever she'd gone and gloating, "Ye will never make it back across the bridge in time ta save your beloved Doon."

Jamie clutched Vee's arm. His manner became clipped and efficient as he pulled the new queen to his side. "The fastest way to the riverbank?"

In spite of the panic on her face, Vee remained calm. "Up the stairs and out the back door." Before her words were finished, they were moving toward the exit.

Duncan crossed the room in a half dozen determined strides. My stomach plummeted as he reached for me. I longed for him to take me in the shelter of his arms and kiss me senseless. Instead, I grasped his powerful hand and let him drag me behind Jamie and Vee.

Just before the door, I pulled away long enough to scoop up Aunt Gracie's journal and the upended duffel. I stuffed the book into the bag and thrust it at Vee. "Take this. Whatever you do, don't drop it." There were questions in her eyes but she slipped the strap horizontally across her torso and rushed into the pitch-black corridor.

Duncan waited at the doorway, his eyes voicing a particular question. He would never return to Doon if I didn't. Or at least if he didn't think I was going back. Before he could say anything, I grabbed his arm, tugged him into the hallway, and whispered, "I've changed my mind about staying in Doon."

Feeling physically sick, I watched as wonder crossed his face, followed by relief and a new determination to get to the bridge. Duncan's hands pressed into my back, urging me to climb the stairs two at a time. As we raced through the darkened house and out the back door, I thought of Aunt Gracie. How before she died, she'd promised me she was going to recover. But she couldn't.

The clock from Alloway's main strip started to toll the hour. *One!* The low muffled clang reverberated through our bodies as we dashed toward the trail that would get us across the bridge.

Once on the footpath, Duncan interlaced his fingers with mine. Anchored to his side, I had no choice but to match his long gait stride for stride. Just ahead of us, Jamie propelled Vee in a similar manner while Fergus sped past us to take the lead.

My side ached. *Two!* My lungs burned from lack of oxygen. I ignored my protesting body and pushed through the pain. The distance separating the cottage from the bridge seemed impossibly far. Yet I refused to abandon hope.

I focused on the bend that led to the Brig o' Doon. *Three!* Fergus rounded it first and declared, "I see the brig!"

In front of me, Jamie and Vee seemed to run even faster — if such a thing was possible — as they caught their first glimpse of the portal that would lead them home. *Four!* With a shout, Jamie urged us on. "Keep going!"

We sprinted through the curve. Ahead, the Brig o' Doon was barely discernible in the haze of the riverbank. Duncan's fingers tightened over mine in wordless assurance, and his pace quickened. *Five!*

I was doing the right thing. I had to believe it. But we were running out of time. As we neared the mouth of the bridge, thick tentacles of mist reached for us. All that remained visible of the Brig o' Doon was the lamppost on our side. *Six!* If not for that dull yellow halo of light, we'd have lost our way for certain.

The disembodied voice of Fergus echoed from the oblivion. "I'm across!"

My timing had to be perfect. As I took the first jarring step onto the cobbled stones of the bridge and the mist swallowed us, my hand slipped from Duncan's.

"Mackenna!" he called out in alarm.

"Right here." I struggled to keep my response as reassuring as possible. *Seven!* Although he was only inches away, I couldn't see any part of him. How I wished in that moment I could see his ridiculously gorgeous face one last time. "Keep running!"

Then I stopped.

Eight!

Using the parapet wall as a guide, I quickly edged my way backward toward Alloway. I wasn't sure how far I'd crossed, but I needed to ensure I was past the halfway point before the last toll.

Ahead, I heard Jamie exclaim, "We've made it!" followed by Vee's bell-like laugh of relief and Duncan's hoot of victory. *Nine!*

Now for the hard part.

Duncan's voice held a sense of urgency. "Mackenna? Where are ye?"

Ten!

I labored to make my mouth speak the terrible truth. "I'm not coming."

I heard Duncan rush toward me instantly, followed by the sounds of a struggle as Jamie and Fergus restrained him. His voice wavered with disbelief. "But you said —"

"I lied." If he could find a way, he would come after me. The only way he would stay where he belonged was if he never wanted to see me again.

Some promises couldn't be kept, despite our best intentions. *Eleven!* A sob hitched in my throat as I stepped back onto the firm ground of Alloway and waited for the final toll.

From the other side of the Brig o' Doon, Vee gasped. "Kenna, what are you doing?"

"Come ta me!" Duncan's frantic plea caused me to sink to my knees in an effort to hold my ground and not to rush to him. The ache in my chest was excruciating.

"Mackenna!" Already his voice sounded distant — coming from someplace far, far away. "Please!"

Twelve!

The mists began to dissipate. For several moments, I stood in shock and watched the Brig o' Doon reappear. Staring at the vacant passage, I struggled with the reality of what I'd done. I'd abandoned my best friend and broken trust with the boy I loved.

I could only hope when Vee went through the bag and found Uncle Cameron's ring that she would understand. Like her, the rings belonged in Doon — I did not. She'd probably still be furious, but eventually she would forgive me — and she'd help Duncan to do the same. In time, he would find someone who could make him happy and move on. Unlike me.

Stars filled the sky as I walked numbly back to the cottage. Now that the kingdom was safe, I wasn't afraid of Addie. Even if Vee hadn't stripped her of her power, she'd still lost. But I needn't have worried, because the chamber under the cottage was as empty as a tomb. She'd disappeared, hopefully for good.

All traces of Doon were gone from my life — as if it'd never been more than a terrible and lovely dream.

ChAPTER 41

Veronica

The journey back to the castle was bittersweet. Doon was saved. And by some incredible twist of fate, I'd become its queen — which hadn't really sunk in yet. In my heart, I knew it meant I would never have to leave the land and the people I loved. But it also meant I'd never return to the mortal world again.

Would my mom miss me or even care that I was gone? Most likely she'd be relieved when I didn't return. She'd move on with Bob, and maybe start a new, even more dysfunctional family. What excuses would Kenna make for my disappearance?

Kenna. Something cracked deep inside my chest. *What will I do without the girl who shares my brain?*

My stomach clenched. It wasn't like before, when she'd moved to Arkansas. There would be no late-night phone calls or texts. This separation was permanent. I couldn't conceive that I'd never hear her voice again.

She'd made the choice to pursue her dreams, and I couldn't fault her for that. But when I looked at Duncan — his broad shoulders stooped, his face a mask of anguish — I wished with all my heart she could've accepted the dream her life would've been with him in Doon.

I stumbled over the uneven ground as loss clouded my vision. Jamie grasped my arm to steady me, his eyes searching my face. I gave him a watery smile, my gaze lingering on his beautiful features, and my heart gave a violent twist. I'd almost lost him forever too.

With a soft smile, he tucked my arm through his and we fought our way through the thick forest together.

Silence greeted us as we entered the village. Every window was dark. As if in repose, the colorful buildings rested snuggly against one another. Had we failed to save the people of Doon after all?

I glanced questioningly at Jamie. His brow furrowed and he stopped in the middle of the street. "Listen," he whispered.

Duncan and Fergus turned toward us. We all strained to hear the gentle melody that floated on the breeze, swelling and retreating on the gentle wind.

"They'd be in the Auld Kirk," Duncan said with quiet determination.

"Of course!" Jamie beamed, the tension leaving his body for the first time since we crossed the bridge.

"Come on!" Fergus motioned to us and then set off in a loping stride. Duncan, Jamie, and I followed on his heels. Despite my exhaustion, energy surged through me as we ran in the direction of music that became clearer with every step.

Give us strength to face the darkness,
Faith to keep us safe,
And be our protection in times o' trouble.

The hymn, clear and pure, rose into the night air, causing my heart to swell within my chest.

Never will we fear, for You are our mighty shield.
Because we have made You our refuge,
The Most High our dwelling place.

We raced up the stone stairs of the church. Duncan and Fergus pulled opened the double doors, and all four of us stood in the entryway.

No evil shall befall us or our own,
No scourge shall come near ...

The entire kingdom of Doon stood united, their voices lifted to the sky, singing a prayer for their kingdom and the safe return of their king. Jamie's eyes met mine as he took my hand, and we stepped into the sanctuary.

Fiona was among the first to see us. With a cry of joy, she ran down the center aisle and hurled herself into Fergus's waiting arms. People surrounded us, their exultations and questions blending into a dizzying cacophony. Sofia flew toward us with a huge grin. Respectfully, I stepped to the side to give her access to Jamie, but stumbled back when she threw her arms around me. "You saved him, didn't you? You beautiful girl, you saved us all," she whispered urgently into my hair. Surprised, I met Jamie's intense pride-filled gaze over Sofia's narrow shoulder.

"She did save us all," Jamie said in a reverent tone I'd never heard him use before. "In fact, it's a story all of Doon needs to hear."

After giving Sofia a brief hug, he held his hand out to me. Ignoring Jamie, I turned back to the tiny Italian girl, searching her lovely face. "But Sofia ..."

I trailed off, unsure how to frame all the questions racing through my mind. Why was she not mad at me? How did she feel to see Jamie holding my hand? How long would she go on loving him?

With a wide smile, she leaned close to my ear and whispered, "'Tis all right, Veronica. I've had a Calling o' my own."

My eyes widened, and I stared at Sofia in amazement. A quick glance at Jamie's face told me this was not news to him. I arched an eyebrow and frowned. "You knew about this?"

"Aye, though in my defense it was a recent development," he said, his lips sliding into an apologetic grin.

And just like that, I melted.

"Come." Jamie took my hand and pulled me against his side, whispering, "Your highness."

I smiled up into his handsome face as he led me through the crowd, to the front of the church. But as we climbed the steps to the altar, my feet began to drag. How would these good people accept the news that their newly crowned king, who'd been reared for the position since birth, had been usurped by an ordinary American girl — one who was thought by many to be in league with the devil?

But as Jamie recounted the harrowing events of our ordeal, beginning with Gideon's enthrallment and ending with our final defeat of the witch, it became clear by the appreciative reaction of the people that I had nothing to fear.

"So, my good kinsmen, without further ado, by way of the Americas, with a wee bit of help from the Ring of Aontacht and by her strong faith and valiant self-sacrifice, may I present your new monarch. Queen Verranica!" Jamie swept into a deep bow and then dropped to a knee before me, his head bent low. The crowd rose to their feet, cheers and applause echoing to the rafters.

Humbled beyond all words, I swallowed the emotion threatening to spill out. Reflexively, I searched the crowd for the flaming hair that signified my best friend, and found Duncan's sad smile instead. My heart ached for Kenna's — and also for Duncan's — loss. But I had to believe she was here in spirit and that she would want me to grab on to happiness with both hands.

I turned to Jamie, grasped his shoulders, and pulled him to his feet. When his eyes met mine, they were dark pools of mystery. What could he possibly be up to now?

With a raise of his hand, the people quieted. Admiration rushed through me at his commanding presence, inspiring me to gain control of my shaking limbs and the sobs tightening my chest.

"Good people, as the tradition dictates, a reigning monarch must fulfill the Completing before the commencement of their official Coronation." Translation: I needed to choose a king before I could be crowned. I stared at Jamie, unable to believe he'd bring this up now.

"I, for one, would like to know who her choice for coruler will be," he said with a playful grin.

As the room erupted in laughter and applause, I cupped my hand over my mouth and leaned closer to him. "What are you doing?"

Jaime put his arm around me and pulled me against his side. His breath skimmed the sensitive skin on my neck as he whispered, "Ye have to choose, love."

"But don't I have until the next Centennial to reveal my choice?" I loved Jamie with all my heart, but this tradition was so archaic. We hadn't even discussed how we felt about each other in private, and he wanted to do this in front of the entire kingdom?

"Nay. When ye took my place, you became queen before this Centennial ended, so you're actually a wee bit behind."

Some part of my exhausted brain recognized he was talking me into a corner — forcing the issue in typical Jamie fashion. Pulling away from his intoxicating embrace, I clenched my teeth against the sudden doubts crowding inside my head. I knew the Calling was supposed to lead you to your soul mate, but what if it was wrong? What if our fairy tale didn't have a happy ending? The logical part of my brain told me to trust this blessing, but the neurotic, abandoned little girl inside me warned that Jamie would ditch me just like my father did.

I needed more time.

Drawing in a deep breath, I turned to tell him, and found the Golden Boy from my visions. With a soul-searing look, he closed the remaining distance between us. His clean scent — soap and summer storm — engulfed me as he leaned down to my ear. "Verranica, I will never leave you."

I stared up at my beautiful prince, tears gathering in my eyes. How did he always know exactly what I needed to hear? Then a tiny voice inside of me answered: Because the Calling is real and your destiny is standing right in front of you.

My heart hammering in my chest, I clutched his hand, took a step back, and lifted my chin. "I choose you, James Thomas Kellan MacCrae, to be my king and coruler." My voice rang strong and clear, prompting a mass intake of breath from the crowd.

A slow, dazzling smile spread across Jamie's face as he tucked a strand of hair behind my ear. In words meant only for me, he said, "Verranica, when ye called me out for doubtin' our Divine Ruler and told me I had to put the people of Doon before my own desires, I knew you were my perfect match, and we were meant to be together. I'm verra sorry that it took me so long to trust what was between us.

"But, in my heart, 'tis always been you. When I saw ye that

first time in my dreams, I felt as if I'd known you all my life. And over these past weeks, I've only fallen more in love with you. You challenge me and make me laugh. Just lookin' at you makes me want to sing."

Jamie loves me! I felt the smile in my heart before it reached my face.

"And if ye need more proof of my intentions" — he reached into his jacket and pulled out a crumpled cream colored square — "open this."

It was the envelope from his coronation, containing his choice for queen. My hands shook as I took the rumpled packet. I couldn't believe he'd been carrying it throughout everything. I flipped it over, and the MacCrae crest, a regal lion's head, stared back at me from the blue wax seal.

From the crowd, someone sounding suspiciously like Fergus shouted, "Open it!"

I glanced at Jamie with a tentative smile, ripped open the flap, and pulled out the folded slip of paper. Written in a bold script was a single word:

Veronica

Suppressing a squeal, I lifted my head to see that Jamie'd dropped to one knee before me — again. "Verranica Welling, I love you with all my soul. I will happily be your king, if you will consent to be my love, my wife and my queen for all of our days in Doon and beyond."

This time, I didn't need to think about my answer. "Yes, Jamie. Yes!" I pulled him to his feet and jumped into his arms.

The responding roar from the people of Doon was so loud, it almost shook the beams of the old church. Suddenly, all the feelings I'd bottled up inside chose that moment to pour out.

"I love you. I love you. I love you," I repeated as I kissed his cheeks, his nose, his dimpled chin, and his perfect mouth.

His responding laughter, beautiful and deep, warmed me all the way to my toes. As my feet slid back down to the ground, he arched a golden brow and said, "I'll be expecting this treatment ever' day for the rest of our lives, ye know."

"In your dreams," I teased.

He chuckled low and sexy as he took my face in both his hands and kissed me until I knew I'd never be cold again.

After several earth-shattering moments, whistles and cat-calls broke us apart. Stepping off the dais, hand in hand, we made our way toward the people — our people. Somewhere in all the well wishes, hugs, and tears, I became a part of Doon in truth.

Finally, I'd found the place where I belonged. My destiny.

epilogue

Mackenna

I stowed my intern orientation packet under my folding chair and concentrated on the rhythmic voice of Adrenaline Theatre's artistic director, Weston Ballard. Butterflies tapped through my stomach, choreographing a frenetic rendition of *All That Jazz*. We were on the stage, seated in a circle, doing our first icebreaker of the season. Thanks be to Kander and Ebb, the patron saints of Chicago, we were not playing Scene Freeze.

Chills raced up my spine as I struggled to direct my mind away from the most horrifying night of my life and back to the present. Today was huge — the beginning of everything I ever wanted. Well, not everything. Mostly everything.

And I could — I would — live with that. It's not like I had a choice.

"For the next eight and a half months, this theater will be your home. It will be your privilege, your possibility, and your passion. It will be your sanctuary."

I focused on the cadence of Weston's voice as he strolled among us. The speech no doubt was the same one he delivered each year for incoming interns. But the way he lingered in my space seemed special.

With precise diction and perfect projection, Wes continued, "Let's get started with a creative exercise. I want you to envision the most fantastical place imaginable."

I drew in a deep breath and held it for two beats. As I exhaled, I relaxed my shoulders and let my mind wander.

Tendrils of mist, thick and damp, began to roll in from backstage, engulfing the other interns. I stood and turned stage right. The artistic director's hypnotic voice grew hushed, like a footnote, as the building vanished. The murky outline of a wild forest became discernible through the haze. And directly in front of me, the Brig o' Doon appeared — beckoning.

It had to be a dream, except I was wide awake and standing at the mouth of the bridge.

The mists coalesced to take on a familiar form — one that caused my heart to leap with joy. I hadn't thought about my imaginary friend, Finn, in ages. He'd appeared that first summer in Alloway, when I was lonely for the company of other kids. Like Peter Pan, he'd filled my childhood with magic and, inevitably, captured my first kiss.

He looked just as I remembered. His lopsided grin, equal parts smirky and awestruck, promised benign mischief. His large brown eyes sparked with confidence as he raked his fingers through his dark hair to form chaotic peaks.

Holy Hammerstein! I knew that gesture — it was imprinted on my heart.

Before my eyes, Finn grew into a tall and broad shouldered boy of eighteen. His dark gaze crackled with expectancy as I drank in the ridiculously gorgeous face of Duncan MacCrae.

"Come ta me, Mackenna — "

I listed to one side, and the cold metal of the chair snapped me back to my surroundings as I gripped the edges to keep from sliding off. I was still on the empty stage with the other interns. The mists and bridge were gone. So was Duncan.

Weston's speech continued, "Nowhere — not even that place you just went, is better or more real than where you are. The Adrenaline Theatre — this is your calling."

He was wrong. I knew what a Calling was — and it was exactly as Vee had described, a waking dream that feels more vibrant and tangible than anything else in life.

My imaginary friend wasn't a delusion.

Duncan Rhys Finnean MacCrae and Finn were one and the same. That familiar, elusive something I'd felt when I was with him made perfect sense now. How could I not have seen it before? The handsome, flirty prince with the easy smile wasn't a fling — he was my destiny.

Not only was I crazy in love with him, but I suspected he'd been appearing to me — Calling to me — since I was six years old. And in the end, I'd betrayed him ... broken my promise and his heart. The monumental weight of my mistake paralyzed me like the gravity of a foreign planet.

Now that I'd let him go, would either of us ever get to live happily ever after?

aCKNOWLEOGMENTS

We would like to thank all the people who've shared this journey: rooting us on, picking us up, and sharing in our triumph. You are the Destined, and we could not have done this without you!

Extra special thanks to:

Nicole Resciniti, who loved this project enough to want to represent it — twice. And who worked tirelessly to make the dream a reality. You are a godsend!

Jacque Alberta, editor extraordinaire, for loving this story enough to want to share it with the world. *Sara Merritt,* marketing maven, and the devoted people at Blink for making it happen.

Melissa Landers, our not-so-silent third partner, for your hours and hours of labor on this project, for being Switzerland, and for being so much more that a crit partner.

The *DARING HonestlyYA Crew* — *Jenn Stark (writing as Jennifer McGowan), Kristi Cook, Kim MacCarron, Jen McAndrews, Lea Nolan, Mari Bates,* and *Pintip Dunn.*

Mike Heath and Magnus Creative, for our gorgeously epic cover.

The guys of *Combatants Keep,* for *repeatedly* demonstrating that pivotal medieval sword-fighting sequence Jamie and Duncan play out in the tournament scene.

Ashley Klaserner, Daria King, Dinah Luneke, Jennifer Heisey, Noël Albers, Mary Plye, Angie Grogean, Kathryn Miller, Zoe Jordan, Sienna Condy, Malin Coughlin, and Lucy Briand for being early readers and for loving this story.

Our village — Mindy McGinnis, Liz Coley, Julie Cross, Mark Perini, Amanda Brice, Jessica Lemmon, Tina Ferraro, Cinda Williams Chima, Linda Keller, Tonya Kappes, the fabulous women of OVRWA (past and present), and our Seymour Agency sibs. Your support and faith in us is truly humbling!

Carey would like to personally thank:

God — first, last, and always — for giving me a life more abundantly and richly blessed than anything I could ever conceive of.

My family — Michelle, Tori, Jessie, Mary, Dylan, Sean, Beth, Mark, Jamie, Ty, Gram, Dad, Shey, Jani, Josie, and Mom. My undying gratitude to each and every one of you for enabling me to pursue my dream. I love you like crazy!

Harrison, Athena, and above all else Aaron — for taking up the mantle of my dream with willing hearts. For sacrificing more than you should. Somewhere in my youth or childhood, I must've done something very good to deserve you.

Lorie Langdon, my first crit partner, constant spiritual supporter, the best cowriter in the universe, and the other half of my brain — I'm still amazed you don't throat punch me after some of our revision sessions. Thank you seems inadequate.

My MargaRITAs, and my AMAZING crit patners — Jenn Stark, Kristi Cook, Kim MacCarron, Jen McAndrews, Erica O'Rourke, Vanessa Barneveld, Shea Berkley, and Shelley Coriell. I couldn't ask for better "go-to" girls and thank God for bringing us together. I can't wait until we can all say, "I knew her when."

Brianna Ahearn for her valuable insight, and enthusiasm. I'm so glad you're on the journey with us.

Meredith Briski, a dear friend, early reader, and someone wise in all ways of things YA, who had a vision for Kenna's own book long before the rest of us.

My personal cheer squad: *Melissa Dietrich, Kevin Stout, Gina Dierig, Erin Kotch, Angela Combs, Margaret Szemprech, Carol Wade, Lorie Jones, Debbie Burress, Amy Maier, Susan Campbell, Dave King, Roger Cady, Denice Bachmann, Holly Snider, Don Overton, Bob Luderman,* and *Claudia Liff.*

Lastly, those I have likely overlooked in my haste to meet my editor's deadline. I'm so sorry. Email me and I'll make it right in book two!

Lorie would like to personally thank:

My Savior King, my Dream Giver, my Protector, *Jesus Christ* — the One who makes all things possible.

Tom Moeggenberg for being my real-life hero, the one who lifts me up when I fall.

My boys — *Ben* and *Alex* — for *never* doubting that their mom would be a published author, and for repeatedly asking if they could be in the movie. Love you guys!

Mom, for inspiring me to dream BIG dreams, for instilling in me the love of writing, and for believing in me even when I don't believe in myself.

Leon Jennings for being my prayer warrior, wise mentor, and the best grandpa in the universe. I can almost feel the warmth of your smile shining down on me.

My family — *Dad, Brian, Toby and Jerry, Tracy, Grandma Darlene, Aunt Sue* and *Uncle Adrian, Aunt Barbara* and *Uncle*

Harold, Aunt Deb, Angie, Pam, and *Katie.* Thank you for your enduring encouragement and support.

Aunt Gaye and *Uncle Floyd,* for introducing me to travel and culture, and, best of all, to the magical world of *Brigadoon*!

The girls who keep me sane — *Kelly Moeggenberg, Laurie Pezzot,* and *Tricia Lacey.* Thank you for your prayers, for making me laugh, and for occasionally forcing me to get out of my writing cave to enjoy life.

JR Forasteros for pulling me out of my darkest moment by making me face my greatest fear.

And of course *Carey Corp,* who helps me to see the world in a whole new light, pushes me to be a better writer, and lets me crash on her couch when I need a safe place to land. I wouldn't want to be on this miraculous journey with anyone but you.

CPSIA information can be obtained
at www.ICGtesting.com
Printed in the USA
LVOW08s0113170817

545324LV00003B/5/P